THE HEROIC ADVENTURES OF
Donny Coyote

THE HEROIC ADVENTURES OF

Donny Coyote

KEN MITCHELL

COTEAU BOOKS
WWW.COTEAUBOOKS.COM

This is a work of fiction. Names, characters, places, and incidents either are the product of the author's imagination or are used fictitiously. Any resemblance to actual persons, living or dead, is coincidental.

Edited by Geoffrey Ursell.
Cover and book design by Duncan Campbell.
Cover photo (detail), "Las Vegas at Night," by Johner/Photonica.
Author photo by Don Hall.
Printed and bound in Canada at MarcVeilleux Imprimeur.

National Library of Canada Cataloguing in Publication

Mitchell, Ken, 1940-
The heroic adventures of Donny Coyote / Ken Mitchell.

Based on Don Quixote, by Miguel de Cervantes Saavedra.
ISBN 1-55050-263-8

I. Cervantes Saavedra, Miguel de, 1547-1616 Don Quixote. II. Title.

PS8576.I88H37 2003   C813'.54   C2003-905035-1

1   2   3   4   5   6   7   8   9   10

COTEAU BOOKS
401-2206 Dewdney Ave.
Regina, Saskatchewan
Canada   S4R 1H3

Available in the US and Canada from:
Fitzhenry & Whiteside
195 Allstate Parkway
Markham, Ontario
Canada   L3R 4T8

The publisher gratefully acknowledges the financial assistance of the Saskatchewan Arts Board, the Canada Council for the Arts, the Government of Canada through the Book Publishing Industry Development Program (BPIDP), the Government of Saskatchewan, through the Cultural Industries Development Fund, and the City of Regina Arts Commission, for its publishing program.

for Jeanne

The Making Of A Hero

CHAPTER 1
Direct Action

In the little city of Moose Jaw, out on the windswept plains of Saskatchewan, lived an unusual young man named Donny Coyote. He had few assets except a collection of old comic books and a used Rocky Mountain bicycle, but he liked his job and was a respected citizen in his community. He earned enough from his wages at the Cansave Recycling Depot to buy necessary items like food and comic books and videos.

His favourite meal was the Big Breakfast Bonus at Smitty's Pancake House beside the Canadian Tire store on Main Street. Most of the time he ate his Kraft Dinner alone in a compact little bachelor apartment on High Street, on the third floor above the Kwikprint shop. His friend Doc Pearce had helped him find it.

Donny Coyote (it said "Donald" on his driver's licence) didn't know much about his past or his parents. He knew – Doc had helped him do the research – he had been left at an orphanage in the outlying town of Assiniboia by an unidentified donor who had written down his name as Coyote, or maybe Coyotl. Perhaps the donor was named Coyote, or perhaps the Orange Benevolent Home named him Coyote because of the small birthmark on his lower back. It was red in colour and resembled a running coyote. The home guessed his age to be three months old at the time of entry. At two years, he was given a complete physical examination by his official guardian, the Province of Saskatchewan. His stubborn silence was identified as "post-natal retardation" in the home's records, but he slowly learned how to talk.

Coyote no longer remembered the Orange Home, though he still felt the pangs of hunger, and could still see the starkly engraved drawings in the old Bible. After his eyes were tested at the age of ten, he was given glasses, and he learned words like "run" and "play." After a while, he began to read comic books. He grew into a youth blessed with a lean, muscular physique, which allowed him to work long and hard at any job he liked. Coyote's greatest skill, however, the one that impressed his friend Doc Pearce, was his wild imagination. In his brain was a vast cartoon-like realm of monsters and aliens and superheroes, characters generated from his world of comic books. More than anything, Donny Coyote wanted to be a superhero, a real superhero. He had collected comic books ever since the age of twelve. Before that, he had watched heroes on TV: Hercules, Spiderman, Mighty Mouse, The Incredible Hulk. Comic books were better than TV. He liked to read the balloons in the drawing and memorize the way the characters talked. It was like entering another world.

Coyote had learned to read even though the teacher in the Orange Home thought he was retarded. They said he was never adopted because of his poor eyes, which were slightly crossed and magnified by his glasses to the size of headlights. The glasses perched on his long canine nose, making him look rather like a short-sighted dog. He finally got placed by a social worker named Margaret St. Denis, who took a professional interest in his reading development. She arranged for him to go to his first foster parents, the Hustons, and recommended that he take a Special Ed class in reading.

The Hustons also gave him an allowance so he could buy more comic books. After a while, he owned huge stacks of second-hand comic books. He started watching more TV, and collecting videos, posters, and buttons. He owned a box full of fantastic hero gadgets – a piece of real Kryptonite, the Phantom's Ring. A pair of the Wolverine's claws, made out of genuine Adamtium.

Donny stored his comic collection in stacks of cardboard boxes in his bedroom closet. His friend and reading mentor, Doc, had helped him organize the collection, and showed him how to order from dealers' catalogues.

Dr. Robert Pearce was a Professor Emeritus of Cultural Studies from the University of Minnesota, and had retired to Moose Jaw. When Coyote asked why he had moved there, he said because it was north of North Dakota. It was Doc who warned Coyote to be careful with professional comic traders in the US, who were always trying to steal rare editions from unsuspecting amateurs.

Coyote took up serious collecting with Doc's advice. After he got his job at Cansave, Coyote's closet contained a complete run of *Superman* and the *World's Finest Action Comics*, all of *The Vigilante* and *The Punisher*, most of *Batman*, some original *Captain Marvels* and *Mary Marvels*, plus an assortment of old Dells: *Red Ryder, Tarzan, The Lone Ranger*, and *Little Lulu*. Little Lulu wasn't a superhero, but she and Tubby and Annie made Coyote laugh out loud. He liked Little Lulu.

Coyote shared his Disney-like visions with Princess Di, his favourite reading tutor. She had helped him for years, along with her father, Doc Pearce. She sometimes disapproved of the adventures of his various heroes – Spiderman, The Hulk, The Exterminator, for example – but still encouraged Coyote to act on his heroic beliefs. Together they had patrolled the rusty banks of the Moose Jaw River, looking for pollution caused by oil refineries and railway yards.

They had joined causes, and carried banners for peace, justice and security with various oppressed people in Moose Jaw. She inspired him to think globally and act locally, to recycle his household trash, to intervene for the weak and helpless, to *take action*. She had given him a Crumb cartoon to tape on his wall. KEEP ON TRUCKIN'. Princess Diana Pearce was like a saint to Coyote, and his devotion sent him down the path to his first adventure.

It started one morning in late winter when the popcan kid came into the Cansave Recycling Depot the eighth Monday in a row. Coyote's heart went out to him, this kid in ragged clothes, without socks. He looked like he hadn't eaten for two days, his bare feet flopping around in a pair of busted-down basketball shoes. In the meantime, the Saskatchewan winter had dumped mountains of snow on the streets, blasting out of the Arctic like an avalanche.

As usual, the kid was dragging a few garbage bags full of popcans and plastic bottles, at least twenty bucks' worth, while his old man slouched with a set of earphones in their pickup truck, banging time with his hands on the steering wheel. Coyote and Sandra and the other workers had seen that truck pull up every week all winter. To Coyote, it looked suspicious. The garbage bags were always new and the cans unflattened, like they'd been stolen from the hospital charity bins. Sandra was suspicious too, but she didn't want to get involved.

"Forget it, it's their business," Sandra said. "For all we know, they could be charity volunteers."

Coyote said the real point was about the kid, who should at least have a pair of socks and be shown how to wipe snot off his face. Plus he looked like he hadn't had a bath for six months.

Sandra could see trouble coming – so she said in all the later interviews – and everyone knew she had a talent for spotting, or maybe even finding, trouble. She threw Coyote her fiercest look, warning him to keep his mouth shut or she'd inform Wendy he had a bad attitude. Wendy was the supervisor, with the power to punish Cansave employees who mouthed off to the clients. Wendy had already fired two guys for mouthing off at clients, Dwayne and another guy no one remembered any more.

All the employees stopped work to hear what Coyote would say to the popcan kid. The week before, he had told them he would speak up. "Hey kid, how about asking your old man to step in here?" he said.

"Who?"

"Your old man."

Sandra rasped, "Donny, you better stay outta this!"

"What are you talking about? What old man?"

"The guy sittin out in the purple Chevy. With the Oilers hat."

"That guy? Gerry? He just gives me a ride. I don't have no old man. Gimme the money, squintface."

"We don't have to give money to under-fourteens. Anyway, I just wanta ask him something."

"Look dork-brain, he ain't my old man, okay? Get it straight."

"Well, what is he?"

"He's my uncle, okay?"

"Whatever."

"Donny, I'm callin Wendy right now!" Wendy had gone to the Social Services office to turn in their weekly wage-sheets.

The boy went to the door and yelled, "Hey, Uncle Gerry! Come in here a sec. This dumbnuts wants to talk to ya."

"Are you crazy?" Sandra hissed at Coyote. "Wendy's gonna ship you back to the pogey bin for this! You'll be on welfare the rest of your life!"

"What is it?" Gerry wheezed, waddling through the door. When he got closer, Coyote could see it wasn't an Oilers hat, though it had the same colours. It said 'Born to Bingo.' Coyote's eyes weren't good for distance, despite his thick glasses. "You his uncle?" he said.

"You got a beef? I'm his Uncle Gerry. Whatsa problem? My little nephew tryin to pass off some fake cans on ya? Heh heh."

"Where are you guys getting these cans?"

"What's it to you, four-eyes? You give a shit where some poor welfare family finds a few deposit cans? Gimme a break."

"Another thing. Couldn't you get him a pair of socks? And show him how to wipe his nose."

"What are ya, some Social Services welfare cop? Gimme the goddam money and we're outta here."

"I'll give it to you if you stop at Zellers on your way to the liquor store. There's lots of money here for a pair of socks."

"Hey, who's in charge here? Lady! Yeah, you. Do I gotta put up with this shit?"

Sandra puffed up defensively. "I awready warned him not to talk to clients."

Coyote turned to the boy, who stood with the door open, ready to run. "Had breakfast yet today, kid?"

The boy stared at Donny Coyote and at the man in the fake Oilers hat. He had dark grey eyes with gritted centres that looked like they could drill through cement. They looked like the crusts of dirty snow in the corners of the Cansave parking lot. "Not since yesterday."

"Here, take this cash." Coyote handed him the money. "Make your uncle stop at Burger King. There's enough for a Xtreme Bacon and Cheese Whopper."

"Say, what is this? Where's the goddam foreman? Lady, are you in charge?"

"The supervisor's away at the moment," Sandra said. "If you want to make a complaint, you have to write it down."

So it went, one argument leading to another. Gerry tried to grab the money, but the kid wouldn't let go, even after Gerry kicked his butt and yelled the fuck word at the top of his lungs. Sandra ran to phone Wendy, after the kid ran out the door with the money and took off down the street. Gerry started screaming about compensation, and throwing bags of popcans right over the counters and clear across the building, making all the workers run for cover. Coyote had a third degree in martial arts, so he grabbed him and held him down until Wendy came and called the cops.

That afternoon, Wendy put Coyote on Behaviour Modification, and took him off his job on the can crusher. He had been on the can crusher ever since Dwayne's sudden departure last year. Wendy put Coyote on unit counting for a whole week, and gave Sandra the crusher position. It was unfair, and Coyote felt it served them right when the cans all came out twisted. There was no appeal for Behaviour Modification, because it was in the employment agreement Cansave had signed with Coyote's legal guardian, Saskatchewan's Department of Social Services.

"You need to have your behaviour modified," Wendy explained, even though she admitted in her monthly report that his behaviour had been "appropriate for the situation." She also testified later at

Gerry's trial, where she allowed that Coyote had been right in confronting him. The boy was a runaway from Regina who had been taken in by "Uncle Gerry," a convicted pedophile and welfare fraud. The police gave the story to the newspaper and the paper interviewed the Deputy Minister of Social Services, who also agreed Coyote had acted correctly. The paper put Donny Coyote's picture on Page Three of the Moose Jaw *Times-Herald,* with a long story about his brave intervention and his courage under fire. He kept it folded in his wallet, to show people who didn't know who he was. It came in handy for ID.

HERO BLOWS LID ON CHILD ABUSE

Thanks to quick action on the part of CANSAVE depot employee Donald Coyote, a tragic tale of child abuse and exploitation was exposed in Moose Jaw yesterday.

Gerald Clarence Barnes, 45, who operates a homecare facility for foster children in downtown Moose Jaw, has been charged by police with 23 counts of fraud, theft, and sexual assault.

Barnes has a long record of convictions for fraud and child pornography in several Western Canadian cities, but his lawyer said he would fight the outstanding charges all the way to the Supreme Court. If convicted, Barnes faces a lengthy term of imprisonment. Judge Rod Williams called him "a menace to society".

Mr. Coyote, the unlikely hero of this story, is a four-year veteran employee at the CANSAVE Rehabilitation Program, where Special Needs Adults recycle used clothing and deposit containers. He collared Barnes in a daring citizen's arrest at the recycling depot early yesterday morning, while Mr. Coyote's supervisor, Wendy McSimmons, called police.

Meanwhile, public officials and welfare authorities have applauded the heroic actions of Mr. Coyote, a 25-year-old sorter at Moose Jaw's community sheltered workshop for the mentally challenged. Despite a vision impairment, Mr. Coyote recognized Barnes' behaviour as suspicious and took action that led to the arrest.

"He is a hero, no doubt in my mind," Mayor Ray Brown said. "I'm forwarding Mr. Coyote's name to the Governor-General for a national bravery award."

There was a huge picture of Coyote grinning above the headline, flexing his biceps for the camera. Of course, Sandra Dollar was totally bummed out by this turn of events. She had been scheming for months to get Coyote's job, and had no sooner got it than the press turned him into a big public hero, and she had to give it back.

Sandra was always informing Wendy when employees broke the rule on talking to clients. Sandra could speak to clients because she wasn't mentally challenged. She merely had a social handicap. She said Coyote made people think handicapped adults were all weirdos, when they weren't. Sandra had a photocopy of her IQ test, which was in the nineties, and good enough, she said, to enter any university in the province.

Coyote didn't deny Sandra Dollar was smart, smart enough to get a real job on Main Street, but she was ugly as a toad. Dwayne once said if he had a dog with a face that ugly, he'd shave its ass and teach it to walk backward. Even though Sandra was ugly and chippy, Coyote got along with her, as he did with most people. Her problem was that being a lifelong victim of other people's screw-ups and biases, she was too pushy for her own good. She said she was a radical feminoid and told people she was saving up for a sex change operation because she was fed up with being an oppressed female.

Sandra's file in Wendy's office said that she suffered from Body Dysmorphic Disorder, which Wendy interpreted as Aesthetically Challenged. Sandra had been smashed in the face with a baseball bat by her second pimp when she was fourteen, an estimated twenty years before. Donny Coyote admired her because she didn't take crap from anybody, which was why they were friends, and went on being friends, more or less, even after he became famous.

But she wouldn't stop bugging him about his heroic intervention, even after he finished Behaviour Modification. "Gotta keep stickin yer oar in, don't ya Donny? Know what happened to the cat, don't ya?"

"You're just pist because they put my picture in the newspaper."

"Who cares what they put in that lousy rag? They waste a million trees a day promoting bigger idiots than you. That newspaper supported Johnny Cretin for Prime Minister. Cretin and his cradle of crooks."

"I never voted for Cretin."

"No, but you believed the son of a bitch."

"Anyway, Wendy says I done the right thing."

"Aa, what does she know? I'm telling ya, Donny, lay off this macho, he-man, hang-em-high, vigilante kick you're on, or you're gonna get yourself whacked! Why do you always have to play the hero?"

"I can't help it," Coyote said, with a shrug of his shoulders. "Princess Di thinks it's cause I read comic books."

Sandra started mocking him as "Our Big Hero," telling the clients to ask for his autograph. Sandra said she hated comic books. "If yer such a big fuckin hero," she said one day at work, "why don't you come over to South Hill and try kickin butt in my neighbourhood? Easy to be a shit-disturber here on the nice side of town, but how would you make out with all the riff-raff and low-life? You got any idea what it's like over in the gulag? You won't see Dale Goldhawk going to South Hill! People getting shot up, knifed. Suicides every day. Glue sniffing, needles, AIDS, the works! And worst of all – wife beating! Why do you think I got a job down here?"

"I thought welfare got you the job."

"I still got freedom a choice, smartass. No, I did it to escape from my asshole of a husband. That son of a bitch put more scars on me than a hay baler. Only reason Delvis lets me out of the house is so I can earn money."

"So why don't you take off?"

"I did once. When I came to Moose Jaw. I heard about the women's shelter on South Hill. He followed me, natcherly."

"That didn't work?"

"Wade, my own shit-wit brother, told him where I was, so Delvis came after me and wrecked the place, smashing windows and everything. They put him in jail for a month, then let him out so he could take anger counselling. The social worker said I should go back and live with him again but a week later, déjà view all over again. He sweet-talked me into renting this shack we got over by the stockyards. Son of a bitch can be charming on days he's sober."

"So can I help somehow?"

"Ya can't fuckin help, so forget it okay? Know why I got no teeth? He knocked 'em all out! What can you do about that, Our Big Hero?" She snorted. "Nothing! So grow up and get real."

"You should tell the police."

"We need somebody to go over there and lay down the friggin law! The cops refuse to intervene because of human rights!"

"Well, you have to see it from the police's side. People have rights."

"Don't let'em bullshit you. Women and kids take all the abuse over on Garlic Heights. You want to tackle violence, Captain? You got a serious challenge on South Hill. The Ku Klux Klan used to hold rallies over there! Downtown is the centre of fuckin civilization in comparison."

That was when Coyote decided to take action. On Friday, his next day off, he would commit to action, instead of wasting the day at Harry's Video Arcade. Princess Di was always urging him to take direct action. Taking action might cheer Doc up, because if Doc saw him at Harry's Video Arcade, playing Killer Force or Spawn-Fighters, he would get depressed and start drinking and they'd have to spend the day doing something useful, like cleaning the ceramic tiles on Thunderbird Viaduct, or polishing Doc's car, a '78 Ford Pinto.

If he showed initiative, Coyote hoped Doc might lend him the car to drive to South Hill and look for innocent victims to save. When he thought about all the helpless women and children being abused by perverts and drunks that called themselves husbands and parents, his brain sizzled with fury. His fists ached to pummel the evil out of people. He trembled with anger at how cruel people were to children, and the law didn't do sweet toot about it.

That was why society needed superheroes – to protect the helpless and downtrodden. Ordinary officials of law and order like the city police and the FBI and the Mounties were overwhelmed, unable to handle all that injustice. They were trying to do their jobs, but they didn't have the heart of a true crime-fighter, someone who could instinctively detect the evil hidden in the human heart. A person who could take Action. A person like – Donny Coyote's brain gonged like a bell – *Captain Coyote.*

CHAPTER 2

Captain Coyote's First Mission

ll day Friday, Coyote studied his comic book collection and looked around for bits of costume, and weapons for his utility belt. He reread the adventures of his various heroes, to remind himself of their various strategies and their powerful oaths under combat conditions: *Holy Moley! Kemo Sabay! Great Caesar's Ghost!*

When Coyote arrived on his bicycle at Doc Pearce's Redland Avenue house at supper time on Friday, he found Doc in a good mood, at least a good mood for Doc. Princess Di was home from university for the Easter holidays, a lucky break. Doc was always happier and more generous when Princess Di was home.

"Donny, come in and grab a chair!" Doc called through the door. "Just in time for supper. You must be famished, burning up all that energy to save the world." Doc was making Spanish rice for supper, as he did every Friday.

"I try hard, Doc, like you say. Hi, Princess."

"Hi, Donny."

Doc said, "Did Your Highness hear about Donny Coyote's triumph in the struggle for eternal justice?"

"What triumph?" P.D. asked, zipping through the kitchen.

"He nailed a child molester single handed. Just last month. There was a big story in the paper."

"My hero!" Princess Di sat down on the bench in the kitchen nook. She always liked to hear Coyote's latest adventures, no matter how busy she was. She was supposed to be preparing a lecture to the Moose Jaw Action Committee for the Status of Women that evening. "Princess Di" was a nickname Doc had given Diana. But she had been named, Doc said, not after the princess but after Diana, the goddess of the hunt, because of her flaming red hair.

Coyote thought her hair was redder than The Human Torch's, like long flowing curls of fire which blazed around P.D.'s gorgeous face. The fierce mane made her seem even more passionate than she really was, which was pretty passionate. Doc gave her the nickname when the real princess married the Prince of Wales, long before she was killed in the car crash. Doc would buy copies of the *National Enquirer* at the supermarket, so he could tape their screaming headlines on the refrigerator. "Di Goes Topless in Majorca!" "Lady Di Denies Gay Lover."

P.D. had become a feminist at the age of fourteen, and didn't find Doc's nickname amusing, but she was stuck with it. Now she was completing a Ph.D. in political science at the University of Saskatchewan. Doc said then she would be P.D., Ph.D. Dr. Diana Pearce.

Coyote handed her the clipping from the *Times-Herald*. He blushed as she read it aloud, and nearly at the end she gave him a moist kiss on the cheek. "I'm so proud of you. You really are a hero!"

"Thanks."

"And she's home for the whole weekend, Donny! What a treat for a couple of trouble-makers like us, eh? A superhero and a washed-up academic."

P.D. frowned at him. "You're not a washed-up anything, Dad. You took early retirement. And you're in good company. Think of all the hockey players and tennis stars who retire long before they're fifty. Look at Wayne Gretzky." She took a handful of broccoli spears and mushrooms from the fridge and piled them beside a bowl of blue cheese veggie dip. "You have ten years of good scholarship in you. You write wonderful papers! So don't pretend you're some worn out has-been."

"I've given up, Princess. My brain cells are atrophying. And I drink too much. When you're not here, I collapse into dipsomania."

"I did notice the collection of bottles."

"That's this man's influence. Donny's my recycling specialist. Your creation, in a way. A dedicated environmentalist."

"So, your career continues to expand, Donny. What's next? Planning to take on the corporate globalization agenda?"

Coyote shook his head. "Something better! Actually, I came to ask Doc – if nobody's using your car tonight, Doc – maybe I could borrow it?"

"To?"

"Drive over to South Hill and look around for – trouble."

"Jeezzzus," Doc wheezed. P.D. clutched his arm. "What's wrong with this neighbourhood? Not enough crime on Redland Avenue? No distressed damsels on Mortgage Heights?"

"People at the depot were saying I could expand my horizons, maybe – freelance a bit. There aren't enough heroes working the street."

P.D. laughed, allowing a drool of veggie dip to drip onto the bosom of her T-shirt. Doc got annoyed when she laughed at Coyote, but it never bothered Coyote. Her laughter made his backbone shiver like when he heard Katie Kool or Roy Orbison singing on the radio. When she laughed, he would stop talking and listen with his mouth open. This made her laugh more, and he became enchanted by her melodious sound. To stifle her giggling, she pushed a broccoli floret between her teeth. She didn't want to upset Doc, to give him an excuse to take a drink.

"You want to take my car out cruising for trouble?"

Coyote had driven Doc's Pinto before, but Doc was always with him, like on their trips to Minneapolis or up to Saskatoon, or when Doc was feeling low and needed him to drive to the liquor store. "Sandra was telling me a lot of bad stuff goes on over there."

"I'm not sure I trust Sandra Dollar's view of the world. She's a chronic liar, as I recall."

"Yeah, but I thought, I'd, you know, check it out. It's a good way to use all the PR I got on TV."

"Donny, Donny. The world is a lot more complicated than what you see on TV! Your comics are more realistic than the crap they show on the news. And you can't save all the victims in the world. Think of all those big cities. It's not humanly possible."

"You said it wasn't humanly possible to collect the complete *Superman* – and I did. With your help, though."

"I've lived in those big cities, Donny. Toronto. LA. Minneapolis. I've survived worse neighbourhoods than anything you'll find on South Hill. You want to know why I drink?"

"About the car, Doc. If P.D. doesn't need it tonight..."

"Let him take it," she said. "I drove a rental car down from Saskatoon. Don's a big boy now. God knows, the people on South Hill could use help, too."

"Thanks, P.D.!"

With a shrug, Doc handed Coyote the Pinto keys. "You're responsible for any damage, right?"

"Sure, Doc. But I never put that ding in your back door."

"I never said you did. But you have to be responsible. Be back by midnight?"

"Maybe a little later than midnight. I still gotta get my costume together."

Doc froze. "Costume?"

"Just some stuff I collected. A mask, a cape, that kinda thing. Utility belt."

"Jesus."

"It'll be fun, Doc. I'll be okay."

"Call if you run into any trouble."

Coyote drove first to the Canadian Tire store to buy masking tape, so he could stick white racing stripes along the side. At his apartment, he got out the Captain Coyote costume he had been collecting. The best part was a Calgary Flames hockey shirt he had found in the recycled clothing bin at Cansave. It had a big flaming C on the chest, and he had felt-penned "oyote" behind it. There was also a fancy cape he had salvaged dumpster-diving on Connaught Avenue. It looked like an English policeman's cape, navy blue with a red satin lining, his favourite colours. He stood in front of the bathroom mirror to pull on his aviator's helmet. It was a real World War I leather helmet with goggles that fitted over his glasses, covering up his disability. It made him look like The Phantom.

Before he could wear the costume, however, he had to get initiated, like The Phantom and most of the other heroes. He took off the clothes and folded them carefully into a plastic grocery bag. He might find a place to get initiated on South Hill.

Cruising down Main Street toward the railway tracks, Coyote enjoyed showing off the racing stripes on Doc's Pinto. The Friday night traffic was heavy, and a couple of times he revved the engine as he sped through a yellow light. Of course he would have to rename the car, if he kept using it. Maybe "The Coyote Mobile." He could glue a flaming C on the side of it.

He turned west along the railway tracks toward Thunderbird Viaduct, the big bridge that crossed the rail yards and the river to South Hill, arching across the Canadian Pacific tracks like a rainbow over the sky. He had crossed it hundred of times on the bus going to Empire School for Manual Training, but this was the first time Coyote had driven to South Hill by himself.

As the Coyote Mobile glided up the curve of the viaduct, he felt like Superman, soaring over the spidery network of railway tracks below. The light of the setting sun flowed along the tracks, making long red streaks all the way to the horizon. A train shunted along, its line of box cars rattling and swaying. Coyote could see the Agpro grain elevators silhouetted in the west. He could see the pink glitter of Thunder Creek, running now in the April thaw. A meadowlark perched atop a lamp post on the viaduct, warbling at the setting sun. Coyote stopped and rolled down the window to listen, and heard its melodious summons to action.

As the Coyote Mobile rolled off the bridge onto Fourth Avenue, it entered South Hill's main street, a strip of shops and crumbling apartment blocks. Where should he start? Walk into Merle's Barbershop looking for suspicious activity? Take up surveillance on Karl's Konfectionery and Post Office? No, first the initiation. He needed a public proclamation, an official beginning.

Coyote stopped at the Mohawk gas station. Doc and Princess Di bought Mohawk gas because it used ethanol, an environmental fuel. Environmentalism was the first "ism" Coyote had learned from Princess Di. She was the one who organized the campaign to start the Cansave recycling depot, and helped him get his job there, his first real grown-up job with benefits.

"Fill?" the gas attendant said.

"Two bucks' worth. I don't suppose you reckanize who I am?"

"I dunno. You look kind of familiar."

"Donny Coyote – maybe you seen me in the paper, the time I caught that child molester?"

"Oh yeah. That's it. Check the oil?"

"Tonight I'm gonna become Captain Coyote. Where do you think is the best place on South Hill to make a public announcement?"

"Could try the hotel."

"Hotel?"

"Yeah. The Billard Hotel, around the corner on Home Street. Well, it's a sorta hotel. They don't rent rooms no more. Just a bar really."

"Oh yeah, I know the place. Next to the stockyards."

"That's it. So what happens when you turn into Captain Coyote? Grow long hair and fangs and stuff?"

"No, I just put on my costume. After I'm announced, I'll probably patrol around, check out the scene, look for emergencies, whatever."

"If anybody needs a tow, we got 24-hour towing here."

"Well, it's really violence I'm looking for. Disasters. Crimes. Kind of like that Goldhawk guy."

"Captain Coyote, eh? Can I get your autograph?"

"I don't mind." Coyote printed his name neatly on the man's cigarette package.

"Hm. Got any super-powers?"

"I practise *tae kwon do.* It's like karate."

"This your car?"

"My friend Doc loaned it to me for the night."

"Kinda low-tech for a hero, ain't it? A Pinto?"

"Well it's cheap on gas. That's a plus."

"A hero has to drive something with muscle."

"Muscle?"

"Gotta go power these days. Tell you what. My brother's got a used-car lot out on Number Two Highway. Four Aces Salvage. He gets lotsa muscle vehicles. Slightly used, but good power – you know? Once he had a Stingray, couple of Trans Ams. Here's a card. Go and check'em out."

"Geeze, I might just do that. Thanks!"

As he drove off, Coyote could not believe how well things were going. In no time flat he had a name, a costume, the possibility of his own car. Just a few more gadgets for his utility belt, and he was ready for action. If he was lucky, there'd be a total asshole at the hotel, a biker or some other scumball, hassling a woman or a visible minority. He'd cut him down with a *tae kwon do* chop, paralyze him with his special Coyote grip and drag him off to face the wrath of Princess Di. He'd drop the slime bag at her feet like a dead rat and watch him grovel, begging for mercy. "Don't let Captain Coyote punish me any more! I promise to get my life on track!"

P.D. would be pleased, so pleased she might come back to live in Moose Jaw and join the mission. As a team, they could accomplish great things. They could both look after Doc, and try to keep him from getting depressed. Maybe she could be his loyal companion – like Lois Lane or the Fox Woman. After they cleaned up South Hill, they could take on the city of Moose Jaw, then the whole world, like Superman and Dale Goldhawk, saving people from the clutches of brutal thugs and shyster lawyers. There were hundreds of victims crying out to be rescued, a thousand abuses to be crushed, a million injuries to be healed.

He drove past the Billard Hotel, a three-storey brick building overlooking the railway siding. Its red and blue neon sign winked on and off like a beacon – Billard! Beer! Billard! Beer! The parking lot was full of big livestock trucks, with a few pickups jockeyed into one corner. The Billard was only a block from the Moose Jaw Stockyards, bathed in the odour of cow manure. Coyote remembered going past when he rode the bus to Empire School.

There was nobody in the hotel lobby, but a sign with an arrow said TO THE BAR. Coyote wandered down the hall until he saw the bar door, belching noise and clouds of cigarette smoke. Peering inside, he could make out a jumble of cowboys and truckers crowded around the pool game, and two girls sitting at a table near the door. They looked like nervous teenagers, maybe runaways, with their gym bags piled on the chair beside them. They were probably hitchhikers who'd ridden in with the cattle freighters.

"Excuse me," Coyote said, "Where's the manager?"

"Get lost, four-eyes," the younger-looking girl said. The name Wanda was tattooed on her arm.

"Not so fast," the other one said. "This buckaroo might be lookin for a good time."

"I'm really looking for the hotel manager. To arrange something."

"Talk to Darren over there," Wanda said. "He's the bartender."

"Will my car be okay in the parking lot?"

"You have a car?"

"Well, it's Doc's car. An old Pinto."

"Coo-ul."

"So what's a dummy like you doin driving around in an old Pinto?"

"Doc let me borrow it. So I could fight injustice and evil."

"Oh, oh. A Jesus freak! C'mon, Marla. Let's go sit at the bar."

"Wait! I'm not gonna hurt you."

"You look kinda pervy to me."

"I'm not a pervert! I'm a hero. I was in the paper a couple weeks ago. You mighta seen me. I saved a kid at the recycling depot."

"Hey, I read about that," Marla said. The black makeup on her eyelids was so thick he could hardly see her eyes, but they looked tawny coloured. Wanda had brown eyes, deep brown eyes like a deer's, and they were nice, but Coyote liked tawny-eyed people. P.D. had tawny eyes.

"You're the dude who busted that honky pedophile! You're that Coyote!"

"That's me! And tonight, I'm going to become Captain Coyote. I only hafta make the announcement. Do you need protection?

"Not from you, Butt Head!" Marla snorted. "We escaped your kind of protection in Medicine Hat! Pimps were comin onto us like cockroaches!"

"I'm not a pimp!"

"Pull the other leg, it's got bells on."

"But I could save you from the pimps! Or whatever you need!"

Marla looked at Coyote suspiciously. He was weird, but sounded sincere. "Oh, that's different," she said, turning to Wanda. "Anything we need?"

"We got needs, that's for sure. Ever stroked a pussy, Captain?"

"I like pussies."

Their laughter made him feel good, and he sat down at their table. They seemed embarrassed when they couldn't stop giggling, so he said, "Go ahead and laugh. I don't mind. If people laugh, I'm doing my job, right?"

"Yeah, right, Captain!"

"Hey, Captain. Let's do something. You ever try lap-dancing?"

"No..."

"How's this feel?"

"Well, okay, but –"

"What the hell is going on here?" someone yelled in Coyote's ear. He leaped to his feet, dumping Marla onto the floor. A Bluto-like waiter stood over him, a guy with arms that swung from his shoulders like sides of pork. Was this to be Captain Coyote's first combatant? He crouched into a *tae kwon do* stance. This called for a cool, deliberate approach, not a frenzied attack.

"It's okay, Captain," Wanda said. "Relax. This is Darren."

"You heard me, doorknob! What the hell is going on?"

"Are you the hotel manager?" Coyote inquired.

"What if I am?"

"I'd like to request an announcement. About Captain Coyote – my new identity."

"Is that so?"

"And also the use of one of your rooms to put on my costume." Coyote showed him his plastic shopping bag, a Safeway bag, the kind Doc called a Moose Jaw briefcase.

"No rooms at the Billard, Jack. These broads awready tried that one. They coulda told you that."

"Maybe I could use your bathroom."

"What are ya, a dipstick? You wanna drink or not?"

"Maybe a glass of water."

"Hey, what the fuck is this? Who is this guy?"

"He's Captain Coyote. A hero."

"Shit, that's different! We love heroes. Heroes are big spenders! If you got hero's money, pal, I can rent the whole third floor to you."

"Well I don't have money right now –"

"You can't afford a lousy beer?"

"I don't drink beer."

"Well you better order something or you can't sit in here. You want food? We got a shitload of classy pub grub: hamburgers, fishburgers, chickenburgers, french fries, pizza pockets, pepperoni, you name it."

"How about a BLT?"

"No BLTS. Can't do BLTS in a microwave. Hey you slags, clear your stuff off the chair, and let Captain Critter sit down."

"We were here first!"

"Coyote," Donny said politely. "Soon to be Captain Coyote."

"Yeah, and once these two piranhas get their fangs into you, you'll know the meaning of the word victim. You want a menu, Colonel?"

"I could try the chickenburger."

"Delicious. Frozen fresh. Two minutes in the microwave. Anything else?"

"Well, one thing. Do you have a PA system with a microphone here? I'd kind of like to get started. I'm here to clean up crime on South Hill."

"Shoulda bin here last week when the Pelletier brothers hit the place. It was like WWF Wrestling in here. Coulda used you then. Say, you look pretty tough. You a weight lifter? Ever worked as a bouncer?"

"Well – I have a few martial arts skills."

"Captain Coyote, huh? What kinda crimestopping do you specialize in?"

"Oh, a little of everything. I stop kidnappings. Robberies. Damsels in distress. That kind of thing."

Darren looked interested. "Damsels in distress?"

"Do you know any?"

"Hey, Captain, maybe – maybe you could help me out of a little jam."

"Captain Coyote will never refuse a request for help."

"Right on! I knew you were a trustworthy dude. You want an assignment?"

"Count me in."

"You arrived just in the nick of time. My feature entertainer choked up on me tonight. Weaselled out on his contract. Can you imagine? The night the truckers roll in from Medicine Hat! But hey, maybe we're in business! How much would you charge to show us your costume?"

"Oh, I don't do this for money."

"Atta boy! Look. I gotta clear this with Mr. Klovik, the owner. He might set you up with a tab for a couple of drinks. All you gotta do is come out on stage so I can introduce you. You can make your speech. We got a fancy stage all set up with coloured lights, and a huge sound system."

"This would be – my initiation?"

"Why not? If yer a hero, you gotta be initiated! Right?"

"Oh yes. Batman. The Phantom."

"Fuckin aye. How did they do the Phantom?"

"He was initiated on an island off Madagascar, after his father was killed by pirates. The king of the island found him washed up on the beach, and arranged the ceremony. The Phantom had to say, 'I swear to devote my life to the destruction of piracy, cruelty and greed, and my sons will follow me!'"

"Yeah, we could do something like that. Lissen, don't heroes need a sidekick?"

"You mean, a faithful companion?"

"You gotta have one! Look at Batman and Robin. Superman and Lois Lane. They all had them. Well, how about these two chickadees, just waiting for something to do?"

"Oh, I'm not sure they're suitable."

"Hey! What the fuck's wrong with us?"

"I was planning to, you know, advertise for a faithful companion. I might even go to the States to look for the right person. It's not an easy job. Anyway, I'll do that after the initiation. First we have to find a VIP official for that."

"VIP. Like who?"

"Well – the Queen, for example. Or the president."

"President Bush? Of the United States?"

"Or President Reagan. I think he's still alive."

"Shit!" Darren thought for a moment. "How about the mayor?"

"You know Mayor Brown?"

"Well, not personally. But Mr. Klovik does. He's in like Flynn with Brown and all those yahoos on city council. Klovik can arrange it. Don't go away, Captain. We'll get the mayor right over here. Just let me zap your chickenburger in the microwave." Darren lumbered toward the bar.

The girls turned their full attention to Coyote. "Hey, this could be your lucky night, Captain! Wanda and me've done lots of initiations."

"No kidding!"

"We usually charge mucho buckos, but we'll do this one for tips. Seeing as we're already here."

"Tips?"

25

"You got no money, right?"

"You'll love it," Wanda said.

"Wanda and me done a zillion wedding stags in Saskatoon."

"Marla has this awesome trick she does. First the guy pulls a fifty-dollar bill out of his wallet, lies down on the floor and rolls the bill up and sticks it between his lips, see? Then she dances over top of his face and lowers her body over it – and pulls it out!"

"Geeze, I dunno. I was thinking of something kinda – formal."

Darren returned with a grin. "One chickenburger, Captain. And Mr. Klovik wants to see ya. He's got the mayor lined up! You want a beer?"

"Just a glass of water, thanks."

"Water? We don't serve that crap! Have a beer! You can share it with your faithful companions."

"Go for it, Captain!"

Captain Coyote had to think about it. His crime-fighting career was about to take off. And he'd met two damsels, maybe not in distress, but needing protection. Of course, it would be better if President Bush or the Queen came to do the honours, but Mayor Brown was no slouch either. Even Sandra would be impressed. Coyote had met Mayor Brown once before, when the city paved the back alley behind Cansave. The mayor had driven all the way from city hall to open the repaved alley, so he should jump at the chance to launch a real local hero.

CHAPTER 3

Initiation at the Billard Hotel

Before Coyote could lick the chickenburger's mayonnaise off his fingers, Darren had pulled him behind the bar, and down another hallway to the back of the building. They descended a flight of stairs and entered the basement office of Jason Klovik, owner of the Billard Hotel. At first Coyote thought Mr. Klovik was dead, a swollen carcass lying on a busted-down sofa, before he realized the man's deathlike stare was focused on a hockey game on TV. The set was dangerously perched on top of a pile of old pizza boxes sitting on a huge iron safe. Darren waited for a commercial break and said, "Mr. Klovik, this guy says he can do the show tonight."

"Oh yeah? Ever done a peeler act, kid?" The sofa seemed to be disappearing under the crush of his body.

"Peeler what? I'm talking about an initiation. A heroic initiation."

"Okay, whatever. Darren'll take care of it. So...what's your name, bub?"

"Coyote. Donald Coyote. Soon to be Captain Coyote."

"What do you charge, Captain?"

"Charge?"

"For the initiation. What's it gonna cost me?"

"Nothing! You're doing me a favour!"

"Yeah, I can see that. And you got your own costume?"

"Right here. But we still need a dignitary. My first choice is President Reagan, but I guess the mayor's okay. Is that right you know Mayor Brown?"

"Old pal of mine. So's the police chief, and the health inspector. I know'em all. But I'm not sure they heard of you."

"Oh, not yet, but I'll soon be famous. All I need is the public initiation to get started. The mayor has to say a short vow."

"How's it go?"

"It goes, 'Do you, Captain Coyote, swear to dedicate your life to the cause of justice and the destruction of evil?'"

"Hang on, I'll write it down. Gimme that again. The mayor says where's the justice? Overthrow of evil. Fuck, I dunno. Does the mayor gotta say this, or can I do it?"

"It has to be somebody official. It could be the police chief."

"Oookay, we'll start working on it. Whatever the talent says. Need anything else? Couple beer? Free nachos? Hey, what can Darren bring ya?"

"Milk would be nice."

Klovik pulled a cellphone out of his shirt pocket and muttered into it as he watched the hockey game. A few minutes later, Darren returned with a styrofoam cup of milk and a bottle of beer for Klovik. When he opened the door, raucous bar noise from upstairs pounded through the office, and Klovik gestured at Coyote to turn up the volume on the hockey game. Colorado and Detroit were playing. Klovik said to Darren, "So here's the deal. We pronounce him Captain Coyote, then let him do his act."

"I dunno about an announcement, Mr. Klovik. Our mike is on the fritz. I'll try to get it working."

"Say, Captain, if you're interested in money, we could auction off your costume. Give you a fifty per cent split."

"No, I don't think so."

"Okay, just walk out on stage, and leave the rest to me and Mayor Brown," Klovik said. "Anything else?"

"Maybe we could publicize it first."

"Don't bother. The locals won't come near this place tonight. With all these freighter cowboys in here? Like gas and water. Don't mix. The cowboys are on a tear, drinkin paralyzers like they was water. This place will be a zoo! But, hey, truck drivers are people, aren't they?"

"I guess."

"That's the spirit! They're gonna appreciate this, General."

"Captain."

"Should I tell the girls to get dressed, Mr. Klovik?"

"Yeah, sure. As soon as the game's over. Listen – just a tip, kid, keep your eye on them two munchkins. I mean, they're okay for your show, but mind your wallet, know what I mean?"

"Wanda and Marla? You think they're dishonest?"

"Shit, no! None of my beeswax. But you get my message, Colonel? We don't get a lot of heroes in here, so we gotta take special care of them, right Darren?"

"One other thing," Coyote remembered. "Could I borrow one of your hotel rooms? For a changing room?"

"Naa – the rooms are all booked. But there's a toilet behind the stage. Kind of a private can for the talent. You can hang out there. That's where Garry The Grasshopper changed into his costume."

"Garry the –?"

"Grasshopper. The football mascot? He was a big hit the night he came."

"He came here? Garry the Grasshopper?"

"Yeah. Him with a van full of cheerleaders and a karaoke machine. They were on their way back from a game in Calgary, musta bin half a dozen of them, all drunker than skunks. Boy, the place jumped that night! They sang every Elvis song he ever recorded." Klovik looked up with a flicker of interest. "You sing?"

"No, afraid not."

"Well, I hope you're entertaining. Oh, one other thing – no fucking on stage. I personally don't care, but I could lose my liquor license. The liquor inspectors nearly shut us down when they saw Garry the forni-cating Grasshopper. Heh heh. Four cheerleaders!"

"Listen, I don't do that sort of stuff."

"That's okay. You can talk, right? Hey, I used to be a hero myself before I retired to the hotel business."

"A hero? What was your professional name?"

"The Magician, they called me. I was a Super-salesman."

"Oh."

"Hell, I could sell anything. Travelled all over the States. Started out flogging World Encyclopedia, then aluminum siding, swimming pools, home renovations – ended up in stocks and bonds."

"The Magician, eh?"

"Hey, I can read the numbers off a credit card at a hundred yards."

"Geeze. Telescopic vision?"

"You said it. Better than Superman."

"I'm still working on X-ray."

"It's a great life being a hero if you can take the heat."

"So you retired and bought this hotel?"

"It's not that bad. Just looks cheap. It was all I could afford at the time. But it's a real gold mine. You interested in buying into a high-vol-ume liquor license? Hey, I seen worse! Come in the summer if you wanta see crowds. We have a mud pit in the beer garden. Women's wrestling. Wet T-shirt contests!"

"Sounds like fun."

"I'm saving my best idea for the tourist season. We're gonna dig a tunnel right through that wall, all the way under the CPR tracks to River Street. We'll call it the Ole Whiskey Smuggler's tunnel! The tourists will flock through here like shit through a goose. The mayor already approved the permit."

"Speaking of the mayor – you'll call him about the vow?"

"Leave it to me. You be ready to go in twenty minutes. Darren's gonna fix the mike and rehearse them two bimbos from the Hat, make sure they're clued in. Anythin else from the kitchen?"

"No, thanks."

"Okay, that's – three-fifty for the burg and milk. Two bucks each for the beer. Seven-fifty, not counting the tip."

"Oh. I don't have any – money."

"No money?"

"I thought the food was free – because I was –"

"Where'd you get a dumb son of a bitch idea like that? When I was a hero, I carried a wad of money that thick! You wanta be a hero, you gotta carry it by the friggin bale. Garry the Goofball had dough. So did my buddy Flash Boyko, the king of plastic siding. They had loot fallin outta their pockets. I mean, you can't be a hero when you're a deadbeat! Would the Phantom stiff me for a chickenburger?"

"Darren said it was free."

"Well, forget about the mayor then. He won't come all the way across town for a cheap bastard like you. I'll have to introduce you myself!"

"Maybe I'd better wait and do my initiation next week."

"Okay, okay! We'll put your food on the tab. But remember I occurred a big expense bringing those girls in. I got a bar full of cowboys screaming for entertainment, so it's time to fish or cut bait, General – we're about to launch your career. But forget about the mayor."

The entertainers' washroom behind the stage was small and filthy and stank like a septic tank, but at least there was a mirror so Coyote could check his costume. He swirled the big purple cape over one shoulder and straightened the seams on his black sweatpants. He adjusted his goggles and checked the weapons he had assembled on his utility belt – cattle prod, lasso, and a blackjack he had made with a billiard ball stuffed inside an old gym sock. Finally he took the Phantom Ring from his pocket and slipped it onto his right hand. As he studied his image in the mirror, he heard the microphone squeaking in the bar. The amplifier was warming up.

"Okay!" Darren's voice screeched through the wall. "Is everybody ready to boogie?" A roar from the crowd rattled the door of the toilet. Coyote stepped into the corridor.

"We have some fantastic entertainment tonight in The Ponderosa Lounge of the Billard Hotel. Ladies and gentlemen, with no further adieu, please welcome – a new hero for the twenty-first century, Captain Coyote!"

That was Coyote's cue. He ran onto the stage to a thunder of applause. Dozens, maybe hundreds, of fans were lined up in front of the stage, cheering raucously. They were laughing, too, which made him feel good. People had laughed at Batman and Captain Marvel. A hero had to have a sense of humour. He stood at the microphone, peering out of the spotlight into the dark smoke-filled room. Coloured lights winked and flitted everywhere. There was a sudden burst of the theme from *Superman* out of the speakers, and Wanda and Marla pranced on-stage in tiny bikinis, bumping and rolling their hips as they sidled toward Coyote, until they stood on either side of him.

Mr. Klovik appeared in the bar at the far end, a sweaty mountain of flesh rolling through the crowd. When he arrived on stage, he snatched the microphone and yelled, "Shaddup, you assholes!" The crowd quieted to a general mutter.

"The mayor was supposed to come tonight but he couldn't make it, so it's recumbent on me to introduce our star performer. We're fortunate to have with us tonight, one of the great heroes of all time, Corporal Coyote – and his beautiful companions, all the way from Alberta, Marla and Wanda! Giv'em a big hand!"

The crowd went crazy. The whistles and yodels of the truckers rose in a piercing climax. Klovik waved them to silence. He lit a cigar and pulled a maroon Gideon bible out of his back pocket, raising it in his right hand.

"First we gotta initiate him. It is indeed a great honour for me to declare that Corporal Coyote is a public hero dedicated to the power of justice and the bashing of evil. Ashes to ashes, dust to dust, amen. Here's your badge, Captain."

Klovik held out a Ronald MacDonald Police Patrol badge, its silver letters glittering in the lights. It wasn't a real badge, Coyote could see. It was a kid's badge, but Klovik had thoughtfully written across it in red marker, CORPORAL COYOTE. It was a neat gift, and tears of gratitude filled Coyote's eyes as he pinned it to his chest.

A cowboy yelled from the rear of the hall, "Take it off!"

"Yeah, take it off!" another bellowed.

Coyote thought they were yelling about his mask, which he had vowed never to remove in public, or to reveal his civilian identity. He ignored their hoots. The crowd broke out in a chant: "Take it off! Take it off!" Wanda and Marla laughed, and started clapping to lead the applause. Coyote gestured no, no, and signalled at Klovik to start the theme from *Superman* again.

As he reached for the microphone, somebody grabbed the waistband of his sweatpants and yanked them down to the knees. He looked around in astonishment. It was Darren! When Coyote bent over to pull his pants up again, the mob howled with glee. It was embarrassing in front of two girls: Captain Coyote, a hero of the twenty-first century, with his powder-blue jockey shorts exposed to the whole bar! He tried to hop back to the washroom, but a cowboy scrambled onto the stage, blocking his exit. Captain Coyote leaped to avoid him, but it was Wanda the cowboy grabbed for. He began yanking on her flimsy costume, trying to rip her bra off. Coyote reached for his utility belt. His hand fell on the grip of the electric cattle prod.

Without a plan, he drew his weapon and jabbed it into the cowboy's crotch. The man shrieked as though he had been knifed and leaped off the stage, crashing onto a beer table and rolling to the floor. The hall fell silent, and the two girls fled screaming offstage. When two big truckers climbed onto the stage, Captain Coyote grabbed the microphone stand, and swung it furiously in a circle, slamming both assailants, groaning in pain, back into the crowd. A can full of beer flew through the air and exploded on the floor beside him.

"Take it off!" a cowboy yelled. "Take it off, ya limp prick!"

Captain Coyote spoke into the microphone to calm everybody down. "Now settle down, folks. We'll be finished in a minute. I just hafta make a short speech and –" But his voice inflamed their fury all the more. Bottles, cans, beer glasses, ashtrays came flying through the clouds of cigarette smoke, smashing all around him.

"You fools!" he yelled. "Don't you know who I am?"

Klovik rolled onto the stage and tried to grab the microphone, but Coyote finally rebelled at his bossy attitude. He grabbed the front of Klovik's grease-stained shirt, and shouted in his face, "You lousy double-crosser!" Coyote was startled to hear his voice booming out of the big speakers. "Are you trying to pull a fast one?" it bellowed.

"This was your dumbfuck idea!" Klovik screeched, pulling the microphone away. "You got your initiation! Now beat it before these dipsticks wreck my lounge."

"We wanta see tits!" a voice yelled out of the flashing glare of lights.

"Shut up, you idiots!" Coyote roared at full volume. "My assistants won't come out till you settle down!" A final glass shattered at the back of the room, and astonishingly, there was silence. "I have a couple things to say," Coyote said.

"Giv'er hell, Captain!" Darren shouted.

"If you want to see Marla and Wanda, I'm sure they'll agree to entertain, but first you have to behave."

A mutter of sullen agreement arose from the truckers. The two girls peeked around the corner of the stage.

"I'm sorry, I have to leave now – I'm going to look for real trouble. But first, I want to re-name my loyal assistants – Wonderful Wanda and Marla the Magnificent. Gentlemen, raise your glasses."

With a confused murmur, the drinkers lifted their beer bottles and shot glasses in the smoky haze.

"To Marla and Wanda."

"To Marla and Wanda!" the crowd murmured.

"Three cheers for Captain Coyote," Darren yelled out.

"Hip – hip – hurray!" the truckers yelled.

Coyote's throat choked with emotion. He was so broken up he could hardly speak. "Thanks, guys. For the honour you have bestowed on me tonight, I am truly grateful. But now I have to go and challenge the forces of evil." He marched offstage.

Darren caught up to him at the exit. "Sure you won't stay for a couple beers, Captain?"

"No thanks. I'm on duty now. My work is waiting for me out there."

"What is it you do, exactly?"

"I patrol the streets – halting crime, fighting abuse, and all forms of evil."

"Evil – in Moose Jaw?"

"It's everywhere – where people least expect it. In homes, businesses, even playgrounds. Tell Mr. Klovik I'm sorry about the damage."

"Aaa, forget it. He got his money's worth. Listen, I think you'd make a useful kind of bouncer. Come around if you'd interested in part-time work. When you're off duty." Darren clapped his arm around Coyote's shoulder and eased him out the door into the parking lot, where his Coyote Mobile waited.

CHAPTER 4

Busting the Criminals

Coyote left the Billard in a state of elation. He could hardly wait to tell Doc about his initiation. When Cansave opened on Monday morning, he would tell Sandra and Barry and Nolan and Wendy all about the great event. He might even wear his costume to work – in case more child-molesters or other suspicious characters showed up. He needed to upgrade the weapons for his utility belt – though the cattle prod had been very useful – and he would search the donations bin more closely. And he would have to look for a car, because Doc's Pinto wouldn't always be available. Tomorrow was Saturday, and he planned to ride his bicycle to Four Aces Towing out on the highway, and see if they had any hero-type cars on their lot.

With his head full of plans, Coyote did not notice the Astro van parked at the curb, until a hair-raising shriek stabbed at him out of the darkness. He peered through the van's tinted glass windows and could make out some faint shapes moving inside. Then he heard a voice growl, "Burn the little cocksucker!"

Donny Coyote might have looked for help in such a situation, but Captain Coyote's heart leaped with joy at the criminal's disgusting command. Coyote believed in luck, but this was too good to be true. His first crime in progress. He stepped to the passenger door and banged sharply with his knuckles. "This is Captain Coyote!" he called. "Anybody need help?"

"Hellllp!" the voice yelled again.

That was all Coyote needed. He wrenched the door open. The street lights lit up a weird scene of torture. Two men in ball caps were holding a street kid about sixteen years old. He had long hair and his shirt was torn open. One guy held the boy's hair twisted in one hand, with his other arm around the kid's throat. The man's cap said RAIDERS. He wore a pair of dark glasses. The other gangster was holding a cigarette lighter, glowing red-hot, to the boy's bare chest. His cap was a green-and-white Riders.

"Can I help or something?" Captain Coyote asked politely. He had stumbled upon another case of child abuse, but he held his cool.

The Raiders guy said, "What the fuck do you want?"

"I'm Captain Coyote. What is going on here? I heard a cry for help."

"Me!" the boy yelled. "That was me! You a cop? Make them lemme go!"

"You're interfering in a private business discussion, asshole," the one with the lighter said. "This little jerkoff developed sticky fingers – handing out merchandise. Now he doesn't want to pay up."

The boy twisted out of his grip and slumped to the floor of the van, but the Raider yanked him up by the hair again.

"I lost a gram delivering it to a customer!" the youth moaned. "I won't do it again, Arnie! I swear to god, I won't! I never banged it, I didn't smoke it, I don't even do drugs! I wanna go home!"

"Did he say drugs?" Captain Coyote asked.

"Look dickhead, this is a private van. Who invited you? Who are you?"

"Captain Coyote. I take calls from people in distress. And it doesn't take a psychologist to see this is unfair – two against one. He's just a kid."

"Fuck off outta here while you can still walk, doorknob!"

"If you fellas want to step out on the street, I can even up the odds."

"Git'im, Boze!" Arnie yelled, and lunged at the caped crusader with the hot cigarette lighter. Coyote knocked it out of his hand with a sharp *tae kwon do* chop. He whipped the blackjack from his utility belt and slammed it into the roof of the van. The boom echoed inside the Astro like a freight train.

"Holy shit!" Boze yelled, scrambling to the back of the van, perhaps going for a weapon. Coyote swung his blackjack at the passenger window, which burst like a balloon.

"Hey, don't!" Arnie said. "You'll wreck the motherfucker!"

"Then let the kid go!" Coyote was getting worked up now. He bashed out another window, then slammed the roof again, hard enough to lay a deep crease down the middle of it. Arnie shoved the snivelling, moaning boy out onto the sidewalk. He had lighter burns down his back, and serious needle scars on his arms. He was a junkie, just like Dwayne.

"Look here, Captain," Arnie said. "Don't freak out. We're just lookin after business, not botherin the public. Andy works for us – delivering shit. He's our best runner, so why would I hurt him, right? We're just scaring him a bit. Discipline, that's all it is. Tough love. We caught him stealin on the job."

"You'll have to take that up with Canada Employment. I'm saying to let him go. Is that right you owe them money, Andy?"

Andy looked at Coyote in astonishment. Nobody had ever intervened for him before. "No! They owe me money! I haven't got paid for four weeks! They just keep saying I lost the stuff, or that I mainlined it. And I didn't, I swear to God!"

"How much do they owe you?"

"Six hundred bucks."

"Okay, this is easy. You guys pay him his money, or I'll wreck your van. Okay?"

Arnie held up his hands for a truce. "Just a sec, just a sec, awright? Okay, I owe him some pay, but what about the fifteen hundred bucks' worth of cocaine that disappeared? Who's gonna cover that? You?"

Coyote had to think about it. "I get your point," he said. Street justice was a complicated business. He had to be fair to both sides.

"Plus I put up bail twice when he got busted, and paid his medical expenses after he took a shit-kicking down at Costa's. Who looks after the little son of a bitch when he gets sick? Me – right Boze?"

"You."

"Well, I don't know. If he's sick, you should probably send him home to bed. So let's say that cancels out the missing drugs. Tell you what. Just pay his back wages."

"Problem is, I'm flat broke at the moment, Captain, but what I can do, seeing you feel so strongly, is to make him a down payment."

"That's fair."

"We'll go straight down to the ATM at Fourth Avenue and pull some cash. I'll take Andy along to keep me honest."

Andy broke out shrieking again. "No way! Don't let him take me! They'll kill me!"

"It's okay, Andy. Arnie has admitted his mistake. Here's my phone number. If he doesn't pay you, just give me a call, and I'll come and wreck his Astro."

"Are you nuts? Who the fuck you think you're dealing with? He's Arnold Korchinksy! The crazy Ukrainian!"

"That's a racist remark, Andy. I have to warn you. Ukrainians are an invisible minority. How will visible minorities ever be accepted, if we don't show respect?"

Andy stared at Coyote and at the grinning drug dealer. "He's a fucking lunatic! And so are you! You think he's gonna pay me, after beating the shit out of me for six hundred bucks?"

Arnie draped his arm over Andy's shoulder. "C'mon kid, let's make up and quit bothering the captain here. We'll let bygones be bygones. I've seen the light, thanks to Captain Coyote."

They drove off in the dented van, as Coyote walked triumphantly into the parking lot. Captain Coyote's first battle with street crime had been a total victory. It was all about resolving disputes. He could drive the Coyote Mobile home with head held high. Princess Di would be impressed too; she had long ago made him commit to the cause of saving lives and trying to resolve disputes. The only problem was that she didn't like comic book heroes, saying they were too macho and racist. Even so, Captain Coyote hoped she would approve of his new identity. As he drove back across the Thunderbird Viaduct, her face appeared in the Pinto's windshield like a TV screen, glowing brightly.

"Anybody can be a hero," he told her. "But I intend to be a super-hero. I'm going to make you proud of me, P.D.!"

Maybe he would never go back to being Donny Coyote. He felt a new destiny was opening before him like a brand new, original comic book, starring Captain Coyote. People would recognize him on the street, probably start asking for autographs and personal souvenirs. He would be called on by the big world, the world of television beyond Moose Jaw. He would travel the country like Dale Goldhawk, one of his favourite heroes in the fight for people's human rights.

He knew there was a whole universe of cruelty and perversion which loomed in that vast dark region. His mission would challenge evil throughout the brutal wasteland he witnessed every night on CNN – drug dens and biker gangs, terrorist bombings of innocent people. He could go to LA and stop the rioters. Smash the street gangs in Winnipeg. The assassinations in New York. People were shooting each other on the freeways and assaulting their own children on talk shows, just like the scenes from Hell in the Bible at the Orange Home.

Coyote shook his head. He thought of all the preparation needed before he could take on all the evil in the whole world. He needed a proper car, for one thing. And a faithful companion was essential. Most of the legendary comic book heroes had great companions: Batman and Robin. Superman and Lois Lane. Captain America and Bucky. Tarzan, the Lord of the Jungle, had Cheetah, as well as Jane. Princess Di would be a perfect companion, but she was busy working on her Ph.D.

Captain Coyote decided to take a final patrol down Main Street, showing off the Coyote Mobile and checking for trouble on the street corners. Then he spotted half a dozen motorcycles parked in front of the all-night café at the Greyhound Bus depot, and alarm bells went off in his head. The riders wore black leather jackets bearing the colours of the Edmonton Hells Angels. They weren't terrorizing anybody – but they were roaring their motorcycles noisily, and spitting on the street.

"Aha!" Coyote muttered to himself. "A job for the masked avenger." Could he handle the gang alone? It was both a dangerous challenge, and an opportunity. He had to take a chance. As Doc always said, "Better to lose by a card too many, than by a card too few." The city police were too busy with serious crime to check on a pack of rogue bikers. He would order the gang to climb onto their machines and drive out of town. Wheeling the Pinto through a U-turn in the middle of the block, he cut across the street and swerved into the parking spot beside the bikers.

Unfortunately, the April air had turned frosty during Coyote's initiation. The pavement was covered with a slick sheet of ice. When Coyote touched the brakes, the Pinto slid clear across the frozen pavement and bounced over the curb, snapping off a parking meter. The front end of the car crunched over the meter and ground to a stop bare inches from the plate glass window of the coffee shop.

A pair of customers inside sat gaping at Coyote as he crawled out of the Pinto, doubled over and gasping for breath. His head had smacked into the steering wheel, flinging his helmet and glasses off. Everything was blurry. Worse, his vision had doubled everything, and now there were not six, but a dozen black jackets advancing menacingly toward him. He staggered to his feet and reached for a weapon on his utility belt. The blackjack? No. The lasso.

"What's your hurry, pilgrim?" the first two bikers said. They were dressed in dark leather from head to foot, with Nazi helmets on their heads. "You took that parking ticker outta there like a nucular bomb. You're not some shit-disturber, are ya?"

"I'm okay," Coyote said, "It's you guys who are in trouble. Doc's going to be real pist if his car's scratched."

"Pissed at us?"

"It's your fault! I pulled in because you were loitering on the street. P.D. says bikers are trouble."

"Yeah? Who's P.D.?"

"Princess Di. She hates Hells Angels."

"Well, fuck Princess Di. And you too, Mr. Bean. You nearly totalled a couple of expensive machines there with your Dukes of Hazzard driving. I'd say Princess Di owes us an apology."

"Princess Di doesn't apologize! She wouldn't give you losers the time of day. She'd tell you to get lost!"

"Well, tell us where she lives, and we'll see that she gets a chance!"

Coyote's head still buzzed from its crack on the steering wheel, but the threat to P.D. put him in such a rage it cleared his mind, and he could see single again. "You wouldn't dare lay your grubby claws on her. Princess Di is a feminist!"

"Well, why didn't you warn us? I'm quaking in my boots. A feminist! I bet she's got a face like a bag of smashed assholes, too!"

Despite his effort at control, Coyote's temper snapped. He charged straight at them like the Hulk, twirling the lasso around his head. He had forgotten about the icy pavement, however, and as he flung the lariat, his feet shot out from under him. He went flying through the air. Luckily, his cape lifted like a parachute and cushioned his landing on the ice. The bikers roared with laughter as he struggled to get free of the cape and tangles of lasso rope.

"Goons!" he yelled at them. "Stand back, shitheads, or I'll incinerate you with my laser ring!" He raised the Phantom ring menacingly.

They only laughed harder. One of the bikers was a girl with a skin-tight leather jumpsuit and a death skull tattooed on the side of her face. She attacked Coyote in a rampage, kicking him in the ribs with her pointed steel-toed boots. He tried to roll away from her deadly jabs, but was tangled in his cape. She was like a demon, trashing him from every angle as the gang cheered her on.

Finally he yelled at the top of his lungs, hoping someone inside the bus depot was watching. "Help! Call 911!" But her boots just kept hammering on his ribs.

At last a police siren began whining in the distance. Somebody had phoned from inside the bus depot. Laughing and yelling like maniacs, the bikers pulled the she-devil away from him and jumped onto their motorcycles. They revved and popped the engines as they roared back to life.

Humiliated, Coyote crawled back to the Pinto to find his glasses. If he could make out their license plates, he could memorize the numbers and track them down later. But his glasses had disappeared under the seat, and the biker convoy escaped, heading up Main Street to the Trans-Canada Highway. The battered hero collapsed on the pavement and wept with bitterness, his brief taste of sweet victory turned to ashes in his mouth.

CHAPTER 5

A Faithful Companion

The police arrived quickly enough, but wasted a lot of time cross-examining Coyote about the smashed parking meter under the Pinto. They also made him take a breathalyzer test, even though he explained that he never drank alcohol. He showed them his driver's license and Doc's car registration, and after they took the details, they called a tow truck to lift the Pinto off the parking meter. A sympathetic waitress in the bus depot verified Coyote's garbled account of the gang's attack.

A reporter-photographer arrived from the Moose Jaw *Times-Herald* to get the news story, and somebody said a crew from the cable station was on its way. Maybe, Coyote thought hopefully, there would be an upside to his crushing defeat after all – some good PR. He could see headlines like: "Local Hero Drives Biker Gang From City."

"Wait a minute, wait a minute!" the police officer snapped. "Before everybody starts mouthing off to the media, let's get the facts here. First we gotta figure out who's committing what crime. Citizens should not be intervening in criminal matters."

"But I am not an ordinary citizen, sergeant. I am Captain Coyote."

"Did you by any chance have anything to do with a 911 call we got from the Billard Hotel before midnight? Some kind of riot?"

"Well, I took care of the riot. I was being initiated there as Captain Coyote, hero and crime fighter."

"You've had a busy night, Mr. Coyote. We had to ship four patrol cars to the Billard, but the fun was over by the time they got there. We busted them for unlicensed strippers. I guess you'd already left the scene."

"Well, yeah – after I stopped the riot."

"Tell you what. We're going to call Dr. Pearce and make sure this car was being driven with his permission. Plus somebody has to pay for the tow truck, but wait, let me guess. You have no money, right?"

"Temporarily."

"Are you feeling ready for an interview?"

"As soon as I find my glasses, if they're not busted. But I wish you wouldn't call Doc. He doesn't like phone calls in the middle of the night."

"Let's find out," the officer said.

Each piece of bad luck kept connecting to the next, as they sometimes did, especially when police made phone calls. When Doc walked into the police station at 4:06 that morning, he was stressed out, and Coyote could see he'd had a drink before coming down. His hands were shaking and his face was deathly pale. He calmed down when he realized that Coyote was not injured, except for the lumps and scrapes from the biker girl's boots. The police mechanic said the damage to the car was minor, just a small dent on the bumper, no damage to the frame or wheel alignment. The police agreed not to charge Coyote with careless driving, if Doc took responsibility and drove the car home.

Coyote was more worried now about Princess Di's response to the accident than he was about the bikers, who were long gone. Would her and Doc ground him permanently? Take away his licence? Put the kibosh on his dream? He decided against laying assault charges. It might be better if he forgot the whole biker episode, and gave up seeking revenge. Besides, it wasn't good PR for a superhero to get the boots put to him by a girl. Who would be the faithful companion of such a dork?

Doc did not speak all the way home, which was scary. Princess Diana, at least, was asleep after her action committee speech, and Coyote was grateful when Doc didn't wake her up. He and Doc sat in the kitchen while Doc drank coffee and fixed the broken frames on Donny's glasses. After that, Doc just sat for a long time, trying to say something that he didn't know how to begin.

"I'll pay to get the bumper re-chromed. I was trying to do the right thing, Doc."

"I know that."

"I just didn't see the ice."

"Jesus Christ, Donny – I don't care about the car. It was your kamikaze assault on the general public. Who are you going after next? Muslims? And what is 'doing the right thing?'"

"My initiation worked out pretty good. You wanta hear about that? Over on South Hill."

"You know how much I hate middle of the night calls."

"I was thinking too fast, maybe, and then I lost my temper. They insulted P.D. I'll be more careful next time."

"There won't be a next time. I'm calling a halt to this sideshow."

"Sideshow?" Coyote said.

"The initiation. This costume. Your 'mission,' the whole ball of wax. It's nuts."

"No, it's not. Princess Di likes the idea."

"Well, okay, I kind of like the idea too, it's just – why do you take everything to extremes? Tell me about the initiation."

"It was great, Doc! At the Billard Hotel on South Hill. I made lots of great contacts, and the mayor nearly came! Everybody thought it was a joke at first, but when they realized I really was a superhero –"

"Yeah?"

"Doc, they cheered me like crazy! I helped a couple of girls get some easy work. And on my way home, I rescued a kid from a couple of drug dealers. This is cool, Doc! I'm almost ready to go on TV, like Goldhawk."

"I knew it, watching TV. If you'd stick to comic books –"

"Don't worry, I won't borrow your car again."

"I don't care about the damned car! It's more serious than that. I can't turn you loose on unsuspecting humanity!"

"No, I guess not..."

"On the other hand, the bastards need clowns like you. The last of the romantic heroes!"

"That's me, okay."

"Let's just take it easy for a few days, will you?"

"Sure. Doc, what do you think about me buying a car?"

"What??"

"I could borrow the money easy –"

"If you had wheels, God only knows where the cops would be calling from next."

"I need it for a bigger mission, Doc. There's bad stuff happening all over the world, not just in Moose Jaw. Like all the shootings and murders in the States. I feel terrible for those people. Remember the time we went to Washington, DC? But I was thinking I could start in Montana."

"Montana?"

"Yeah. It's just across the border. Montana is good. Or if I got really serious, I could go all the way to Los Angeles."

"Why the hell would anyone go to Los Angeles?"

"That's where the worst trouble is."

"Anyway, let's talk. About the car."

"It would be like a Batmobile, you know? A guy told me they had some good cars at Four Aces Towing."

"What will you use for money? You spend every dime you earn at Cansave on video games. There isn't enough left to rent a tricycle!"

"I was thinking about putting up my – you know –"

"No, you can't sell your *Action Comic*."

"Well, just for collateral at the pawn shop. Or some of the others. Like traders or horror comics. You don't like horror comics anyway."

"We can talk about this another time."

"Doc, this is something I have to do! Once I get a car, I can hire a faithful companion and we'll make a crime fighter team! I just gotta get organized, so if I need to sell a few comic books…"

"Don, that collection of comic books is your entire life savings. The pawnshop traders will skin you alive."

"You don't think I should be an action hero?"

"I didn't say that."

"Let's ask P.D. It was her that got me started."

"I know."

"Does she know about the police?"

"I didn't want to wake her. It's real late. Why don't you go home and get some rest? The sun will be up in a couple of hours. Come over tonight at supper time. I'll treat you to a mushroom pizza. The Princess will be here, and we can let her be the judge."

With that, Doc wandered off to bed.

Despite Coyote's battered condition, he didn't feel tired at all. He put his helmet and goggles on to ride his bicycle back to his apartment on Fairford Street, dreaming about his upcoming mission. The sun was rising over the park on the first warm day of spring, but he barely noticed. Green sprouts of grass were already edging the sidewalks. People were moving out to their front porches to sit in the morning sun and drink cups of coffee.

Coyote saw all this, but was focused on the action going on in his head like a movie, a cartoon movie. In the movie, he had a complete costume and a flashy new Coyote Mobile. With some money borrowed on his comic book collection, he could buy a new one easily, and have cash left over to upgrade the weapons on his utility belt. He could invest in a smart phone, to help him stay in touch with 911. If Doc didn't let him pawn the comics, he could quit his job at Cansave and get ten months' worth of holiday pay, on top of his final payout cheque.

He rode past the recycling depot to see if Sandra was there, and sure enough, she was. Cansave was usually closed on Saturday, but Sandra often went in to pick through the donations bin. People left more valuable stuff on the weekend, for some reason. Once there was a real fur coat that she got two hundred bucks for at the pawn shop.

"Holy shit," she said. "What happened to you?"

"Had a run-in with some Hells Angels."

"Never fuckin listen to me, do ya? Didn't I say you were headed for a thumpin?"

"It wasn't that bad. Tell you one thing though. They won't be back in Moose Jaw for a while."

"Jesus! What planet are you from? Look at yourself!"

"What?"

"You look like you fell in a hammer mill. And take off that ridiculous helmet! I'm not gonna talk to somebody through a fuckin condom!"

"Okay!" Coyote took off his helmet and goggles. "Whaja find today?"

"Not much. Pair of Calvin Klein jeans."

"Neat. Where'd you get the black eye?"

"Delvis went on a rampage last night and busted the bathroom wall down. I hadda send my kids over to the KFC till the police came. No way I'm going home today. Wendy said I could hang out here and answer the phone."

"Jeeze. You need any help?"

"Aaa, same old shit, don't worry about it. Whadda you been up to?"

"Hey – I got initiated last night."

"Well – yabba dabba do!"

"It was spectacular! They had coloured lights and everything! Beautiful girls!"

"Where did this extravaganza go down?"

"In the Billard Hotel!"

"That dump? I wouldn't be caught dead in the Billard."

"It was awesome, Sandra. Better than a rock show. You shoulda been there. On the way home, I rescued a teenager from the clutches of a drug gang. Then I ran into the bikers."

"Is this gonna be spewed all over the newspaper too, like the last disaster?"

"I dunno. Maybe."

"You just can't stay out of trouble, can you? You're lucky you're still alive."

"Anyway, I'm thinkin of quittin my job to become a professional superhero."

"Yeah? Who's gonna pay you to do that?"

"Oh, I'd be kinda – freelance. Like Dale Goldhawk."

"Aaa, the fuckin TV network pays him. Nobody's gonna pay you! You told Wendy yet?"

"I just thought it up last night."

"She'll put an end to that wacko idea. A turkey like you isn't allowed to just up and quit. She'll tell yer social worker, and that'll be the end of your heroic career."

"Margaret won't care."

"Like shit. Margaret's a social worker. She's paid to care."

"Anyways, I'll tell her. I have to take direct action, Sandra, like saving the environment. Anyway, I thought you'd be happy if I quit. You'll get to work on the can crusher."

"Aaa, that's another dead-end slot like all the others. I'm thinking what I'm really cut out for is a good management position. Anyway, Wendy isn't gonna let you quit because you want a change of image. You're her media star. She needs you."

"She could hire Dwayne back. Jeeze – maybe Dwayne's available. I need a faithful companion. I should talk to him."

"He's a fuckin druggie!"

"Dwayne's cool. He's not wired any more."

"Bullshit."

"He just chips once in a while."

"What the hell do you know about Dwayne chippin heroin?"

"I seen him at the video arcade."

"Don't hang out with that asshole! If you wanta be a hero, you gotta have a better partner than that. Somebody you can count on."

"I'd like to ask Princess Di, but she has other commitments."

"Then you're shit outta luck, aincha?"

"Giss so."

"Tell you what."

"What?"

"I could take a few days off, maybe try it for a week or two. If yer interested."

"Jeeze, Sandra – I dunno."

"Dumbfuck! With an opportunity like this starin ya in the face?"

"Oh, you'd be good, Sandra, but – I might go to the States probably, and you have a family to –"

"Hey, what is this sexist bullshit? Mothers not allowed to work? Don't mothers get to be faithful companions? Or is it just rich-bitches like Doc's princess who get the call? There's equity laws in this country against that kind of thinking, buddy boy!"

"But who would take care of your kids?"

"Aaa – to hell with them! I've been thinking about pulling the plug on the whole operation, anyway. Let that sonofabitch Delvis take care of things for a while. Margaret's always telling me what a rotten role model I am, so giv'em a chance, I say. How much do companions make?"

"Well – I couldn't pay much, at least until I'm famous."

"Hm. I guess I could work for expenses. You do pay expenses, right?"

"Let me think about it, okay?"

"But if we get on TV, you gotta let me talk too."

"Anyways, I have to buy a car first. I was going to sell some comics but Doc won't let me. If you put some money in, maybe we could do it!"

"Well, I got a month's holiday pay coming, plus this week's wages, maybe six hundred bucks in all. If you're serious about expenses."

"We could go out to Four Aces Towing tomorrow and have a look at their used cars. If we like something, we could be ready to go by next Saturday, right after we get paid."

"Hoo-haa! Oh yeah, one more thing."

"Yeah?"

"I want a professional name too!"

"Like what?"

"I dunno. Who are some other faithful companions?"

"Well, there was Tonto. Batman's friend Robin, the Boy Wonder."

"Na."

"Bucky. Tubby. Little Beaver."

"Little Beaver?"

"Yeah. He was an Indian kid. Red Ryder's friend."

"Something suitable for a strong, independent woman."

"Well – there was Supergirl. Or Lois Lane."

"Middle-class phoneys."

"Well – how about Wonder Woman?"

"Wonder Woman?"

"Yeah. She was a great comic book star. Wonder Woman had a pair of magic bracelets that made her invisible. Classy outfit with high blue boots and tight shorts. She also had kind of a golden lasso. She was a descendent of the Amazons."

It was hard, though, for Coyote to see Sandra as Wonder Woman. On the way back to his apartment, he tried to imagine her in a halter and skimpy shorts. She usually wore mismatched sweat outfits that covered her potato-shaped body. By the time he got home, he was exhausted. He didn't even turn on his TV or look at his comics. He rolled out his sofa bed and fell into a deep sleep – before having the strangest dream Donny Coyote had ever dreamed.

CHAPTER 6

A Comic Inquisition

C oyote stood in a courtroom that looked an awful lot like the principal's office in Empire School. But instead of Mr. Bullmer, a judge sat on the other side of a high counter, dressed in black robes. The judge wore a long white wig, and held a hammer in one hand.

"Stand up, birdbrain!" a voice yelled in Coyote's ear. He was jerked to his feet by a Mountie standing beside him. The Mountie wore a Stetson hat, red coat, and leather boots. He whacked Coyote over the head a couple of times with his gloved hand. Coyote turned to look, and even though it was obviously a dream and couldn't really be happening, he almost pissed his pants. The Mountie wasn't a real Mountie. He was Sandra Dollar! She pulled a billy club out of her belt and whanged Coyote over the head again. "Step forward, shitwit!"

He shuffled toward the counter to face the judge, whose face was hidden by the fluffy white wig. A pair of slender hands emerged from the long black sleeves and parted the curls of the wig. This time Coyote's shock was staggering. The judge was Princess Di. Even more astonishing, the front of her black robe had fallen open, and underneath it, she had no clothes. Princess Di was stark naked. And there he was, staring at her soft pink skin.

She said, "The court will hear the case against Captain Coyote, alias Donny Coyote." It was P.D. speaking, but her voice had turned cold and her eyes hard.

Sandra jabbed him in the ribs with her club. "Step to the front," she barked.

"Where is the alleged comic book collection?" Judge Di sniffed.

"Here, Your Majesty," Sandra said. She pointed to a wheelbarrow beside her, full of cardboard boxes. His collection of comic books. The boxes were bashed and busted open, with loose pages falling out. He had a feeling he was being paddled up Shit Creek, and he could hardly breathe from the panic in his chest.

The Mountie plucked a comic from the pile with the tips of her fingers. "Shall I rip out the offensive parts first, Your Majesty?"

Judge Di smiled graciously. "That won't be necessary, sergeant. Who is representing the defendant?"

"I am, Your Majesty," Doc's voice called out. He came rushing through the door in the nick of time. Coyote started breathing a little better.

"Very well. The accused is charged with the possession of obscene and hateful comics. To wit, books violent and degrading to women and other victims of patriarchal culture. This is the charge. How do you plead?"

"I plead for mercy," Coyote said.

"Shut your face!" Sandra yelled, whacking him over the head with her club. She turned to the judge. "I read as many as I could stomach, your majesty, and they all spout the same disgusting line! The oppression of women! This is a pile of stinking male chauvinist crap, denying the existence of females! I say we should incinerate the entire collection! It's too late for this asshole, except to make an example of him to save other innocent minds."

"What sort of punishment do you recommend, sergeant?"

"Cut his balls off!"

"Don't get bloodthirsty, sergeant. This isn't the Dark Ages. I am determined to be fair. And I'm not sure we should be burning books, even if they are hate comics. That could be interpreted as censorship."

"How about shredding them?"

"May I speak to the issue?" Doc said. If anybody could save Coyote's comic books, it would be Doc. When he was a Professor of Cultural Studies in Minneapolis, he had studied comic books, and had his head crammed full of all kinds of information. Doc and Donny Coyote had spent long evenings discussing different comic book characters and the techniques of the artists that drew them. Princess Di sometimes joined these discussions, which could grow heated and wordy. Although he rarely understood what they decided, Coyote was always entranced by their professional rhetoric. It was like Doc and P.D. had their own superpower, which Coyote often found himself practising while he punched the can crusher at Cansave.

"Your Highness," Doc said, "the essence of Mr. Coyote's defence is that, far from degrading women or minority groups, his library of comic books actually projects the highest values of civilized society – the victory of good over evil, and the elevation of women to the status of superior beings." Coyote nodded approvingly.

Judge Di glared at them. "Well, I'll take a look at one," she said.

Sandra selected a comic book off the pile. It was Coyote's prize collector's item, a copy of *Action Comics No. 1*. On the cover, Superman hoisted a car full of crooks over his head, ready to smash them against a rock. Judge Di frowned and flipped to the first page. "This was the first appearance of Superman?"

"As a comic book hero, Your Highness," Doc said. "Of course, supermen were a staple of literature and poetry long before 1938. The Greek heroes, the Norse Gods. Odysseus. King Arthur and the Knights of the Holy Grail were all supermen. The creators of the American Superman were actually a pair of cartoonists named Shuster and Siegel. They stole him from a novel of Philip Wylie's called *Gladiator*."

"But he was the first comic book superhero, right? The first to fly through the air, possess superhuman strength, see through women's clothing, and so forth. Correct?"

"Correct."

"As the name suggests. Super – man." Judge Di picked up a black felt pen and drew a circle on the cover around MAN.

Doc flinched and said, "It's also quite valuable, Your Honour. That is one of six known copies in the world. With the rest of Mr. Coyote's collection, it represents his life's savings. That comic book in mint condition is worth over fifty thousand dollars."

"That's ridiculous! And outrageous. It's worse than pornography. Blatant sexist propaganda promoting patriarchal domination – to brainwash boys into brutish aggression and flaunting their supposedly superior physical power."

"Does Your Majesty genuinely believe there is a conspiracy to create male heroes to ensure male domination? Really, heroic narrative is a cultural tradition that has been with humans since the beginning of time."

"Well, it's going to end. If such nonsense turned this naive young man into 'Captain Coyote,' acting out dangerous fantasies to save the world from evil-doers, then the public is obliged to intercede, if only to protect him from his own delusions. The influence of his reading material is painfully obvious."

"On the contrary," Doc said. "Donny Coyote is a perfectly ordinary young man inspired by the mythology of heroes. His desire to become one is no more pernicious than the public adoration of your name-sake – Princess Diana Spencer. A feminist hero of our age, largely created by the news media."

"That's different. Hers was a story about her struggle for identity, and the cost to her personally. If she was a feminist model, it was because she affirmed her independence in a doomed struggle against patriarchal and monarchist authority, which was determined to crush her. She was a powerful role model, a nurturing mother and peace-maker. She was real and – genuine!"

"Well, that's debatable. And history has a way of deconstructing such iconic figures. But my point is that her success wasn't the result of a feminist plot. So why would it be different for Superman? He was just one of hundreds of 'heroes' created for impressionable young readers. And he was nothing when he first appeared in *Action Comics.* A blip. A piece of blatant plagiarism. But Siegel and Shuster's Superman articulated some deep social need of the 1930s. No one could have predicted his commercial success. As usual, the mass market recognized the power of such mythology long before we anthropologists began to analyze it."

Judge Di frowned. "Perhaps we could defer the theoretical debate until I have studied the entire collection. What else is there?"

Sergeant Sandra reached into the box. "Have a look at this! *Captain Marvel.*"

"A Superman clone created by a rival publisher," Doc observed. "As you can see by his costume, the symbol on his shirt, and the powerful muscled physique. The same archetypal figure."

"But he didn't come from Krypton?"

"No. Captain Marvel's identity was conferred on a crippled American newsboy, Billy Batson, by a bearded old wizard through a magic spell. When Billy Batson said 'Shazam,' he changed into Captain Marvel. Shazam was an acronym made from the names of classical gods. S for Solomon's wisdom and so on: Hercules' strength, Atlas's stamina, Zeus's power, Achilles' courage, and Mercury's speed."

"No women gods, I see."

Doc grinned. "Apparently not."

"Well, it's not funny," Judge Di snapped. "You wouldn't joke about rape or genocide! Such garbage has poisoned the minds of a whole generation of North American men! Send *Captain Marvel* to the shredder!"

"To the shredder!" Sandra hooted. She picked up two whole boxes of Fawcett comic books and dropped them into the shredder bin. Coloured streamers spewed from it like a fountain.

Coyote felt sweaty and sick. If *Superman* and *Captain Marvel* made her angry, what would his other comic books do? *The Punisher,* for example. Or *The Hulk!* Judge Di looked so mad, the entire comics collection could end up destroyed. But that was nothing compared to Coyote's real problem – the growing erection of Mr. Private.

Every time Judge Di waved her arm or slammed her hand on the desk, her black robe opened and revealed more of her naked body. When she moved, the tips of her breasts trembled, throwing shadows on the smooth pink surface of her stomach. Coyote was embarrassed by Mr. Private's response and covered the front of his pants with his hands.

"What else is in this vile collection?" she demanded.

"They're just fantasies, Your Majesty!" Doc said. "Like fairy tales. Comics are like cultural dreams. Nobody has to defend dreams."

"Darned good thing," Coyote thought, appalled and humiliated by what was happening in his own dream. Mr. Private was growing more urgent by the second.

"Superheroes clearly have a powerful influence on the male imagination," Judge Di insisted. "It's not just random storytelling. It's a strategy of the patriarchal elite to exclude women from power because they lack physical prowess. Why don't comic book heroes use their minds, their emotions? They're mere glorification of brute strength."

Coyote tried to look small and insignificant, despite the protrusion in his jeans.

Judge Di turned to face Doc and Coyote with a somber look. "Are there any female comic book heroes?"

"Of course," Doc said. He handed over a copy of *Sensation Comics*. "Wonder Woman. She was a descendant of the Amazons. This may upset your male conspiracy theory."

"Go on." Judge Di leaned back in her chair. The robe fell open to expose a red triangle of bushy hair.

"In the background story, Aphrodite the Goddess of Beauty says, 'My women will conquer men with love!' That was the wonderful premise of Wonder Woman's entire character. When the Amazons were defeated by Hercules and his army of gods, they escaped to Paradise Island, which men were forbidden to enter. Their leader Hippolyta created a small statue which came to life as Diana, the Princess of the Amazons. When she was fifteen, Diana received a set of golden bracelets, bracelets the Amazons wore as symbols of their folly in submitting to male domination."

"No doubt created for a young female audience."

"Perhaps. But it was young males who actually bought it. *Wonder Woman* was as big a hit as *Superman!*"

"The costume looks like something Bill Clinton might design."

"Well – Wonder Woman was a shapely woman, Your Majesty. And she was as colourful as any male superhero. I think the star-spangled shorts and bra were pretty snazzy myself. In this first issue, she left Paradise Island with an American flyer who crashed-landed there during the Second World War. Steve Trevor was a military intelligence officer. Naturally, they fell in love. The Amazons forbade her to have anything to do with him, but Diana nursed Steve back to health with her healing rays."

"And she wasn't just Steve's sycophantic sidekick?"

"No, no, she was the hero! Steve Trevor faded from the story line after a few issues. Like other heroes, Wonder Woman had a dual identity. In daily life she was Diana Prince, a private nurse who cared for Steve.

"In her public heroic life, she rescued women in trouble. She had the power to summon a glass airplane, and she had a golden lasso that caught fleeing criminals. Once roped, they had to do her bidding. The Amazons had given her a pair of gold bracelets called 'cuffs of antisubmission' that could deflect bullets. Wonder Woman took great delight in beating the crap out of bad guys."

"I assume this was written by a woman."

"I'm afraid not. A psychiatrist named William Marston wrote the comic strips in his spare time."

"Oh?"

"Yes. Dr. William Marston. The inventor of the lie detector. Am I digressing?"

"No, it's all adding up now! Look at this stuff. Women in bondage! Whips and shackles. What was Marston, a pervert? Spankings! Aggh – get rid of it."

"Good riddance," Sandra said, flipping the comic into the shredder's grinding rotors, and *Wonder Woman* joined the growing mound of confetti.

"Well, I've seen enough," Judge Di said. "Court is adjourned until I can view the rest of the comics. The defendant will now enter my chambers for a personal interview."

Doc and Sergeant Sandra turned to see what Coyote would do, but he stood paralyzed. If he moved a single step, Mr. Private was going to explode. The black robe slipped off Judge Di's shoulders, leaving her naked in the middle of Mr. Bullmer's office. Coyote could not move, immobilized between terror and desire. Then the door to Mr. Bullmer's office swung shut, and the keyhole slammed Mr. Private right on the head.

CHAPTER 7

Coyote's Second Mission

Coyote awoke in his bachelor apartment with his shorts all sticky and his body streaming sweat. He was horrified at what had happened in his dream and dashed off to take a shower. Washing himself ferociously in his shower stall, he suddenly remembered his comic books.

The yawning emptiness of the closet was worse than his dream. They were gone, every single box. All his *Punishers,* his *Supermans,* his *X-Men.* And *Action Comics No. 1!* He stood in numb shock for several minutes, trembling as he tried to figure it out. He went back and stood in the cold shower to help him think, forcing his body into the icy stream for a good fifteen minutes. Nothing helped. He just couldn't make sense of their disappearance, or the dream about Princess Di that kept running through his head.

He got out and looked at his watch – eight o'clock! He was already late for Doc's supper invitation. He ran for his bicycle and pedalled frantically up the hill to Redland Avenue.

The Pinto was gone from the driveway in front of Doc's house, and Coyote got a sick feeling in the pit of his stomach. But, nearing the house, he could see Princess Di sitting on the porch in Doc's wooden swing, a dark expression on her face. She looked even more upset than she did in his dream, but she was wearing clothes.

Coyote was so embarrassed by what had happened that he could not face her. He tried to keep riding past the house, but she saw him and called out, "Donny!"

"Hi, Princess."

"Have you seen my dad?" she said, her voice jagged from anxiety. He shook his head, unable to speak. Did she know about his strange dream? Had Doc gone to inform the police about it?

"Why?" he stammered. "He's – not here?"

"He'd left before I got up this morning. Before ten. No message."

"Oh." This was not a good sign. When Doc didn't say where he was going, he was heading for the liquor store, and he could be gone for days. But was it because of the comic books and Coyote's dream? Or the accident with the Pinto? Princess Di stared at him, hoping for an answer. He could not meet her tawny eyes, which felt like they could see right through him. He fiddled with the brakes on his bicycle and finally said, "Princess, do you think Doc might've stopped by my place, while I was sleeping?"

"It's possible. Why?"

"Well, you know my comics?"

"Comics?"

"My collection. Of superheroes."

"What about them?" She did not like comic books the way Doc did. Doc thought comics were better than TV and video games. P.D. thought – well, as she did in his dream.

"They've gone missing!" he blurted.

"Really?"

"You think Doc might've borrowed them while I was asleep?"

"Donny, I hope you're not accusing Dad of stealing –"

"No! It's just – I can't find them."

"Oh, they're buried somewhere in your piles of junk. Don't you keep them in old boxes in some cubbyhole?"

"Yeah, but I looked everywhere. They disappeared."

"Well. Try to look at the bright side, Donny."

"Bright side of what?"

"There's an old saying – it's an ill wind that blows no good. You know what that means?"

"Yeah. Bad news."

"Yes, but – bad news with some good news. The cloud with a silver lining."

"You know some good news about my comic books?"

"Think of it as an opportunity to liberate yourself from the shackles of your childhood fantasies. The longer you're stuck in a world of comic absurdity, the harder it is to face the real world. Know what I mean? This could be your chance to grow up."

"I am grown up."

"Escapism is not a career, Donny. You're not a little boy any more. Anyway, it's Dad I'm worried about. I have to go back to Saskatoon on Monday –"

"You think maybe he went to the liquor store?"

"Well, he was pretty upset by your accident last night."

"I told him I'd fix the damage!"

"He's not worried about the money. He's worried about you."

"It was an accident, Princess!"

"A fight with a biker gang at two o'clock in the morning?"

"Jeeze, it's not like I planned it!"

"Well – I have to say it bothers me too. Donny, it's not the damage to Doc's car, it's him being dragged down to the police station in the middle of the night to rescue an irresponsible...!"

"Hero?" Coyote suggested.

"Child! It's too much, Donny! You make me sorry I ever asked you to commit to social action! I never expected my dad to be a casualty in your war on crime! All he does is worry about you, and you go and pull some idiotic stunt like that. It's not fair!"

Princess Di started a long speech about ingratitude and selfishness, until Coyote couldn't follow the words, which tumbled and crashed against each other. Instead, he watched the angry rise and fall of her breasts under her dress.

Suddenly he was experiencing X-ray vision! He could see her

breasts through the cotton fabric, jumping in fury as she gestured. He felt Mr. Private beginning to rise, and forced himself to concentrate on her speech about the evil of comic books.

Her indignant fury ended in a sharply worded threat: "Maybe we should stop this Captain Coyote nonsense before you cause some real trouble!"

Coyote was aghast. The last thing he expected was Princess Di's opposition to his mission. A cold thought pierced his brain like an icicle. Could P.D. have removed the comics? Had she been duped by an evil conspiracy to divert him from his chosen task? Nobody but Princess Di had the power to do that.

Coyote had loved her since he was sixteen, the first day Doc had invited him for lunch at Redland Avenue. He was living at the Hustons then, and Mrs. Pearce was still alive, and she cooked meals for him on Friday night in their big kitchen. P.D. was still a senior at Central Collegiate, and the student council president. Coyote and Mrs. Pearce would listen to her practise her speeches in the living room. He could still quote whole sentences from "The Youth of Tomorrow" and "Beyond the Gender Question."

"Princess, I need my comics, you see, to borrow some –"

P.D. broke down and shouted. "Oh, why don't you get just lost!" Then she twirled on one Birkenstock, and ran into the house.

Coyote was devastated. He waited a while on Doc's front porch, uncertain what to do next. He wanted to go and find Doc, but did not have a clue where to start. Doc could be anywhere if he was on a bender. Or was it about the dream, and the comic books he had defended in the dream trial? Maybe he removed them to keep them safe from the Mounties. But surely he would have left a note.

Donny Coyote sat alone on the porch swing until the night air grew cold, and he pedalled back home, numb and depressed. P.D. had never told him to get lost before. Coyote knew he had to try to sleep. He was scheduled to get up early on Sunday morning, because he and Doc were volunteers to serve the homeless breakfast at Soul's Harbour. Maybe Doc would show up there.

Coyote slept very little that night, rising like a zombie in the morning and stumbling down to Soul's Harbour on Manitoba Street. Doc didn't show up. After working his shift, Coyote went to the Cansave depot, hoping to find Sandra there rifling through the clothing bins. She went through the pockets of donated clothes, and sometimes found money and other neat things like key chains or lighters.

Sandra grinned when he arrived, showing her gaps of missing teeth. She held up a cracked motorcycle helmet with a dangling chin-strap. "Here, Donny, you can wear this instead of that cheesy flyer's hat. And look! Somebody left a carpenter's tool belt, just the thing for a real utility belt."

Coyote was suspicious. Why was Sandra suddenly interested in his costume? She wore a T-shirt which declared in big green letters GRAB YOUR OWN ASS. About six inches of belly protruded between that and her pink sweat pants, stuffed into a pair of cowboy boots.

"What's that outfit for?" he asked nervously.

"I'll need a costume if I go along as your faithful companion."

"I don't know, Sandra. I've been thinking about it and – why do you want to go?"

"Could be a barrel of fun."

"It's not supposed to be fun, it's hard work."

"Yeah? Beating up on losers?"

"That's just once in a while, when they get aggressive and out of control. Anyway, I might go somewhere for a while and freelance, you know? Maybe get a business card made, and I could start working as a security guard. I'd like to try the States."

"Well I gotta admit, it takes balls, Donny, quittin your job and hitting the road without a clue where your next dollar's comin from. I respect a man of action. That's what convinced me to join up with you. We could kick butt."

"I dunno, Sandra."

"What's wrong? Chicken?"

"No, it's just – I'm not feeling too good."

"What is it?"

"A real bad headache. It might be a migraine."

Sandra didn't have any aspirin, but she broke open the first aid box in Wendy's office, and handed him the bottle of Tylenol. Then Coyote went home to his apartment and watched TV, but it only made him feel worse. He kept turning to the news to see if Doc had been in a car accident, then he'd go to the closet and look at the empty space and take more Tylenol and try to sleep. He got up early Monday morning and rode past Doc's house, but the car was still not there. He was afraid to go in and face Princess Di.

Dragging himself in to work, Coyote tried to concentrate on crushing the cans flowing past the unit counter. When the rush died down at lunchtime, Sandra said, "You nearly got me talked into this expedition to the States. But I needa know: what's in it for me?"

"You mean money?"

"There's gotta be some compensation. Else why do it?"

"There's other rewards for beating down evil. Honour. Fame. Good PR. Sometimes you get money, but not like regular wages. People feel grateful when you save their town, or straighten out their teenagers, or whatever."

"Yeah, but how do you collect? Invoice them, or what?"

"Oh, it's usually a verbal contract. We provide security, people offer us a place to stay, maybe ask us in for supper, or order up a bucket of fried chicken. If it's a rich community, like Regina, they might have even fancier rewards. They might give us official positions. Like Sheriff, or District Attorney. Least that happens in the States. Everything's easier in the States."

"Bullshit!"

"I see it all the time on TV! If I build up a reputation as a crimefighter like Batman or Dale Goldhawk, I could get a job with a real security service. Maybe even the President's secret service. The sky's the limit."

"Yeah, right. You ever been across the border?"

"Couple times with Doc to Minneapolis. You?"

"Millions of times. I was born down there, eh? In Lewistown,

Montana. I'm a descendant of Gabriel Dumont. Of course, my people don't recognize the border."

"Your people?"

"The Métis people."

"I didn't know you were Métis."

"Lot you don't know. My family's real name was Douleur. I'm thinking of changing it back. What about your people?"

"I don't have any people. I came from an orphanage."

"You got no idea who your parents were? Dropped off by Indians, I bet."

"You think so?"

"Had to be, with a name like Coyote. Well, you're gonna have trouble crossing the border, unless you got me along to advise you."

"How come?"

"Cause you can't prove your heritage! They stopped me just because they thought I looked Indian. Course, they said it was because I had a criminal record, but that's just bullshit. I don't recognize criminal records. Anyway, things are better in the States. I don't mind giving it a shot. When do you wanta leave?"

"I dunno, Sandra. Maybe I'll try this country first. To work up my résumé."

"Listen, I gotta get out of town before the end of the month. Delvis is only waiting for me to get paid so he can grab the money. If we got to the States, he'd never find me."

"Maybe if we got some experience, we could get a job in the secret service."

"The what?"

"Secret Service. The special bodyguards for the President. Also they get to take out his enemies. Like that Saddam guy. Well, they didn't get him yet, but problems like that."

"Are you nuts? Get a job from the President of the USA?"

"Sure. Might as well reach for the top."

"You don't know where he lives!"

"I do so. He lives in California. Near Disneyland somewhere."

"Bush? Like hell. He lives in Washington, DC."

"I mean President Reagan! He was the only real president."

"Aaa – you moron. You don't know anything about politics."

"Yes, I do. I know you have to be a lawyer to get into politics."

"What an idiot! Reagan wasn't a lawyer. He was a fuckin movie star."

"That's what made him such a great president. He was already a hero. Maybe that's why he won the election. The most important thing for a president is to look like a hero. You can just tell he's a great guy. He'll be happy to see us."

"Okay, you talked me into it. But if there's no pay, you have to cover my travel expenses."

"All we need is food and maybe gas, and I have an American Express Card. Doc gave it to me."

"You got an American Express Card? In your own name?"

"Yeah, Doc pays the account from my trust fund."

"Hey, we're laughing, Donny boy! Don't leave home without it! He don't care if you use it?"

"Doc's gone off somewhere, and I hafta quit worrying about him. He's got problems of his own. Anyway him and Princess Di are against my plan. I guess she thinks I'm wrecking Doc's life."

"I tell ya, I wouldn't want her breathing down my neck. Spoiled rich kid. She's one a them middle class feminists, born with a silver spoon in her mouth."

"Princess Di is a wonderful person, Sandra. You're jealous because she's so good at social action."

"Me, jealous of that Barbie doll? You wanna make me hork? What do you think of my costume?"

"I dunno," he said. "Maybe a different T-shirt."

"Hey, there's a thousand classy T-shirts to pick from here. Lookit this one. 'Take Me Drunk, I'm Home!'"

"Maybe something with stars. Wonder Woman had stars and stripes on her suit."

"Donny, I got a whole garbage bag full of nearly new T-shirts. There's an entire friggin truckload here! If we can't get security jobs, we can set up a roadside stand selling T-shirts. Lookit all these vintage T-shirts waitin to be recycled. Has to be a few bucks in this, eh? Say, what are we gonna be driving?"

"I'm going to Four Aces Towing after work to look at vehicles. They were recommended."

"Them yahoos? Better take me along, else you'll get totally ripped off."

Coyote tried to talk Sandra out of going along on his mission several times that day, but she grew more determined than ever. After work, she borrowed a bike from Chip Elliott, who worked on the loading dock. They rode out to Four Aces Towing, an old Esso station converted to a wrecking yard. Dwight was in the shop, tearing the hoist off a grain truck. He didn't have any cool cars like a Mustang or a Jeep right then, but thought he might have some in a few days.

As they were leaving, Coyote noticed a one-ton pickup truck near the back gate. Somebody had constructed a log cabin out of spruce slabs on the back of it. The cabin had windows and a shingled roof, and a reinforced steel door on the back. Cut in the door with a welding torch was a sign that read, "Wally's Welding."

"How's the motor in that camper truck?" Coyote asked.

"Camper? That's a mobile welding shop. I took it in a trade last fall. You a welder?"

"No, but it looks cool."

"That'll getcha noticed on the highway, okay."

"How is it for gas mileage?"

"Well, you couldn't ask for a better engine."

"Really?"

"Hundred and five horsepower flat-head six, eh? It'll do twenty klicks to the gallon easy. Course, you're not going to win any races but – how far you planning to go?"

"To the States."

"He gets these crazy ideas," Sandra said. "This guy's Captain Coyote. You know – the big hero?"

"Oh yeah – my brother said you might be by. I can give you a great deal on this baby. Twelve hundred bucks drives it off the lot."

"Is she in good shape?"

"Maybe a tad slow on the highway, but you earn that back on gas mileage. She'll make it to the States easy. Gas is cheaper in the States too. Less'n two bits a litre."

"Can we look inside?"

"Sure. Specially equipped. Two built-in work-benches above the wheel wells, which you could easy convert to bunk beds, if you plan to camp. Throw a couple of sleeping bags up there. Could easy adapt that propane forge in the corner into a little cook stove. Plus a bench vice and a box of welding tools. All thrown in free."

"We'd need a radio," Sandra said. "How's the radio?"

"Tell you what I can do. I could patch in a radio and an eight-track tape deck from that old Chrysler over there."

"Hey, that's not bad, Donny. What do you think?"

"It looks all right. But it's a lot of money."

"How much you guys got to spend?"

"Well, maybe a thousand. Right, Sandra?"

"Yeah. A thousand, tops."

"I could let it go for eleven hundred."

"What else can you throw in?" Sandra asked.

"Whatever you need. Here's a jack and wheel wrench. It doesn't have seat belts, but I could rip the seat belts out of that Plymouth Fury beside it. Free gas can."

"Filled with gas?"

"Goes without saying. You won't get a better deal in Moose Jaw. Nobody's got one of these babies sitting on their lot. I can't hold it forever, though. You got cash?"

"We'll bring the money next Friday. Go ahead and put the radio and stuff in. What about license plates?"

"Well, that's up to you guys. Tell you what, I'll put on a set of dealer plates that expire in a month or so. Get you across the border, anyway. After that, who cares?"

The deal worked out better than Coyote had planned. Sandra and

Coyote gave notice to Wendy the next day, and by Friday their April pay cheques were ready to go, with holiday pay. Wendy tried once more to talk Coyote out of quitting, but when she saw that he was serious, she gave each of them a sleeping bag from a box of seconds that had come from Home Depot. They also snagged a couple more bags full of T-shirts, and a compass and a bottle opener for his utility belt.

Princess Di had returned to Saskatoon but left a message at his apartment saying she was worried about Doc, but she had a pile of her own work to do, trying to finish her thesis. Coyote was also worried about Doc, who could disappear for days on one of his drinking binges. You never knew which angel was in charge when Doc went on a binge. P.D. didn't believe in angels, but she still talked about Doc's good angel and bad angel. Once Doc had woken up in a youth hostel in Spearfish with a bad angel, and not a clue how he got there. Princess Di had to drive down and kick the bad angel's butt around the block before she could bring Doc home.

Coyote knew from Alateen meetings that Doc was the only one who could challenge the power that alcohol had over him. All Coyote could do was be a good example, acting in a way that made Doc proud, proving he was independent. Even if Doc did take the comic books to hide them somewhere for safekeeping, Coyote still trusted Doc. Doc knew what was right to do, even if he didn't always do it right. There might be a good reason the comics went missing during his dream.

He didn't understand all the weird things Doc said, or why he did such dumb things on a drinking jag, but Doc didn't always understand Coyote either. Probably nobody understood Coyote, except maybe P.D. He didn't care.

With Sandra's and Coyote's money together, they closed the deal at Four Aces on Saturday morning and drove the new Coyote Mobile back to Doc's house. Coyote had a key. Sandra said they'd be doing Doc a favour by cleaning out his fridge before the food went rotten, so they borrowed a plastic cooler and filled it from Doc's fridge.

Sandra also thought of stopping at the food bank, and they got a bag full of potatoes, some pizza pops, and a whole box of smokies and pepperoni sausages, plus a bag of doughnuts and a cabbage, which Sandra promptly tossed in the dumpster. She insisted on stopping at the beer store and buying two cases of Bushwakker at her own expense, in case they didn't come across beer stores along the way. They were set for a couple of weeks.

Coyote's main objective was to find the President's house – Reagan or Bush, it all depended which direction they went – while looking for opportunities along the way. They could look for good jobs to put on their résumé. They would just head south on Number Two Highway, keeping their eyes peeled for crimes in progress, environmental disasters, and victims of abuse.

They were in no particular hurry. If they happened to find a town where there was lots of scope for fighting crime, they'd just settle down for a while and get to work. The news media would no doubt follow their progress along the way, so the heroes planned to ride the tide of good PR to ever greater assignments. If there were tough questions at the border, the US officials would be forced by public demand to allow them through.

Once they became famous superheroes, Coyote planned to call Doc and Princess Di and let them know he was okay. Then they could come and visit. P.D. would be so proud of him, she might even decide to join the mission.

Truckin On Down The Road

CHAPTER 8

The Russian Drones

Their first leadership argument broke out before they reached the edge of town. Sandra wanted to take the wheel as the official driver, as driving was included in the faithful companion's job description she was compiling in her head. Coyote was just getting used to the operation of the new Coyote Mobile, and decided the leader of the mission should drive the first day, or at least till lunch time.

A hot argument ensued, which filled the Coyote Mobile with a furious din until Sandra yelled for him to stop. He pulled over to the side while she jumped out in a big snit and slouched around to the back door of the camper. She said she'd rather ride in the back than sit in the company of a boneheaded boss, and would prepare an official grievance for the day when she'd have to report him for Unfair Labour Practices.

After a few miles, Sandra slid open the little window in the back of the cab. "So, how does the old bitch handle?"

"You mean, the Coyote Mobile?"

"You're not really gonna call it that, are ya?"

"Why not? It's a good way to promote our name, plus it advertises that we're a professional action team. You got a better name?"

Sandra thought a long time, rejecting several possibilities that almost came to mind – and finally came up with The Wonder Wagon, which even she admitted sucked big time.

"Good," Coyote said. "It's settled. Maybe we can find a sign painter in Wood Mountain and get the name painted on the side. Like Ghost Busters. Plus we can order business cards and personalized license plates."

It was a gorgeous morning for driving, straight south from Moose Jaw into the warmth of an early May morning. Coyote felt happy to be alive and on the road. There was nobody to stop them doing what they wanted, no questions to answer, or permission to get. They were free to go wherever the roads and his new highway map took them. He wanted to share his feeling with Sandra, but she was still in a sulk about not driving.

In the distance ahead, the high ridge of the Missouri Coteau loomed over the southern horizon, showing green along its high crest as the last traces of snow melted down its slopes. Doc said the ridge marked a north-south continental divide. On this side, all the water ran back to the Qu'Appelle River and Hudson Bay, and all the way to the Arctic Ocean. On the south side, the creeks flowed down to the Missouri and south to the Gulf of Mexico.

Sandra muttered through the window, "I don't suppose you got any idea where we're stopping tonight?"

"I'd like to camp at Wood Mountain," Coyote said.

"What the hell for?"

"Well, there's a campground there, according to the map. Also a personal reason."

"Personal?"

"That's where I was born."

"What a bullshitter! I thought you were born in an orphanage!"

"No, I grew up there. Doc found out a couple years ago when he searched the records at the Orange Home. They said my mother came from Wood Mountain, and that's where I probly born. Doc and me went there once, but there's nobody by the name Coyote. He figured my family had all left."

"Well, it wouldn't hurt to check it out. On the other hand, if you're an example of what people produce in Wood Mountain, maybe we shouldn't look under too many rocks. What else is in Wood Mountain?"

"There's a big rodeo at the park in the summertime. Doc said my dad might've been a rodeo rider."

"Hey, that'd be okay! They need security at rodeos."

"It'll be a good place to rack up some experience. That's the first thing the president will ask for."

"I can't believe you're serious! How far is it to Washington, anyway?"

"Dunno. You could check the map."

"Naa. I don't read maps."

"How come?"

"Cause I can't!" Sandra snapped. "Workers' Comp says I'm 'spatially challenged.' Hey, if I could read maps, I wouldn't be going on this goofy expedition, I'd be a truck driver."

"Well, it's down that way, about five thousand kilometres. California is about the same in that direction. Could be five days driving. Maybe six."

"If we went to California, we could go through Las Vegas, right?"

"Sure. It's on the way."

"Lots of opportunities for security work there. Place is crawling with the Mafia and other gangsters."

"Sounds possible."

"Stick with me, Coyote. I know which side of my bread is buttered. We could really rock Las Vegas."

They passed over the crest of the coteau and looked out over a series of vast plateaus falling off to the south. And as they approached the final ridge, Coyote spotted a squadron of Russian Drones hovering along its peak. There was a whole flight of them, Soviet robot attack planes, exactly as they had appeared in No. 43 of *Blackhawk Comics*. Captain Blackhawk and his squadron of fighter pilots shot them down in the final nick of time, just as they were being launched at New York.

"Russian Drones! Sandra, look!"

There were ten or twelve of them in a long wavering formation, their propellers whirling in the air. They were attached to pylons standing below the ridge, where they couldn't be detected by American radar stations beaming sonar waves from the Montana border.

"What are you talking about? Those are wind turbines, you bonehead."

"No, I can prove it! That's them! Same huge propellers and everything. These are even bigger than the ones in *Blackhawk*. Sandra – we have to warn the Americans. This could be our introduction to the president!"

"You're nuts! They're turbines on the tops of power poles."

"I'm telling you those are launching pylons. Just like in *Blackhawk!*"

"What a shitwit! See that cable going up the pole? That's a power line."

"Sandra – you don't understand. They're revving up their engines for takeoff. When they reach supersonic speed, they'll disconnect and fly south to destroy American cities. We have to stop them!"

"Wait a minute. If they're Russian, what are they doing in Saskatchewan?"

"They put them where the CIA could never find them – because it's so isolated. There aren't any farms through this area. Look – they're aimed straight south! Right? It's time for action!" He pulled the Coyote Mobile over to the shoulder.

"Hang on," Sandra said. "Let's stop and call the cops at the next pay phone. Just don't go messing with them, okay? There's a big wire fence around the base of each one."

"There's no time to lose!"

Coyote veered off the highway and through a Texas gate into the high country pasture where the Drones were moored. "I realize they look like wind turbines, but that's why they're so dangerous. These drones could have nuclear warheads on them. Captain Coyote must take action. You can get out and wait here if you're nervous." He stopped the Coyote Mobile and let Sandra scramble out the back.

"Okay," she yelled, "but it'll be your ass that's going on the chopping block."

Captain Coyote lifted his new helmet from the dashboard and strapped it on. He floored the accelerator, and the truck went careening along the ruts through the buffalo grass toward the pylons at the top of the ridge. The trail was so rough that boxes and tools were bouncing around in the back, but he kept the gas pedal jammed to the floor. The motor roared at full power as the Coyote Mobile bucked and lunged toward the nearest drone. It finally stopped, tires skidding on the grass, near the base of a drone.

Coyote jumped from the cab and grabbed the bolt-cutters from his utility belt. The only way to climb the fence, which was probably electrified, was to clamber onto the roof of the truck and leap over the wires onto the metal tower. The drone's propellers whirred thirty feet overhead, in a high-pitched, menacing whine. They were nearing top speed, about to take off at any second.

Coyote climbed quickly up the pole, only to be abruptly halted by a metal shield near the top. He could not maneuver around it, or get close enough to the aircraft to smash it with his bolt-cutters. He would have to cut the electrical cable. He thrust the bolt-cutters' jaws at the power line and, gritting his teeth, slammed the handles together.

An explosion shook the air simultaneously with the cry of "Hawkaaa!" bursting from Captain Coyote's lips. A lightning bolt blasted out of nowhere, sending an electric arc shooting down his arms in a writhing web of blue neon, whipping around his head and down his back, zapping every nerve and muscle in his body. He felt like he'd been smashed in the head by a post maul. The jolt hurled him off the tower, flying through the air in a long arc. He hit the ground with a bounce or two and rolled down the slope like a tumbleweed, stopping at the base of the next drone.

His breath knocked out and his head twisted against the fence, Captain Coyote looked up in triumph. The drone's screaming propeller was slowing to a stop! He collapsed on the grass, stunned, his brain a whirling panorama of fireworks and sparks and shooting stars. He couldn't remember who he was for a minute, or what he was supposed to be doing. He knew now how Superman felt when struck down with Kryptonite.

Captain Coyote's fatal weakness might be that he drew lightning. But how could lightning strike on a sunny day, with not a cloud in the sky? And at the precise moment he attacked the drone! It had to be a Russian booby trap of some kind. He slowly cranked himself to his feet, mentally preparing to attack the next Drone.

He looked for his bolt-cutters, and eventually found them lying in the grass a few yards away. The lightning bolt had split them up the middle, leaving the wooden handles smouldering stumps of charcoal.

Sandra came wheezing up the trail. "Donny! Are you okay, Donny?"

Coyote tried to move his jaws to answer, but they refused to unclench. He suddenly felt weak, and fell to his knees.

"What the hell are you doing?" Sandra said. "Praying?"

His voice box was paralyzed, but he could still see, for his glasses had miraculously stayed on his face. Everything was out of focus, though, and Sandra looked downright weird. Her eyes spun like drone propellers.

"That was fucking spectacular, man! I told you that was a power turbine! Jeeze, that was better than the Chinese fireworks at the Regina fair! Can't you talk, or what?"

Coyote gestured victoriously at the dying drone.

"Yeah, I tried to tell you, but you wouldn't listen! Maybe next time you'll learn."

Coyote finally pried his jaw loose. "I'm gonna finish them off. Out of my way."

"Don't be a *dumbkopf*. Let's just climb into the Coyote Mobile, and be on our merry way. You better lay down in the back while I drive. You look kinda rough."

Captain Coyote staggered over to look into the side mirror of the truck and was shocked by what he saw. A blackened chunk of plastic, the remains of the helmet, covered the left half of his head. The bare right side looked like a flame-roasted haunch of ham, still smoking. The right lens of his glasses had turned black, and stared out of his soot-covered face. His hair on that side was all burned off, and the skin covered with a layer of black crud. His face looked split down the middle, half twisted like The Joker's.

"Come on, gimme the keys. Let's get outta here before somebody comes to check on this busted turbine. There's probably an alarm on it. Just trouble looking for a place to happen, aren't you? Like that kid with the pop cans."

"I was right about that kid," Coyote muttered. "And I'm right about the drones." But there was a tremor of doubt in his voice.

"They're not drones! They're wind generators! Jeeze, yer a stubborn son of a bitch."

"Doc says you gotta be stubborn to be a good comic book collector."

"Big deal. Anyways, I thought you said your collection went missing. You don't even know where they are."

"Don't worry, I'll find out who took them."

Sandra laughed. "Maybe the Russians came and stole 'em in the middle of the night."

She drove the Coyote Mobile across the hills, as Coyote gritted his teeth in pain. He was counting the kilometres to Wood Mountain, where he hoped they could stop and find a drug store. He wanted to buy some Firebrass Balm for his burned face. He had forgotten to pack Firebrass into the first-aid kit, which was in a special compartment in the back. Also he had to fix his bolt-cutters, a crucial weapon in the fight for justice.

"Justice, my ass!" Sandra said. "When are we gonna get real weapons? We could use a few more megatons of firepower."

"Guns?"

"Hey, buddy, we're heading for the land of deadly force. We need a Kalashnikov or one of those Uzis."

"We can't afford machine guns, Sandra. Anyway, superheroes don't use guns. The secret is to use the special weapons we've got."

"Who says?"

"The Green Lantern. He lost all his magic power when crooks robbed him of his power ring, and he vowed to work with whatever material was available."

"Green Lantern? Never heard of him."

"Don't sound ignorant. He was one of the first big heroes. He had a smartass sidekick, too, a kid named Doiby Dickles. Anyway, they stopped at the next oak tree they came to and cut off a branch. A big thick one as long as two men – for a cudgel. He beat on crooks with that."

"Well, let me know when you spot an oak tree. There are no oak trees in Saskatchewan."

"Chokecherry might work, if we see a big one. The thing is I could use a real cudgel. I need more than a pair of bolt-cutters and a black-jack. Heck, with a good big cudgel, I could've knocked those drones right off their stands!"

"Spare me the Schwarzenegger movie. The way you look, it'll be a few days before you tackle anything more dangerous than a bottle of beer."

"It's only a burn. And a few bruises. I'll be okay."

"What a fruitcake! I'd be, like, screaming my head off if I got a jolt of power like that. Jeeze, there was sparks coming out your ears and everything! Wasn't it painful?"

"It hurts, but I never complain."

"How come?"

"Hero policy. Not even Wonder Woman complained. Pain's no big deal. Anybody can put up with physical pain. I learned that at the Orange Home."

"There you go again. Male chauvinist bullshit! If you assholes ever had to experience childbirth, with half your guts dropping out, you wouldn't even say the word pain!"

"I didn't."

"Pardon me?"

"Well – it was you who brought it up. I was just explaining –"

"Anyways, I'd rather listen to a person groaning in agony, than put up with an idiot who sits there holding it back and causing other people stress."

"You should be watching the road, anyways. I'm okay."

"As long as the pain rule don't apply to faithful companions, then we understand each other. If I get zapped through the head with 20,000 volts of electricity, expect serious screaming."

"Go ahead. There's no policy for faithful companions. In fact, lots of them yell in pain. It might even be part of the job description."

"Speaking of job descriptions. When do we stop for a meal, Captain?"

"We'll be in Wood Mountain in a couple of hours. But I'll get the cooler out if you want some lunch. I'm not hungry myself."

"Well, I'll say one thing, Coyote. You're easy to get along with." She pulled the truck over to the side so Coyote could climb into the back and get the food cooler. "While yer at it, dig one of them Bushwakkers out for me, willya? You made me awful thirsty up there on the wind turbine."

"What do you want to eat?"

"How about a couple of them pepperoni sticks?"

Sandra guzzled down half a Bushwakker before Coyote could get the food box opened. She belched so loud it rattled the passenger window. "Shit, that's good stuff!" She burped again. "None of that commercial piss for superheroes, eh Donny? And you won't find restaurants that make food as good as this, not even McBurgers." Holding two pepperonis in her left fist, she slammed the gearshift into low and the Coyote Mobile lurched back onto the highway.

"Well, enjoy it while you can. That beer is all we get for the whole trip."

"Jeeze, what a party-pooper! As soon as I start enjoyin myself, you gotta throw cold water all over. Here I am bustin my ass to put this outfit somewhere, and all you do is bitch and moan. Here, have a puparoni!"

"I'm not hungry."

"What are ya, anorexic? You gotta learn to consume!" She rolled down the window to chuck the empty bottle into the ditch. "Pull me another brewsky, okay?" Coyote was horrified. "Sandra! We can't litter the countryside. That's the first rule of being a hero. It's not just fighting bad guys. We have to set an example. That bottle is deposit-refundable. Children will be watching our every move!"

"Yeah, yeah. There's a package of beef jerkies there too. You wanta try them?"

"Here."

"Atta boy. Hey – brighten up. I bin thinking about this security business. Y'know, that could be a good racket. Okay, it's a little dangerous, but we're ready to take risks – right?"

They reached Wood Mountain by late afternoon, but the village seemed deserted. A single grain elevator tilted crookedly over the railway track. They drove the length of Main Street, a two-block stretch of abandoned stores and decrepit houses. There were a few cars around, parked in various yards, but not a soul could be seen in the streets. Hoping to find more signs of life in his birthplace, Coyote was cruelly disappointed. The businesses were all boarded up and for sale, except for a quonset hut that looked like a curling rink at the end of the street. There was a gas pump in front and a sign said, "Trail's End Café and Gas Bar."

As the Coyote Mobile clanked to a halt beside the pump, the proprietor stepped out the door. He had dark skin and wore a blue turban wrapped around his head. He studied them with a mix of hope and suspicion.

"Hi there," Coyote said.

"Good evening, gentlemen."

"We're looking for some people named Coyote."

"There is no one by that name in Vood Mountain."

"You sure?"

"Most assuredly sure. I have lived here for three years, since I purchased this café, and the only coyote I have heard of was an artist who lived here before my time. They say he drank copiously every night at the old hotel and wandered up and down the street, howling at the moon like that rascally wild canine."

"I don't suppose you have any Firebrass Balm in your store?"

"Pardon me? Is it a cigarette?"

"Salve. For my face."

"I am sorry, no. Perhaps Vick's Vaporub?"

"Hm. Where's the campground?"

"It is two miles east of town. A fine facility. Unfortunately, it will not be open until the first of June."

They decided to try the campground anyway, and found the gate open. At the far end, a Southwind luxury motor home was parked in a grove of poplar trees. While Sandra lit a fire in the barbecue pit to cook their smokies and Kraft Dinner, Coyote looked for a good big cudgel. They would need one if they ran into another terrorist plot. He took a hatchet from the toolbox and walked over to the poplar trees.

As Coyote passed the super-extended mobile home, he heard heavy metal music blaring inside. A party was underway, with women's voices shrieking and the sound of stomping feet. He chopped down a poplar and lopped off a couple of branches to make new handles for his bolt-cutters.

Suddenly a pair of three-wheeled motorcycles roared into the campground and pulled up beside the Southwind. Coyote knelt in the bush to watch the marauders, in case they harassed the tourists. He could finish peeling and whittling the grip of his cudgel. In the meantime, his stomach groaned with hunger, and his burnt face ached like it had been smacked with a plank. Sandra would be guzzling beer and eating all the macaroni, but Coyote stayed at his post. As the party in the Southwind grew louder and wilder, he crouched, waiting for the tourists to call for help. Once or twice he thought he heard a scream, but decided it was from the rock music. He finally fell asleep, and awoke stiff and cold just before dawn. The park was silent.

Returning to the Coyote Mobile, he discovered Sandra had polished off the whole case of Bushwakker and passed out beside the van, where she snored like a gas mower. There were at least nine empty bottles lying on the ground around her. Sandra's drinking was going to be a problem on the mission, that was clear. She refused to get up at eight a.m. for morning assembly. When Coyote tried to wake her at ten o'clock, she just snarled and turned over, her belly protruding below her shirt.

After a breakfast of Kraft Dinner, Coyote spent the morning organizing his equipment in the van, and pounding nails in the wall to hang his tools up. He put labels over them with a red felt pen, and set everything in its place. He fitted new handles on his bolt cutter. He carried the empty bottles to the camp recycling dumpster. At noon, he tried to shake Sandra awake.

"Hey, Sandra, let's go. Your belly's gettin sunburned."

"Where's that fuckin racket comin from?"

"Robins up in the trees. Means it's spring."

"Tell'em to shut the fuck up! Hey, any beer left?"

"You already drank a week's supply."

"Toldja we'd have a good time on this trip." She belched and hiccuped in the same instant, silencing the robins. "I'll be responsible for filling the cooler with beer."

"Let's have lunch first."

"You have lunch. I'm not hungry. I'll drive back to town and find a beer store. There has to be one in Wood Mountain. Shoulda asked that rag head."

At that moment, a racket burst out at the far end of the campground, as the motorcycles began revving their motors. They pulled onto the exit trail, their purple helmets gleaming in the noon sun.

"Bikers!" Coyote muttered. "This could be trouble, Wonder Woman." He reached for his utility belt. "Get ready for action."

"You think those punks hit on the people in the big RV?"

"That's a Southwind. Probably belongs to some movie star."

At the motor home, several terrified faces peered out the windows, as the bikers roared toward the exit.

"I've got to stop them, Sandra."

"How come?"

"Just to question them. You have to look evil straight in the eye. Only a hero can recognize it."

"Be my guest."

"If they're just ordinary punks and scumbags, I'd let you deal with it. But you're not trained enough to face a supercriminal."

"Hey, they're all yours, captain. Personally, I'm against violence. But if some asshole starts beating on me – watch out! This is one woman who can defend herself."

"Good attitude, Sandra."

As the motorcycles approached, Coyote stepped to the middle of the trail and waved them to a halt. They screeched to a stop, the dust rolling in clouds. Their license plates said they were from Nebraska. They had cool purple helmets, with high-tech radio headsets, and they wore dark sun goggles and white bandanas across their faces like road bandits. Coyote walked around the Americans' machines. The one on the left pulled the scarf away from his face. "Nice day, mister," he said. "You the camp attendant?"

"I'll ask the questions here. You from Nebraska?"

"Yeah, my partner and I are optometrists, heading up to a convention in Edmonton. Are those prescription eyeglasses you're wearing?"

"I said I'll ask the questions. Were you harassing the people in the Southwind?"

"Not at all. We partied with them last night for a while. You know who that Southwind belongs to, right?"

"Who?"

"Katie Kool. The country and western singer."

Coyote was stunned. Katie Kool was one of his biggest musical heroes. He was her most diehard fan. "Stand back, Sandra," he said, elbowing her to one side. "I'll deal with this."

"That's far enough, you bozos," he said to the bikers. "Just shut off your motors till we can interview those women you were terrorizing."

"Terrorizing?" The bikers looked at one another, amazed. "We're not terrorists. We're optometrists. Let us by!" They released their clutches and the bikes plunged forward, charging straight at Coyote.

He swung at the nearest biker with his cudgel, and would have knocked him clean off the machine if the man hadn't jumped first.

Sandra tried to wrench the rider's helmet off as he rolled on the ground. The other biker swerved around Coyote and took off for the exit.

Concerned for Katie Kool's safety, Coyote sprinted across the campground to see if she was okay after the night of terror. A girl sat on a canvas deck chair beside the door, watching Wonder Woman and the biker fight over the helmet.

"Miss Kool?" Coyote asked.

"Katie's inside. What's going on over there?"

"My partner is sorting out the biker who harassed you last night."

"Look! The other one's coming back."

Coyote turned in surprise. The second bike had indeed turned around and was roaring back to rescue his fallen comrade.

"Donny!" Sandra shouted. "Get back here. He's tryna grab my helmet!"

Before Coyote could move, the motorcycle ran right into Sandra, its headlight ploughing into her stomach. She dropped like a stunned cow, and the first biker jumped back onto his machine, clutching his helmet. Both motorcycles drove over Sandra's thrashing body, and sped out of the campground to the highway. The dust settled for a few minutes, as Coyote and the girl watched Sandra crawl toward the Coyote Mobile. She climbed inside, apparently looking for beer.

A woman with buzz cut hair and a red cowboy shirt stepped through the door. Coyote recognized her right away, from Muchmusic TV.

"You can breathe easy, Miss Kool," he said. "You're safe!"

"And you are –?"

"Captain Coyote. I don't have my costume on right now. I used to be Donny Coyote, a hero from Moose Jaw. Friend to those who have no friend. Defender of the downtrodden. I have a reference from Dr. Diana Pearce."

"Reference? For what?"

"Protection and security during your stay in Wood Mountain."

"I've already got security." She and the girl carrying the deck chair stepped back inside the trailer, and she snapped the screen door shut. "Anyway, we're leaving."

"That's too bad. Are you going by way of Moose Jaw?"

"Why do you want to know?"

"Well, if you don't mind, you could stop at the newspaper and tell them how we saved you from those bikers. We can use some good publicity."

But someone inside the motor home started the engine, and before Katie could reply, the Southwind had lumbered out of the campground, following the motorcycles to the highway.

When Coyote got back to the Coyote Mobile, he found Sandra draining a bottle of Bushwakker she had discovered.

"Thanks for the help," he said.

"We took care of them, eh? Didja remember to ask Katie for a reference? With her endorsement, we could get real security work in the States, get a classy group of clients. The Americans will appreciate a gonzo action team like ours." She raised the empty beer bottle in a salute. "After all, we are Canadians!"

CHAPTER 9

Lost in the Badlands

By the time the two adventurers got the Coyote Mobile loaded up, their spirits began to lift. They had triumphed over the forces of evil, despite the tire tread marks across Sandra's stomach and the painful burns on Coyote's face, which was beginning to blister a bit. The day's luck had already improved. Sandra had found the missing case of Bushwakker under the van, and stashed it in the truck's spare tire well, until they could get ice for the cooler. They pulled out onto the road.

"I gotta hand it to ya, Captain, you really hammered that son of a bitch."

"I'm more worried about your stomach."

"Aaa, a few rubber burns. They had me outnumbered, but I still scared the yellow shit out of them. Do I get to drive the truck today?"

"I thought I'd drive till we get to the border." He checked the gas gauge. The highway sign said fifty klicks to the border.

"Hang on, Captain – power down. Aren't we gonna go to town and claim our reward?"

"Reward?"

"Hey, we barely averted a serious crime, right? Wood Mountain owes us big time for this. We gotta collect our fee."

"We could go look for the mayor, I guess. But we never offered them security protection."

"Never too late. A one-elevator town like this could use a total security package."

"Good idea. It is my hometown after all. Maybe a fire-police-ambulance combination. We could make the Coyote Mobile into an EMS vehicle easy. Let's see if there's a town office."

"Whatever. If we're gonna risk our life and limb taking on biker gangs, the town's gotta pay, right? That's how security contracts work."

Coyote stopped at the gas pump in front of the Trail's End Café and Bar. "How much do you think it's worth?"

"It's worth whatever they got, ya dipstick! You gotta learn how to collect the fees, Donny, or I'll have to take over as leader. Think global, act local. All we're askin is for expenses, like food and drink. Plus we need some gas, right?"

"Yeah, we're almost down to empty."

The old Sikh with the enormous blue cloth around his head emerged from the café, staring back and forth between the Coyote Mobile and Coyote's burned face. He was dressed in old pyjamas, and looked depressed.

Sandra got out and sauntered over.

"You vant gas?" he asked, studying the day's T-shirt. It said HOOTERS!

"Regular unleaded."

"How much?"

"Depends. How much was our protection worth?"

"Protection?"

"You never heard about the punks we kicked out of the campground this morning? I don't think a tank full of gas is too much for that kind of security, eh? Plus we wouldn't object to a bite to eat. Whatever you got – hamburgers would be fine. All we need is some compensation."

"Compensation? For what?"

"For expenses! For beating the shit out of that biker gang! For keeping this community safe for you and your ungrateful family!"

"My family?"

"What are ya, deaf *and* cheap? What kinda dork are you? All we're asking is a lousy tank of gas, maybe a couple of cokes."

"My friend, if you had trouble at the campground, you must report to the RCMP. For gasoline, you must pay me money."

"Okay, where's the nearest detachment?"

"No police here. Are you driving to the border?"

"Might be."

"There is a Customs Office at West Poplar. He has a direct line to the RCMP detachment in Mankota."

"Okay, forget compensation," Sandra said, switching to Plan B. "Just put the gas on Mr. Coyote's credit card. American Express."

"Sorry, I don't accept American Express."

Sandra glared at him. "Then we're not gonna patronize your lousy raghead store. We're outta here! Lay rubber, Captain!" Coyote drove off without laying rubber. He turned reluctantly out to the highway, because they really did need to fill with gas. He checked the gas gauge again.

"Stupid place," Sandra said. "Trust you to get born in a tight-assed dump like Wood Mountain."

"Maybe there's a gas station in West Poplar," Coyote said. "Or we could go back and pay cash."

"Forget it. Keep going. Don't forget, gas is a hell of a lot cheaper in the States. No taxes. We can fill up there."

"Do they have real cops at the border, or just customs guys?"

"Who cares? They're all hooked up to the same computer. We'll be lucky to make it across. Gotta hope the guy's asleep, and we can sneak past."

Coyote concentrated on the winding highway that rose across the Wood Mountain benchland before sloping down toward the border. After a while Sandra said, "I been thinking, Captain."

"About the gas?"

"No. Look – I got a few blots on my record – you know about that – so maybe we shouldn't go through customs. There are other ways to get across. Otherwise, sure as hell, they're going to check ID. Find out who's who, what's what. I could end up in jail."

"The police don't put bonny fido heroes in jail."

"You think you're pretty hot stuff, don't you?"

"No."

"You actually like getting your name in the paper!"

"Newspaper is okay – but TV's better. For publicizing our mission. Look what happened when they put Superman and Batman on TV. Everybody started watching them, not just kids who read the comic books. TV is awesome, Sandra. When we get to California, they'll be covering every move we make. We could be TV stars."

"Well, you better hire yourself a makeup artist!"

"Why?"

"To cover your ugly mug? And it's time to do something about those burns. Your face looks like you zapped it in a microwave."

"The first town we come to, we'll find a drug store. We have to have a decent first aid kit."

"What's that – a six-pack of beer?"

"Very funny. I mean bandages and stuff. Plus I need some Firebrass."

"Some what?"

"Rawleigh's Firebrass Balm. You can use it for anything – burns or cough syrup, even on snake bites."

"Never heard of it."

"It's hard to find. I'm not even sure Rawleigh's makes it any more. But one drop fixes anything. They kept a big five-gallon can of it at the Orange Home, and when I left, they gave me a jarful."

"Jeeze, whudja do with it?"

"I used it whenever I got the flu, or diarrhea, or when I had to cut off a wart. Good for pulled muscles, too, when I'm lifting weights. And once I caught my finger in a bike sprocket and sliced the tip right off. I picked it up off the ground and ran home and rubbed Firebrass Balm on it, and stuck it back on and wrapped it in a cloth. It healed as good as new. See?"

"Yuk! What a scar."

"It's magic stuff. If some terrorist blew us up with dynamite, I could stick us together again with Firebrass."

"Better than Krazy Glue, eh?"

"Wish I had some now. Doc put mine somewhere for safekeeping. My skin feels like it's still burning up."

"Quit whining. Remember, a superhero has to take pain."

"Taking pain is different than liking it. It's better to slather ointment than just grin and bear it."

The gas needle was falling rapidly past the E for empty, and the map showed no towns all the way to the border. The countryside looked deserted as they crossed the Big Muddy badlands. They saw one ranch, and after that, nothing but dust until they got to Opheim, on the Montana side of the border.

"And when are you gonna take that stupid belt off? It looks dumb."

"You know the old motto? Be Prepared."

"Sez who? Ronald Reagan? You can't walk into a customs office looking like a complete dork."

"That reminds me. I need a new helmet."

"That biker's helmet woulda been great. The built-in headset was cool!"

"Real cool."

"You seen me try to rip it off his head, eh?"

"We could buy a couple in the States. They probly take American Express."

"My point is – it could get ugly at the border. They might dig up a couple of old drug charges on my record. And I don't want to go back to Canada. I'm starting to think how good life is in Las Vegas."

"Don't worry about the customs guy. You stay in the car. Let me talk to him."

"Fat chance you got with a face like yours."

"Sandra, we can't avoid the border crossing."

"I'm working on a plan. Anything left in our food cooler?"

"Jar of Cheez Whiz. Couple of doughnuts, going kinda stale. Some pizza pops, but they turn soggy when they're thawed out."

"Jesus. Always complaining. Pizza pops too good for superheroes, or what?"

"Oh no, I like pizza pops. If they're not too soggy. Salami and cheese is my favourite, but the food bank gave us all Hawaiian." It wasn't a perfect diet, balanced with P.D.'s food groups, but it was mostly nutritious. At the Orange Home, he had been weaned on oatmeal porridge, buttermilk, and bologna sandwiches. He said, "Heroes have to accept whatever's available. I bet that Sikh guy would've given us a bag of chips and some milk, if we'd asked nicer. We could've bought some gas. It's not like we're broke."

"What a loser! No wonder all your friends take advantage of you."

"If you do good deeds, you get rewarded. What's your plan for crossing the border?"

"Listen, I have to water some bushes. Turn down the next side road."

"There are no side roads, Sandra. You should have gone at Wood Mountain."

"There's one there! A grid road. Hey, I just had another idea. There's gotta be a farm down here, right? We can kill two birds with one stone."

Sandra's ideas always made Coyote nervous, because there was no telling how they'd work out. Ideas were one thing, but she had a lot of weird notions that led to trouble. He said, "Let's not go too far off the highway. We're nearly out of gas."

"That's what I'm gonna take care of. There's got to be a ranch along here somewhere. They always have big jeezly tanks of tractor gas sitting around the yard waitin to be emptied. Look. Over there!" She pointed to the horizon, where a shelter belt of caragana bushes lined a field. "Let's check it out."

Coyote turned onto a trail leading to a cluster of abandoned buildings. Sandra disappeared into the bushes to take a leak, squatting over the rough bark of a fallen tree while she studied the deserted sheds.

"Hey!" she yelled. "I see the fuel tank! We're in luck. Plus we can look for old tools or a coil of copper wire lying around we can salvage."

Sandra filled the Coyote Mobile from the rusty gasoline tank. They looked around but couldn't find anything except a lot of broken-down machinery. "What now?" Coyote said.

"Just keep heading south on this road toward the border."

After a few klicks, the road curved toward a range of hills, and they passed a sign reading, "BOUNDARY. Badlands National Park. Limited Access. No Services."

"Hey," Sandra said. "I think we just found a way across the border."

The further they drove, the more dry and barren the landscape became, until they ended up in a maze of towering clay buttes. They stood like abandoned sand castles on the high plateau. The trail disappeared but they drove on, wandering back among the hills, tracking across deep ravines.

Suddenly the motor sputtered and died and refused to start. There were no trees around, no houses, no garages, nothing. The only sign of life was a hawk drifting across the sky. Coyote looked at the map, but it only said they were somewhere inside a huge green patch labelled Parks Canada. There were no roads marked.

"National park!" Sandra sniffed. "Typical. Not a hamburger stand in sight."

They decided to eat whatever was left in the food cooler, which turned out to be stale doughnuts and pepperoni. Sandra voted that they crack the case of beer, but Coyote ruled the vote out of order until they had set up camp. The badlands would be dark in an hour. First, a good night's rest; they could fix the engine in the morning. He would find a phone to call the CAA to come and fix the motor. Even if they walked back to the highway and all the way to Wood Mountain, the Trail's End gas station would be closed for the night. The sky turned red, then purple, and finally black.

They were about to vote again on the beer, when Coyote spotted a fire burning in the far distance, halfway up the hills along the horizon. If it was tourists or park wardens, they might have a cellphone. They set off for the campfire, crossing a dry creek bed and stumbling through a field of gopher holes in the darkness. As they got closer, they could see people moving around the fire, and a corral with horses in it. There was a covered wagon parked beside the corral, with a couple of canvas tents on the other side. A pile of saddles was stacked by the corral.

"Cowboys!" Coyote said. "We're in luck. Real cowboys!"

"I doubt it," Sandra snorted. "You see any cows? Cows can't exist out here."

They were dressed like cowboys, though, most of them, with red bandanas and big white hats. They all stared at the two ragged heroes approaching the fire, and one of the cowboys raised his arm and waved them in. They were eating steaks off of big styrofoam plates. Coyote and Sandra could smell beef grilling on a barbecue.

A big cowboy in a beat-up hat came over to greet them. "Hidy, folks. Hope yer not lost?"

"Kind of. We turned off the highway by mistake and the motor in the Coyote Mobile gave out."

"Well – then you need help! You coyote hunters or something?"

"No, I'm Captain Coyote. It's my special vehicle, see. This is my partner, Sandra, also known as Wonder Woman. We're on a mission to eradicate crime, protect innocent victims, and save the environment. We're headed for the States."

"What part?"

"Well, Montana for a start."

"Zatso? At's where we're from! Just yonder that way, on the Montana side." He pointed to the horizon, a black line they could barely make out below the bowl of stars. "We're ridin out of the Shamrock Western Corporate Retreat Centre, four miles east of Opheim. I'm the wrangler, Dunk McIlwaine, and that's Slim over at the chuckwagon. Fella watering the horses is old Willy. These are some buckaroos we brung along on the ride." He waved to the rest of the group, who watched from the circle round the fire. They were all seriously over-weight, way too fat to be real cowboys.

McIlwaine explained that the buckaroos were guests at the Shamrock ranch, clients he was guiding on the three-day Marlboro Man Ride. They had crossed the border into the Canadian badlands on the first day, riding twenty miles, and the buckaroos were feeling sore and miserable. They had flown to Montana the day before from Boston, Massachusetts, where they all worked as investment analysts for large financial corporations. Their companies had enrolled them in the Shamrock Western Experience, a program to enhance corporate morale through outdoor male bonding.

The result was doubtful, for they were all in a state of passive resistance. They weighed at least two hundred and fifty pounds each, a couple of them over three hundred, all dressed in plaid shirts, with gaudy bandanas around their necks. The seams of their wide-cut denims strained at the thighs as the buckaroos shuffled around the campfire, moaning.

Dunk said they had been hoping to meet some real Canadian outlaws in the badlands.

"We're not outlaws," Coyote protested.

"Course, we know that. But you could pass for outlaws, that's all! Just to give the buckaroos a thrill, you know. We'd be glad to share our grub, if you and your lady are hungry."

"Jeeze, that's great. So you don't mind if we camp here for the night?"

"Happy to give you a corner of our tent. Got any sleeping bags?"

"Yeah, but we left them back in the Coyote Mobile."

"Don't suppose you have any beer?" Sandra said.

Dunk and Willy laughed raucously. "If only!"

Coyote's eyes lit up. "As a matter of fact, we have some. A whole case. It's in the back of our van. We can bring it when we get our sleeping bags."

"Hell, we'll ride over and collect it, if you got beer!"

The joy on the cowboys' faces a great professional insight to Coyote. A free lifetime offer of 24-hour security service could never produce such delight and celebration. Beer could become a tool in the eternal struggle for justice! He would stock more of it in future. Dunk called to the chuckwagon for Slim to throw on another couple of steaks for their guests. They could hear the meat slap the propane grill, and smell the beef sizzling.

"After you eat supper, we'll ride out and get your stuff. And see what we kin do about your truck. Sit down and rest your ponies a bit."

Dunk pulled a couple of saddles to the fire for the guests to sit on. "Where you folks planning on takin yer crime mission?"

"We're not sure of the exact route yet. First we have to cross the border, then we'll look for opportunities in Montana, and work our way to the President's. We might stop in Las Vegas along the way and clean it up."

"Canadian Snowbirds flockin south, hah? Only it's the wrong season! The birds are flying north. Look."

It was true. Far above, they could make out an enormous flight of Canada geese beating northward, their Vs etched against the stars in the night sky.

"What kinda opportunities are you looking for?"

"Mostly people in trouble, victims who need help," Coyote explained.

"You and the missus both?"

"Oh, we're not married! She's just my faithful companion."

"My professional name is Wonder Woman."

"Zatso? Hey, Slim! Them steaks nearly done?"

"Two minutes! There's a pail here if those guys want to fresh up."

"At's okay," Sandra said. "My hands are clean enough."

Coyote nudged her toward the water pail. "As Wonder Woman, you have to be cleaner than Mr. Clean."

"Piss off, willya?"

But she rinsed her hands and face in the bucket, and as they returned to the campfire, he gently suggested, "Also, don't try to grab all the food. Or the beer when it comes. Let others get their share."

"Why the fuck didja tell them about the fuckin beer? That's all we got!"

"They got a right to it. It's the law of the plains."

"Forget it, dipshit! On the trail, it's every man for himself. Right, you guys?"

The buckaroos, stuffed to their shirt collars, nodded solemnly.

"Is there anything for us to eat off?"

Dunk pulled a wooden crate out of the wagon and set it down for them to use as a table. Sandra pushed Coyote away, though there was room for both. She was just being obnoxious, to embarrass him in front of the gawking buckaroos. One of them made a comment on her rudeness.

"But I don't mind," Coyote said.

"If he doesn't like it, he can sit somewhere else," she snapped. "There's room over by the horses."

"Don't pay any attention to her," Coyote explained. "It's just food does this. Also beer. Usually we get along."

"Sounds complicated," Dunk said. "But that's companions for ya. Complicated as hell. Here comes yer dinner."

Slim carried a barbecued steak in each hand, steaks so huge they hid the styrofoam plate underneath. They were so big Sandra couldn't tell which steak was bigger, and had to measure them with her fingers. She grabbed the biggest one with both hands, and ripped a bite out of it.

"Ever notice," Sandra asked, waving her slab of meat amiably at the buckaroos, "how good food tastes when you don't have a fancy table with napkins and glasses and all that crap?"

She raved on for a while about her eating habits, making the buckaroos snicker nervously.

"I hate people telling you how to eat," Sandra mumbled, through an even larger mouthful. "Know what I mean? 'Chew it slow, don't guzzle your drink, wipe your mouth! Don't burp! Cover your gob when you sneeze!' Who can enjoy food with all those stupid rules?"

"Amen," Dunk said. "Finish up and we'll go and collect them barley sandwiches from your truck."

"I'm with you, bub."

"How's the steak, Captain?"

"This is great food, Dunk. How about a round of applause for the cook?"

A huge cheer went up for Slim, who stepped into the campfire light, blushing and grinning like a cat. He opened his mouth to speak. "We -we - we -" he stammered, unable to get past the sound of w.

Dunk explained, "Slim's got a slight stammer, but what he's tryin to say, we eat real simple on the trail, but it's good and there's plenty of it. There's a big pot of beans when you guys get your fill of cow."

Sandra took off to the chuck wagon, where a tank of beans bubbled on the propane stove, next to a mound of baked potatoes, and a stack of hot biscuits wrapped in tinfoil. After the main course, they could finish off a pan of rhubarb crumble. Sandra was silenced by the generosity, while Dunk explained that the Shamrock Experience featured western gourmet meals on the trail.

Coyote ate a whole plateful of beans before starting on the crumble. Sandra was right about one thing: food did taste better outside, even if it was just a bonfire hot dog, or an egg sandwich at a picnic. She might be only one rung above criminals, but sometimes she was no dumbbell when it came to philosophy.

"Bet this is how they ate in the old west," Coyote said, licking the last morsel of rhubarb from his plate.

"Think so?" a buckaroo asked.

"Oh yeah. That's the great thing about being on the frontier. Life was simpler those days, when everybody rode on horseback. No roads, or fences or houses. We can all sleep on the grass tonight, and imagine we're back a hundred years, when this really was the frontier, full of Indians and cattle rustlers."

"You know somethin about Western history?" Dunk said, turning with interest.

"Don't get him started, okay?" Sandra said.

"Well, I know a bit about cowboys. Red Ryder, Gene Autry. Roy Rogers and Dale Evans."

Dunk's weather-beaten face broke into a grin. "Fantastic! Hey – why don't Willy and me ride back to your camper to get the beer and stuff, while you guys tell these fellas all about the old West. They expect me to know that shit, but hell, I come from Flint, Michigan. Willy hails from San Francisco. Slim here's a local boy and knows the lore, but folks don't have the patience for his speech defect. He's a real poet, but most people don't got the patience to listen to somebody stammer."

The buckaroos round the fire nodded. They said they were waiting to hear some cowboy yarns, so Coyote squatted beside the fire just like Walt Disney did on TV. He began, "Once upon a time, before farmers

101

came and ploughed up the land and polluted the environment with fossil fuels and pesticides and chemical fertilizers, the cowboys and Indians used to roam out here on the open prairie with the buffalo. They lived together in a world of nature. There was always food, because they grew everything they wanted, like beans and potatoes, and they only killed animals in the winter, when they needed meat.

"In those days, people never fought over their stuff. They shared everything they had – horses and tools and food, just like you guys. If they had coffee and beer, they shared that too. That's the law of the plains. If you have two saddles, and the other guy doesn't have any, you give him one of yours, or even a horse, if you had lots of them."

"Yeah, a real paradise," muttered Sandra, who loathed the wide open spaces.

"It was a paradise! The streams ran with crystal clear water, all the way from the glaciers in the mountains across to the plains to the shining sea. The rivers were full of fish. Forests covered the plains in the days before acid rain, and people didn't build houses out of plastic and aluminum. They salvaged logs from the forest and cut them into walls. Presto, log cabins."

"What about the winter?" asked a skeptical buckaroo. "Isn't it forty below in January?"

"No problem! Not if there's veins of coal running through the hillsides, big chunks of it popping out of the ground like shiny black turnips. And in the spring, the sun felt good and warm and full of natural energy, so people lived outdoors all the time. The rain would wash them, and the sun would dry them off again. Life was so good they celebrated every season of the year. That was before ploughs and bulldozers were invented to rip Mother Nature open, and pillage her goodness, a richness intended for all creatures, and not just multinational corporations. Also, they didn't wear a lot of clothes in those days."

Slim looked up, startled. "Even the w-w-w-"

"Even the women. No store clothes. They used buffalo hides and flour sacks, recycled stuff. No polyester jackets and nylon pantyhose."

"Not so good for women, though – eh, birdbrain?" Sandra

resented the attention Coyote was getting. "Or did they have to go around naked?"

"Well – they only covered what had to be covered. If a girl had a good figure, she didn't wear bathing suits and tight pants. She let herself hang out."

"Now yer talking!" Slim said.

"And they'd wear flowers in their hair, crocuses and dandelions, fancier than the Queen's fancy hats. Girls could walk anywhere by theirselves, in town or countryside. There were no rapists or pimps to bug them, and if a girl wanted to see her boyfriend, that was her own business."

The circle had fallen silent under the spell of Coyote's stories, a mix of Princess Di's philosophy and his comic books. One of the buckaroos cleared his throat. "If you don't mind a personal question, Mr. Coyote, what do you do for a living?"

"Now, or back home?"

"Now."

"Well, I'm a superhero. I do rescues, security, and environmental action programs. My partner and me are on a mission to protect the weak and the oppressed."

The buckaroos fell silent, and they could suddenly hear Dunk riding back to the camp at a full gallop. He pulled to a halt with the bags tied behind the saddle and waved Sandra's box of Bushwakker brew. Everyone applauded. He handed her the box, and Sandra ripped the top off while the buckaroos roared approval. Dunk wrenched the caps off the bottles and passed them around. Coyote took one because Sandra elbowed him in the ribs, meaning to take it so she could get it from him later.

"I checked your gas line," Dunk said. "Some idiot went and filled your tank with diesel fuel. Carburetor's all bunged up. Slim can probly get it fixed in the a.m. Slim's a whiz with a socket wrench. Whaddaya say, Slim?"

Slim stepped forward into the campfire's light. "W-w-w-w-"

"'Will do,' he means. How about a poem, Slim?"

Slim was about fifty, with a mop-like moustache that covered his mouth and made him look like Gabby Hayes. He cleared his throat and launched into a recitation of "The Cowboy's Love Song," which had been published in *Montana Cowboy Song and Poetry Annual.*

After placing his hand on his heart, and shaking his head to settle some disturbing memory, he closed his eyes and took a deep breath. "This is dedicated to W-w-w-"

"Wendy!" Dunk and Willy sang out.

The cook continued:

> *I know you love me –*
> *Though you keep your mouth real shut –*
> *I can tell by the look in your eye –*
> *And the curvaceous tilt of your butt.*
>
> *I know you think deep thoughts inside*
> *That lump of gristle called "brain,"*
> *And so I giss you'll be my bride*
> *As the band plays our marriage refrain.*
>
> *But why this frost across your face?*
> *How come you slap my hand?*
> *Am I the loser in this race?*
> *My love tossed in the sand?*
>
> *I suppose you think that only gays*
> *Put their heart upon their sleeves*
> *But here I stand in my cowboy's rags,*
> *Straight from a herd of beeves.*
>
> *A smart guy said "clothes make the man"*
> *If that's true, I'm just a clod.*
> *But underneath these denim jeans*
> *Is a regular cattle prod.*

Here the cowboys and buckaroos yelled and applauded Slim's clever, though naughty, lyrics. Slim picked up the pace and carried on:

I don't care for dancing jigs,
Don't croon my tunes to sleep,
But if you like a tool that's big
Mine's passable, and deep.

I'll say again what I said before
About your luscious charms:
Each mole and birthmark I adore
And the tattoos on your arms.

I bragged about your gorgeous thighs
To the guy who pumps my gas.
"You mean," says he, "She takes the prize
because you like her ass!

"Neath that T-shirt and bandana
there's mounds of quivering flesh
but every cowhand in Montana
has clutched them in greasy caress."

Hurt by his taunts, I called down his lies
and challenged my gas jockey friend,
so hard I blackened both his eyes –
and he met his untimely end.

Oh, I know your love does not come cheap
but I'll slave to make you mine
though the further I crawl, and grovel and creep
the more my savings decline.

My horse and dog, my dearest friends,
I'd sell them in a flash
to buy a diamond for your hand
and help us tie the sash.

*And if you balk, I swear to God
and the muse of cowboy verse
I'll rage and rant and kick the sod
and make this song a curse.*

The buckaroos cheered and stomped the ground as Slim's face glowed with pride. They asked if the poem was based on some incident from life, but he refused to comment.

In the following quiet, Coyote asked if the Shamrock outfit had a first aid kit. He needed some salve for his face, which looked like he'd stuck it in a flaming can of gas.

"Why didn't you say something?" Dunk said. "We got just the thing. Slim, fetch some gunk from the chuck wagon."

"Gunk!" Coyote said. "What kind of gunk? Axle grease?"

"Better. Rawleigh's Firebrass Balm."

"You have Firebrass?"

"That's all we got, Captain. The only thing we use."

Slim fetched the salve from the chuck wagon and plastered it onto Coyote's broiled head. At last, his face felt soothed. Exhausted by the day's events, Coyote dragged his sleeping bag to a patch of grass a few yards away from the tents. The others would stay up for hours to drink and talk, but he needed sleep. He laid on his back, watching the stars and listening to the geese honking through the night sky. Nestled deep in his sleeping bag, Coyote was just drifting into a dream about Princess Di and him riding a horses across the prairie when someone yelled, "Hey! There's a car coming up the trail!" That woke him up again.

"Oh no!" Sandra's voice brayed. "It's the fuckin cops!"

CHAPTER 10

A Cowboy Story

C oyote crawled out of the sleeping bag and reached for his glasses. When he finally got them on, he could see a pair of headlights stabbing out of the darkness beyond the stalled Coyote Mobile. "Who the hell could that be?" he heard Dunk say.

"You not expecting somebody from the ranch?"

"Mr. Nostbakker brings supplies in the morning. He's never druv out in the middle of the night."

"It's the fuckin cops," Sandra repeated. She was staggering from the three bottles of Bushwakker she had snagged, and was looking for a place to stash her empty.

Willy scratched his head. "Why would the cops be comin out here?"

"Aa, the captain and me had a rumble with a biker gang up at Wood Mountain. We kicked butt. You know cops. They probably need to ask a few questions."

"You guys runnin from the law?"

"Well – not really –" Coyote said.

"I knew it!" Willy exclaimed. "Fugitives!"

It wasn't the police, though. A pickup, with searchlights on the roof and a rifle rack on the back window, pulled up at the fire. A sign on the door said, "Shamrock Corporate Retreat Center, Opheim, Montana. R. Nostbakker, Exec. Director." The knot in Coyote's stomach tightened as Ricky Nostbakker stepped out. He wore blue jeans and cowboy boots like the buckaroos, but looked more like an accountant than they did. "Hi, boys. I brung out the groceries, to save a trip in the morning. Also an urgent message for Dunk."

"Message?" Dunk said.

"Kinda private. I'll tell you later."

Slim and Willy unloaded the truckload of supplies: a flat of eggs, bag of horse feed, propane tank, slab of corned beef, pancake mix, maple syrup, a box of frozen steaks, and a case of Coors. Coyote was stunned. What a generous boss! On impulse, Coyote stepped forward and asked Mr. Nostbakker if he could help them get some gasoline, after Slim cleaned out the diesel fuel.

"Atta boy, Captain!" Sandra said.

Nostbakker regarded her curiously. "Who are these turkeys?" he asked Dunk.

"Couple of Canadian missionaries. This is Captain Coyote and his companion, Sandra Wonderwoman."

"That your camper sittin back there on the trail? Custom welding?"

"That's an old sign. We're actually professional superheroes."

"Then I'm shit out of luck, ain't I? I'm looking to get an iron shamrock for my gate, and the nearest welder's in Malta, hundred miles away."

"We could work something out," Sandra suggested. "Maybe find an old iron gate we could trade you for gas."

"Aa, don't worry. I can give you all you need. Shit, I got a fifty-gallon drum of it in the back. How far you going?"

"Las Vegas direction," Sandra said.

"Feelin lucky, are ya?"

"We're going to California to meet the president," Coyote said.

"Isn't he in Washington?"

"Not Bush. I mean the real president – President Reagan. We're going to volunteer for the secret service."

"Say – you ain't part of that Freemen outfit holed up down Jordan way, are ya?"

"Freemen?"

"Bunch of kooks and vigilantes, declared themselves a free republic. Got a bunch of rocket launchers and bazookas and I don't know what all."

"Dunk said we could camp here, if that's okay with you."

"Fine by me. We got a special permit to bring our Marlboro Man tours in here, but far as I know the park's open to the public. In the morning, you can join these buckaroos for breakfast. I brung plenty of food."

"We noticed."

"These boys from Boston got big appetites."

The buckaroos had such big appetites they wore custom-fitted denims provided by the Shamrock Center. Coyote felt sorry for their horses.

That day they had ridden eight miles from the ranch, across the border into Badlands National Park. Tomorrow they faced thirty miles of rugged buttes before they reached the town of Fir Mountain at the north end. There they would enjoy a Canadian rodeo and a night's rest in a motel before a long two-day ride back to Opheim.

Mr. Nostbakker's message to Dunk changed all that, for the day's luck now sent the heroes spinning in a totally different direction.

Nostbakker approached the old wrangler and solemnly removed his Stetson. "Thought I better tell you personal, Dunk," he said, avoiding his eyes. "There's bad news from the Opheim Hotel."

"Not burnt down!"

"Just a real bad accident. They called me from town this morning."

"They lost their liquor licence?"

"There's gonna be a funeral. Your friend Chris went and killed himself last night. He slashed his wrists in the men's can after closing time. They found him this morning."

"Dead?" Dunk's face turned pale, as if he had been slashed himself.

"As a dog," Nostbakker murmured.

The news made Coyote sick and dizzy, being close to such a horrible event. If they had come a day earlier and stopped at Opheim, they could have prevented the tragic death. "Who was he, Dunk?"

"Just a kid who lived at the hotel. He came out west dreamin of bein a cowboy, just like me. Then he went and got wired on Marcella Henderson."

"I thought she came first, and cowboyin came later," Nostbakker said.

"Nope. Other way around. This Chris fella – Chris Thomas was his name – came driftin into town last year around the time of the fall rodeo. He was a tourist, but he wore rodeo duds, big leather chaps and spurs, and a fancy red neckerchief. He caught one sight of Marcella riding her big chestnut quarter horse in the steer roping event, and that was it. He never knew what hit him.

"When he found out her old man was Clayton Henderson, who owns the Opheim Hotel and Bar, Chris went and got a job there so he could get to know Marcella. Clayton was always desperate for help, so he hired Chris on the spot as a manager. He needed him to tote supplies and clean toilets."

Nostbakker put his hat on. "Another thing, Dunk. Chris left a note for you, wrote in blood."

"To hell! His own blood?"

"I woulda brung it out, but the sheriff insists on keepin it for evidence at the inquest. A real long note – sort of a will. Wrote it out on a hunk of paper towel. He wants you to be the executor of his estate, yuh see. And he asked for a special burial."

"Special burial?" Dunk said.

"He wants to be buried beside the rodeo grounds where he first saw Marcella! And he requests that she be invited. Well – you'll have to read it yourself."

"Oh, he had it bad," Dunk muttered.

"It was a hell of a sight."

"The body?"

"The signature. Wrote in his own blood! Clayton brung it to me, he can't barely read no more, and the sheriff come from Malta. Blood all over the men's john, too. Maybe he was a dumb kid from the city, but everybody says he went out cowboy style."

"What else is in the note?"

"Oh there's a whole list of final instructions on what to do with his body, or parts of it, but don't worry, it'll never get that far. A funeral has to be something the undertaker will agree to perform. And which Clayton Henderson will allow. He gets a say cause he's payin for it. That Chris had a weird imagination."

"He was a philosophy student," Dunk explained to Coyote, "and wrote poetry."

"And you were his friend?"

"The only one," said Dunk. "Except for Ambrose, I guess."

"Ambrose?"

"Ambrose Schwartz, the old wino that hangs out in the bar. He was Clayton's original bar manager, thirty years ago. Him and Chris useta cry in each other's beer, and I'd listen to their sad stories till the bar closed. What the hell – it beat TV. Sometimes, I'd close the place for Chris if he passed out."

"Dunk, there's another thing. Chris's note said if you were not around, Ambrose would be the executor! And now Ambrose claims he's in charge because you're out on the range, and he plans to carry out the will as the deceased intended."

"I see."

"Clayton phoned the ranch tonight and told me to come out and talk to you. It's not normal, the stuff he requested, Dunk! All hell could break loose. Anyway the funeral's tomorrow, so I'll even give you the day off."

Dunk took his hat off and studied it. "Is that with pay, Mr. Nostbakker?"

"I can't stretch that far, Dunk. There's an awful pile of money riding on this particular tour package. I'd have to hire a replacement. Those Boston companies purchased the Marlboro package, and these fellas got their hearts set on being Marlboro Men."

"Willy could take them."

"Insurance company says there has to be two experienced wranglers at all times. Slim don't count." Nostbakker eyed the two heroes. "Either of you ever wrangle horses?"

"No, but we could learn!" Coyote said. "I always wanted to be a cowboy."

Dunk shook his grizzled head. "They can't do it, Mr. Nostbakker. Anyway, I'm not that keen to go. Chris wasn't a real close friend. I just felt sorry for him. Ambrose can look after it."

"Dammit! You got me over a barrel, Dunk. Okay, I'll give you the day off with pay. You can all ride back to the ranch in the morning and try out the automatics on the firing range. Those who want to can go into Opheim and attend a genuine cowboy funeral. I guess that's a real western experience, right?"

A sullen mutter rose among the buckaroos, as Nostbakker continued. "It's guaranteed to be entertaining, if Marcella shows up. She's worth a morning's ride, anytime. And I hear Deacon Bobby Pickens has offered to preach the eulogy."

"Sure, let's take a break!" Blair, one of the executives, piped up. He had the blotchy red nose of a scotch drinker. "I've had it with these stupid goddam horses."

There was a murmur of agreement among the buckaroos, who quickly decided the funeral might be a good bonding exercise, as long as they didn't have to ride to get there.

"Hey, I got an idea," Wonder Woman said. "Now that we have gas, we can give you a lift in the Coyote Mobile. We can drive on that trail, can't we, Dunk?"

"Passable most of the way. There's one dangerous patch, crossing Rock Creek Canyon. Bad sink holes, like quicksand."

"What about crossing the border? Going through customs?"

"No need, far as I see. But somebody has to stay and look after the horses."

Willy finally agreed to remain in camp and tend the horses. Nostbakker said the buckaroos would get credit for full participation in the Marlboro Man Ride, if they went and bulked up the funeral crowd.

Coyote didn't want to crash a stranger's funeral, but Dunk said he needed them for security. There would be a reception afterward at the hotel, and things could easily get out of hand. Coyote and his companion could wear Security armbands.

"Well, if that's agreed, I'll get back to the ranch," Nostbakker said, "They're showing Lonesome Dove tonight on satellite. Slim, come and clean out the fuel filter, and we'll fill these guys' gas tank. Then they can leave at dawn."

The heroes' luck in finding the cowboys cancelled out all the bad luck at Wood Mountain. When Coyote drove the Coyote Mobile back to the campfire, they had already cracked the second round of beer. Dunk began conducting an impromptu wake for his dead friend. Coyote was practically falling asleep on his feet, but Sandra wanted to party, even if it meant listening to stories about a dead drifter. The cowboys piled brush on the fire until it was blazing to the heavens. Coyote sat in a daze, faint with pain and exhaustion.

"Where was Chris from?" someone asked.

"Nobody ever asked, and he never told," Dunk said. "Clayton figgered he come from Russia or Quebec, because of his funny accent. He'd bin to university and could fling around fancy words. 'Conceptualize.' 'Manifestation.' Oh, he could rattle off a speech on demand, if he was drunked up and Marcella wasn't around. He went into shock as soon as she came near the bar. He was always sneaking off to the men's can to write his feelings about Marcella. He'd get drunk at closing time and read them out loud."

"Even though she – never liked him?"

"Maybe she did, at first. He looked kind of cool in his bronc riding outfit. Marcella's all cowboy herself, and who knows what happened at the rodeo. But after she found out he was a phoney, she wouldn't give him a sniff. We're talking about a gal who could bulldog a yearling at the age of ten."

"She gave him the bum's rush, eh?" Sandra cackled.

"Yeah, but he refused to quit. That's when he got the job at Clayton's hotel."

"Jeeze. Sounds kind of sad," Coyote said. He thought about Princess Di, and wondered if Marcella could be as beautiful and smart as P.D. He hoped she would come to the funeral.

"Oh, Chris was pathetic, but kind of entertaining. He could forecast the weather, though he was usually wrong more than right. Claimed he could predict the future – like an astronomer. Kept blathering on about the Age of Aquarium and planting by the phases of the moon. Always telling the cattlemen to plant more lentils and soybeans. Hemp. That kind of thing. He was a crackpot."

"But he wanted to be a cowboy?"

"Yeah, but who was gonna hire a guy like that?"

"A w-w-w–" Slim stammered.

"Yeah, a wimpy son of a bitch, fer sure. Things came to a head last winter, the last time he proposed to her. Real dumb. First, she tried to get him fired, and when Clayton wouldn't cut the string, she took off organizing kid's rodeos for the Sioux and Cheyenne reservations. Hasn't been back since. I think she's riding at a rodeo this weekend in Lewistown. A real cowgirl."

"You think that Marcella's rejection made him – suicidal?"

"Marcella takes particler pleasure in rejecting young guys."

Slim's head bobbed excitedly. "I heard she liked to go riding in her w-w-w–!"

"There's nothing she can't break – horse, man or mule. She can fix a tractor and brand a calf. First woman to ride a Brahma bull in a state rodeo. Team penning? Barrel racing? She's won every trophy going. Marcella shoes her own horse and repairs her own saddle. She's a true cowgirl."

"What about her father?"

"Clayton's as hopeless as everybody else at tryna keep her in line. Marcella's mother died when she was a baby, see, and he swore that the girl would have everything she asked for, to make up for her mother. He bought Marcella a horse when she was ten, and on her sixteenth birthday a Pontiac Firefly, and when she turned eighteen he gave her a gold Visa card. Then she made a tragic mistake."

"With Chris?"

"No, before that. Another guy. She was just a kid at the time."

"But this mistake – changed her?"

"Might say. Made her different anyway. Quit takin an interest in men. I think that's why Clayton encouraged Chris in his courtin, even though she wouldn't have anything to do with him. Clayton needed a manager even more than a son-in-law. Bein a rancher, he had no clue how to run that hotel himself. But when Chris learned to keep the books and clean toilets, Clayton suddenly saw him as a marriage prospect, havin already thrown a shitload of suitors out the back door. Chris was a workaholic compared to Ambrose. Everybody figured that was part of the deal, right? Whoever won the hand of the fair Marcella could end up with the only profitable business in town. Clayton was picky about who Marcella took an interest in."

"Sounds like a slut to me," Sandra observed meanly, in the same tone she used on Princess Di.

"Oh, she was a hot tamale. There was always half a dozen cowhands jostling round her in the bar. She could play any game in town. Hell of a pool shark. Shuffle board. Could punch the centre out of a dart board. She grew up in there!"

"So Clayton tried to auction her off, like some trophy," Sandra said.

"Well, if you had a million bucks tied up in a business, you'd want a say in son-in-laws too. It ain't easy to find a manager. Too many temptations. All that cash flow. Clayton figured if he could trick Marcella into marrying Chris, they could run the family business. After all, Chris had been to university, even had half a degree. Even so, he went along with Clayton's scheme, and wasn't getting paid. But he had a roof over his head, and semi-decent food to eat, and all the beer he could drink as long as he kept it under control."

"And nothing happened?"

"Well, Chris tried to impress her by buying an old broken-down palomino, which he tied up in the hotel parking lot. Then he popped the question. Kiss of death. She took off in a horse trailer full of gear to organize the Sioux rodeos."

Sandra smirked. "And she's travelling with a gang of cowboys?"

"That's no big deal. She does that all the time. She can handle them."

"I bet," she snorted.

"You're just trading in gossip," Coyote frowned. "Will she come for the funeral?"

"Some say she'll be back. Others swear she won't. But every cowhand in the county will be there to find out, you can bet on that. Some of them got her name tattooed on their butts. Oh, she's a character."

"Someday, maybe she'll find a real cowboy," Coyote said.

"Like you?" Sandra leered. "Dumb-ass! She'd rip your head off!"

When Coyote blushed, Dunk slapped him on the shoulder. "You're welcome to try, Captain. Anyway, come along to the funeral. We can use the extra security."

"What do you say, Sandra? An assignment for our résumé!"

"Even better – it's how we get across the border. If they catch us, we were just driving these guys to a funeral! Perfect excuse."

The party carried on, despite Coyote warning them they should all get a good night's sleep. He dragged his sleeping bag over to the far side of the Coyote Mobile, where it was quieter. He wanted to set a good example, so Sandra would not stay up all night and drink herself shit-faced, guzzling all the Coors she could grab. He felt good lying on the grass, where he could feel the wind ruffle his hair. In the morning, he would ask Dunk if he could ride one of the horses back to the ranch. It should be easy to learn, if the buckaroos could do it for a day.

If Sandra drove the Marlboro Men in the Coyote Mobile, Coyote could ride a horse across the border into the States! If he ever met Marcella Henderson, he would have to be a master cowboy.

The Firebrass Balm cooled the heat pulsing in his face, and Coyote drifted into a blissful sleep, hoping Marcella would appear riding a horse into his dream.

CHAPTER 11

A Cowgirl Story

The clang of steel on steel woke Coyote at dawn, along with Dunk's American twang singing out, "Rise and shine, buckaroos. Breakfast is hot!" He was stiff and cold, for the temperature had dropped overnight, and his bones ached from lying on the cold ground. The buckaroos crowded around Slim's propane grill, attacking his Canadian-style breakfast, featuring stacks of pancakes with real maple syrup, back bacon with mounds of scrambled eggs, hash browns bulging with green onions, big quart bottles of ketchup. The two heroes joined the huddle at the end of the chuck wagon. Even Sandra's hung-over, bloodshot eyes bulged in amazement at the feast.

Overnight, a cold weather front had blown across the badlands, and the grey morning sky threatened the misty pastures. Banks of cloud blanketed the coulees. Wandering horses appeared out of the mists and vanished back into them. While the buckaroos finished their breakfast, Dunk and Slim set forth to saddle their horses. This was Coyote's opportunity to learn how to ride. He ambled over to the wranglers, wearing a cowboy hat he'd found in the stuff from the Cansave donations bin. Dunk was pulling a cinch tight on a big horse of mottled gold.

117

"I was hoping I could ride along with you guys back to Opheim. Wonder Woman needs some practice driving the Coyote Mobile. Do you have any spare horses?"

"Sounds like yer feelin better."

"That Firebrass is great stuff. I feel like Superman this morning. After a breakfast like that, I can do anything."

"You like to try out that pinto or my old buckskin?"

"Anything, as long as it doesn't go slow."

"This is Starbuck, my best trail horse. Broke him myself when I first took up riding. You climb aboard while I throw a saddle on the paint." Dunk adjusted the reins for Coyote, then the stirrups.

Starbuck looked like Roy's horse Trigger, Coyote thought, just a shade darker. His hands trembling with excitement, Coyote swung himself into the saddle. He paused for a minute to savour the altitude so high above the ground. Standing up in the stirrups, he could see the tops of the buttes marching into the prairie badlands. His heart swelled with feeling, as his stomach had been stretched by breakfast.

"He's neck-reined, so all you gotta do is twitch him one way or t'other. There's nuthin to learn. Just sit natural and step into his weight. If he wants to run, jest let him go for a while. Only make sure you can stop him."

"How do I do that?"

"Haul back on the reins, like a sumbitch. If you can do that, all the rest is style."

Sandra and Willy stuffed the six overweight buckaroos with their Marlboro backpacks and suitcases into the rear of the Coyote Mobile for the trek across the border. Willy stayed with the horses, waving at the caravan as it disappeared into the mist. Dunk and Slim trotted along in front, while Coyote gamely followed on the big buckskin. The Coyote Mobile trailed behind, bouncing between the badger holes and boulders, its springs squawking in agony from the weight of the buckaroos.

Dunk explained that they were following the coulee side of Rock Creek as it flowed southward across the border. Its rocky channel laid down a trail of sorts through the harsh landscape. They had to ride in large circles around a few pools of muddy water left from the spring runoff, and quicksand lurked.

In the old days, Dunk said, Rock Creek trail had been a popular route for smuggling stolen horses and other contraband across the border. Horse thieves like Dutch Henry and his gang had crossed here from the badlands of Valley County, Montana. The wolf dens in the maze of buttes had been converted into cowboy camps all along the border, the north end of an outlaw route that ran along the Rocky Mountain foothills all the way to Mexico.

"Slim claims Butch Cassidy was the one who laid out the trail, and him and his bunch would steal horses all along the route – from ranches, Indian reservations. Then he'd ship 'em over the border to Canada for sale. Dutch Henry, he was the only one ever caught by the Mounties for horse-stealing. One of his pals, the Pigeon-toed Kid, got shot in Saco running from the law."

In no time at all, Coyote learned how to stop Starbuck and make him turn on command. By the time they reached the border, he had mastered trotting and loping. It was easy when there was so much space to let the horse run free. It felt like another super-power. Coyote thought of changing his plan, of working with Dunk and Slim in Montana and becoming a cowboy hero, like Roy Rogers and John Wayne. That's how President Reagan had started his career – as a cowboy in the movies.

As they climbed the creek banks toward the top of a ridge, Dunk pointed to a couple of rusty iron pins sticking out of the ground near the crest. "Survey stakes," he said. "The American border."

"That's it?"

"Take a look. Says, 'Boundary Commission of 1882.' They stuck them here when they surveyed the 49th Parallel that year."

Coyote dismounted to study the markers. "You mean we're actually standing on the American border?"

"Yep. Put one foot across that line, you're in the US of A. The Land of the Free and the Home of the Yankees. Kin you feel the difference?"

Coyote stood still and quiet to get the full effect. It *was* different. Stepping across the line was like going from a black and white movie to full colour. The air smelled like ritzy bathroom freshener, and he could hear a choir of angels singing God Bless America like they did at hockey games. He had entered another magic kingdom, like Disneyland, a cartoon place where the colours were brighter and the sounds sweeter.

"It's amazing. Canadians must be different from Americans, eh, Dunk?"

"Not that I can tell. Only difference is that a Canadian says he ain't American – when any fool can see he really is."

They kept riding south, as Coyote grew to like being a real cowboy, loping across the Montana badlands. Travelling like the wind, the three riders soon left the lumbering Coyote Mobile behind. They rode to the top of one of the castle-like buttes, overlooking miles in all directions, a vast jumble of canyons and coulees. Near the horizon, Coyote spotted a little town. "Is that Opheim?"

"Nope. Opheim's the other side of the ridge. That's Nostbakker's Authentic Western Town."

Dunk explained that five years before, Nostbakker's cattle business, the Shamrock Ranch, had gone bankrupt, and been converted to an ecotourist destination site, Nostbakker's Authentic Western Town, with the help of a state senator and a federal Economic Initiatives Grant. He converted the corral and old bunkhouse along with a couple of feed sheds into a frontier street scene, with a saloon, barbershop, sheriff's office, and livery stable. It looked like the western town shown in all the movies. His plan was to offer wealthy Japanese and Swiss tourists a taste of the old west, complete with a staged gunfight daily at the stroke of noon.

It was a good idea, but in the wrong location, three hundred miles from the nearest airport. Nostbakker's Authentic Western Town had also gone bust, and the Shamrock Ranch – all 27,000 acres – was taken over by the Boston bank that held Nostbakker's mortgage. The bank's head office, and its affiliated financial investment company, saw a future for the ranch as a training facility for prospective CEOs to develop male bonding skills.

The rural isolation was a bonus, and it soon opened with the former owner in charge. It quickly obtained a high approval/satisfaction rating among investment houses along the eastern seaboard. After Marlboro Cigarettes signed on as a major sponsor, the executive director was prepared to guarantee that following one session at the Shamrock Western Experience, graduates were certified Marlboro Men and permitted by law to state this on their company letterhead. They arrived as corpulent slugs, and left as hunks.

Sandra delivered the potential hunks to the ranch by noon, and they all went for lunch in the dining hall. As they relaxed with a final cup of Edie Nostbakker's powerful coffee, an Econovan full of cowboys roared up the driveway. The driver wore a black cowboy outfit and a preacher's collar around his neck. As he stepped out into a cloud of dust, he settled a big Mexican sombrero with silver dollars in the hatband, just like the Cisco Kid's, on his head.

Dunk nodded to him. "I expect you're headin for the funeral, Deacon."

"I am, brother."

"You plan to officiate the ceremony, Deacon?"

"Well, I ain't sure, Brother Dunkin. I phoned the Opheim funeral parlour to offer my services, but according to the words of the feller's last will and testament, there will be no words of prayer from a Christian pastor, or from any other of the world's organized religions. Only cowboys are to be allowed to speak. Fortunately, I am so defined on my employment record, and if called upon by the Almighty voice, I will attend to the spiritual needs of the deceased.

"After all," he went on, "the young man died in the embrace of Satan, lusting after Clayton Henderson's daughter. The struggle for his soul will be loud and tumultuous, and will shake the foundations of the earth. If just half the stories about him and that woman are true, this will be an apocalyptic event."

"Let's hope not. Thing is, he apparently asked me to run the show, and I'll call upon you for a blessing."

"Thank you, Brother Dunkin. I am ready for the challenge, as cowboy or as pastor. I don't believe I've met these folks."

Dunk introduced Deacon Bobby Pickens and the cowboys, who all worked at the Bar M, west of Opheim in the Montana badlands.

"Captain Coyotey?" the preacher asked with a derisive squint in his eye. He had a deep suspicion of everything Canadian. "Is that with a K?"

"No, a C. Two C's. And we say 'Kiyoot' in Canada, not 'Coyotey'."

"Are those weapons on your belt, Captain? I never seen a Canadian with weapons, ceptin a Mountie."

"They're just bolt-cutters and a cattle prod, Deacon. Also a black-jack. And a gas mask. Like most heroes, I don't believe in guns. These just even the odds when we have to get tough with a gang of crooks."

"You're some kind of – Canadian bounty hunters?"

"Well – I'm a superhero, actually. This is my faithful companion, Sandra. Otherwise known as Wonder Woman."

"Hello ma'am." The deacon winked at Slim. "Seen much action this trip?"

Sandra cut him dead. "Yeah, we kicked the snot out of a biker gang up in Wood Mountain."

"We were saving a show business star from a vicious attack," Coyote added, to keep the record straight.

"Showbiz?! Who was that?"

"Katie Kool."

Deacon Dickens looked like he had been struck between the eyes with an axe. "The punk vegetarian?" He stared at the two heroes. "You rescued Katie Kool, the anti-beef activist?"

"We are sworn to protect the weak and defenceless. That was her situation, and we saw our duty. That's my reputation in Canada, you see. I was in the papers last month for saving a kid from child abuse. Maybe you saw it." Coyote took out his clipping to show the preacher, who studied it with interest, comparing the photo to Captain Coyote's singed and battered profile.

"Anyway, I'm an old-fashioned type of hero, like Sir Lancelot and the Knights of the Round Table. I carry a cudgel instead of a gun."

"So – if yer Lancelot, who is King Arthur?"

"Well – President Reagan is, I guess."

"And who's the Queen – Nancy?"

"Well, my real ideal is Princess Di."

"The one got kilt in the car crash?"

"That's the English one. I mean the one in Moose Jaw. She's a perfect woman."

"Y'mean – Wonder Woman here isn't your girlfriend?"

Coyote looked horrified. Sandra responded in kind, jabbing her finger down her throat.

"It's time to head to the funeral parlour, fellas," Nostbakker said. "I can hear the music starting from here."

It was true. From off in the distance came a whispery screeching Coyote recognized, a country music version of "Rock of Ages." He remembered the song from the Orange Home, where they'd sung it every Sunday.

The Coyote Mobile got in line behind Nostbakker's truck and the cowboys' Econovan, and the funeral convoy rumbled toward the sound of the loudspeakers. The Opheim Funeral Parlour was about three miles away. The parlour was located beside the Mr. Beef Drive-in, and both parking lots were packed full. The whole town had turned out for the event. Coyote recognized Ambrose right away, dressed in a shiny black suit. He was staggering around with a fistful of crinkled papers in one hand, weeping through a pair of rheumy eyes, and waving the mourners inside. Dunk gave the two heroes Security armbands to wear.

A plain wooden casket sat on a platform at the front, the lid removed to show the corpse of Chris Thomas, the cowboy fool who had tried to win the heart of Marcella Henderson. He looked pale, younger than twenty-two years. Stacked around him in the coffin were his notebooks, filled with poems dedicated to Marcella.

The chapel was actually the former Oddfellows Temple, and furnished with the Oddfellows' gothic wooden chairs. There was a podium of black oak carved in ornate patterns. The hall was filled mostly with men, but a few wives attended with their husbands, drawn by the rumour that Marcella Henderson might be coming. They all asked, "Is she here?" "Is she here yet?"

The undertaker glided to the podium. "Ladies and gentlemen, dearly beloved, if any. We are gathered here to carry out the final wishes of Mr. Chris Thomas, who as you know died suddenly of tragic causes at the Opheim Bar. In his will, Mr. Thomas requested that his body be interred at the Opheim Rodeo Ground, at the very spot where he first laid eyes on Marcella Henderson.

"As a confirmed suicide, Mr. Thomas was not eligible for burial in the Opheim cemetery. Therefore the rodeo committee, advised by Clayton Henderson, gave permission for his grave to be dug between the rodeo parking lot and the rear bleachers on the south side, where the outdoor toilets used to be. That's otherwise useless land, because of soil contamination, so this is a win-win situation for everybody – the town, the rodeo committee, and the late Mr. Thomas. The interim executor of the estate, Ambrose here, hired Boyd's Backhoe and Bobcat to dig the grave. But I see the official executor of the will, Dunkin McIlwaine, has arrived. Dunk?"

"I object!" Ambrose declared thickly. "I'm in charge of the will."

"You have a copy of it?" Dunk said.

"It's a photocopy from the sheriff's office."

"Let me see." Dunk grabbed the document and glanced at it. "It says there will be no religious ritual of any kind. However, I asked Deacon Bobby Pickens to say a piece at the gravesite, so can we agree to that, if he leaves Christianity out of it, Ambrose?"

"Over my dead body."

"I'll take that as a yes. As for the rest of his instructions, we'll have to see how events unfold. Did anybody think to invite Marcella?"

"Well, I sure didn't. She can rot in hell before I talk to her!"

"You're not in charge, Ambrose. Here – give us a hand haulin the coffin over to the rodeo ground. Boys!"

The six casketeers stepped up, their Stetsons clapped to their chests. With Dunk and Ambrose directing, they bent down and lifted the coffin onto their shoulders and carried it out the door. They placed it on the old grain wagon waiting at the curb behind a team of big plough horses. The cold wind had turned bitter, and blew through them like a knife. Dunk climbed onto the wagon seat with Ambrose, and drove the hearse along Main Street to the rodeo ground. The crowd followed in trucks and vans. At the edge of town, a ramp of faded and dusty bleachers faced a field of churned-up sod, a perfect cowboy's grave.

Boyd had hitched his Bobcat onto one end of the bleachers and pulled them around so that they didn't face the outdoor toilets on the far side. The audience quickly filled the bleachers. A few early-season tourists, attracted by the procession, joined the crowd, despite the freezing wind. The wagon pulled up beside the mounds of clay where Boyd sat patiently in his Bobcat, while the undertaker set up a podium and mike stand in front of the bleachers.

As the cowboys set the coffin down beside the grave, Dunk said, "Ambrose, are you sure this is the spot?"

"I remember it like yesterday," Ambrose sniffed. "He was standing beside that mound of dirt when the jade first galloped past. We sat many times on the top pole of that very corral, while he pointed to the site and told me his heart-breaking story."

"Clayton, is Marcella coming to the funeral?"

The crusty old patriarch cleared his throat. "I called her in Pierre last night, and she said she can't. She's driving to Lewistown today. She entered four events at their spring rodeo."

"She wouldn't dare show her face!" Ambrose hissed. "Not with her victim lying there white and stinking in his coffin."

"Can it, Ambrose!"

"Let's get on with it!"

"The will says that Marcella Henderson's supposeta read Chris's poem, the one he wrote that night, to the assembled throngs. After the poem, the parts from his corpse are to be offered to her as a token of his undying love. Doesn't say what happens if she ain't here. Who's got the parts?"

"They're in this mini-casket," the undertaker announced, holding up a red fishing tackle box for the mourners to see. A dull rain began to fall, and somebody passed Coyote an umbrella to hold over the microphone.

Dunk stepped to the microphone. "Giss I'll have to read it myself, but first I wanta remind folks that even though Chris was a stranger in Opheim, he was special to some. So no laughing or snickering."

"Give'em hell, Dunk," Wonder Woman snarled. "We'll keep these yahoos in line."

"Chris mighta bin a loser, but he had an original mind. He knew plenty about astronomy, and physicstics and psychology. He knew poems by Kahlil Gibran and Rod McKuen and B. S. Elliott. But his real talent was writing his own poems."

Just then a Dodge Ram pickup swerved off the highway and cut across the ditch. It bounced across the field, horse trailer rattling along behind. Displaying his Security armband, Coyote edged forward.

"It's Marcella!" somebody gasped.

A burst of energy in a white Stetson hat leaped out of the truck cab. Marcella was more beautiful than Coyote could have imagined. She had flashing dark eyes, and wore black denim jeans and a two-tone deerskin jacket. She was short, about five feet tall, and strode with quick, catlike movements to the edge of Chris's grave. She glanced briefly into it before turning to face the crowd. Her eyes grew tense, as if expecting a fight. She seemed to recognize some of the cowboys, glaring briefly at each.

Unsettled by her ferocious eyes, Coyote ducked behind Sandra to observe.

As Marcella moved to the casket, Ambrose ran forward. "Where are you going, you Jezebel? Have you come to gloat over your victim? A final triumphant thrust of your knife?"

"Let's get one thing straight, Ambrose. I did not come to eulogize this poor son of a bitch. I stopped here on my way through town because I had to throw his silly lie back in his teeth. Is that clear? I did not lead this guy on!"

A few in the crowd hissed, but most stared slack-jawed as she grabbed the microphone and launched into a tirade. "I'm fed up with being blamed for his pathetic grovelling. It makes me puke the way men can't leave me alone. You're the ones egging that kid on. It was you who created this ridiculous sideshow."

"Where's your decency, woman?" Ambrose hissed through broken teeth. "It's Chris's funeral!"

"And why am I the chief mourner? I was not responsible for his suicide!"

"He killed himself because you denied him his manhood!"

"I told him to back off, cause he was crowding my space. I never gave him any cause to chase after me. And it wasn't even me he wanted. It was just my body. He was stalking me. I can't help the way I look. It wouldn't have happened to some slack-assed cow from Missoula."

"Give me that microphone," Ambrose wheezed.

"Let her talk, Ambrose!"

"Go for it, Marcie!"

"I know you all think I'm nuts – because I do man's work. I'm not interested in getting chained to a kitchen to bake pies the rest of my life. Don't get me wrong. I appreciate all the support from the men in this community when I made Montana Ladies Bronc Champion three years in a row. But that doesn't give you the right to humiliate me!

"I need my freedom – no different than some bitch coyote loping across the badlands. I love rodeo work and breaking horses and hunting deer, so I don't plan to settle down as a ranch wife. But that doesn't make me into Britney Spears. Okay, I have a good figure. I never tried to hide it – but I don't flaunt it. So it's not my fault that grown men turn into slobbering fools at the sight of it – and the drunker they get, the harder they slobber. Well, if I do settle down with a man, it won't be with one who only wants to fuck me.

"Is it so weird not to have a boyfriend? What's the big attraction in a penis? Who needs it?

"I don't need a husband for protection or to manage a bank account. I can take care of myself. And I'd rather wrestle cows in the muck, than get hitched to a pair of walking testicles. So you can take that boy's memento and bury it in the same hole where you buried his brains. I don't want it." Tears glistened in her flashing eyes as Marcella tossed the microphone to Ambrose and strode off the platform.

Coyote motioned at the crowd with his cattle prod, and they parted to give her a clear path through. He saluted as she passed, and as she shook her head to fling away her tears, one of them struck the burnt side of his face, causing a spark of pain, like an electric kiss. His cheek went numb.

The crowd watched in silence as her truck tires spun clods of mud across the rodeo grounds. In a few seconds, she was gone, heading south-west toward Lewiston.

"Jeeze!" Sandra declared. "What was that about?"

"That's just Marcella," Dunk said. "She was always opinionated."

"What a bitch!" Ambrose muttered.

Coyote turned on him with a raised fist. "Don't start bad-talking Marcella!" He assumed his *tae kwon do* attack position, and the circle of mourners retreated in alarm.

"Donny, back off, okay?" Sandra said. "You can start breathing again. She's gone. Good riddance!"

"You, too. Just leave her alone. The next person who slags Marcella will get their block knocked off. So nobody better mess with her, or they'll deal with Captain Coyote."

"Relax," Dunk growled. "This ain't Canada." He gestured to the pallbearers. Giving Coyote a wide berth, they picked up the coffin and began lowering it into the hole Boyd had dug. "Okay, Reverend. Your turn. Then Ambrose can read the poem."

Deacon Pickens mumbled over the coffin, while Ambrose dropped Chris's pages of verse one by one into the grave. The men raised their shovels to fill the hole. Dunk pounded a wooden cross into the dirt. Ambrose stepped to the podium with Chris's final poem shaking in his hand.

"I'm gonna read his poem," Ambrose quavered into the microphone. "Then I intend to have it engraved on the tombstone I'm ordering from Billings. I'll accept contributions at the reception." After a couple of shaky starts, he began:

Here lies a jilted cowboy
stiff as a poplar rail
who never dogged a steer
and never rode the trail.

He died his lonely tragic death
pursuing a fickle girl
which says an awful truth about
the follies of the world.

Ambrose collapsed on the microphone in a shower of tears. Dunk and the cowboys and buckaroos laid wreaths of sagebrush, while Ambrose grabbed at their hands and blubbered his thanks. The mourners began shuffling toward the Opheim Hotel and Bar, where Clayton Henderson had set up the reception. They were worried that Clayton might not have ordered enough liquor for the event, as he was known far and wide as a tightwad. Would the booze run out before four o'clock, or would it last till six or seven? The buckaroos were scheduled to be at the Shamrock Center at five for a mid-experience evaluation. The heroes' security duty was over, and Coyote was feeling anxious to hit the road.

"We could stay for the reception," Wonder Woman suggested.

"No way. We did our job, and now we look for our next assignment. I thought we might go to Lewistown, and check it out. Maybe get the security contract for the rodeo."

"But we gotta collect our fees for this one first, captain. That's the deal, isn't it?"

"I'd say we got our reward when Dunk sneaked us across the border."

They stopped at the hotel to say goodbye to Nostbakker and Dunk, who assured them they were welcome to return, especially when crime got worse in the fall. It seemed to be seasonal in Montana, where the homicide rate shot up every winter. In the fall, cattle rustling was epidemic. Some of the Boston buckaroos suggested the heroes should bring their crusade east, if they ran out of work in Montana. Boston was desperate for law and order, like every other city on the east coast, and there was great potential for an anti-crime campaign. There was more crime on Union Street in one day, they said, than in all Montana in a year.

"Why are we going to Lewistown?" Wonder Woman demanded as they headed down the grid road out of Opheim. "Because that ditzy Marcella babe's going there?"

"Nope. Because of the rodeo opportunity. Dunk said he'd give us a reference to get on as their security."

"Nothing to do with Marcella Henderson?"

"It might be cool if we happen to run into her. I wouldn't mind watching her ride broncos. What's wrong with that?"

"I'm gonna have to keep an eye on you. Ambrose was right. I know her type."

"Just shut up about Marcella. Lewistown is on the way to California, that's all."

"This better not bugger up our plan to stop in Las Vegas. You want professional security work? That's the place to hit. Rich pickings. Think of all the protection those casinos and clubs need. The whole city's overrun with Mafia types. The sky's the limit."

CHAPTER 12
Fighting the Yankees

The cloud thickened over northern Montana as the Coyote Mobile chugged across the rolling plains. The heroes agreed that the USA was more scenic than Canada. The sky was bigger, the plains flatter, the grass thicker and greener. And it was only May! They were in the land of wider horizons, stretching further than the eye could see. This was the vista that brought the settlers to the great western frontier of America – an endless expanse of grass and sky. Their prospects were perfect, except for the horrible Canadian storm following them from the freezing Arctic. They crossed the Missouri River south of the Bearpaw Mountains just as the rain turned to sleet, and then to a curtain of snow drifting across the highway. Sandra had taken the wheel, after proving her skills on the trek across the border, but she was unnerved by the chasing storm. At the next highway junction, she stopped. They could see nothing but blowing snow in all directions.

"Which way now?"

Coyote studied the map and the road signs. "Well, down that way is Jordan. Stay on this road to get to Lewistown."

"Forget that Jezebel, will ya? We gotta find a place to stop for the night. No way I'm camping outdoors in this shit. Jordan. Isn't that where those Yankee vigilantes were holed up?"

"What vigilantes?"

"The Freemen. A buncha rednecks who declared independence from the States, and set up a republic of bald-headed men at Jordan, Montana. Complete wackos. They refused to pay taxes, and they had their own army and flag and everything."

"Jeeze, yeah, I remember them. Think they might still be active?"

"This country is full of nutbars like that. Yankees. Didn't what's-his-name live out here somewhere. Kazinski?"

"The Unibomber? You're right – Montana. Could be good work in Montana."

"Let's stay off the main highways in case the border cops are on the lookout for a Coyote Mobile."

"I say we go to Lewistown. There's bound to be work opportunities there. It's a real city. We're running low on cash, and I don't like to use Doc's credit card."

"That's why we're going to Vegas – remember? Let's move it!"

"I'm sure there's as much crime in Lewistown as there is in Las Vegas."

"That's the nearest city going west?"

"Yeah."

"Y'know, I think I got relatives in Lewistown."

"Really. You never told me that."

"Betcha I could track them down."

"Their name Dollar, too?"

"They spell it Douleur down here. That's the old way. They'll probably put us up. The camping routine is giving me the heebie-jeebies. I hate sleeping outside. I'm startin to get panic attacks and stuff – and look at this fuckin weather!"

"You should've thought of that before we got all the gear for camping."

"Hey, I signed up in good faith. You never said nuthin about camping in snow."

Twenty miles past the Jordan turnoff, they reached the Judith Gap, and ran head-first into a raging blizzard. The brooding clouds overhead collapsed and dumped a soppy mix of snow and rain, burying the countryside. Sandra's response to the treacherous piles of icy slush alarmed Coyote. She jammed the accelerator to the floor, trying to out-race the storm. She ignored his request to slow down, even when he escalated to a demand, and finally a direct order. She refused to sur-render the wheel, now that she had control, and the Coyote Mobile careened and spun through the icy slush like a bumper car, the head-lights shining on a screen of white fuzz.

"Sandra!" Coyote said. "I command you to pull over and park on the shoulder. You can't drive in a blizzard. We have to stop and wait it out. We have an emergency kit, let's use it!"

"Sign said Lewistown, ten miles. We kin get there before dark, and score a decent room for the night. I'll look up my relatives."

"We'll never make it alive if you don't slow down –"

"Hey, back off. Who drove this rig across the border? Me, right. Don't go dictating. I'm getting you to Lewistown. It's you who's freakin out over the weather."

"Also, I don't believe you really have relatives in Lewistown."

"You think my relatives won't put us up? For your information, my great-great-uncle was Gabriel Dumont's kid brother. They spent a cou-ple years in Lewistown back, oh, a hundred years ago. You know who Gabriel Dumont was, Professor Einstein?"

"Yeah, I know who he was. He fought at Batoche." Coyote and Doc had gone to the site of the Northwest Rebellion the previous summer.

"That's right. And after the battle was over, he skipped over the border to Montana, just like us. They would have shot him down on sight. Anyways, I got lots of my cousins down here. They'll be good for a couple meals."

"Yeah, maybe."

"And if my connections don't work out, we can stay at a motel. Just as long as we're not camping. I'd like to sit on a real toilet for a change. Maybe even take a shower. I'm finished with the boy scout routine."

Coyote protested, "But that's why we bought the Coyote Mobile. We're driving to Yellowstone Park. We have to camp."

Sloshing into the outskirts of Lewistown, the Coyote Mobile passed a yellow portable sign at the side of the highway. The sign declared, "Custer Motel and RV Park. BAR, MINIGOLF, FREE BREAKFAST. Canadians Welcome. C$ at Par."

"Hey, good deal," Sandra said. "Let's try this place. I'll check the phone book." She went to the pay phone beside the front door of the office and looked for the Douleurs. There weren't any, but there was a Zebediah Dumont, who sounded like some old guy who wouldn't give them the time of day. A sign beside the door warned guests not to leave belongings in their cars at night, except at their own risk.

"Bingo!" Sandra cried.

"How come?"

"Doncha see? They have no security! Bim, bam, boom, we hire on as their security personnel, protecting the customers' cars and belongings, in exchange for a night's room at the Custer Motel. Win-win situation all around."

"Yeah, it might work. Our sleeping bags are getting soaked in the back, so we can't camp anyhow."

"Roof leaks. Must be an inch of water sloshing around in there. Tell you what, Donny. I'll check out the bar while you work out the security deal with the front office. If all else fails, give them your credit card. The sign on the door says they take American Express. This is our kind of place, buddy."

"What are you going to do in the bar?"

"Look for relatives – anybody who looks like me."

"Hey, Sandra. Lay off the beer tonight, okay? If you stay sober, we can have a game of minigolf later. My treat."

"Minigolf in a goddam blizzard?"

"It could be fun."

"Anyway, I hate golf. Lawyers golf. Politicians golf."

"Minigolf is different. Doc and me played it in Fargo. It's more fun than foosball. Anybody can play. It's cool."

"I get cool in bars. Whyn't you come along for once? They have games there too, and VLTs. You like video games, doncha?"

"Yeah, but not ones in bars. Bars make me think of Doc and how I have to show a good example. I promised Princess Di."

"Okay, let's go check out the gun stores then. You'd like that, right?"

"Guns?"

"Yeah – we're in the States. There has to be a zillion gun stores."

"Well okay – let's get our room first."

The manager flatly rejected Captain Coyote's proposal to guard the motel parking lot in exchange for accommodation, but did accept his credit card.

"Room Number 13," the manager yawned. "Past the ice machine."

Coyote hesitated. "Thirteen?"

"That's all I got. Take it or leave it."

While Sandra checked out the lounge, Coyote parked the Coyote Mobile beside the door of Number 13, and hauled the food cooler and wet sleeping bags into their room. He met up with Sandra in the dining room, and they had the steak special as they planned the evening. Coyote insisted on going to find Marcella's rodeo, but Sandra preferred to hang out in the lounge, hoping a relative might appear. She believed hundreds of them were living in the area. What's more, she had found out about a gun dealer called Bernie's Pawn and Gun Emporium, a hundred yards up the highway. Bernie's didn't close till midnight. They agreed to meet at ten for a shopping expedition to Bernie's Pawn and Gun.

Coyote located the Lewistown Rodeo Grounds on the far side of town, only to find them buried under a carpet of ice and snow. The corral and holding pens were deserted. A sign nailed to the gatehouse said, "Rodeo Cancelled." Feeling more jinxed and betrayed by his luck than ever, Coyote drove back through the storm to the motel. He parked the Coyote Mobile among some trees at the end of the lot, and went to meet Sandra in the lounge. She hadn't found any relatives, but had somehow bummed enough drinks from strangers to get half-loaded. Now she was fired up to get some real weapons before they ran into another gang of criminals like the creeps at Wood Mountain. She said Stone Age weapons like Coyote's were useless when it came to whacking modern gangsters.

Bernie was a cheerful guy who giggled a lot, anxious to please his first customers of the evening, no matter how weird they looked. He was used to weird. Careful to obey state law, he required the heroes to print their names at the top of a registration form. That was just a habit. They didn't look like real customers, and were either criminals – technically not eligible for gun ownership – or penniless vagrants who didn't have the down payment on a box of .22 cartridges, let alone a Saturday Night special.

They were also as thick as straw stacks. When Bernie tried to explain the registration form, their eyes glazed over and they began edging away. One moved toward the display case of submachine guns, and the other to a promotional video on pepper spray and stun grenades. In the end, all they purchased were two canisters of pepper spray. As defensive weapons, these didn't require registration, and Coyote was allowed to charge them on his American Express.

"What state's next?" Sandra said, as they trudged back through the snow.

"Well – Wyoming, if we go through Yellowstone."

"I hope the gun laws are looser in Wyoming," Sandra said. "This is ridiculous. The world has gone nuts when every lunatic and serial killer can buy weapons by the dozen, and heroes have to suck wind."

"Don't complain. We did okay. Pepper spray is better than guns for lots of things."

Coyote was desperate to get some sleep, but Sandra was convinced that her relatives would still show up in the Custer Motel Bar. She insisted that Coyote join her, and thought she could find somebody to pay for their drinks.

At eleven o'clock, the bar was filled with a variety of folks, mostly cowboys and ranchers out for Monday Night Keno. The place was jumping, with slot machines clanging and cowboy music blaring from the loudspeakers. After a while the noise and smoke made Coyote's brain ache, and he started to feel woozy. The machines whirred and clanged and bonged as the symbols flashed across the screens: six-guns, cactus plants, bucking broncos. It was like the roulette wheels at the Moose Jaw Fair, watching the number roll along the gutter of the wheel, wobbling as the wheel slowed, dropping into a slot. Whenever Coyote played, his ball always fell in the wrong slot, and he had to keep playing to win it back. He hated gambling games because they made him lose control and turn into a numbered ball, one ball in a mixed-up bingo globe of numbered balls, and there was nothing he could do to stop them rolling. The numbers sucked money out of him like a Rainbow vacuum cleaner.

Coyote shook his head, trying to stay focused. He was exhausted after the long day – crossing the border on horseback, guarding the funeral, driving through the blizzard. His burnt face ached, and his shoulder was still sore from the fight with the optometrists.

Sandra ignored his complaints. She was having a good time in the lively crowd. After her first three or four Coors, she joined a group which had gathered around a loud character in camouflage fatigues. He was buying rounds of drinks and said he was raising money for a Timothy McVeigh memorial fund.

"Betcha he's one of those Freemen!" Sandra muttered. "Let's listen and see what we can find out. I'm gonna show that dumb manager he made a big mistake not going for our security deal."

Coyote stood up to go to their motel room. Though worried about the trouble Sandra could get into in the bar, Coyote was too wiped out to babysit her. People were staring at his blistered face and pointing at him. He needed sleep. Tomorrow the roads would be clear, and they would make for Yellowstone, where he could relax in the peaceful embrace of nature and forget about the eternal fight for justice.

No sooner had Coyote's head fallen on the pillow than he began to dream about Marcella Henderson. They were riding along the banks of the Missouri River, he on Starbuck and she on her paint horse. They were both naked except for cowboy hats, and her rich dark tresses cascaded over her shoulders and breasts, covering her nude body. Their horses leaped into the river and began swimming across it, drawing closer and closer together until Coyote's knee was touching Marcella's. Suddenly Princess Di appeared on the opposite river bank, mounted on a gigantic white horse and dressed in judge's robes. The angry look on her face was terrifying to see, and Coyote jumped off into the mud at her feet. She lifted her gavel and slammed him over the head.

"Donny, wake up! Quick!" Sandra was bellowing, bashing him with her fist and pointing out the motel window. A beam of light from the parking lot slashed across her face, making it look even more jagged than usual.

"Those goddam Yankees!" she hissed in his face, her breath foul with beer. "They're attacking the Coyote Mobile."

Coyote grabbed his jeans and his belt and ran to the window. The snow had stopped falling, but the white blanket on the ground silhouetted a group of men swarming around the Coyote Mobile at the far end of the parking lot. He cleaned his glasses and peered at them. "What are they doing?"

"They're trying to break in! There's at least six of the bastards."

"Did you call the cops?"

"Are you nuts? We're illegal aliens, remember?"

"Get your pepper spray. We'll sneak up on them in the dark and surprise them."

"Okay – let's blast the suckers." Sandra jammed her can of spray into the waistband of her sweat pants. Coyote clicked his own onto the utility belt. He didn't have time to put on his whole costume.

"Who are they, do you know?"

"Ah, some guys I met in the bar. Real dorks, sound like those Freemen. They're all McVeigh fans, eh. Survivalists and suchlike from the badlands. I mighta said something to piss them off. I was telling them about the Coyote Mobile, and how we had a bunch of weapons inside. Coulda bin a mistake. I giss that's what they're lookin for."

"Okay, I'll take charge now. We're going into action. I've got my cudgel. You take the bolt-cutters."

"To do what, exactly?"

"First we stop them from wrecking our vehicle. There's no choice, Sandra. Our entire future is out there getting hijacked in the parking lot. And I might add, this wouldn't have happened if we were camping outdoors."

"No," she said, "or if we had a gun or two." She patted the pepper spray in her pants. "Lead the charge, sarge."

Coyote was impressed by Sandra's display of bravery. Maybe it was true about the awesome power of beer. Still, the odds were at least six to two, or even one and a half, depending on how Sandra was counted. Their weapons would even things up.

They eased quietly out the door, and snuck toward the thugs surrounding the Coyote Mobile, which looked like it had been hit by a train. The steel door was pried off the back, and two of the attackers were loading stuff into the back of their pickup truck, its motor idling in the darkness. It was piled with the heroes' garbage bags of clothes and all their welding tools, even the spare tire. The others were wrecking the Coyote Mobile engine right in the motel parking lot. The hood had been torn off the motor, and they had smashed a window to get into the locked cab. Two Yankee marauders were hunched over the fenders, bashing the motor with hammers.

"You sneak around and grab the keys out of their truck," Coyote whispered, "the second I start the attack. Then come at them full tilt with your pepper spray from that side!"

Sandra moved off into the darkness. Captain Coyote took the gas mask from his belt and pulled it on over his glasses. Approaching through the shadows of the trees, he felt like an invisible angel, or an alien from some other dimension.

The crooks never saw him until he suddenly popped up in front of them out of nowhere. They stared in horror at his scowling gas mask. Coyote hit the button of the pepper spray.

"Cops!" they yelled, as clouds of spray stung their faces. "Run!"

They fumbled toward their truck, bouncing off each other in the cloud of gas, yelling from the pain in their eyes. Sandra attacked from the other side, hitting them with another blast of pepper spray. Coyote charged from a third direction, swinging his cudgel in a fury and mowing them down like ten-pins. Sandra went after the biggest marauder with the bolt-cutters, slicing a chunk out of his ear. The Yankees stumbled in a blind panic out of the parking lot while Coyote chased behind, cudgelling their legs in righteous fury as they ran cursing down the icy highway into Lewistown.

The heroes had no time to celebrate their victory. With all the noise, the motel manager would be calling the cops. The last thing they needed now was police attention. Sandra admitted that staying at the motel had been a mistake, and the sooner they got back to the countryside and found a safe place to camp, the better. Coyote pressed the starter of the battered Coyote Mobile, and they held their breath as it fired up with a muffled roar. They drove to the door of Number 13 to collect their stuff, and began flinging it into the van through the wrecked door. But they were not quick enough. As they drove away, the horde of Yankees returned with a truckload of reinforcements. They swerved in front of the Coyote Mobile, preventing the heroes' escape.

Coyote leaped out and whipped the pepper spray from his belt. He blasted away. A weak cloud of fog spurted from the nozzle and died. Their heroic attack had backfired, for the gang was now twice as vicious, and came at them like a pack of riled-up bears. The big one led the attack, bleeding from the nick out of his ear.

"The keys, motherfuckers!" he yelled. "Where's our keys?" The Yankees kicked their heads, stomachs, backsides, whatever they couldn't cover with their elbows and hands. Coyote's mask and glasses got knocked off and he couldn't see who was pummelling him, but he heard a sudden clink of keys as Sandra pulled them out of her pocket. She threw them jingling into the snowbank. "There they are!" she shrieked.

"Cummon, let's go!"

"Not before we smurf these bastards!"

"We give in!" Sandra yelled. "Don't. No more. We quit!"

Coyote gritted his teeth, lying curled up in a ball to cover his head and stomach.

One of the kicks to the head must have knocked him unconscious, because the next thing he knew, he woke up on the frozen expanse of the parking lot. His eyes were swollen shut. His head felt like a diesel engine. He couldn't open his eyes, but the warm sun on his face told him it was morning. At least he wasn't in a hospital or jail. The police hadn't come.

"Donny?" he heard Sandra moan. "You okay, Donny?"

"Can't see."

"Lemme look. Yeah, your right eye's completely shut. The left one might open a squint. Let me rinse the gravel out." She shook a bottle of liquid. "Concentrate on something for a sec."

"Yikes!"

"They worked us over like the city dump, buddy. I haven't got boot-fucked like that since I was in Pinewood."

"Pinewood?"

"Women's Correctional Centre up north where I spent some time. I found a bottle of wine. Care for a slug?"

"Naw. I wouldn't mind getting some Firebrass, though."

"There must be a store somewhere in town."

"How is the Coyote Mobile?"

"Seems to run okay. You ready to travel?"

"Maybe in a few minutes. Where's my glasses?"

Sandra looked around and found Coyote's glasses, which had been stomped on during the battle. Both lenses were cracked and scratched, so his vision was worse than ever. The pain in his head was humungous, but no worse than the humiliation of getting sucker-punched by such a gang of losers. They sat in the Coyote Mobile to catch their breath.

"It was my fault, Sandra. I should have known they'd come back for their truck."

"Yeah, you should've. Pretty stupid idea from the start."

"Next time, we'll just call the police. They're used to dealing with petty criminals. It's pedophiles and organized crime we should concentrate on."

"That a new hero rule? We only go after the big shots?"

"It's just common sense. Superman doesn't grab every jaywalker that crosses the street. He has to focus on the biggies, like Lex Luthor. We have to do the same. Otherwise, we waste time trying to do too much."

"If I was in charge, things would be different."

"That's not the issue, who's in charge. I have to be in charge."

"How come?"

"Well, I'm the only initiated hero, for one thing. Here's a new rule for you. Just ignore the next gang of Yankees or any other hosers. Don't even bother with them. If they're aliens or child molesters, or real super-villains, come and get me and I'll organize a devastating counterattack."

"Pardon me while I puke in my hat. Listen boss. I can take care of myself. Nobody pushes Wonder Woman around. But I better be rolling in dough by the end of our trip, if I'm doing all the dirty work. I'm a tough cookie, okay? But next time I'll just let you sleep when a gang attacks – I'm tired of getting the crap beat out of me."

"Could we discuss this after I clean up?"

"Hey. End of conversation. Can you walk to the motel room? Might as well use the shower there, seeing as we paid for it. Here – take my arm."

"I've been thinking about all this bad luck, Sandra. I'm sure it's just temporary."

"That's how luck goes. Sometimes up, sometimes down. Our luck's been stuck on rotten for a long time. Which makes me real nervous going to Yellowstone Park. They have grizzly bears and wolves and so on in Yellowstone, right?"

"Yeah, but it's safe. Families take their kids all the time."

"They take their kids to Vegas, too. Why don't we just go straight there? With my connections, we could get a lot of work."

"Doc always wanted to go to Yellowstone. Him and Mrs. Pearce and me and Princess Di were supposed to go before Mrs. Pearce died, but we never did. There's spouting geezers there, and sulphur pots, and huge waterfalls at the top of the Rocky Mountains. It's on the Continental Divide."

"Who cares about that crap? I thought we were looking for criminals."

"Well, there must be crime in Yellowstone Park. Poachers, for example. Environmental trouble, for sure."

"Well, at least it's on our way to Las Vegas. Let's grab a shower, then we can take off out of here. The snow's nearly melted."

Coyote felt better after a shower, though he had cuts and bruises everywhere. He could only open one eye. He hoped they might find a drugstore in Lewistown that sold Firebrass. They mopped out the back of the camper and repacked their gear, spreading out the sleeping bags on the benches to dry. They fastened the broken hood down with a bungee cord, and set off for downtown.

"So you're giving up on finding Marcella Henderson?"

"Not giving up. I'll watch for her at rodeo events. I'm sure our paths will cross again. My luck has to get better soon."

"Spit and cross your heart."

"I feel it in my bones. We just need the right town and good people. Some day we'll look back on these disasters and laugh."

"I'm already giggling my head off. Ha ha."

"I mean it. You have to think positive to be a hero. Another thing, we'll never have good luck until we follow the rules. What would happen if we got a security contract, and didn't obey rules? It could wreck everything."

"I'm getting a little sick of your happy-face rules, so just can it, will ya?"

"It takes brains to follow rules."

"That blast of pepper spray wasn't so smart."

Sandra took the driver's seat with smug authority, Coyote being too weak to resist. Though dented and bashed, the Coyote Mobile was still ticking away and pedestrians stopped to stare at its progress up Main Street. Coyote waved at the crowds through the cracked windshield. With its missing back door and rumpled hood, the Coyote Mobile ran ugly but proud, showing people that heroes could take a few licks and emerge triumphant.

"What a wreck," Sandra muttered. "Burns gas like some old lawn mower. Whuddaya say we unload it on some farmer, and buy a decent RV?"

"I couldn't trade the Coyote Mobile in now. She's part of our identity."

"Things have changed. It was okay for Canada, but now we're in the States, that's all I'm saying. We need a new look. Like a couple of cool motorcycles."

"Maybe some day."

"We shoulda kicked that Katie Kool gang out of their fancy Southwind. Don't heroes get to keep the criminal's stuff, like bounty hunters? I heard that somewhere."

"Theft is what we've vowed to stop, Sandra. It's disrespect for property that made those punks wreck the Coyote Mobile. It caused all our cuts and bruises."

"I thought you liked pain."

"I never said I liked it. I said I could handle it."

"Hey, there's a drug store. And a liquor store across the street. You wanta look for your balm while I take care of the food and beer supply? Gimme twenty bucks." She disappeared across the street. Coyote eased himself out of the cab and limped into Bonanza Drugs.

The druggist took one look at Coyote as he approached the counter and said, "You really need to see a doctor, son."

"My partner's driving me to emergency. Do you sell Firebrass Balm here?"

"What is it, a hemorrhoid suppository? Cold medicine?"

"It's a special medicine that heals cuts, cures poison, and it's full of Vitamin D."

"Son, you need to get those injuries tended by a doctor. The Medical Center's out on the western edge of town."

"You don't know where I can find Firebrass?"

"Never heard of it, son. Try Wal-mart – or the Medicenter. It's on the highway."

Sandra's shopping was more successful. She sat in the driver's seat with a case of Budweiser, a bottle already clutched in her fist. She also had two plastic shopping bags filled with potato chips and cheezies.

The Montana Medical Center was in a huge mall filled with medical, dental and social services. They found Emergency at the third entrance. Inside was a sign that Sandra read out loud to Coyote. "NOTICE: Medical Care for Those Who Cannot Afford to Pay. This state health care facility by law must provide services free or at a reduced charge to persons who cannot afford to pay for medical care."

"Hey, that's lucky, cause our health cards won't be any good here."

"Forget it, takes too long. This is an emergency. Gimme your American Express."

With the credit card, they got two plastic ID cards, and a nurse escorted them down the hall to a medical cubicle. "The intern will be here shortly," she said.

Wonder Woman sat down in the only chair. "Are we gonna take shit-kickings like this every assignment, Captain? The mission could turn into a real downer."

"The great superheroes overcame worse defeats than this, Sandra. Look at The Phantom – wandering the planet for years to avenge his father's death. Every one of those heroes faced destruction a hundred times. It will be the same for us. But any minute we could become famous. All it takes is one TV camera at the right place and the right time and – bingo – superheroes."

"Yaaa, bullshit."

"It's true. Things change. Look at all the times Batman was captured by the Joker or the Penguin. Humiliated by the Cat Woman."

"Yeah. That Cat Woman was cool. Remember the time she hung Robin from a trapeze, tied up in a cat's cradle? Two hundred lashes with his own utility belt!"

"That's nothing. How about when Captain America was captured by Herr Dr. Krautschlinger, the Nazi spy hiding out in California? When Captain America entered the Nazi castle, he fell through a trap door and came to in the dungeon, tied hand and foot. Upside down. Helpless. They gave him a Nazi enema!"

"Bastards. What's in it?"

"A gallon of ice-water mixed with sand!"

"I'd beg for a clean bullet in the head."

"That's the great thing about heroes. Whatever pain you think you've suffered, one of them has suffered worse."

"Is that supposed to be comforting?"

"You have to look on the bright side. We've still got our reputations. The worst thing is a bad public image. That was The Hulk's big problem. At least nobody filmed those Yankees beating us up. That could look bad on TV."

"The real question is – when do we turn in this junk heap, and trade for something with more zip?"

"Well, let's see how it goes in Yellowstone. We'll need her there, for sure."

"And who's gonna drive us to Yellowstone? Me, right?"

"You have to drive, until I feel better."

"Oh great, pull a sicky. Give Wonder Woman all the work. I can see what's coming next."

If either of them could see what was coming next, they would have turned around and driven back to Moose Jaw. But they could not. And after a couple of hours of waiting, their wounds were stitched and painted with iodine – there was no Firebrass at the Montana Medical Center – and Sandra had herself treated to a back massage. The mall's optical outlet was able to replace the broken lenses in Coyote's glasses, but the prescription in one lens was a bit off, and though he could see again, his right eye was even fuzzier than before.

CHAPTER 13

The Adventure of the Corpse

B attered and bandaged, the heroes remained thoughtful as they crossed Montana toward Interstate 90. Coyote was thinking about Marcella Henderson and his dream of riding horses naked across the river. The dream would come back to him at strange times, like when they were passing waves of grass shimmering in the wind, or he saw a flight of clouds chasing each other like horses. As the Coyote Mobile entered the Yellowstone River valley, the sun was beginning to set. They turned onto Interstate 90, a big four-lane highway.

"I been thinking..." Coyote began.

"Oh, oh – here comes trouble!"

"Maybe there's a reason for all our bad luck. Like we're doing something wrong."

"Ha. Everything you do, like. Time for reorganization, I say," said Sandra.

"Exactly. We're nearly broke, and we haven't actually earned any money yet. We have to raise some cash."

"You want my opinion, you need to take a tougher line in the security negotiations. Like that Custer Motel. If you'd let me do the talking, I could've got us a written security contract. I could've negotiated us a fat retainer plus a decent room, and we'd still be on the payroll.

Problem is you don't know to negotiate, Captain. You're too gullible. You got flim-flammed by a pathetic desk clerk."

"The problem was you getting mixed up with that gang of Yankees."

"That's got nuthin to do with it. Put me in charge. I could've got the motel to buy our gun permit, and we woulda had the firepower to blast those punks. Did you see that Uzi in there? Wouldn't that've been useful! Don't tell me about negotiations."

"I wasn't. I'm saying we have to pick better assignments. Turn over a new leaf, eksetera. We need to take on some really big potatoes."

"Like who?"

"Terrorists. Or white-collar crime syndicates."

"Yeah? You wanta take on the Mafia?"

"I was thinking about big companies that steal resources, or illegally pollute the environment."

"Excuse me. Polluting the environment?"

"That's a bigger crime in America than bank robberies."

"There is no money in saving the goddam environment!"

"Anyway, I'm in charge and I say we're going to Yellowstone Park. We could apply for ranger's jobs. What could be better than joining the park service – and protecting Mother Nature? One of America's greatest natural parks is being threatened by ranchers and mining companies, and bullied by the tourist industry. Doc told me about it from a book. The animals are endangered."

"So what?"

"The park used to be full of timber wolves, but the government put a bounty on them. Then they were all shot and poisoned by the local ranchers, and completely wiped out in their native habitat. When the wardens realized that predators were part of the life cycle, they decided to bring the wolves back. So they imported some timber wolves from Canada, and there's eight packs of them now. Still endangered, of course."

"You want to protect some lousy wolves?"

"Same with coyotes. They nearly wiped out the coyotes in the

1930s. Doc and me watched a documentary on Discovery Channel."

"About coyotes?" Sandra said.

"It proved they don't attack any cattle or sheep or deer. Mostly they eat mice and insects, but everybody thinks they eat chickens and dogs, so they hate them and kill them at every chance."

"We shot the bastards where I grew up," Sandra said. "Not easy to shoot either."

"People have tried to exterminate coyotes for a hundred years, but there's more of them than ever. Now they're moving in to cities. All over North America. They can adapt to any environment. Doc says they're smarter than humans."

"I knew there was a moral to this speech."

"Well, I can't help being – you know, proud of them."

"Because your name is Coyote? Don't make me barf. What was this plan about scoring some cash?"

"I bet the Ranger Service would be interested in hiring us. But we should get proper résumés done up. And business cards. That's what I mean about getting organized. If we snagged a job there, we could earn a salary and save the wilderness!"

"Is it even open this time of year?"

"The restaurants and stuff might not be open, but there must be somebody there. The map says the gates open in May, so we could see at least see if they're recruiting. They'd probably like to hire a guy named Coyote."

"You wanna bet on it?"

But Sandra's negativity could not squelch the ideas that bubbled out of Coyote's brain, lively as the water burbling along the Yellowstone River beside the road. He was looking forward to the great Yellowstone Park. Doc had always promised Coyote they would someday visit the world's first nature preserve, created by Teddy Roosevelt, the last great president. Doc wasn't a fan of modern presidents, the way Coyote was.

Coyote wanted to reach the park before the gates closed for the night, but their vehicle went even slower as it approached the mountains. The sun had gone down, and the sky was pitch black. It felt like they were travelling through outer space. Then Coyote noticed a cluster of bright flashing lights winking in the side mirror. The lights were following the Coyote Mobile, dipping and spinning along the curves and ridges of the valley. They danced in and out of sight – sometimes there, sometimes not – speeding up and slowing down again.

"Don't freak out," he muttered to Sandra. "There's strange lights following us."

Sandra looked into the driver's mirror and nearly swerved off the road. "I can't believe this. It's the fucking cops again!"

"No way. Cops have red and blue lights."

"If they're not cops, it's the INS. They musta spotted us on satellite when we crossed the border and sent a squad car after us. We'll never shake them on a freeway. Look for an exit ramp!"

"It doesn't look like a car. They're just lights – flying in formation. I think they're UFOs."

"You ever seen a UFO? Don't talk like a wingnut. You don't even know what a UFO looks like!"

"Well, they don't go to Canada. But there's millions of UFOs in the States. I seen them on TV!"

"You mean flying saucers? Driven by some rubber space cadets with big eyes?"

"UFOs usually appear as bright lights sweeping across the sky. Just like these. You can see them, right?"

"Okay, it's a possibility. They're probably attracted to weirdos like you. What happens if they are UFOs?"

"The most important thing is to stay calm. Till we find out if they're hostile."

They were approaching Livingston, Montana, where they turned off the interstate toward the park on No. 89, a highway that wound through the mountain ranges like a roller-coaster. The shoulders of the road were littered with dangerous fallen boulders. Sandra pushed the Coyote Mobile to its top speed, despite the hair-raising curves and the loose steering in the front end. Still the lights followed. Rounding the base of a steep cliff, she swerved to miss a rubble heap of smashed sandstone and wrenched the old truck to a bucketing halt on the shoulder, glaring into the mirror.

"Let's see what comes around the curve. Get set to stomp the little bastards!"

A blaze of flashing lights came whirling around the corner, almost blinding the heroes with their brilliance. To Coyote's astonishment, the dazzle came from a set of white strobe lights mounted on an ambulance, which was driving straight at them at a hundred klicks an hour. Its big halogen headlamps lit up the Coyote Mobile hulking at the edge of the road, its ass end sticking out across the yellow line.

The ambulance driver swerved sharply to the left, and the ambulance careened up on two tires as it tried to miss them. It clipped the back corner of the cabin, driving the Coyote Mobile's grill into the pile of rock. The ambulance cleared both lanes and crashed into the iron guardrail overlooking the Upper Yellowstone canyon, its lights still winking like flash bulbs. Coyote could make out some big red letters on the side: EMS. Emergency Medical Services. They had caused an ambulance to crash!

Coyote went into shock. Their luck was getting worse. Or was the Coyote Mobile a jinx, a lightning rod attracting bad luck and disaster? Forgetting his cuts and bruises, Coyote leaped out and ran to the ambulance, while Wonder Woman puffed along behind.

She was elated. "This is fantastic, Donny. Our luck has turned!"

"What are you talking about?"

"That goddam ambulance hit us. A government vehicle smashed into us. Think of the compensation!"

"Oh, I don't think we can –"

"Millions. We'll be rich. Suing the government. Just leave this to me, okay?"

The back door of the ambulance banged open and a medic hopped out. To Coyote's great relief, he was unhurt. The ambulance was tilted to one side, its motor still running. The attendant shook his head, stunned by the impact of the air bags. He wore a crisp blue medical uniform, and a rapster's red silk bandana tied around his head.

"You okay?" Coyote said.

"Whew. Yeah."

"Nobody hurt?"

"Naa. This thing has a chassis like a Russian tank. How about you?"

Before Coyote could speak, Sandra collapsed on the ground, writhing in pain. "Man, are you in trouble!" she moaned. "You ran right into us!"

"You guys were parked in the middle of the road!"

"Hey. We were parked on the fuckin shoulder, man! There's our tracks. We pulled over to let you pass!"

"And why are you driving a log cabin in the mountains at night, anyway?"

"We're camping in Yellowstone National Park," Coyote explained. "Is your patient okay?"

"Patient?"

"In the ambulance. Is he okay?"

"Na. She's dead. It's cool."

"Dead!" Coyote gasped.

Sandra's face went pure white. "Holy shit!"

"Don't panic. She started out that way. I'm delivering a corpse to the organ transplant centre in Jackson Hole."

"You're carrying a dead body in there?"

"Yeah. This EMS is not an EMS. It's a HODEV – a human organ delivery vehicle. Some kid's on life support at Jackson Hole and needs a liver ASAP."

"You got a good liver in there?"

"Well – it's in the body of a deceased. We refrigerate the corpse at the moment of death, and employ it as a container for its various valuable parts. It's part of the new USDHSS plan to speed up organ shipments around the country. ROA. Regional Organ Allocation."

"Jeeze."

"It's the only fair way of distributing surplus body parts, and cheaper than cutting them out and flying them by helicopter. Less traumatic for the deceased's loved ones. They consign the happy cadaver to us, and we maintain it until the call comes from some lucky recipient. All done via the internet! You want to see her?"

Coyote shuddered, but Sandra said, "I wouldn't mind taking a look. Never know when you'll see your next corpse."

"There could be infections," Coyote suggested. "We don't know how she died."

"Heart attack. There's no danger of contamination. You're completely safe. This is the most antiseptic vehicle in Montana. It's also a mobile counselling centre. Step inside." The attendant opened the side door of the ambulance and waved them inside. He pressed a button on a refrigerated cabinet. The glass top slid open to reveal a middle-aged black woman, her eyes closed as if sleeping. She seemed at peace on her mission, and Coyote's heart went out to her. A real hero, he thought.

"So you guys weren't hurt?" the medic said.

"Not hurt? Where do you think these scrapes and bruises came from? I'm in agony from whiplash. The government's gotta pay for this!"

"Give up, lady. Those injuries were treated at least twelve hours ago. Probably happened when you smashed this rattletrap the first time."

"I can't turn my head. We're suing for medical expenses and post-traumatic shock!"

"Forget it. What are you guys, anyway? Welders?"

"We're heroes," Coyote said. "From Saskatchewan."

The medic stared at their ragged clothes and scarred faces, trying to figure out their agenda. "What kind of heroes?"

"You wouldn't recognize us out of uniform, but I am Captain Coyote, and this is my faithful companion, Wonder Woman."

"I see." The ambulance driver started edging toward the cell phone in his EMS. "Excuse me a minute."

"Right now we're doing security contracts, but we also have experience stopping child abuse, disaster rescues, environmental protection. That's why we're going to Yellowstone, to offer our skills as rangers. This is our vehicle, the Coyote Mobile."

"What are you, some kind of trickster?"

"You mean – The Joker?"

"No, like the trickster. Coyote is a character in native stories. He's always playing jokes on other animals. That's what this is, right? A joke?"

"No joke," Coyote said. "We offer the best protection!"

"Sounds like a scam to me."

"Well, it's not."

"Anyway, your job's not so great!" Wonder Woman said. "Hauling dead bodies."

"I've had worse. Don't I look happy? And I lucked into this job, really. Not many people want to be organ transplant counsellors, until they see the pay. Check out the risk factors. They're not extreme, as long as you avoid body fluids."

"Yuck. So how's the pay?"

"That's the best part. Ninety-five thousand a year. And I was getting desperate for a job. I trained to be an English professor."

"Bullshit!" Sandra snorted.

"It's true. I wrote a Ph.D. thesis on John Milton, just when all the universities stopped hiring. Had a couple of sessional appointments, till even those dried up. Nobody reads Milton any more, so I really got hung out to dry. I had to pay off a huge student loan, with a useless degree. Eight years of education, *pfft*. I decided to try something different."

"It's different."

"I wouldn't mind," Sandra said. "The money sounds good."

"How much do heroes make?" the medic asked.

"We don't have a set rate, but usually forty bucks a day for expenses."

"I'd make a good organ transplant counsellor," Sandra said.

"It's nature conservation we're pursuing right now," Coyote reminded her.

"We better get there soon then, boss." She turned to the counsellor. "Is there a place along here to buy food at this time of night?"

"Well – you might find something open in Gardiner, the town at the park entrance. But I can help if you're short of food. I carry emergency rations." He reached into the food locker beside the body cabinet.

"Any pepperoni sticks?" Sandra inquired.

"More like health food – fruit roll-ups, granola bars, that kind of thing." He piled boxes of snacks in their hands.

"Jeeze. Thanks," Coyote said. "I'm sorry about the fender-bender."

"Forget it. But I'll have to file a police report. Can I see your registration?"

"We're trying to avoid police attention at the moment," Sandra said, winking her blackened eye. "Couldn't we keep this private?"

"I have to report any accident. What shall I tell them?"

"Smashed into by a USO. An Unidentified Stationary Object. Driven by a Hero with a Hound-Dog Face."

The organ transplant counsellor laughed and wrote it down. He said it had a Miltonic ring to it. Even Coyote laughed. Every once in a while Sandra came up with a good line. He could imagine it painted on the side of the Coyote Mobile: "Captain Coyote, the Hero with the Hound-Dog Face."

He repeated it as they drove south to the park. "How did you think of that, Sandra?"

"I dunno. After those punks worked your face over, it just came to me. 'He looks like an old hound dog, his face all swollen up like that.' You like it?"

"The public might go for it. Dogs have a better image than coyotes, I guess. Captain Coyote – the Hero with the Hound-Dog Face. Did you work on it, or did it come in a single flash?"

"More like a flash. No big deal."

"I'll make sure you get credit. We'll paint it on the side of the truck."

"The name or the face?"

"Both."

"You don't need the face. Just stick your snout out the window. Same effect."

All the way to Gardiner they debated the pros and cons of Captain Coyote's face on the side of their vehicle, while finishing off the EMS emergency rations. Coyote found a campground on the edge of town, a pleasant park nestled in a stand of lodgepole pines. They were the only campers.

After a night's rest, they would get totally reorganized, maybe fix the Coyote Mobile's leaking radiator. Coyote had to find some Firebrass Balm. Then they could put on clean T-shirts and go to join the greatest conservation service in the world, the Yellowstone Rangers.

CHAPTER 14

An Earth-shaking Discovery

The sun rose the next morning on a very different landscape than the sandstone hoodoos of the Lower Yellowstone. Gardiner was located high in a green mountain valley, nestled between the saw-toothed ridges of the Rocky Mountains. The snow which had blanketed the Rockies only two days before was already vanishing in the sunshine. Below the campground stretched a meadow where Appaloosa horses frisked in the morning sunlight, and herds of thick-bodied cows grazed.

After they cleaned up the back of the van and plugged the radiator, the heroes went looking for groceries and medicine. Gardiner was practically deserted, its motels and restaurants still closed for the season. There was no drug store. They did locate a hardware store on a side street and were able to stock up on tools and weapons to replace the ones stolen in Lewistown. They also found an open Chevron station, and while Sandra filled the vehicle with gas, Coyote went to the washroom to examine his battered face. It was looking better, at least. His eyes were open, but were both so blackened that he looked like a racoon.

When Coyote got to the counter with the credit card, Sandra had piled up four packs of beef jerky and a carton of beer to go, but he made her put the beer back. He had to rely on Sandra to do the talking because his face was such a mess. But he insisted he was well enough to take the wheel and drive into the park. The Park Service needed them. Innocent tourists were always being attacked by starved grizzly bears or packs of foraging wolves. There would be fires to put out and trails to be blazed. Once they got the routine down, Coyote would start a campaign to restore the wilderness to its original condition for future generations, as Teddy Roosevelt had dreamed. He also had to remember to buy a souvenir for Doc from Yellowstone Park.

At the big log gate, a girl in a Mountie hat greeted them. Her extra-sized name tag said Ranger Natashya Bzrychekyovitkowski-Boyd. The winter snow pack was still melting in the higher mountain passes, but the roads were clear for traffic. The combined fee for Yellowstone and Grand Teton National Parks was only $20 for a whole week, which could be charged on Coyote's American Express card. So far, their luck was holding. The ranger girl told them no hunting or fishing was allowed in the park, and no campfires. She came out to inspect the Coyote Mobile.

"You did say Coyote Mobile?" she said. "For transporting – coyotes?"

"Just us. It's my name, see? Captain Coyote. You might've heard of me."

"I can't say that I have." Ranger Bzrychekyovitkowski-Boyd studied the welding sign on the back door, which was held shut with wire and wooden boards. "You're not planning to do any welding, are you?"

"That's an old sign, before it was the Coyote Mobile. We haven't got our new sign yet. If we become rangers, we could put a Yellowstone sign up."

Ranger Bzrychekyoivitkowski-Boyd looked inside. "Well, we're always recruiting. I'll give you an application form to take to Admin Headquarters. That's at Mammoth Hot Springs, five miles up the road."

"Jeeze, thanks!"

"Have a good one."

Cheered by her enthusiasm, Coyote drove up the winding mountain highway in a whistling mood. He wouldn't mind a snappy uniform like Natashya's. The rangers probably rode horses, too.

The crags rose higher on all sides as the road climbed toward Mammoth Hot Springs. Even Sandra's attitude had improved by the time they circled the main building to the parking lot. The five-acre lot was already half-full, a vast expanse of camper trucks, RVs, mobile homes, tent trailers, and buses. The Coyote Mobile proceeded with slow dignity past the staring tourists. Coyote parked in a stall beside the building that said, "Reserved for Administration."

A sergeant in the Recruitment & Training office gave them numbered tags and more application forms. They were told to return at 10 a.m. the next day, to attend an orientation session for applicants in the Albright Visitor Center. In the meantime, they were welcome to explore the wilderness wonders of the first National Park. The sergeant handed them two Big Snack coupons and a fancy brochure of the Yellowstone Circle Tour, which included many self-guiding features. Hiking trails wound in all directions, as well as climbing, birdwatching, cycling, dirt biking, and snowmobiling trails.

After Yellowstone Falls, they could drive past a series of craters and hot springs to the resort village at Yellowstone Lake, before reaching the greatest attraction of all, Old Faithful Geyser.

Most visitors, of course, preferred to admire Nature from inside the comfort of their cars, and drove their RVs from one glorious attraction to the next, passing each other recklessly on the dangerous curves as they rushed to do the Circle Tour in a day. There were handy Big Snack drive-ins at each nature attraction.

That morning, however, the alpine meadows of the Blacktail Plateau were still emerging from winter's snowy cocoon. Deer and foxes could be seen ambling among the early-blossoming flowers, gazing shyly at the few passing vehicles and disappearing into the pine woods.

"Won't it be fantastic," Coyote exclaimed, "to work in a park like this?"

"I suppose I could get used to it."

"Think we got a chance at those ranger jobs?"

"Well – I might. You haven't got a hope. They're bound to have some kind of IQ test. Notice the funny look that sergeant was giving your Captain Coyote badge?"

"He was reading it. What's wrong with that?"

"Hah. He wrote down the number."

"I don't care. What makes you think you'd get a job?"

"Didn't you notice the affirmative action statement on the form?"

"What's that?"

"Where they asked you to check off if you were woman, native American, a visible minority, or physically disadvantaged. I got all four. I'm practically guaranteed."

"You said you were native?"

"I told ya – Gabriel Dumont was my great-great-uncle. The legendary hero of the Canadian Métis. My family name is Douleur."

"Yeah – but you can't *prove* you're Métis. Only you might be."

"I don't have to. Let'em prove me wrong. They got their facts, I got mine. The blood of five Indian nations run through my veins. Hey, look out!"

A bear cub suddenly appeared at the edge of the road, emerging from the pine forest a few feet from the asphalt. The innocent cub strolled onto the centre line of the road, gazing in defiance at the approaching van.

"Don't slow down!" Sandra yelled. "Keep driving!"

"I'm watching out for the bear!"

"Hit the gas, you dipshit. Papa Bear and Mama Bear are probably sitting around the corner waiting for us!"

"That is amazing. A live grizzly cub!"

"Don't stop. Don't stop!"

"We have to let him cross, Sandra. Look!"

"What are you, suicidal? Didn't you see the signs warning about bears?"

"He's so cool. I bet he's hungry."

"You're his food, birdbrain. Get out of the way. I'm taking the wheel before you get us killed."

"I'm going, I'm going!"

Coyote eased the Coyote Mobile around the bear cub sitting in the middle of the road. As they passed, a huge mound of fur rose out of the bushes in the ditch and a six-foot grizzly sow craned her neck to look at them.

"See, what did I tell you? Talk about narrow escapes!"

"Calm down. They weren't going to attack. Remember, it's our duty to protect this wildlife."

"Oh sure – protect grizzly bears. From what? Jesus, you're dumb. Park Rangers! I bet we get assigned to cleaning the toilets."

"That's important work too, Sandra. If we join the park service, we'll have to do everything. You don't get to pick just the fun jobs, like putting out fires."

They climbed the mountains at Dunraven Pass, and stopped at an observation turnoff that looked out over the mountain ranges. The sun, already in decline, bathed the Rocky peaks in an orange glaze, igniting a spectacular show of colours across Yellowstone Canyon. Several other vehicles were parked at the turnoff, and a family sat at a picnic table with several boxes of Big Snacks. Coyote put a quarter in the binoculars so he could scan the mountainsides, hoping to see a wild elk or a bison, maybe even a coyote.

Sandra refused to get out of the Coyote Mobile to look through the glasses. "Come on, let's get outta here and find a decent motel. It'll be dark soon, and being this high up in the mountains gives me the creeps. I feel a panic attack coming on. I might have to go on disability."

"Well, let's stop at Yellowstone Falls for the night. There's a campground there. We still have lots of emergency rations. You'll be okay sleeping in the Coyote Mobile."

Coyote drove down the back road to the Falls Lookout. From a mile away, they could see the mist of the Lower Falls, its white plumes of spray floating down the canyon, turning pink against the evening sky. Coyote couldn't take his eyes off the sight. He wanted to get close enough to touch the thundering power of the waterfall.

The brochure showed a footpath down to the falls called Uncle Tom's Path, and Coyote drove till he found Uncle Tom's parking lot, where several campers already were parked. Even from the top of the canyon they could feel the power of Nature, shaking the mountain of rock under their feet. After some persuasion, Sandra agreed to leave the truck and venture down Uncle Tom's Path. It took a long series of switchbacks down the face of the canyon, and around a bend in the river to the foot of the waterfall. The tremor was so powerful, Sandra found it hard to walk.

"You have to get over your fear, or you'll never be a ranger!" Coyote yelled over the roar.

"I don't want to be a goddam ranger!" she shrieked back in a fury.

The farther they descended, the louder grew the pounding of the waterfall, until it sounded like a continuous blast of noise. Sandra moved slower and slower, clinging to the face of the cliff. They came to a plank footbridge across a crevice. Halfway over, Sandra grabbed the wooden railing and clamped her arms round it, terrified to move in either direction. Coyote couldn't budge her. The harder he tried to pry her loose, the tighter she gripped the rail. She finally agreed to let go if they could go back to the top of the canyon, and Coyote gave up the attempt.

Back at the parking lot, Sandra climbed into the rear of the Coyote Mobile and huddled in a corner, trembling and gasping for breath. She was completely traumatized by her fear of heights and the shaking of the ground, not to mention being surrounded by wild animals.

"Get me out of here!" she moaned. "I have to find a decent motel!"

"Now?"

"I can't stand it. This wilderness is gonna kill me!" She finally made Coyote promise to drive to Yellowstone Lake Village, twenty miles away, where there was a hotel and a campground with flush toilets. He could drive back in the morning by himself if he wanted to see the Yellowstone Falls. She gradually calmed down as the Coyote Mobile chugged down the road to the village.

"Maybe there's a liquor store. I'd feel better after a cold beer."

"Okay, we'll get some beer, and see how things look in the morning. I'd sure like to get a full night's sleep before the interview."

"I am not going for no stupid interview!"

"Sandra, listen to reason. This is important. We are committed to saving the wilderness, and the best place to start is Yellowstone Park. I know we live in a modern society with cars and planes and computers etcetera, but technology is killing the planet. We have to restore America to the Age of Nature. That's our challenge – a mission for the new millennium."

"You're too late. Humans are in charge now."

"But if Yellowstone could be restored to its original shape, with its wildlife and ecology preserved, that would show the whole world it can be done. We can have paradise again. If they can bring back animals like the wolves and coyotes, we can do it for other exterminated species. We could see herds of buffalo again, thundering over the countryside. The whooping crane and burrowing owl. They're counting on us!"

"That is the dumbest mission I ever heard of."

"Nature is connected with everything. And we have to do it one animal, one waterfall at a time. You have to think big. Of course, first we'll have to show the Rangers we can do the grunt jobs like security work."

"Well, do it without me. Either we start for Las Vegas in the morning, or I'm going on my own. If I can catch a bus outta here."

Coyote stared at her, his chin stuck out defiantly. "Okay, you got it. First thing in the morning, I'll drive you to the nearest bus station. But I intend to stay and restore the first park of America to its natural state."

"Feel free, shithead. Just don't come cryin to me when you get eaten by bears. All our other disasters are nothing compared to what's comin next – and I don't want to witness it."

"Then you're just a quitter."

"Quitter. You ungrateful dumbfuck, I gave up my family, resigned my job, compromised my reputation, so I could take off on a stupid quest, and this is the abuse I put up with. Might I remind your lordship that you once promised a big fat salary plus expenses. Now we're stuck in the asshole of nowhere surrounded by wild animals."

Unfortunately the Lake Village hotel was still closed for the season, and the campground was full. Even the overload campground was full. Sandra began screeching with fury, and he could only calm her down by stopping at a Big Snack – it was open till midnight – and picking up more supplies on the credit card: pepperoni sticks, a case of pop, four bags of corn chips and a six-pack of Budweiser. They drove back to the parking lot beside Uncle Tom's path, hoping they'd still find space. Sandra swore she'd be dead before morning, even though Coyote guaranteed her that the parking lot was perfectly safe, with several campers parked nearby.

Coyote crawled into his bunk in the back and started drifting off to sleep, but the thunder of the falls kept Sandra awake. She drank four cans of beer to calm her nerves, but this only made her anxiety worse because she had to pee so much. As she refused to step into the bear-lurking darkness outside, she solved the problem by putting a milk crate on her bunk, hoisting her butt onto the side window, and pulling her pants down.

This ritual kept waking Coyote up, and he realized he was in for a long and sleepless night, making it hard to do a good job interview. He groaned in protest. Then Sandra insisted on starting one of her long, beer-fuelled stories about her abused childhood, trying to drown out the thunder of the falls.

"Once upon a time I knew this guy called Dave Hogg –"

"Is this a fairy tale?" Coyote asked.

"Quit interrupting! Dumbnuts. Why would it be a fairy tale?"

"That's how fairy tales start, once upon a time."

"Well, so did my life and all my fucking problems. So shut up. Where was I?"

"A guy called Dave Hogg –"

"Once upon a time when I was a kid and living on the farm out at Gravelbourg, there was this good-looking young school bus driver named Dave Hogg. He was a pretty cool guy with a Fonz haircut, and could crack funny jokes. He took a fancy to this town girl named Betsy Gronerud. She was in Grade Twelve, and her old man was totally freaked out by it. Larry Gronerud was president of the chamber of commerce, and always running for the Liberals. He owned the biggest machinery dealership in town. In fact, he would have won, except the Conservatives always ran a guy connected to Derek Burntswine, the sleazeball Balboni made a senator –"

"Wait a minute. What happened to Dave Hogg? If you include everybody who ever lived in Gravelbourg, this will take all night."

"Dave Hogg was the driver of the school bus, and had the hots for Betsy Gronerud. She was seventeen and kinda chunky, not real fat, but a size 14 at least, and a moustache on her lip – not just a few hairs either, a real fuzzball – but he thought she was the cat's pyjamas."

"She was a friend of yours?"

"Yuk. I never hung out with creeps like her. She was always sucking up to Dave in front of her girlfriends, a clique of real brown-nosers from town. They stood there waiting for our school bus to arrive every morning, so they could make eyes at Dave. But I got the real story through a friend of a friend, who swore on a stack of Bibles. After a while, Betsy stopped putting out for Dave Hogg, so he dumped her the night before the high school grad. Oh, she was some pissed. Proceeded to make his life hell, phoning his house at all hours of the night, sending threatening love letters, etcetera. She spray-painted her name on the side of his bus."

"It's hard to shake a girl loose once she gets a grip," Coyote agreed.

"Sheddup. Whaddayou know about it? Anyway, after school one day she was waiting with us at the school bus stop, with this mournful look on her fat mug. After us farm kids piled on, she was going to climb in when Larry slammed the door in her face and took off down the grid road, leaving her in the dust on the sidewalk, screaming her undying love. Well, this caused a riot on the bus and we were all cheering Dave on, because when old man Gronerud found out about his daughter, Dave's bus-driving job was toast. He just took off for the open countryside. Hogg's last ride. If the Groneruds caught up with him, they'd castrate him like a yearling pig.

"About a mile out of town, we get to the first farm, the Cournoyer place, and he's just dropping off the Cournoyer twins when here comes Betsy cannonballing up the road in her old man's pickup truck. The bus takes off again, with us kids cheering Dave on, and he gains a good distance on her before he has to stop at the next road to drop off Danny Mintenko. Again Betsy nearly catches up, and again he takes off with those funny red stop signs flapping against the side of the bus.

"The bus had to go at least twenty miles into the country, with Dave dropping a kid off every mile or so. When the last one was gone, he'd turn the bus west and just keep goin, to Calgary or wherever. There was still five or six of us sitting in the back, cheering him on. Listen, keep track of the kids getting out, because if I lose count, I'll have to start again. The further we went, the rougher the road got, because the municipality never gravelled it that far out. Then he stopped at the Gomersalls and dropped Will off, and then Stephanie Jorgenson's farm, and a mile after that –"

Coyote groaned. "Couldn't you just say he dropped everybody off? If you stop at every single farm, you'll never get to the end!"

"How many have we dropped off so far?"

"How the heck do I know?"

"Shit. I told you to keep count. What a dork. Well, forget that story!"

"Wait a minute. Why does it matter how many kids were dropped off?"

"Well, it doesn't. I asked you to count, and when you quit, the story just flew out of my head, even though there were lots of juicy parts left. Yes sir, lots of blood and gore. Heroic deeds. Now you'll never hear it. Too bad, sucka. Hand me a Bud, willya?"

An explosion suddenly rocked the Coyote Mobile, like an atom bomb going off.

"Omigawd, what's that!"

"Sounds like something blew up," Coyote said.

"An earthquake. The mountains are falling!"

"What is that horrible smell?"

"I mighta farted. Big explosions like that affect my asshole. Doctor says it's a nervous reaction to sudden low frequency sound. My guts go into a huge spasm."

"Well – can't you –?"

"No, I'm not going outside. Turn your head. I'll try and point my ass out the window." She tilted her buttocks at the tiny rectangle of the window. "Be easy if I wasn't so drunk!"

Another explosion split the night air, and the stench hit Coyote with the force of a shock wave. "I thought you were aiming out the window!" he yelped.

"I was, but I can't see a damn thing."

"Well, it's turning light out now. Let's get outta here before I suffocate."

They stumbled out of the stinking Coyote Mobile into the grey light of the mountain dawn, with the explosions going off every few minutes in the canyon below. The fresh mountain air revived him, and after a while Coyote retrieved the food cooler for an early breakfast snack. Sandra felt better in the daylight, too, but insisted on waiting in the truck if Coyote went down Uncle Tom's Path to view the falls. He wanted to investigate the source of the mysterious explosions rocking the mountainside.

At the top of the trail, Coyote saw a sign he hadn't noticed in the dusk of the evening before: PATH CLOSED TILL NOON. He usually obeyed such signs, but he felt he had to investigate the noises. He clambered over the barricade and started down the path. It was not so dangerous in daylight, though he slipped a few times on the rocks, wet from the spray drifting off the falls. He reached the bridge where Sandra had balked the night before, and edged across to gaze at last upon the great falls.

He was not prepared for the terrible sight that greeted him round the bend of the canyon. Expecting to see a majestic waterfall gleaming in the morning light, he was stunned by a scene of massive demolition along the river bank. A pair of bulldozers and a huge Euclid earth-mover clawed and bashed the cliffs, scraping away tons of smashed rock. They pushed the rubble into the river to make a wide flat surface that looked like an airport runway.

Coyote blinked in disbelief. The roar of diesel engines almost drowned out the awesome thunder of the falls. Another blast of dyna-mite went off somewhere on the cliff face, and boulders hurtled through the air, narrowly missing Coyote as they plunged into the river. A park ranger at the foot of the trail spotted Coyote and rushed forward, waving his arms. "Go back. Go back. Didn't you see the sign? The trail's closed till noon!"

"What's going on?"

"Dynamite blasting!"

"But what for?"

"They're building a new road down from the highway."

"You're bringing cars down here?"

The ranger nodded. "Extra parking so people can view the falls. We're trying to finish before the summer rush. Half a million cubic yards of rock. Third greatest engineering feat in the history of the Park Service!"

"But why are they doing it at night?"

"Public safety. You're free to come and view the falls this after-noon."

Crushed by his discovery, Coyote sat at the edge of the river, feel-ing sick and depressed. Of course, common sense said they needed a parking lot for people to view the falls. But Teddy Roosevelt would spin in his grave at this. It showed how far the park had declined. How could they encourage cars, and still have room for bears and moose and bur-rowing owls? It was another savage assault on Nature by the tourist industry. Nature called on Captain Coyote to act.

CHAPTER 15

The Flash's Helmet

Coyote had no time to run back to the top of the canyon and get his uniform. He had to stop the machines in their tracks. Then he and Sandra could go to park headquarters and blow the whistle. But what if the chief ranger had approved the plan? Coyote had to think about that, and thinking dulled the momentum of action. He put the thought aside.

Circling past the ranger guarding the construction site, Coyote made his way along the river's edge to the earthmover, a gigantic piece of equipment as big as a house. It sat with motor idling, as the driver waited for the next dynamite explosion. Coyote climbed onto the frame beside the gas tank. He remembered a GI Joe comic when Joe had poured sugar into a Commie jeep's gas tank and made its motor seize up.

Coyote didn't have any sugar – he made a mental note to get some for future operations – but he had an idea. He hadn't peed that morning yet, and surely his urine would be full of sugar from all the soft drinks he had drunk during the night. He unscrewed the cap of the Euclid's fuel tank and unzipped his fly. He inserted Mr. Private and discharged a full bladder into the fuel tank. The engine coughed twice and fell silent.

"Hey!" the ranger yelled, running across the piles of rock. "What the hell are you doing up there?" Coyote thrust Mr. Private back into his jeans and jumped to the ground, running to the next bulldozer. He still had some left in his bladder, and if he could leap onto the moving tractor, he could disable two vehicles in the same mission. That would cause a stir in the news media!

Before Coyote could reach the bulldozer, however, four rangers appeared out of the trees and surrounded him. He couldn't resist arrest, which might look bad on his record. But if he was arrested and charged, his defence of the park would be recognized and the charges dismissed.

In the end, the rangers didn't arrest him. After questioning him and discovering that he hoped to join the service, they escorted him to the top of the canyon and tore up his job application. They deposited him beside the Coyote Mobile, where a line of people was waiting for Uncle Tom's Path to open.

Sandra was delighted by the parking lot disaster. She had predicted something like this would happen, and because Coyote refused to listen to her, he'd lost his chance at a ranger job. Coyote's forlorn hound-dog expression looked so funny that she fell down on the parking lot, howling with laughter and pounding her fists. Still chortling, she taunted him with his words from the night before: "'We have to restore America to its natural state!' Our big hero. Ahahahahaha!"

Coyote climbed into the Coyote Mobile and started the motor. He hit the gas pedal and nearly drove over her as he backed up to turn the Coyote Mobile around. She climbed into the cab, still giggling.

"Hey, take it easy, Captain. I was only makin fun!"

"Well, I'm tired of your fun. Now I'll never work for Yellowstone Park. And maybe the place is going to hell, but it doesn't mean I'm giving up on Nature. It's not funny!"

"Why not? You thought those explosions last night were pretty hilarious. Now we're even. I thought you liked laughing at trouble."

"Okay, I'm sorry I lost my temper, but it wouldn't happen if you didn't jabber so much. Faithful companions are supposed to keep their mouths shut. Robin the Boy Wonder was deaf and dumb, compared to you. Tarzan's friend Cheetah would be a better companion than a motormouth like you. Don't worry, I'll get my chance to tell this story, with all the true details."

"When you tell the final true story, will it include how you promised all the fat jobs when we started off on this nutty crusade? What's the story going to say about all your broken promises?"

"My story will tell the truth about every adventure, including the disasters. Maybe I can laugh about it then. Bad stuff happens. And I didn't guarantee you a fat job. I said there could be rewards. Anyway, you refused a ranger's job."

"None of your ideas pan out. And how about a real wage? How much did Robin the Boy Wonder earn? At least Cheetah got a few bananas. He ate."

"You haven't been starving. Whatever we have, we share."

"So far all you shared is a lot of beatings and insults. But I'll try and keep my suggestions to myself, if it makes you happier."

With extra time on their hands, now that the ranger jobs were history, they spent the morning reorganizing their gear so they'd be ready for the next opportunity. Coyote printed an inventory of all their equipment and supplies, and a list of stuff they needed. Sandra was keen to be on the way to Vegas, though, so by noon they were on the highway going south. All Coyote saw of Yellowstone Lake was a glimmer of ice through the cracked windshield of the van. They didn't turn down the side road to visit Old Faithful Geyser.

"We can get jobs in Vegas," Sandra said. "I guarantee it. It's the richest city in the States. Entertainment capital of the world."

"What makes you so sure there'll be action there?"

"Well for one thing, the place is crawling with gangsters, the ones who started the casinos and bars out in the desert in the first place. Just think of the dough there is in security!"

"But we'd end up working for the Mafia. We have to find opportunities that go in sync with our mission."

"There you go again. Negativity!"

"Wonder Woman, we have principles."

"Well, if we don't trade this garbage can in for a real car, we'll be standing on the side of the road looking at them go past. Look – fifty miles an hour, downhill. We'll never make it to Las Vegas at this rate. The sooner we get a real set of wheels, the better!"

"Forget it!" Coyote snapped. "We invested a lot in this old girl, and she's our vehicle. Besides, what's the hurry?"

Grand Teton Park was on the west side of the Divide, a high flat plateau of dense forest, divided by the meandering Snake River along the foot of the Grand Teton Mountains. It too was a protected wilderness for vast herds of elk. By late afternoon, they reached the resort town of Jackson Hole, a bustling collection of restaurants and motels and casinos. They cruised the streets for a while checking for criminals and other threats to public order.

Near the centre of town, they passed The Last Frontier Antique and Craft Shop, with a couple of old people sitting on a bench out front. The man wore a peaked farmer's hat that said, "Don't forget my Senior's Discount!" His wife was dressed in a pale green pantsuit and clutched an armful of plastic shopping bags. Between them on the bench sat a silver helmet. Though battered and dented, its surface gleamed in the sun. Coyote recognized it at once: The Flash's helmet.

"I can't believe it!" he declared to Wonder Woman. "Prepare for action."

"Action?"

"See that helmet on the bench beside the old folks?"

"That geezer with the feed cap? That's not a helmet, it's an old wash basin. He must've bought it in that junk store."

"That shows how much you know!" Coyote replied. "That 'basin' happens to be The Flash's helmet."

"Who?"

"You never read *Flash Comics?* 'Faster than a streak of lightning, swifter than the speed of light, fleeter than thought is ... THE FLASH, reincarnation of the winged Mercury!' The fastest man alive. He wears a helmet with wings on it, and that's it. Same shape, same colour!"

"I hate to disappoint you, bubblebrain, but that is a stainless steel basin. I don't give a shit what your comic books say. After your fiasco in Yellowstone, I am not going to listen to any more of your nutzoid schemes."

"Then I'll have to take care of this one myself." As they passed the store a second time, he pulled over and parked.

"What are you planning to do?"

"Seize the helmet, of course. That is a rare historical artefact, which we'll have to restore to its rightful owner. That old man obviously thinks it's a piece of junk. But until we return it to The Flash, I might borrow it as my personal helmet. I could've used a helmet when we met those stupid Yankees!"

Wonder Woman jumped out of the van. "Okay, I see a bar down at the next corner. The Hole in the Wall. Time for a lunch break anyway, so why don't I go treat myself to a beer? Don't forget I warned you. Just like I did with the Russian Drones. And the Yellowstone National Parking Lot."

"Shut up about Yellowstone, or I'll kick you off the mission team."

"I'm trembling, I'm trembling."

The owner of The Flash's helmet was a senior citizen from Pelston, Michigan, named Vance Bullinicks. He and his wife Bette were driving to the Antique Road Show Festival in San Diego. They were collectors who stopped at every junk store, flea market, auction barn, antique shoppe, and second-hand emporium they saw on their ramble through the back roads of America. In Jackson Hole, they had found a steel depression basin with a winged base, which Vance planned to have evaluated at the Road Show. With nary a smidgen of rust, and only a couple of minor dents, it could be worth more than fifty dollars, ten times what he had paid.

Vance Bullinicks' geriatric eyes watched Coyote approach, taking in his thick spectacles, painful limp, and battered face. He put a hand over his treasure.

"Pardon me," Coyote said. "Do you know what that is?"

"Yessir, I do. And I'm gonna collect on it. Paid only five bucks for it."

"Five bucks?"

"Ask my wife if you don't believe me."

"It's like Vance said," Bette quavered. "Five dollars!"

"That's a good deal, okay. But it wasn't theirs to sell. It belongs to The Flash. Would you be willing to sell it to me at cost?"

"Back off, bub. It's mine. Bought and paid for."

"You let him take it Vance, if he offers you a decent price."

"No way!"

"I have to return it to its rightful owner."

"Stand back from me, punk!"

Faster than Coyote expected, the old man leaped to his feet and took off running. True to its legend, the helmet seemed to lend him speed as he hobbled down the street. He was trying to reach his car, a Chevy station wagon with Michigan plates. Grabbing his cudgel from the Coyote Mobile, Coyote ran after him, catching up to the old man as he was unlocking his station wagon. Mrs. Bullinicks followed behind, badgering the bystanders for assistance.

"It's okay," Coyote explained to the gathering crowd. "It's The Flash's helmet. I'm returning it to him."

"Help. Thief!" the old man yelled, struggling to hold his prize.

Astonished pedestrians ran to gawk at the melee. Someone said a movie company was making a TV commercial for a pizza chain.

"Hand it over, mister. I offered you a fair exchange, but justice demands that you surrender that helmet!"

"Get away. *Thieeeef!*"

"He's the thief," Coyote explained to the crowd. "It belongs to The Flash."

"Who the hell is The Flash?" someone asked.

"Well, in daily life, he was Jay Garrick, a student at Mid-Western U!"

The crowd was confused by the raging claims and counterclaims, but clearly sympathized with the old man. They edged toward Coyote, getting ready to jump him. Fortunately, Sandra had finished her beer and, emerging from The Hole in the Wall to see the mob threatening

Coyote, she jumped into the Coyote Mobile and sent it barrelling toward the crowd at full throttle. The bystanders scattered for safety. Bullinicks released his trophy and jumped into the safety of his car.

Seizing the helmet, Coyote leaped for the back door of the camper as it clattered past. "I got the helmet!" he yelled to Sandra. " Let's go!"

"Good work buddy. Where we headin?"

"Next road out of town. Heading south."

She slammed the pedal to the metal and the Coyote Mobile lurched toward the highway. "So, the old fart was a real beaver, eh?"

"Beaver. You mean, a Canadian?"

"Naa. Beavers used to be hunted for their balls, right? And when some hunter closed in on him, Old Beaver would just bite his nuts off and leave them for the hunter, so's he could escape. What else did the old geek have?"

"Nothing. All I wanted was the helmet!"

"Wash basin," Sandra muttered. Coyote placed the famous helmet carefully on top of his head. He felt humbled by its tradition, elated by its presence. The fastest helmet in the world gave him a feeling of power, the way he'd felt on the horse Starbuck crossing the US border. And he felt his luck change on the spot. He would wear it for the rest of the mission, all the way to the president's house.

"You're not gonna go around in public with that goddam basin on your dome, are ya?" Sandra said, staring at him aghast.

"It's not a basin!"

"It's still got soap rings in it. Look!"

Coyote removed the helmet and examined it. "It might have been used as a basin by the dumb guy who stole it. Sure, it could be disguised as an ordinary basin, but we know better. A little steel wool and a couple of taps with a hammer, and it'll be completely restored. Wouldn't that be something to show the president! In the meantime, if it keeps my head from getting kicked every time you make some friends in the bar – it's worth the trouble."

"Well, if we meet up with real crooks, it won't stop a 45-calibre slug. You'll need more than a washbasin and Firebrass Balm."

"You think Firebrass is useless, but it helped heal my burns."

"Another stupid fantasy – like this wrecked truck. When we get to Las Vegas and snag a decent security contract, the first thing we buy is a good car."

"The Coyote Mobile is doing the job. We can fix her up when we get money."

"Shoulda stole the old coot's station wagon. That mighta bin useful."

"I didn't steal the helmet. I only claimed it for The Flash, as part of our mission. And it's already changed our luck. So to celebrate, let's stop at the next Smitty's Pancake House. We'll order a real supper on the credit card."

"As long as you don't wear that basin inside."

At the junction of Highway 189 they found a Smitty's beside the road, so they went in and ordered double portions of Piggies in a Blanket. Then they drove till they reached a nice-looking campground near the rim of the Snow King Mountains.

In the morning, they would descend across the Rockies to western Wyoming, where their most hair-raising adventure yet awaited.

CHAPTER 16

Freeing the Convicts

Descending the western slope of the Continental Divide, the heroes drove out onto a grassy plain darkened here and there by herds of cattle and the moving shadows of clouds. The Green River wound across a vast plateau speckled with pools of water after two days of heavy rain. A raw, wet wind opposed their progress across the treeless bluffs.

A few miles past Diamondville, they saw a sign pointing east that said, "Rock Springs State Prison 20 Miles." A little farther along the road, Coyote could faintly see a line of orange figures silhouetted on the horizon. It looked like two men on horseback herding a line of cattle along the crossroad. As he got closer, Coyote was astonished to see a file of a dozen men, escorted by two mounted guards with shotguns.

It was a work gang of convicts, probably from Rock Springs Prison. They slouched along the ditch in a ragged line, collecting the refuse abandoned along the road by passing motorists – plastic bottles, pop cans, grocery bags, cigarette butts, broken CDs glinting like rainbows in the mud. Even in comic books Coyote had never seen a sorrier-looking crew. Skin blackened and weather-beaten, shaved heads covered with grey stubble, orange coveralls patched with chunks of silver duct tape, they looked like a parade of fugitive clowns. A prison truck sat a mile down the road, loaded with bags of garbage.

"Must be a chain gang," Sandra observed. "They're wearing leg shackles."

"That's awful. Where could they run to? There's nowhere to go."

"Those mountains, I guess." Sandra pointed toward the Utah mountains, shrouded in thick cloud to the west.

"That's crazy!" Coyote exclaimed. "I can't believe an American prison would send men out in a freezing wind to clean ditches!" He slammed his hand against the dashboard. "It's worse than slave labour. Look at the poor buggers dragging their butts. I thought the government declared chain gangs illegal."

"The Canadian government maybe. The States is no place for wimps and liberals. Here, it's 'do the crime, serve the time.' Don't feel sorry for them. We're on the other side – crime-busters, remember?"

Captain Coyote saw only a band of pathetic raggedy-andys slogging through the mud and wind, victimized by a cruel, inhuman authority. The cold wind scraped on his conscience, as he watched them slouch past in broken boots and patched coveralls, chains clinking at every step. None of them even glanced at the Coyote Mobile, stopped a few yards short of the crossroad. One of the guards stood in his stirrups and waved his shotgun at them to pass.

"It's not right!" Coyote muttered. "We have to help these guys, Sandra."

The loyal companion rolled her eyes. "Holy shit. Again?!"

"Human justice demands that we take action."

"Donny, those walking charm bracelets are criminals, not victims. They're probly all murderers and rapists. Get real."

"I know something about justice, Sandra. I've read a few classics, like *The Count of Monte Cristo.* They're half-starved. Look at their faces!"

As if on cue, the eyes of the men turned to gaze in hopeless despair on the two heroes in their vehicle. They did not ask for help or sympathy, but stared blankly, as if the heroes weren't there at all and they were gazing at the clouds drifting through the distant mountains.

"Let's give them each a can of pop. I'll talk to the guard." Coyote got out and waved at the lead rider, who wore a police uniform with a peaked cap. He glared down at Coyote with suspicion, maybe even contempt.

"Good morning, officer."

"Yo."

"What crimes did these guys commit to get sent out here?"

"Can't tell you, bud."

"Why not?"

"Cuz it's none of your affair. In any case, I don't know. They're convicts, is all. The laziest piles of shit that walk the face of the earth, when it comes to avoiding work. But they voted for this work contract system, so they got it. They get paid for this, if you can believe it. I'm only here to make sure the ditch gets clean."

"You don't know their crimes?"

"Ask the Chief. That's him at the back end of the line."

He spurred his horse on and the convicts passed in front of the Coyote Mobile. As the chief guard passed, he halted the parade. He studied Coyote's battered face, then the lumpish form of Sandra slouched down in the seat. He climbed off his horse. "What's the trouble here?"

"I'm Captain Coyote, a hero from Moose Jaw, Canada. I was asking what crimes these men did to put them in chains."

"Well – mostly they're illegal aliens."

"Aliens?"

"Border jumpers. Wetbacks. The INS calls them 'indefinite detainees.' They did some kinda petty crime to get in here, and after they're released, they're deported. Problem is their own countries refuse to take them – cause they're criminals, see. So they're trapped here more or less forever. Seventy percent of the prison population in Rock Springs."

"Refugees?"

Coyote could see Sandra giving him a dirty look and mouthing words through the windshield.

"Ask'em yourself. A million ways to get caught. They'll brag about their adventures, if you ask'em. They're scheduled for a five-minute break now. Be my guest."

Coyote walked up to the first convict in the line, a young man about twenty who glared fiercely at him. He had the olive skin and large eyes of a Mexican youth.

"Pardon me, what was your crime?"

The youth turned and spat in the mud, shutting his lips tightly. The chief guard advanced on him threateningly and snarled, "Answer the Captain, you stinking wetback!"

"Crime? I am no crime, señor. I am fall in loave, was all I did, I swear to God!"

"Fell in love?" Coyote was shocked. "That's a crime in Wyoming?"

"Listen, pal," the chief said.

"Well, maybe wass not the same loave as you feel, señor. See, I wass fallen in loave with a silk guyabera, at the J.C. Penny in Laramie. I loave being in loave weeth her, so we run away together, me and my beautiful silk sports sheert. The police found her cleenging to my back, and I confessed my loave. Then they find I am from Chihuahua and I got no passport, so now I am on three years honeymoon in the stone hacienda!"

"That's terrible," Coyote said. He turned to the next man. "What about you?"

The second man was a few years older than the first prisoner. He held a mournful look on his deeply lined face, and refused to look at Coyote. He stared at his boots, a pair of thick clogs so scuffed and split that the iron toe caps bulged out of the leather like rusty boils. The man beside him answered, "Guillermo is from Guatemala, and he's here because he likes music too much."

"What. Sent to jail for liking music?"

"Yes. He is our songbird. Our very own canary."

"You mean – a stool pigeon?"

"Oh no, señor. But he sings only when he is in unbearable pain."

"I don't get it. Aren't singers supposed to be happy?"

"Not Guillermo. The day he began to sing, he entered a lifetime of sorrow."

"Is this a riddle?"

"Pedro is pulling your leg, son," the chief explained. "Guillermo claims the police beat his confession out of him, and they don't believe him. Course, they all say that. Nobody ever is guilty. Nobody confesses. Except Guillermo. Cattle rustling, wasn't it Guillermo? Earned him six years at Rock Springs."

"For stealing two lousy cows," Pedro pointed out.

"Yeah, two purebred Charolais – worth twenty thousand bucks apiece, I heard. Guillermo cut 'em up and barbecued 'em!"

"Jeeze. That's still awful harsh. Six years. No wonder he looks so depressed!"

"Oh, that's not why he's so morose. The reason he looks like a whipped poodle, why his cellmates torment him, is because he confessed before the cops 'beat' him. They say he begged for mercy and confessed to a hundred crimes."

"Jeeze."

"Prison justice, go figure. What difference does a confession make, anyhow? An alien's only defence is his ability to invent a good tale. They say if he couldn't lie, he shoulda kept his trap shut."

Pedro nodded his head, grinning. "And now he sings forever."

Coyote turned to the next prisoner in line, a crooked little man in ragged overalls. He had the curly white hair and pale eyes of an albino, and coffee-coloured skin. "This one's a teacher – right, John? He's from Liberia – you know, in Africa?"

"I came to America because I thought I was coming home. As an albino, I was a white man in a black man's country. I didn't belong there. They made fun of my pale skin and funny eyes. My parents turned me out on the street, saying I was a devil. Everyone beat me and spat on me. They said there was a land where white devils lived, across the ocean in America. So I found some diamonds and arranged passage to Panama as a refugee. I lived for six weeks in a shipping container on a bag of rice. They arrested me when they unloaded in Seattle."

Without a word, Coyote stepped forward to embrace the albino. "I'll get you out of here," he whispered, "I promise." The chief guard pulled him away, impatient with such soft-heartedness.

The next convict was an old man with a straggly white beard like a decrepit Santa Claus. "And what caused you to be put here?" Coyote asked.

The old man tried to speak, but tears bubbled up in his eyes. His mouth trembled as teardrops began dribbling down the furrows of his cratered cheeks. The chief pulled Coyote aside and muttered to Coyote, "Four years. Vice charges in Salt Lake City. Taking liberties with old ladies. He's an Englishman."

"What'd he do?" Sandra stood at Coyote's elbow, glaring at the convict. "Molest them in public?"

"The charge was living off the avails of prostitution. They were all seniors over sixty. And him a gentleman of the cloth. He was the head of a millennium religion saving women for Jesus. He met them through the internet and took their money. It was all exposed on TV."

"What will happen to him now?" Coyote asked. He was disturbed by the old man's innocent face and white beard. He had been somebody's grandfather, a respected elder in England, and now here he was, a disgusting old pimp. Not just a pimp but a con artist, cheating and degrading old ladies.

"That's the most disgusting scam I ever heard of," Sandra said.

"Indeed it was disgusting, sir," the old-timer said. "But only if I pleaded guilty to the charge of pimping, which I didn't. The Church of the Universal Spirit never harmed a soul. Oh, I introduced female parishioners to sex tourists from Japan, but never hurt anybody. Our church encourages people to enjoy the ecstasy of their own personal choice, to relieve the loneliness and turmoil that darkens their lives. That's all I ever wanted, and now the government has chained me to a gang of criminals, I who am legally blind and with a long history of hypochondria."

He fell to crying and sobbing, until Coyote finally hugged the old man to make him stop. He passed to the next prisoner, an Oriental youth in his teens. "What about you?"

"I am so innocent!" the lad blurted. "The only way I am here is because I immigrated in the company of my two lady cousins from Fujian, through the help of a snakehead. We were doing so much fun that things got out of hand, and one of my cousins took a silly complaint to the police in Cheyenne. I have no job and no friends, except for the snakehead who was wanting to squeeze my skinny neck. So I turned myself in for protection, and got two years in Rock Springs. Okay, I no complain. I young. Two years is not so bad. But I need dollars to make a long distance call to my cousins in Cheyenne. If you help me, I'll pray for you forever. How about it, sir?" he smiled.

"Let me think about it," Coyote said. At the end of the parade was the weirdest-looking convict of all, a character about thirty. He wore a new, unpatched orange jumpsuit, and was more heavily chained than the others, with a metal bar between his ankles, a hinged device that forced his legs apart. He also wore an iron collar on his neck, and a belt linked with chains to his wrists. He could pick up garbage only by leaning sideways, unable to lift his hands. The cruel shackles made tears come to Coyote's eyes.

"What was this man's crime?"

"Luke is our prize – more jail time than all the others together," the chief said. "Eight attempted escapes since he arrived three years ago. That right, Luke?"

Luke squinted at the chief with hate in his eyes, and turned to Coyote. "A hundred and ninety-nine years!" he snarled. "And they think I should be patient!"

"Maybe you've heard of him," the chief said. "He's famous in the local press for his escapes. Calls himself Gino Pasamonte, but his real name is Ginesello de Parapilla. Course, we all jest call him Cool Hand Luke."

"Go take a flying fuck, bureaucrat. My name is Gino, not Luke or Ginessello or any of your fuckpig names. Gino, that's what the guys call me. I don't give a pigfuck what you call me. Rotting hunk of dog shit."

"Rude sumbitch, ain't he? Well, we can put a clamp on his tongue too, if we have to." The chief's horse snorted in agreement.

"Your name is Gino?" Coyote asked, impressed by the renegade's bravado.

"Anything but Luke. I despise that pigfuck name. These stupid bastards couldn't think up something original. I'd rather be 'Pedro,' or 'Pancho.' I could live with 'Durango.' But I hate that fuckpig Paul Newman movie. I am Gino!"

"Hard to change a nickname, Luke," the chief said. "That's democracy."

"These guys want to know who I am. I am Gino Pasamonte. I give them my permission to call me that. It's written on every page of my film script."

"Film script!" snorted the chief. "That pile of crap. He claims it's insured for fifty thousand bucks!"

"I'd insure it for a million, if I could. Then when you dogshit bastards destroy it, I'll be rich for the rest of my life."

"You wrote a movie script?" Coyote asked.

"Amigo, this script is so dramatic, so realistic, so heart-wrenching, it makes *Pulp Fiction* look like *The Sound of Music*. I may not be a good citizen, but I know the truth, and this truth will burn Hollywood and the American masses to the core. This is bigger than *Citizen Kane*. Bigger than *Titanic*."

"Does it have a title?"

"*The Life of Gino Pasamonte*. What do you think?"

"Not bad. When will it come out?"

"Well – my life isn't over yet, so it's still in development. It starts on the day of my birth, up to when I arrived at Rock Springs. I've been so busy trying to escape, I can't keep up with the scenes in prison."

"They're all the same goddam scene," the chief growled.

"A foul-up in the justice system put me in here, a bail hearing that went screwy. So I left one day, and then things happened, and now I study the asshole of the chief's horse. Lots of detail, eh, Chief? I tell you, my life story is a gold mine. Even if the pigs destroy the manuscript, they can't stop me. I've got a movie agent in LA."

The chief snorted with laughter, which amused Gino Pasamonte in turn, and they laughed together for several seconds. Then the chief abruptly mounted his horse and pointed his shotgun at the convict's head. "Now shut your face, Luke. We wasted enough of these folks' time. The ditch is waiting."

Coyote saw a 12-gauge shotgun being waved across his face, and it made him see red. Pulling the cattle prod from his belt, he pushed the guard's gun barrel to the ground. "Don't point guns," he said. Sandra jumped behind the truck, out of the line of fire.

The chief's eyes tensed, but he lowered his shotgun. "Just back up and get in your vehicle, mister."

"I warn you, we have powerful resources. You are trampling on the American constitution. These men are suffering cruel and unusual punishment."

"What are you, a liberal on steroids?" the chief roared. "You don't have enough geeks and assholes in Canada to bleed for, you gotta come down here and find new ones?" He pointed the shotgun at Coyote's head. "If you're not outta here in five seconds, I'll blow your eyes off."

Coyote had never been intimidated by a lethal weapon; in fact, the threat had the opposite effect. Leaping to one side, he jabbed the cattle prod into the chief's knee. There was a howl of pain, and his shotgun blasted harmlessly skyward. The horse lunged like an unleashed bronco, hurling both rider and shotgun into the mud. Reacting fast, the deputy jerked his revolver from his belt and charged his horse straight at Coyote. The hero took a *tae kwan do* defensive stance and faced the charge, calmly preparing to deliver a brutal hand chop to the horse's chest and drop it in its tracks.

Fortunately for Coyote, the convicts seized their own opportunity and ran in front of the galloping horseman, blockading him. As horse and rider reared toward the sky, the prisoners formed a chained loop around them, yelling like fiends. The horse bucked and plunged, gashing their arms and heads with its hooves. The deputy yelled, "Prison break!" at the top of his lungs. The garbage truck down the road must have heard the shotgun, for it went hurtling down the road to the prison in a flurry of flying mud.

"Grab his gun!" Gino yelled at Coyote, who stood gaping at the fallen chief, unsure what to do next. Sandra ran forward and pulled the shotgun out of the muck. She handed it to Gino, who promptly turned it on her and said, "Okay – we need all your weapons. And your camper."

Sandra was outraged. "What?!"

"You heard me," Gino snarled. "We have five minutes' head start, and we need your rent-a-wreck. You got any tools to cut these chains off?"

"Well, a pair of bolt-cutters."

"Sandra!" Coyote gasped. "You can't free these guys."

"Go get them," Gino said, "or you're dead meat."

Sandra scuttled back to the Coyote Mobile and retrieved Coyote's new set of bolt-cutters, the ones they'd bought in Gardiner. He felt sick as she presented them to the cheering convicts. Guillermo began snapping the fetters off the prisoners' legs, starting with the frenzied Gino Pasamonte.

Coyote made a final appeal to their sense of reason. "Don't do this, you guys!" he begged. "They'll hunt you down like terrorists. There's a better way!"

"What's that?" Gino sneered.

"Join our campaign to stop crime and injustice. Listen up, you guys!"

Some of the prisoners listened, though Gino was focussed on stripping the uniforms off the two guards being held in the mud.

"We'll go straight to the governor of Wyoming, and explain your situation. We'll take him the chains for proof, and get a pardon for everybody. Just tell your stories, like you did for us, and I'm sure he'll pardon you on the spot, maybe even give you compensation."

Gino, fastening up the chief's dark grey jacket and leather belt, laughed. "Good idea, Captain, but we got a better plan. When the warden hears about this little rebellion, they'll be coming after us with dogs and quads and horses, so we have to leave. If there's any gas in your jitney, we might make it to the Wasatch Mountains. Now – the keys?"

Coyote glanced at Sandra, who looked back at him and shrugged. The two guards sat chained to each other in the mud, shivering in their underwear.

"You can't have the Coyote Mobile," Coyote said. "We need it for the mission."

"Chingada!" Pasamonte roared. In a flash, the convicts plucked the heroes clean of their belongings. They were also poked, punched, and pitched into the mud. Their clothes, their money, Coyote's wallet and credit card, their weapons, the food – everything of value was stripped from the camper, except the garbage bag of dirty clothes and The Flash's helmet. But the convicts never found the keys. Sandra had thrown them into the ditch when she went for the bolt-cutters. Gino was furious, and threatened to burn the Coyote Mobile down to the wheel rims, with the heroes and guards chained inside. But they had no time for such a deed, so after a short debate, Gino and Guillermo mounted the guards' horses and took off at a gallop toward the mountains. The others chased after them on foot into the vast expanse of grass, leaving the two heroes bleeding and half-naked beside the hulk of the gutted Coyote Mobile.

"Well," Sandra groaned. "I hope you're satisfied. Feeling sorry for those bastards! What the hell were you thinking about?"

"Justice," Coyote replied gloomily. The two guards were already tottering with their chains toward Rock Springs.

"Next time, listen to me. Pitying those losers was a total waste of time. Like tryna get water from a sewage tank. You have to find a higher class of victim to rescue."

Coyote's spirits had plunged to an all-time low. "Okay, don't rub it in. I should've listened to you." They crawled into the cab out of the biting wind.

"Let's get outta here. We're in deep doo-doo if the police find us now."

"I'd just explain what happened, and offer to help track the convicts down. We really should help those guards. There could be a reward."

"A reward for turning a chain gang loose?"

"For catching them. Remember, we succeeded in keeping this vehicle out of their hands. It almost cost us our lives."

"Amen to that. From now on, let's not mess with any more convicts."

"No more brother's keeper for me. I learned my lesson."

"If you learned a lesson, I should be a university professor."

Coyote knelt on the floor of the cab and stuck his hand through a hole in the floorboard. He flailed it around the muck on the transmission until he pulled out the spare key, dripping with oil. "Good thing I taped it to the frame, eh?"

"You got that part right, anyway. But let's get past the police road blocks before patting ourselves on the back."

Rattling down the highway with Sandra at the wheel, they argued whether to speed out of the area before the road blocks went up, or turn back to Rock Springs and report the escape.

"Yer nuts," she said. "We're illegal immigrants ourselves! Our only chance is to hightail out of here as fast as this heap can move." They were making good speed with the wind blowing behind them. "By the way, if we do get stopped – leave the talking to me."

CHAPTER 17

Adventure at Robbers' Roost

They reached Interstate 89 West without encountering a single police car or road block. Had they managed, through a weird blip of good luck, to escape the chain-gang disaster? They had no money, food, or clothes, but they felt grateful to be alive and free. They could still make their way south to some warmer part of the US. By the time they reached Evanston, it was growing dark and they decided it was safe to stop.

Coyote pulled into a Target Store parking lot, and they parked in the far corner behind a big dumpster to wait until darkness fell. Then they climbed into the back in their underwear and went through the garbage bag of old costumes.

"What next, Mr. Brain?"

"I'll think of something. At least we have the uniforms."

"Yeah, maybe we can hock them for a decent snack."

"And we got almost a quarter-tank of gas. We have to raise some cash."

"Maybe we should cruise the Target Store and see what we can boost. We kin always sell CDs and stuff in the bars. Videotapes are worth their weight in gold."

"Forget it!"

"Well, there's another option. We could go stand by the front door tomorrow morning and panhandle customers."

"I'd rather starve."

"Okay, that's it. I quit. It's time to abandon our crusade. Everyone for himself."

"You're not talking about quitting the mission!"

"You heard me. I'm packin it in."

"I'm sure the bad luck has bottomed out. There's nowhere to go but up, Sandra. Let's just get through tonight, and we can find work tomorrow."

"You bin sayin that for a few days now, haven't you?"

"I'm serious. I really feel like our luck is better. Just to be in uniform is a sign."

"Sign?"

"We should've been wearing our colours when we challenged those guards."

"Colours. You're mindfucked, you know that. And you're not going anywhere with that goddam wash basin on your head."

"Okay, I'll wear it in emergencies only. But we really should wear our uniforms at all times from now on, unless they're being washed."

"Not me. I'm bustin out. I completely lost faith in your management of this operation. We're broker than when we started. At this rate we'll starve before we make it to Vegas. I'd rather go back to Moose Jaw than carry on like this."

"Sandra, what are you talking about – money?"

"Well, that's part of it – plus it's no fun gettin beat-up and frozen."

"I'll tell you what. I can't pay you a big salary, so I'll give you my best comic, *Action Number One*. Doc says it's worth a fortune."

"Big deal, you don't even have it."

"Well not here – but wherever it is, it's still mine, and I'll sign it over to you in writing if you agree to stay in your position."

"Which position is that – the missionary position?"

"Wonder Woman, the faithful companion of Captain Coyote – at least till we get interviewed for the secret service job. I realize now how much I need you. I know we can get along better. Then after we're famous, we'll go back to Moose Jaw, and I'll give you the comic in person."

"I'd rather have the cash in hand."

"Think about it. Doc said it could be worth more than fifty thousand dollars."

"Yeah, but it's still not here. I'll stay if you give me your whole collection."

"Okay, it's a deal."

"You wanta put in writing somewhere?"

"I'll do it right now, on this old gas receipt."

"Plus a commitment to real money, if and when we score a decent contract in Las Vegas."

"I agree. But as of tonight, we'll make our hero identities permanent."

"No more Donny Coyote and Sandra Dollar?"

"We have to be committed."

"Yeah, we'll get committed okay – to the booby hatch! But it's something to consider, switching IDs. Our names must be blinking on every police computer in America. They'll be looking for Donny and Sandra at every motel and gas pump in Wyoming."

"But Wonder Woman and Captain Coyote have no official ID yet! It's a perfect disguise. Makes these dirty old clothes feel better, doesn't it?"

Revitalized, Captain Coyote flipped the purple cape over one shoulder and clapped The Flash's helmet onto his battered head. He climbed into the cab of the wrecked Coyote Mobile with Wonder Woman following, easing her butt painfully onto the seat. She moaned, "What about panhandling for food. Is that against the rules too?"

"Forget your stomach for a while. We have to travel tonight, till the gas runs out. Then, if we have to, we'll walk to Utah, and look for a job."

By the time they reached the pass over the Wasatch Mountains, the gas needle was edging close to E. There was a rest stop on the state line with a sign saying, WELCOME TO GOD-BLESSED UTAH. The sign was lit up inviting them to kneel on the very spot where the followers of Joseph Smith had fallen on their knees to praise God for their deliverance. The heroes had crossed the final and most terrible barrier encountered by the great wagon train that had trekked across the western continent. And now, like the Mormon pilgrims and the Oregon Trail pioneers, they stood at the gate of the promised land – starving, ragged, and penniless, driven on by hope and faith.

"Maybe we should try that," Captain Coyote suggested.

"Try what, dough-head?"

"Pray."

"What – get down on my knees in this gravel?"

Captain Coyote cleared a spot with his feet, and knelt at the roadside in front of the sign. After a moment, Wonder Woman did the same. The instant she placed her fingers to her chin, a miracle happened. Images of beer and food started to ricochet through her brain, perhaps caused by pangs of hunger, but powerful signs of a vision. She suddenly remembered the bottles of Bushwakker beer she had stashed in the spare tire well, and ran to the truck. Not only did she find two bottles of Bushwakker, she pulled out a five-pound bag of potatoes. It was from the Moose Jaw food bank, and she had forgotten all about stashing it there. A genuine miracle! Coyote was astonished and delighted.

They flattened out a chunk of aluminum foil they found in a garbage can. Pulling some wires out of the jumble dangling below the glove compartment, Captain Coyote rigged up a potato roaster on top of the engine. Wonder Woman opened the beer and declared it a tad skunky, but she could handle it till they found better. It had the old Bushwakker bite, far superior to the American piss she had been consuming.

While Wonder Woman drove, Captain Coyote studied the map of Utah. He proposed a route that took them down a network of back roads along the eastern side of Utah. As they were low on gas, they could shut off the motor going downhill, allowing the motor to cool and the potatoes to cook at the proper heat. As they twisted down the mountain passes descending into the great Utah Basin, a delicious smell of grilling potatoes wafted through the floorboards, stoking them with fresh optimism and vision. Coyote declared that as soon as they found a good job, they would be filling their bellies with smokies and hamburgers, with pancakes every day for breakfast.

"How we going to work in security? We don't have any goddam weapons!"

"I'll make us a pair of cudgels in the morning. There's lots of trees here."

"Cutting them how?"

"That tire iron we found in the wheel well. Don't worry. Things are falling into place. Just keep praying. I think we're on the right track."

The Coyote Mobile ran out of gas half a mile from Coalville Creek, where they coasted to a stop beside a campground. It was a perfect place to camp, a whole state away from Rock Springs. The weather had become so warm they didn't need blankets, and they slept on the grass under the van. In the morning, another miracle came along. The campground manager caught them camping without a permit, and when they said they had no money, he offered them each twenty US dollars to empty the garbage cans, and twenty more to haul the refuse to a nearby dump. They could keep all the bottles and beer cans they found.

Before noon, they earned enough to buy a full tank of gas in Coalville Creek, with plenty left over to stop at Smitty's for a Full Meal Deal. The deal was three fried eggs with sausages on a bed of pancakes loaded down with blueberry syrup and Tasti-Taters, with unlimited Pepsi and coffee. There was still money left, so they bought four boxes of pepperoni sticks to keep them going. They discussed staying in Coalville Creek a few days because of its good luck, but decided to push on, looking for opportunities elsewhere.

They followed Number 89, an old two-lane highway with bushes growing to the pavement edge, driving up the Wasatch Valley. Convicts and prisons were far behind them, almost forgotten, and they began to breathe easier. They drove through a series of proud Mormon towns: Mount Pleasant, Ephraim, Aurora. Wonder Woman insisted on turning off at Big Rock Candy Mountain because she had heard it was a place where everything was free, but she just got suckered again.

Presently they saw a sign saying, "Circleville, Home of Butch Cassidy."

"Hit the brakes!" Captain Coyote yelled.

"What?"

"Home of Butch Cassidy! You never saw *Butch Cassidy and the Sundance Kid?*"

"A gazillion times. It's not that Butch Cassidy."

"How many Butch Cassidys can there be?"

"Okay, okay."

The Butch Cassidy Museum was on Main Street, set up in the service bay of a former Texaco gas station. They entered the Museum for fifty cents each. Butch's Colt 45 was on display under a glass counter, framed by piles of dead flies and old newspaper headlines. There were also curled-up movie posters and fragments of an old stage coach, as well as saddles and bullwhips and skinning knives which had been donated to the museum as western artefacts. A sign said that Butch had been born with the name of Leroy Parker to a Mormon family in Circleville.

Captain Coyote was curious to know more about the story of Leroy's life in the mountains east of Circleville, where Mount Dutton and Adams Head reached toward the sky. There Leroy Parker had assembled a band of renegades and changed his identity to Butch Cassidy, so that he could live like Robin Hood and not embarrass his family. One of the stories told of the treasure he had buried in a remote mountain gorge. People still searched the canyons, hoping to find it.

The two heroes decided to drive into Butch's stomping ground and have a look.

They crossed a river valley filled with lush pasture, a perfect area to camp, except there was no garbage collection prospects. The pasture was divided by a beautiful little creek which trickled down to the

Sevier River. They followed a rutted trail along the creek till it rounded a bend near some large boulders. There in a grove of ash trees, somebody had made a small campground with stacks of firewood, and a picnic table made of poplar poles. The water in the creek was from the snow that melted down from the mountains.

"This looks like a great place," Captain Coyote said.

"Great for what?"

"A place we can relax for a while. Maybe till my scabs and stitches heal up. We could stay a few days."

"Yeah, eating what?"

"Well, we got a few supplies. And I betcha there's lots of crayfish in this creek. There's farms around here we could find work."

"I'd rather keep going to Vegas."

"I need a good rest. What's the hurry?"

"I want to do something with my life. You won't catch me lying around wasting time."

But Wonder Woman finally agreed to stay for a couple of days, then another couple. Coyote was good at catching crayfish in the creek, and the bushes were full of ripening berries. On the fourth day, hunting crayfish among the boulders in the creek, he found a hunk of leather sticking out of a pile of gravel among some tree roots. It was an old briefcase, washed along the creek bed in the spring flood. He called Wonder Woman to help him pull it out.

Together they tried to heave it out of the gravel, but the handle snapped off in Wonder Woman's hands, its metal corroded. Clawing the gravel away with their fingers, they scraped until they could pull the briefcase out. It had a strap and lock on one side. The leather was mouldy and half-rotten, but the bag was expensive and had a crest embossed on the strap. Could it be the buried treasure of Butch Cassidy?

The seams of the bag were coming apart, and prying one side open, they pulled out a couple of old shirts, and a pair of rotting elbow pads. Throwing them aside, Wonder Woman pulled out a coil-bound student notebook, and a leather wallet wrapped with elastic bands. A wallet! They both reached, but Wonder Woman's fingers were quicker and stronger. She ripped the elastic off and yanked the wallet open. It was stuffed with American dollars – and not singles, but twenties, fifties, even hundreds – just like in her Big Rock Candy dream. It was the third miracle.

"Yaahooooo!" she screeched. "Coyote, my prayers have been answered. Oh thank you God, thank you. We hit the fucking jackpot!"

She went leaping along the bank of the creek like a jack rabbit, running back and forth between the camp and the creek, vaulting into the air every few steps and squealing, "We struck it rich. Look at it all!"

Captain Coyote, however, was more interested in the notebook that had fallen from the ruined bag. He hoped the owner had left a message or clue to his identity. He turned the crinkled pages, trying to decipher the faded writing, done with a blue ballpoint pen. Sandra was trying to count up the money, carefully stacking the bills in piles, but she lost track of the zeros every time she got over a thousand, and had to start all over again with new piles. Finally she gave up and turned to Coyote.

"So how ya wanta spend your share of the treasure, Captain?"

"I'm not. We can't. We have to hold it in trust till we find out who lost the bag. Of course he might give us a reward, but we can't claim it."

"I don't believe it. A bag of money falls right in our laps, and you don't want it. Butch Cassidy's treasure. A robber's gold. You are nuts!"

"The owner can't be Butch Cassidy. He never went to Brigham Young University." Captain Coyote pointed at the university crest on the bag. It was also on the elbow pads. "It must have belonged to a victim of the The Wild Bunch."

"What's that?" Wonder Woman said. "A rock band?"

"Train robbers. Didn't you read that stuff at the museum? The Wild Bunch was Butch Cassidy's Mormon gang. They lived up there in Robbers' Roost till he died. It was his personal territory. Long before there was a highway through here."

"I thought he died in Bolivia."

"That was only in the movie. Some people say that he wasn't killed in Bolivia, and lived to a ripe old age up in Robbers' Roost."

"Regardless of whose it was, we could still claim it, couldn't we? Why give it to the goddam Mormons? They're haves. We're the have-nots!"

"Shh. I'm trying to read this. It's some sort of a diary. Here's a page dated June 19, 1973. The bag has been here almost thirty years."

"What's it say, smartass?"

"Sounds kinda weird. Listen. 'I should have been a pair of ragged claws, scuttling across the floor of the great salt desert, not trapped in the canyons of Mor-mon-dom, enduring the slings and arrows of right-e-ous religion and the con-tum-ilous whips of Father's stinging words. No longer will I suffer the iniquities of the Church of Latter Day...' Then it's all crossed out."

"It sounds stark raving nuts. What was that about a pair of ragged clues?"

"Claws. I think it's from a poem."

"You're not claimin to be some fuckin poetry expert now?"

"Well, no. Anyway...it's not that poetic."

"Just fast forward to the juicy bits. See what he says about the money."

"It seems like it's written to his girlfriend, or somebody who was cruel to him. He says, 'You tore apart my feelings in public... The super-cil-ious con-des-cension of your voice ... tormented by your cruel taunts and contemptuous smile.'"

"Sounds demented okay. Another loser like Chris Thomas, that kid in Opheim."

Captain Coyote was puzzled over the account, which read like a rejected lover on the edge of suicide, mixed up with a fear of the Mormon church. The journal also lamented the greed of corporate power, the corruption of American politics, and the morality of the advertising industry. Just like Chris. Just like Ted Kaczinsky. The owner had composed a final rant to the world and checked out, maybe drowning himself in this very creek, briefcase in hand.

Wonder Woman finally got the money counted. "Fourteen thousand, six hundred and fifty-seven dollars," she announced, stuffing the greenbacks into her bra. "I don't mind carrying it till we find the owner."

"Better to keep it in the bag."

"Hey, it's safe with me. The keeper of the cash. Security's our game, right? We could borrow it, just till we get back on our feet financially."

"No, I don't think so."

"Think of it as an advance on the reward, which is due to us by law anyway. As long as we keep track of our expenses, it's legit. It's just accounting really."

"Well – maybe."

"Now we're talkin. How about this, eh? I never seen so much moola in one bundle. It almost compensates for all the shit-kickings we took. Anyway, you work on the diary, and I'll be in charge of the money. You write the expenses down, and keep a proper account for him. And hey, I'll quit chirping about doin all the dirty work. I can take a lot of abuse for carrying this stash of cash."

"Let's just keep our goal in focus – to find the owner, or his next of kin."

"Brilliant. And who might his next of kin be?"

"This guy obviously came from a wealthy family."

"Well, they're not going to need the money!"

"No – but they're more likely to reward us. Maybe even more than what's there, if they get closure on their son."

"Aa, yer fulla shit."

The two heroes slept very little that night on Little Sevier Creek. The argument continued: should they search for the relatives or go to Las Vegas? Spend the money or put it in the bank for safekeeping? Wonder Woman's miracle had changed everything, even their relationship. She was re-energized by the change in their fortune. She was ready to take charge of her destiny, seize the opportunity, and live life to the fullest, now that expense money was at hand.

In the morning, they packed for Las Vegas, planning to stop in the town of Panguitch for supplies for the final push. Captain Coyote was cleaning up their campsite when he spotted a strange figure peering at them from the creek bed. "Hello there!" Coyote called, stepping toward the creek.

The figure leaped up and scurried over the pile of rocks into the trees at the top of the bank. Coyote was too amazed to give chase. He tried to describe the creature to Wonder Woman, who had seen nothing, and thought it must be a figment of Captain Coyote's overactive imagination.

Believing he had found the owner of the case, Coyote climbed the creek bank and ran down the road. He spotted the man running along the ridge. He looked a bit like Spiderman, leaping over crags and bushes, landing on his hands and feet. All he wore was a pair of ragged denim cut-offs, so rotten and ripped his hairy butt hung out of them. He looked like Hercules's companion, the goat kid.

When the man reached the peak of the ridge, he stopped and turned to face Coyote. He raised his hands to his mouth and tried to shout, but a horrible rasping noise came out of his throat. Then he stepped behind a clump of brush to hide, leaving his long hair and beard stuck out in all directions, a mass of tangled knots which made him easy to spot. Wonder Woman caught up and they watched for several minutes, but the wild man didn't stir from his hiding place.

"I bet he's the owner of the briefcase."

"Naa – more likely the murderer."

"He looks weird enough," Coyote agreed. "Did you notice his butt sticking out of his drawers?"

"Pervert."

"He's probly disturbed. I should talk to him."

"What? You already forgot about the convicts?"

"I'm sure he's the owner," Coyote said, squinting at the fuzzy silhouette. "He was probably watching us all the time. He must know we've got his bag."

"Captain, can't you let sleeping dogs lie?"

"If it is him, he's been living the life of a hermit for over twenty-five years!"

"I'm not climbin up that goddam cliff to face a lunatic."

"You stay out here, and I'll go up the ridge behind him. That way he's between us, and can't escape."

"What if there's a gang?"

"Who would join a gang with somebody who looked that crazy?"

"But he does look dangerous. Better leave him be."

"How come you're so gung-ho, you'll attack a nest of Yankees single-handed, but now you're afraid of a scrawny hermit?"

"Hey, every situation is different. Depends on how much beer I had, probly. Gimme one six pack, I can take on a whole bar. Maybe I should carry a beer keg, for whenever you need extreme action."

"Come on, we'll go up together. Let me do the talking, though."

"Tell him we'll give him a good return for his investment, maybe ten percent. But first he has to prove he's the real owner. I'll hold onto the dough till we got legal proof."

Captain Coyote grabbed her arm, and together they picked their way up the spur of rock to the clump of bush – only to find that the hermit had disappeared. The scraggly hair was a fringe of dried sage he had stuck on the rocks to trick them. Beyond the ridge, a jumble of gullies and plateaus climbed the mountainside to Robbers' Roost.

"What did I tell you?" Wonder Woman asked. "It wasn't him who stashed the money. He's just some local wacko."

"Look up there." Captain Coyote pointed to a faint trail above them, leading to a stand of pine trees on a rocky ledge. They climbed the ravine to check it out, and at the top stumbled onto the hermit's crudely built den. He had made a hut from pine and aspen poles against the cliff face, covering it with piles of leafy branches. There was a mound of ashes in a fire pit at the centre of the shelter, rimmed by a circle of stones. Leaning against the back was an old rusted-out racing bicycle.

"This is definitely the owner of the briefcase," Coyote said.

"How do you figure that?"

"I could tell from the notebook he was an environmentalist. Only an ecology student would carry a bike up here."

Though the camp was deserted, no doubt the hermit was hidden in the jumble of rock above, watching them. *"Helllo,"* Coyote called, and the rocky canyon echoed with his voice. But the wild man refused to show himself, so they descended to the road again. When they did, Coyote was surprised to see another man with a rifle approaching. He had obviously spotted their Coyote Mobile in the meadow below. He wore a camouflage jacket and jeans, and a battered cowboy hat, but most noticeable was the high-powered rifle he carried at the ready position.

"You guys looking for something?" he called.

"Nothing serious. There's a weird guy who's got a den up on that ledge. Thought it might be somebody we're looking for."

"Who you looking for?"

"Well, we don't know his name. He looks like a hermit."

"You the guys set up in the old pasture down bottom?"

"Yeah, we camped there a few nights. Is there a problem?"

"Nope. Public campground. We just keep our eyes on things around here. I'm a warden."

"You like a volunteer warden?"

"I'm tracking a pair of coyotes that took some of our lambs this spring. You come across any sign of coyote?"

"Not us," Wonder Woman said.

Captain Coyote scanned the mountainside helpfully. "Is he a hermit?"

The hunter shrugged. "Showed up about twenty years ago, drove a bicycle out here from Salt Lake City. People back at Marysvale first saw him, riding along the highway, packin his brief case on the back of his bike."

"He's an environmentalist, right?"

"Nobody knows what he is. Eddie Malick down in Centerville was the only one he ever talked to. Said he was looking for the loneliest part of the Wasatch, and Eddie told him to try Robbers' Roost. Go up that draw another eight miles, and you'll get an idea how rough this territory can be. This here's just the beginning.

"Anyway, a year later Eddie spotted him. He was driving along about here looking for deer, when he ran smack into a big tree lying across the road. When he stopped to pull it clear, this wild man came yowling out of the scrub and scared the hell out of him. Eddie took off running down the road, and this hermit jumped into his truck and stole Eddie's lunch. That's what he was looking for. Hamburgers, to be exact.

"Well, you can imagine the whoop and holler that caused in Centerville. The sheriff called a search party to go and see what this fella's about. They was eighteen of us came up here, and we beat the bushes for two days before we found his den, up there in a big deadfall full of pine roots. Eddie finally reckanized him as the same kid who rode up the highway on his bicycle. His clothes were nothing but rags, and he was all scratched and covered with sores. But it was him. Sunburnt till he was black."

"What did he say?"

"Only thing I ever heard him say was 'hamburger,' but Eddie says he sounds like a preacher when he gets goin. Hates the Mormons. I guess he went a little crazy when he gobbled Eddie's hamburgers. He hadn't tasted meat for a year, except for some a few lizards and crawfish. He was sick of dandelion greens, anyway. Big Macs drove him to highway robbery."

"What's his name?"

"Never offered one. We call him the Hermit with the Hairy Ass. Too shy for his own good. Kinda throwback to the old days, I reckon. Giss he read too many stories about Butch Cassidy and The Wild Bunch. Just went bush. But we started leaving meat for him on a regular basis – it's no big deal to shoot a deer and drop it off for him at the side of the road. A hind quarter seems to last him about six weeks. He's grateful for the meat."

"How do you know, if he never speaks?"

"He talks to Eddie, preachin salvation. Eddie took an interest, started spending time up here. Sometimes he'd sit out here with some venison in his truck, two, three days, waitin for the hermit to show. Last fall he came up to Eddie's truck and sat on the tailgate. All of a sudden, he started twitching, and his eyes rolled around in his head, and his tongue started going in and out, like one of those video games gone haywire.

"When Eddie went to help him, the hermit attacked him like a swarm of bobcats, swinging at him, spitting and yelling in a fury. 'Fred, you rotten son of a bitch,' he screams, 'I'll kill you, you treacherous bastard!' He was punching and biting Eddie, trying to gouge his eyes out, till Eddie jumped inside his truck and pulled his Winchester off the gun-rack. By the time he turned around, the hermit had disappeared back in the bush. Pretty rare sightings ever since. He's probly curious about you two."

"Who was this Fred person?"

"Got me. No Freds in Centerville. Probably the name of one of his demons. There's no denying he is nuts. Some folks argued we should sedate him and take him to the doctor. In the end we decided to leave him be, and lay on the meat. Either of you named Fred?"

"My name's Captain Coyote. This is my loyal companion, Wonder Woman."

"Hidy do. Lucas Barbell."

"Actually, we're on a mission to help people like him. He could be suffering a mental disease."

"More like a social disease," Barbell sniffed. "The hermit's more dumb animal than human bean. Course that don't lower him none in the opinion of most people. He's kind of a Centerville mascot. Our only outlaw since ol' Butch cashed out."

"We have to help him," Coyote said. At that moment, he felt a tug on the back of his cape. He turned around to find the hermit crouching at the side of the road, gazing at him. Tears ran from the creature's brimming eyes, streaking down his grime-encrusted face. He stood up and opened his arms for a hug, like an abused orphan. Overcome with pity, the Hero with the Hound-Dog Face clasped the ragged vagabond to his chest. But he had to wonder: how could he possibly help him?

CHAPTER 18

The Hermit with the Hairy Ass

The hermit emitted a rusty croak. "Do you know me?" he rasped.

"I don't think so," Coyote stammered. "I'm Captain Coyote. And this is Wonder Woman. I guess you know Lucas Barbell."

"Why did you come? Did the Temple send you?"

"No, we're from Canada. Sort of wandering heroes."

"Do you know who I am?"

"Well, I know a bit about you. Brigham Young –"

"Forget that stuff," the hermit snarled. "I left that life behind."

"Did you write your life down in a notebook and leave it in a brief-case?"

The hermit dismissed it with a wave. "I don't talk about that stuff now. No interest."

"Your secrets are safe with us," Wonder Woman reassured him.

The hermit's gaze stayed focused on the face of Captain Coyote. "I am Malachi Carnahan," he rasped.

"Well I be goddamned," Lucas said. "He has a name."

"You obviously had some terrible experience," Coyote said. "If you want to tell us about it, maybe we can help."

"How?"

"Well, like help you see it wasn't your fault. Even the best people go blaming themselves –"

"But it was my fault! You see –"

"— if you want to talk –"

The hermit's words, once begun, gushed from him like a spring. "If you are heroes, I want to thank you for stopping. But I'm a terrible host. I have nothing to offer you."

"We were more interested in your old briefcase," Wonder Woman interjected. "If you're not using it –"

"It contained my journal and a sum of money I no longer need. I plan to leave it to some worthy group of citizens working to improve the public good. They can hold the journal on condition it not be published until after my death."

"What was that about – citizens for the public good?"

The hermit turned to Wonder Woman. "You know of such a group? People dedicated to defending human rights?"

"Well, as a matter of fact – we specialize in sec –"

Coyote clapped a hand over Wonder Woman's mouth, and carried on. "Our mission in the US is to lead a campaign against evil and oppression, Mr. Carnahan. Maybe you'd like to join us. We're on our way to join the secret service – but we're taking freelance assignments along the way – defending human rights."

"To beef up our résumés," Wonder Woman said.

"Please carry on with your story," Coyote said. "Why are you living in the wilderness like an animal?"

"It's a long history. I don't suppose you have any – hamburgers?"

"I toljuh," Barbell said.

Wonder Woman's face lit up. "We got something even better. Beefy pepperoni sticks!" She ran back to their camp to retrieve them from the Coyote Mobile's cooler. The hermit stared after her, fingers twitching nervously. When she returned with the packages, Carnahan ripped the first one open with a famished snarl. Saliva flew as he gobbled down all ten pepperoni sticks, two or three bites for each.

"Thank you, Lord!" the hermit cried. "Thank you, bountiful Lord!"

He burst into tears and, giggling insanely, insisted they all go to his camp to feast on the rest. Lucas Barbell volunteered to go and fetch the six-pack of Coors he had left cooling in the cab of his 4x4.

Stumbling and falling among the rocks and bushes, Carnahan ate the second package on the way to his lair. Periodically he would stop and mumble a prayer of thanksgiving, waving his arms at heaven. They climbed for twenty minutes, until they reached the stand of ponderosa pines. The hermit sat them down on the circle of rocks and stumps around his fire pit, where he usually entertained the wild animals.

As the hermit ripped open the third package of pepperonis, Lucas offered the beer around, and Wonder Woman took two cans. The hermit passed the sausages around and stared at the ground.

Captain Coyote reminded him, "You were going to tell your story."

The hermit sighed and raised his face. "I'll give you the condensed version, on one condition. You have to listen to the whole story, no interruptions or questions. If you agree to do that, I will give you the entire contents of the briefcase, to be held in trust for improving humanity. Agreed?"

No one spoke. Captain Coyote bit his lip, remembering his promise not to interrupt Wonder Woman's long boring tale of the school bus hijacking. She was thinking the same thing, for she winked, and nodded in agreement. They could keep their mouths shut. Barbell nodded too, though he had little idea of what the briefcase had contained.

"We'll listen to it," Coyote said.

"It's painful to dredge the past," Carnahan's strange voice squawked. "But I must exorcise it from my mind. The humiliation of my youth was so agonizing. The stupidity. The naiveté!" He banged his head a few times against a rock.

"Poor bastard," Barbell muttered.

"First I should tell you that my family has always been Mormon, and proud members of the Republican Party. I personally led the national Mormon Youth for Nixon in the 1972 presidential election. Remember, this is in total confidence."

They all nodded solemnly.

"I grew up in Manti, where my Father was an elder of the temple and sold real estate. I belonged to the Young Men's Improvement Association. My parents thought of themselves as plain, ordinary folks, but we had a lot of money."

"How –?" Wonder Woman began, before Coyote choked off her words with an elbow in the stomach.

"My father's dream was that I would enter politics, and he had me enrolled in law at Brigham Young. I planned a graduate degree at Yale and on to Washington. However, I took a theatre class as a minor elective – and it changed my life. I got a small part in a student production of *Oklahoma*. I met – Carrie. Oh, God, thank you – I can speak her name at last!

"Carrie was the most talented person I'd ever met – a true performer. We fell hopelessly in love. Not only could she act and sing and dance, she was an intellectual of the highest order, doing an MFA in multi-media production. Unfortunately, she was a liberal Democrat, or her family was – and there was no way my family would ever tolerate that. In those days –" The hermit's speech ground to a stop. He stared at the ground for a while, lost in painful memory.

"Our relationship became intimate, and Carrie moved into my apartment. I managed to hide it from my parents for a while, but they suspected something was up. They would've been shamed by the entire community if it became known that Carrie and I were 'living in sin.' Of course, we planned to marry later on.

"A year before graduation, Father and Mother arrived from Manti in the company of a Mormon elder. It was an intervention. Carrie was banished from our apartment while the elder gabbled on about Joseph Smith and the laws of the temple. I was outraged and humiliated. Toward the end of it, Father took me by the arm and said, 'I have exciting news, Malachi. Boris Uhaul just phoned. He wants you on Capitol Hill.'

"'Senator Uhaul?' I said, 'From Washington, DC?'"

Carnahan looked at the blank faces sitting around his dead campfire. "You've heard of Senator Boris Uhaul?"

"I think I heard of him," Lucas allowed. The other two shook their heads.

"Dad had received a personal call from Senator Uhaul. He wanted a tutor for his youngest son Freddy, who had been accepted at Annapolis. It was an incredible opportunity – the kind of assignment Father and I had always hoped for. I should've been overjoyed, but I didn't want to be separated from Carrie, even for Senator Uhaul."

At the mention of Freddy, Coyote and Lucas exchanged glances. It must've been the Fred he had raved about.

"My life was turned upside down. They wanted me to register at the Naval Academy, and attend his classes, which I could transfer to my degree at Brigham Young. It was also a chance to meet President Nixon, who was then beginning his death struggle with the left-wing news media.

"Carrie was devastated by this turn of events, when I phoned her to explain. She saw it as a nefarious Mormon plot to destroy our relationship. Of course she could also see it was a great opportunity for me, so we decided to postpone our wedding plans. It meant a long separation, but I thought love could withstand such pressure. We spent our final night in Provo making passionate vows of undying love.

"The next day I landed in the nation's capital. A limo took me straight to Senator Uhaul's mansion in Virginia. He and Mrs. Uhaul were very grateful that I had come to help Freddy, who was not home at that moment. They said he was a bright boy who suffered from some mental disorder called 'attention deficit.' They hoped he could overcome it with a good start at Annapolis. The entire family was supportive, except for the senator's eldest son, Ferris Uhaul. He seemed suspicious of my appointment, and resented the help I had been hired to give Freddy.

"Then Freddy arrived, and we met for the first time. He was a smart kid, but this attention disorder was a real problem. When I reached out to shake his hand, he grabbed me round the neck and tried to wrestle me to the ground. He was a very intense young fellow, exploding with energy, the complete opposite of Ferris. I could see that tutoring him would be a challenge, but I felt I could do the job. Later Ferris took me aside and explained that I was really more of a chaperone and bodyguard than a tutor. Freddy had behaviour problems and needed constant supervision. He was also having an affair. Well, that wasn't so bad, I thought. I could sympathize.

"But as soon as we started the fall term, I discovered that Freddy was gay, and his 'affair' was with the son of a congressman – a black Democrat from Detroit. The other boy was only fifteen, but had an apartment in the Watergate Hotel, where they let their passions run loose. When the boy's parents found out about the affair from the doorman, all hell broke loose. They were as distressed as Senator Uhaul, for the two lovers presented a modern political dilemma. Neither family could tolerate the scandal of breaking up a mixed-race relationship.

"Senator Uhaul expected me to keep him informed on all the activities of his wayward son, who had ingenious ways to give me the slip after classes, so he could head back to his love nest at the Watergate. I really didn't want to know the intimate details of his private life, but I had to do my job – well, you know what that's like. To top it off, Freddy was failing in his studies. The senator said we had to break up the affair before the news media splashed Freddy's secret life all over the tabloids.

"I was desperate, but I finally thought up a plan, similar to my father's. Separate Freddy from his lover, by transporting him out west. We could transfer to Brigham Young to save his academic year, and things might work out. Freddy was violently opposed, but the Uhauls loved the idea. They agreed to pay all expenses. I would be re-united again with Carrie. We were in touch by phone every day, longing for each other.

"Father assembled a few GOP elders to meet us at the airport, me and the political heir to the Uhaul dynasty. The reception went well, as Freddy could be very charming when he was the centre of attention. I became his personal attendant. Carrie was also waiting by the arrivals gate, wearing the peach-coloured cashmere sweater set I had given her on her birthday. I was overcome with desire, yet I dared not touch her, or even speak to her in front of the massed Republicans. But I sneaked her into the taxi with Fred and me.

"Right away I knew something was wrong. Freddy was completely fascinated by her and turned into his most seductive self, holding her hands, touching her back. And she responded! They were practically entangled by the time we got to the hotel, while I carried the bags to his room, totally humiliated. I managed to drag Carrie off, and we spent a night together at last.

"But things got worse. The next day I planned to take Freddy on a tour of Salt Lake City. He was not interested. He wanted to go and see Las Vegas. And while I was arranging the car rental, he pried open my briefcase – the one you found in the creek – and found my journal as well as Carrie's love letters. When I came back with the car, he was laughing his head off, reading aloud from her flights of passion, sneering in my face. I realized he was out for revenge. I figured I'd have to kill him, to stop him from wrecking our lives.

"I tried to warn Carrie about this psychotic monster. She, unfortunately, was already stricken. She'd agreed to go with him to Las Vegas. In vain I pointed out he was too young, too unstable, too Republican. But she had been charmed by his disgusting charisma, drawn to his magnetic aura. She suggested all three of us could take a trip to Las Vegas –"

"Las Vegas?" Wonder Woman blurted. "That's where we're going!"

Captain Coyote tried to silence her, but it was too late. "Go on," he said to Carnahan, who sat stunned.

"To hell with you then!" the hermit muttered, his chin sinking to his chest.

"She's sorry she interrupted," Coyote said. "She doesn't know anything about Las Vegas. Finish the story."

Carnahan waved them vaguely away.

"We're listening," Barbell insisted.

The hermit's beard seemed to wilt as he stared at the ground like a beaten dog, retreating into a private world. His lips twitched and trembled, and he hissed a few words. They edged closer to hear.

"What did he say?" Coyote whispered.

"Something about the Mafia," Barbell said.

"He said 'Sinatra'," Wonder Woman said.

"Sinatra! Frank Sinatra?"

"That sleazy little cockroach wop!" Barbell declared. "I'll never forgive what he did to Ronnie Reagan."

Captain Coyote went rigid. "He did something to President Reagan?"

"Sinatra only pretended to be his friend, and then porked Nancy in the guest room! He was a front for the mob."

"Hey," Coyote objected. "That's a dirty lie! You can't say that."

"What the hell do you know?"

"No mob could get near President Reagan."

"Are you brain-dead? Sinatra was a plant from day one."

"Bullshit!" Coyote shouted. "And only a lying son of a bitch would say it!"

"You got a nasty tongue yourself, boy!" Without warning, Barbell lunged across the fire pit and slugged Coyote in the jaw.

Reacting instinctively, Wonder Woman slammed her can of beer against the back of Barbell's skull and dropped him to the ground.

"Nancy Reagan was married to the greatest hero in the States!" Coyote yelled, winding up for a devastating uppercut to the hunter's chin. He would have committed a serious assault if Carnahan had not suddenly emerged from his trance and emitted a sharp, high-pitched squeal. He fell to the ground with his eyes rolled back in his head, trembling violently and flopping around the fire circle, flailing and kicking.

"Look out!" Coyote yelled. "He's having a fit. Hold him down!"

Carnahan fought like an enraged bear. He screeched and tore at everything in sight, foaming at the mouth, crushing the beer cans as he rolled over them. He scrambled toward the old bicycle and lifted it overhead. Swinging it at them like a club, he tried to force them to the cliff edge. Then he threw it right at Coyote, barely missing him before it hurtled to the rocks below.

They tackled him from three different angles, and despite his biting, clawing, kicking, gouging, and bare-knuckled pummelling, managed to wrestle him to the ground. They could hold only one arm or leg each, so there was always a fourth battering them as he rolled about on the rocks, flinging himself in all directions. Finally he broke free, and with a mighty leap past the entrance of his den, soared off the face of the cliff.

They listened in horror for the *whump* of his body on the rocks, but there was only silence, and the faint whistle of the wind.

"Where did he go?" Barbell said. Coyote stepped to the entrance and looked out. The cliff dropped fifty feet straight to the bottom. Below and slightly to the right was a narrow ledge that only a mountain goat could land on. The Hermit with the Hairy Ass had flown into the wilderness. Coyote was devastated. It was like the time Mrs. Pearce died.

"I guess that means the money's ours, eh?" Wonder Woman said with a chuckle. "Finders keepers, losers weepers. Whaddaya say, boys?"

"I don't want any part of it," Barbell replied. "Any money that fella owned must be as cursed as a parson's dawg. I wouldn't touch it for all the silver in Utah."

"Do you intend to report this to the police?"

"Not likely," Barbell replied. "This has got to be a family secret, boys. If he's dead, no one will ever find him. If he's alive, well – I reckon he's entitled to his privacy."

The heroes set out for Panguitch, where they had planned to load up on supplies and upgrade their uniforms, which had become stained and ragged beyond description. Wonder Woman drove and gave dictation. Captain Coyote printed the list of their needs. His list read: Firebrass Balm, pizza pops, sleeping bags, Chitos, beer, toilet paper, milk, new underwear, Pepsi, uniforms, pepperoni. They would postpone buying new weapons, however, because Utah did not permit sales to out-of-state buyers.

"Nevada's the place," Wonder Woman grinned. "Now we can afford some firepower, there's no turning back."

"But we can't use that money," the captain protested. "It's for citizens acting in the public good."

Wonder Woman hissed, "That's us, booger-brain. He was talking in code. He practically forced the money on us to carry on the mission!"

"That's what he said?"

"Who else was he gonna entrust? Not Barbell. Nope. A pair of genuine heroes who happened to be in the right place at the right time."

Panguitch was not large enough for a Value Village, so they postponed new uniforms, but there was a good convenience store that supplied everything else on their list, even Firebrass Balm. They decided to try Cedar City, near the Arizona border. The map said it was a big place, so it should have a slew of used clothing stores. Wonder Woman needed a more dazzling costume for her entrance to Las Vegas. Captain Coyote was less excited, though he could see the importance of looking professional. But he was depressed after his fight with the hermit, and distracted from the mission. They had not only failed to rescue Carnahan from his exile, but had almost killed him, certainly driven him farther from civilization than ever.

Coyote had beaten the hermit to save him, and even if he survived his dive off the cliff, the poor guy had ended up with even more pain and suffering. What's more, the blows Coyote endured had left him aching all over, and stiff as a board. He would not be able to drive for a couple of days.

The hermit's strange curse on Las Vegas had also ruined Captain Coyote's anticipation of the city. It sounded more like a hell-hole than an entertainment capital. They had travelled forever just to get there, and were more cut up and bruised than ever. Was this an omen of events to come?

He wondered if they shouldn't detour around the place, and go straight to the President Reagan's house at Disneyland. Or did Las Vegas's dangerous reputation mean it was the very place they were intended to go to? A Sodom or Gomorrah where they would face the ultimate superheroes' test. And there would be the added challenge of the hermit's money held in trust.

"Let's just agree not to spend it on beer and gambling," Coyote said. "Only real expenses."

"What's an unreal expense? Pepperoni sausages? Give me a break. This is the hermit's personal loan to our outfit. All we gotta do is keep track of the numbers, see? He knows we'll be good for it. We got a reputation to defend, captain. I notice Barbell didn't raise any objections."

"Okay, as long as we agree to pay the money back, after we get our first contract."

"So we'll get food and drink. What do we need, besides clothes and guns?"

"The uniforms are the most important thing."

"Yeah, these're getting rank. My T-shirt smells like a tank of stewed farts."

It was a typical Wonder Woman observation, which meant it might or might not be true. The days had grown warmer the farther they travelled south, and the inside of the cab had a tendency to overheat from the engine.

When they reached Cedar City, they got separate rooms in the Quality Inn, so they could clean up and make themselves presentable. The Value Village in downtown Cedar City was a treasure trove of recycled garments. Wonder Woman discovered a star-spangled set of stretch pants, and half a dozen outrageous T-shirts, including one that said in bold red letters SUCK THIS. She also found a Lands End gym bag to carry the hermit's money.

To replace his grimy Flames hockey shirt, Captain Coyote picked up a next-to-new Phoenix Coyotes jersey, and three good pairs of tie-dyed jeans. He found a pair of Converse running shoes with plastic wings on the heels just like The Flash's – plus a utility belt with a row of metal snaps to hold his new weapons. His spirits began to improve.

In the morning, Coyote put on his clean new underwear, and the total Captain Coyote uniform, complete with red basketball shorts pulled on over his jeans. He still needed a few defensive weapons for his new utility belt, but they would look for these in Nevada. They stopped at a dumpster to throw out the wrecked briefcase and the tattered rags of old costumes, then sped off to meet their destiny in Las Vegas, the city of light.

The City That Never Sleeps

CHAPTER 19

The Camelot Motel

Down the winding gorges of the Virgin River they rattled, and out across the sun-baked tip of Arizona. The highway swept them through the ancient river canyons to the deserts of Nevada and the Colorado River valley that cut through them. A hundred miles from Las Vegas, the first billboards began to appear: The Liberace Museum, the Magic and Movie Hall of Fame, the Luxor IMAX, conference centres, casinos, amusement parks. They all seemed to specialize in naked girls, hinting at the excitement generated by the City That Never Sleeps. Wonder Woman said she was revolted.

As night fell across the desert, a yellow aura glowed in the sky, like a golden fluff of cotton candy around the incandescent city. The glow spread across the desert sky like fire, extinguishing the stars and planets. When they reached the edge of North Las Vegas, the heroes began looking for a campground, but there were only long stretches of lit-up motels and shopping malls and truck stops along the I-15. They could not cut out through the lanes of traffic to stop. Traffic did not merely flow along the interstate. It blew past like a NASCAR racetrack, five lanes of traffic roaring in each direction.

"We might as well go downtown!" Wonder Woman yelled.

"We have to find a motel out here. They'll be a lot cheaper. The money we save on the motel, we can spend on weapons."

"Yeah, we gotta have firepower. And explosives. We need explosives. This is going to be one crazy operation, Captain!"

Wonder Woman finally maneuvered the Coyote Mobile to an exit ramp at Cheyenne Avenue, and they drove into North Las Vegas. They were soon clattering along Western, and at one intersection passed a huge castle lit up with a blinking facade of neon light. Its stone towers and turrets looked like Walt Disney's TV castle in Fantasyland. The main tower rose seven storeys, with a huge antique clock on its face.

"What about this dump?" Wonder Woman said. "They got a water slide. And a casino."

"That's way too grand for a motel. It's probly the governor's mansion."

"Governor's mansion. As if! Look at the sign, dipshit. Up there. The – Camelot – Motel. You're sure as hell opinionated for a guy who can't see fifty feet."

The castle certainly looked like the real thing. There was a huge courtyard across the street for a parking lot, with a bridge crossing over the road and the castle moat.

"Okay, let's go register. First we'll try to snag a good security deal. Then we can check out the casino."

"Let's find out how much a room costs first."

"Just let me do the talking, okay? I'm going to get us a decent contract straight off the top. Don't you go interfering."

They hauled their bags into the King's Entrance Hall. Though they looked cool in their new costumes, Captain Coyote and Wonder Woman got a few second looks because of the scrapes and bruises on their faces. To Ernesto Palomeque, the Camelot Motel's reception manager, they were Trouble with a capital T, from the instant he laid eyes on them. Except for his glasses, the tall one looked like a hockey player, with his Coyotes hockey jersey. Over spangled tights and high silver boots, his partner wore a lime green T-shirt that said BLOW IT OUT YOUR SHORTS!

"Hey dude," she said, greeting Mr. Palomeque. "Classy operation. How ya fixed for security?"

"I beg your pardon?"

"Security. AKA protection from criminals. Captain Coyote and me offer a full professional security service. Twenty-four hours a day."

"Do you have a card?"

"Our cards are still getting printed but I can get you a résumé in nothing flat."

"I'm sorry, we already have a bonded security service."

"You can never have enough muscle in a fancy place like this. You got a lot of real estate to look after. Our rates are totally competitive."

"What are your rates?"

"Depends, how much is a room?"

"Were you planning to register, sir?"

"That's mizz to you, smartass – and yes, we plan to register. In separate rooms."

"Credit card?"

"Don't you worry about the credit card. We'll be paying cash."

"I'm sorry, mizz, we don't accept cash. To register at the Camelot Motel, you need to show a major credit card."

"Hey, Captain. What's the number of your American Express Card?"

Captain Coyote concentrated for a few seconds. "3735 656952 22001," he said. "Expiry, 12 04."

"Got that, maestro?"

"I should have first mentioned that we don't have a vacancy at the moment. Tomorrow is the Frank Sinatra Memorial Concert. The anniversary of his death. Every place in Vegas is fully booked."

"Bullshit. How come your parking lot's half empty then?"

"Most of our rooms are booked days, even weeks in advance. But if you'd care to wait till nine p.m., there's some possibility of no-shows..."

"Don't jerk me around, sonny. We know our human rights. I'm a visible minority."

Palomeque's brow knotted as he thought. He finally said, "Well, I do have one room available – a double."

"No problem. How much?"

"Eighty-nine ninety-five. Can I have the credit card number again?"

"Okay, here's the security deal. In exchange for the room, we can provide 24-hour protection, transport your cash, lay on the muscle at the door, whatever's called for. We'll be happy to give you a brief demonstration. Win-win all around. We get accommodation. You get extra security."

"I'm afraid not. Will Mr. uh – Coyote be needing medical attention?"

"Just a few scratches, no big deal. He's got his own salve."

"All right, Mr. Coyote. You can sign here. Your room is in the truckers' wing. There's just one double bed. It's the only space I have."

"He doesn't mind sleeping on the floor, right captain? I imagine you got decent carpet on the floors."

"Oh yes, Axminster in every room."

"What all do you offer here for services?"

"Well, The Camelot has over six thousand slot machines, as well as blackjack, roulette, craps, baccarat, and poker tables. There's a cocktail lounge, full massage and fitness centre, the Excalibur heated swimming pool and water slide, and our Virtual Adventure video arcade. In the Jousting Hall on the lower level, we feature a medieval banquet and jousting tournament between King Arthur and the Kings of Europe. Eight and ten p.m. nightly."

"Let me check the place out and get back to you with a complete proposal."

"Will you need a hand with your luggage?"

"Naw, all we got is a few plastic garbage bags. Coyote can take them."

Wonder Woman turned and trotted toward the casino, where the din of gongs and bells from the slot machines rose and fell in bursts of frenzy. Coyote had to sit down and rest for a few seconds, waiting for a wave of dizziness to pass as Palomeque observed him sourly.

"Manuel, carry the captain's bags to his room," Palomeque said. "Room 198, truckers' wing."

"Take it easy," Manuel said as Coyote limped across the lobby. "No rush."

"I'll be okay as soon as I get a shower and rest."

"Looks painful. Down this way, sir. You really should see a doctor."

"My insurance doesn't cover doctors in the States. We're from Canada."

"Try the hot tub in the fitness centre. And definitely a massage."

"What kind of massage?"

"We have four girls working full-time at the massage centre. They mainly serve the trucker's wing. I recommend that you book early. It gets crazy in the evenings."

They walked past the elevators, the casino entrance, the escalator to the Excalibur pool, the Lady of Shallott Beauty Salon, and the massage and fitness centre. Down another long corridor, they arrived at last in the truckers' annex. It was a large wing extending from the rear of the Camelot Motel, built to accommodate knights of the road who made overnight stops in Las Vegas on their long hauls across the US. Behind the Camelot was North Las Vegas's biggest 24-hour garage and fuel depot. Between the two structures, long rows of trucks sat parked, their engines idling through the night.

Manuel unlocked room 198 and piled the plastic bags on the bed. It was a standard cubicle with a vanity, hanging lamp, table and chair, and small bathroom. The bed leg had broken off, and been replaced by a concrete brick. Manuel said not to worry, it had held a 300-pound driver the night before.

Coyote looked at the carpet, which was a bit stained from spilled drinks, but at least had been vacuumed. It looked as soft and inviting as a pillow. He stumbled into the shower, hoping the hot water would rinse away not only the accumulated dust of travel, but also the misery and foreboding which clung to his shoulders. He stood fifteen minutes in the steaming water, letting it soak his aching muscles. But the pain in his head did not stop, nor did the indelible image of Carnahan flying off his Robbers' Roost. The more he thought about the hermit, the worse he felt. After he dried himself, he applied Firebrass all over. He decided to call the massage centre. He'd never had a massage.

A nasal voice answered the phone. "Massage and Therapy Center, Mechelle speaking?" Her rising voice made everything she said into a question. "How may I help you?"

"This is Captain Coyote in Room 198. I was wondering about a massage."

"You want the full body massage or just a quickie?"

"The full deal, I guess."

"We have a trucker's special this week, only ninety bucks. Plus ten percent discount for cash, and if you need one, a receipt for your Blue Cross? But I can't do a full massage till 2 a.m. For a quickie, come straight to the centre. It's only twenty bucks?"

"Maybe I'll try that, and if it works, I'll go for the full deal later."

When Captain Coyote arrived at the massage centre, an attendant handed him a bathrobe and a towel and showed him a cubicle to undress in. She said he had to take off his glasses. There was a knock at the door and a different girl entered. He had to lean close to read the name tag on her halter top. "Mechelle?"

"That's me?"

Mechelle's halter stretched across a pair of breasts the size of honey melons. They were so large Coyote thought there were three of them, and for a few seconds felt the full power of his X-ray vision. He looked at her face, which featured an odd, potato-shaped nose, but a pleasant smile. She wore turquoise eye shadow and sparkles on her eyelids. Her teeth gleamed like pearls, bathed in the room's soft light.

"Remove your bathrobe and lie down on the massage table?"

"You mean – naked?" Coyote felt exposed just showing his chest. He was worried that Mr. Private would act up, though Mechelle seemed very calm and professional. "But can I keep my towel on?"

"Oh, yes. The towel must remain in position at all times. That's one of the rules?"

She flattened him out on the table and stood for a moment, flexing her fingers. "What's that turpentiney smell?" she said.

"Firebrass Balm."

"Well, it feels pretty good. Must be effective?" Her fingers probed into the muscles of his back, penetrating the deepest bruises. Mechelle applied massage oil to her hands, and with a few quick strokes, erased all his surface pain. When she jabbed her thumbs into his shoulder muscles, rubbing out the twists and kinks, he felt blissed-out and sleepy. If she could only reach the deeper hurts, he thought, the ones in his brain.

"Somebody laid a licking on you?"

"Well, it was a build-up of things. The burn happened when I tangled with a Russian Drone just across the Canadian border. And then we crossed the border and ran into a gang of Yankee trouble-makers. My companion –"

The door of his cubicle flew open and Wonder Woman burst in with a twelve-pack of Budweiser under her arm. "Okay, what the hell is going on here!" She had finished her final round of inspection at the casino. "The bell boy said you were up here having a massage, so I thought I better come and rescue you before there's trouble."

"What trouble can I get into with a massage? It feels good."

"More trouble than you think."

"I'm just having a quickie."

"Mr. Coyote was telling me he got scraped up in a fight?"

"It was an accident. Dumb bugger fell out of the car, wasn't wearing his seat belt. *Kapow!* I thought he was never going to quit skidding on the pavement."

"Looks like you fell out too."

"Naa – I turned black and blue just watching him bounce along the road. What the doctors call sympathetic reaction. Hey, how much is a massage? I might get one myself. We're in the same room."

"Pardon me, but what relation are you to Mr. Coyote?"

"I'm his faithful companion, toots. Wonder Woman's the name, and action's my game. So don't make a dumb mistake on the bill. I'm arranging a security deal with the manager."

"I hope you know what you're doing. The last amateurs Mr. Palomeque hired didn't work out so hot."

"That is different. We are total professionals. Ever heard of Captain Coyote?"

"Uh...?"

"Never mind. He's from Canada. Up there he's real big."

"What – like a big star?"

"Bigger than Spiderman. More famous than Goldhawk. He's on TV every night. Okay, he looks like a fuckt-up specimen of male humanity right now, but he's recovering fast. Aren't you, big fella? Oh, heroes gotta take a few shit-kickings. Ask Captain Coyote. One minute you're standing on a pedestal, the next you're swamped in garbage."

Coyote started dozing off, lulled by Mechelle's hypnotic fingers. They worked like magnets drawing the pain from his sorest places, pressing each shoulder and neck muscle, making it snap and relax, snap and relax. "That's good," he murmured. He was happy to let Wonder Woman do the talking, and didn't care if she screwed the story up.

"Yeah, we bin travelling a while, checking out possibilities across the States. Coyote was starting to lose heart, but I talked him into staying with the mission till we got to Vegas. Look at all the scope here. Incredible opportunities. We're just doing the Camelot security until something better turns up."

"Like what?"

"Oh well – like the US secret service. As soon as Coyote's back up to speed. Meantime, we gotta stay focused, stay alert."

"I feel the same?" Mechelle said. "With fate, you never know where you're going to end. Like I took a massage therapy degree at UNLV, so I had a wide choice of career opportunities. Like a medical clinic in San Diego? But the tips totally suck in a clinic?"

Coyote vaguely remembered Wonder Woman taking him by the arm back to the room, and helping him lay out a sleeping bag on the carpet. But afterward he couldn't be sure it happened. He felt like he was walking in his sleep. What confused him was waking up in the middle of a totally different dream, a dream where he was travelling on horseback through some European country like Spain. It was like the countryside in an old *Classics Illustrated,* full of ancient monuments and churches.

After a while he came to an antique palace with a massive jumble of towers and steeples, a castle even bigger than the Camelot Motel. An old man came out of the gate and crossed the drawbridge to greet Coyote and his horse Starbuck. He said he was the Count of Sevilla, and after admiring Captain Coyote's outfit, invited him inside to stay for the night.

The count personally escorted him across the moat and down several passages until they entered a throne room, bigger than Moose Jaw's CPR station. Coyote met the countess, the countess's parents, and the count's brother, the Baron of Torremelinos. He was invited to join their medieval banquet, and got seated in the place of honour at the head table. A row of serving girls carried in huge boxes of fried chicken and barrels of root beer. A chorus of trumpets blared, announcing a dancer who pirouetted onto the stage.

"This," said the Count of Sevilla, "is my daughter, Maritornes."

Maritornes looked like a cross between Marcella Henderson and Mechelle. She had Mechelle's body and Marcella's dark hair, flashing eyes, and sweet little nose. She bowed to the applause and launched into a wild gypsy dance, all whirling red and yellow veils, with flashing heels and sequins. It soon became clear that she was performing for him – perhaps dazzled by his pearl-grey cowboy outfit, complete with a silver Stetson. Maritornes had fallen in love with him on the spot, and begged her father to recruit Captain Coyote to join the Square Table of knights and heroes who lived in the palace. Over a dessert of ice cream and lemon Jell-O, she invited him to her room to get to know him better. He didn't know what to say. Even though it was a dream, and nobody could control what happened in dreams, Princess Di would not approve. But he was so enchanted by Maritornes and her ruby-lipped smile, he said he'd consider it.

While he considered, she took him by the hand to a corridor in the main tower. A staircase led to her bedroom at the top of the tower. When they opened the door, it looked exactly like Mechelle's massage room.

"I knew you'd come," she breathed, drawing him inside and locking the door.

"You did?"

She also wore perfume the same as Mechelle, a blend of ambergris and menthol cigarettes. Gripping his hand, she pulled him to her massage table in the centre of the room.

Maritornes had changed from her sequinned dancing costume and wore a long gown of soft flannel. He could smell its fresh laundry scent as she leaned over him on the table, and he could feel Mr. Private stir in excitement. He reached out to touch her hair.

"I knew you'd come," she sighed. "I dreamed it."

"I think I'm dreaming it, too," he said.

She took his hand and slid it under her nightgown. She had nothing on underneath. She drew the hand toward the gold locket hanging around her neck, and their fingers fumbled over it together, nesting in the deep valley between her breasts. She sighed deeply and climbed onto the table beside him. "How it is now?"

"Okay. I like it."

"Move your fingers. There. Yes."

"This is a great dream. You have beautiful breasts."

"Some girls are embarrassed by their bosoms. Not me. They like to be kissed."

"You want me to kiss them?"

"Why not? It's just a dream."

She lifted her nightgown over her shoulders. Trembling with excitement, he kissed the tips of her rounded breasts. She crushed his head against the swollen nipples, first to one side, then the other side, and down to her belly button. Her belly button smelled like jujubes.

Maritornes reached down and touched Mr. Private, a sensation that sent all the blood rushing out of Coyote's brain. His whole being was getting massaged, and he was faint with pleasure. Maritornes pressed him to the table. Coyote didn't know what might happen next, but it would be totally unique.

There was a sharp rap on the door. "Mechelle!" a man's voice growled.

"Who is it?" she gasped.

"It's me – Trevor."

"Trevor?" Mechelle sat upright.

"Yeah, I found my tool bag. My idiot assistant locked it in the semi." Trevor pounded on the door again.

"Oh!" she said, turning to Coyote, who was now wide awake, clasping her leg. "Then who is – this?"

Trevor's voice bellowed through the door. "Mechelle. Open the goddam door!"

"Oh my god. It's not – Oh, don't."

"Don't what?"

"Kiss me – not there – !"

A fire alarm suddenly erupted in the hallway, a terrible shrieking sound. In the same instant, the door was smashed open and the corridor lights silhouetted the form of Trevor, a powerful-looking truck driver. The light fell upon the massage table and the object of Trevor's suspicions, which Mechelle gripped in both hands. A howl of rage burst from Trevor as he ran at the table, swinging his tool bag over his head. He smashed it down on the naked hero's skull.

Coyote knew then he wasn't dreaming. The pain meant he really had been hammered with a bag full of truck wrenches. This nightmare was real. The blow slammed his teeth down on his tongue, almost biting it in half. He tried to roll off the table to the floor as his mouth filled with blood, but his legs were tangled up in Mechelle's nightgown and he couldn't move. It was worse than a nightmare. Trevor leaped onto the table and began stomping his ribs. Mechelle was yelling and trying to find the fire alarm switch. She finally pushed Trevor and sent him crashing to the floor.

The lights suddenly flashed on, and Mr. Palomeque stood at the door. His eyes popped as he surveyed the scene. "Mechelle, what is going on?"

"Nothing," she said, trying to hide her naked body behind the massage table.

Palomeque stared at Coyote lying on the table, blood pouring from his nose and mouth. "My god. Phone the police. Murder. Dial 911!"

Mechelle grabbed her nightshirt to cover herself, while Palomeque ran to the phone at the desk, and began punching all the buttons at once. "Manuel!" he roared. "Call security!"

Trevor tried to run out the door, dragging his gym bag of wrenches, but Palomeque got there first and locked it. "No one leaves till the cops get here!"

"Oh, Mr. Palomeque," Mechelle cried. "Don't call the police. Please – Mr. Coyote's okay, just a knock on the head. He's a massage client? Trevor got a little jealous? We don't need to call the police. Just get him to Emergency before he bleeds to death. I think he bit his tongue?"

Captain Coyote nodded to Palomeque, trying to stanch the flow of blood into his mouth with his teeth. When he tried to speak, his tongue flapped awkwardly.

"Manuel, cancel the police," Palomeque barked into the phone. "Get that roommate of his down here to drive him to the hospital. They probably can't afford an ambulance!" He hung up. "Here, use this towel. Listen. Do you have medical insurance?"

Coyote shook his head.

"Mechelle, take him back to his room and get his stuff. Him and his buddy have to take care of this!"

Captain Coyote was in no condition to argue, so he stumbled behind Mechelle to Room 198. They could hear Wonder Woman snoring forty feet away, so loud her snores made the door rattle. Coyote banged on the door, while Mechelle called, "Wake up. Emergency. Wake up?"

Wonder Woman flung open the door in a red-eyed fury. "Wake up?" she screeched. "How could anybody sleep in this racket? Holy shit!" She stared at the blood seeping through the towel Coyote held to his face.

"He bit his tongue?" Mechelle said. "You gotta take him to the hospital?"

"Gimme a break! It's the middle of the night."

"He needs his tongue examined. And the hotel won't accept responsibility. There was a kafuffle in the massage centre?"

Cursing bitterly, Wonder Woman dragged Coyote to the parking lot by one arm. When Mechelle offered to remove their stuff from the room, Wonder Woman said, "Tell Palomeque to hold our room, or the deal's off. We'll be back to take up our duties later."

She loaded Coyote into the wrecked Coyote Mobile, and they sat for a minute, trying to decide where to go for medical help. Coyote's second towel was drenched with blood.

"Hey!" Wonder Woman yelled at the parking lot attendant. "This guy's bleeding to death. I gotta get him to a hospital."

"Nearest hospital is Lake Mead Medical Center. Near the Cosmotower." The attendant pointed to a space needle towering over the city in the distance, like a lit-up space rocket ready to take off. "Can't miss it. Tallest structure west of the Mississippi. And the biggest entertainment complex in Nevada."

CHAPTER 20

Sinatra Live!

Far above the glittering streets, the sky-high needle of the Cosmotower rose toward the heavens like a shrine of polished light. Halfway to its tip a pleasure dome revolved a thousand feet above the savage night traffic of Las Vegas Boulevard. Inside, a stranger turned away from his slot machine at that moment to look down on the neon carnival slowly spinning beneath. The dome orbited through the night like a planet, unconscious of the dark night brooding beyond the city's show. If he wanted, the stranger could take an elevator ride to the roof of the Cosmotower Casino and buy a ticket on the Cosmic Roller Coaster, which went looping and twisting around the upper needle, soaring among the stars.

The Cosmic Roller Coaster was tame, however, compared to the ride above it on the tower. A device called the Space Ejaculator offered a trip unequalled in the vast array of amusement parks, virtual worlds, Xtreme centres and electronic circuses that spread for thousands of miles in all directions, through California, Washington, Texas. The Space Ejaculator was a high-power catapult with ten seats. The seats were cranked another hundred feet up to the very tip of the Cosmotower, where a red light glowed. On reaching the top, they were sent plummeting down, hurled by gravity at the

Cosmotower roof below, before suddenly screeching to a stop and bouncing upward again.

Had they been looking toward North Vegas, the stranger and the riders of the Space Ejaculator would have seen the broken-down Coyote Mobile approach The Cosmotower and the rest of the Vegas Strip. It crawled through North Las Vegas's dark and gloomy streets, its battered hulk revealed by a few surviving street lamps, their light slowly fading in the grey advance of dawn.

In contrast to the rest of the cityscape, the view to the north looked like a battlefield from a civil war – block after block of barricaded bars and storefronts, punctuated with flophouses, detox centres, and 24-hour booze cans. On every other corner, Deseret Industries had placed charitable collection bins for the poor. The Coyote Mobile passed the Stupak Mash Village Homeless Refuge and the crematorium of Bunkers Cemetery before entering a long street of dimly lit bars and pawnshops. Here zombie-like figures slid among the shadows, avoiding all contact with people. Others sprawled in the doorways of cocaine joints and hotels, the destitute and homeless, addicts and lunatics, flushed out of the casinos into the gutters of North Las Vegas.

Captain Coyote was appalled by the horrifying scene they drove through, hoping it was a hallucination caused by the pain from his nearly severed tongue.

Wonder Woman swore as she fought the traffic, which got worse with every block they advanced toward the Cosmotower and The Strip. Crossing Owens Road into Las Vegas, the streets turned garish, with endless blocks of casinos and entertainment palaces. Twice she tried to get off the crowded boulevard and back onto the interstate, but the entrance ramps were choked for miles. She was forced to stick to the main stem and crawl along at the speed of a slug.

"What's the holdup?" Wonder Woman yelled at a taxi stalled in the opposite lane.

"Sinatra's Memorial!" the driver yelled back.

"Frank Sinatra!?"

"Yeah. Everybody who ever heard of the guy's comin to town. You think this is bad, wait till tomorrow! Big memorial concert at the MGM Grand – 'Sinatra Live.' Sid Caesar's gonna be there. Kenny Rogers. Every Sinatra impersonator there ever was. I heard Ron and Nancy might be comin'!"

"The President?" Coyote moaned, sitting up on the seat in pain.

"Listen, I gotta get this guy to the Lake Mead Medical Center."

"You're headin the wrong way, pal. Go back a mile, turn off to your right. Lotsa signs, can't miss it."

Wonder Woman swerved into the parking lane and pulled onto a side street to turn around. The pain in Coyote's tongue grew worse, almost making him pass out. He had to stay conscious until they stitched it back together. Then he and Wonder Woman would go to the MGM and meet the President. Despite his agony, Coyote recognized the good luck for what it was. Once again he was in the right place at the right time: a chance to meet the greatest President in history, and achieve his dream.

The emergency ward at Lake Mead Hospital offered pretty good service, considering it was five o'clock in the morning and the place looked like a scene from a war movie. There were only two nurses and an intern on duty. Bleeding victims were stacked on gurneys along every foot of the hallways. Others crouched on the floor, moaning with pain.

The heroes were told to go and wait in line at the registration counter. They found a long lineup of people who looked like illegal aliens. A sign on the counter said, "PLEASE COVER NOSE AND MOUTH WHEN COUGHING OR SNEEZING. US Dept. of Health and Human Services." The line was long and unruly. Above the counter was another sign: "NOTICE: Medical care for Those Who Cannot Afford to Pay." It was the same as Lewistown. To speed things along, Wonder Woman pulled a wad of Carnahan's greenbacks from her bra, and waving it aloft, escorted Coyote back to Admissions. They had cash for emergency treatment.

Captain Coyote was loaded onto a gurney, and rolled down another corridor, even more congested with the sick and wounded, to a tiny curtained-off cubicle. A nurse came after a while and gave Coyote a needle full of Demerol. She sat him up to stitch his tongue together, as Wonder Woman waited outside.

Demerol was something new to Captain Coyote, and he liked it nearly as much as Firebrass for halting pain. He forgot about his swollen tongue, and his stiff back, and all the scrapes and bruises. The drug also unleashed a stream of gibberish from his brain that Wonder Woman could not understand at first. The words were strange enough, and the stitches in his tongue made his speech almost impossible to follow, but she finally figured out she was hearing his account of the night's events.

He narrated his dream of the Spanish castle and its bizarre conclusion, going on at length about the beautiful Maritornes, daughter of the Count of Sevilla, and ending with him and Mechelle naked in the massage centre. He described the rapture of that encounter, and the bad luck in the form of Trevor, an alien with the strength of ten. Perhaps, he gabbled, women in dreams were protected by extraterrestrial beings which earthlings knew nothing about. Then he drifted off to sleep, leaving Wonder Woman confused but impressed.

Captain Coyote was shaken awake in the afternoon by a duty nurse who informed him that since surgery was complete, he had to leave the hospital. To help him along, she gave him another hit of Demerol.

Wonder Woman elbowed his ribs. "You with us, Captain?"

"Mmm!"

"Come on – wakey-wakey!"

"Uh for?" His lips were still numb from the anaesthetic.

"They're kicking us out. Let's go get some rest. I was up all night listening to your nutso rambling."

"Horry."

"Anyway, this so-called mission is starting to look like a disaster. Look at you."

"Rough."

"Yeah, well you at least got some enjoyment."

"Wha'ya mean?"

"Oh, you really spilled your guts, buddy. All about your big dream."

"You can't hell!"

"I won't. I swear!"

"On whuh?"

"On what. On my right tit. Okay. I swear on my right tit I won't reveal your filthy secrets till the day you die."

"And after that?"

"Well, what do you care when you're dead and moldy?"

"I don't heel like arguing," Coyote muttered.

The intern gave Coyote three prescription slips, including one for Demerol. Wonder Woman brightened up. "Let's head to the motel. We can stop at a drug store along the way. We have to let Palomeque know you're okay."

They stepped into a blast of heat outside the clinic as the sun beat a hot tattoo on the pavement. It took a long time to find the Coyote Mobile. It had been towed to a vehicle compound down the street. Wonder Woman had to pay $150 to get it out of hock.

"Let's go fill your prescription," she said. "I could use a hit of Demerol. They used to give me some every time I went to emergency after a fight with Delvis. You really got off on it, eh?"

"It's kinda floaty – happy feeling –"

"You said it. Great high. I'd kill for a hit of Demerol."

"But won' I get – hooked?"

"Naaa. Well – maybe. Who knows? Lotsa people do. But don't worry. Everybody's addicted to something or other. If it's not drugs, it's TV. You're already a food addict, right? Anyway, Demerol isn't like smack. Or crack. It's just brain candy, don't think about it. If you don't like it, I can handle your share. And I don't know why you're complaining. You been high for six hours. Should see the goofy grin on your face. Okay, your pain's gone, but what about me? I'm still aching from the fight with the hermit."

"I don't wanna talk about the hermit."

"Why not?"

"He warned us about Las Vegas. He cursed the place."

"Don't start that crap again."

"Why does it seem like hell?"

"Don't start Bible-thumping on me," Wonder Woman said. "This is just a temporary setback. Don't worry, we'll find Ron and Nancy at this Sinatra bash. Everything'll work out. Forget about that hell shit. I mean, what did we do wrong?"

"We took the hermit's money," Coyote replied. "That started this spell of rotten luck. Remember our good luck in Utah? We wasted the money on dumb stuff like a luxury motel, and going to a massage parlour, and getting into trouble with Mechelle. I forgot my vow to Princess Di and the goals of our mission. I feel kinda – doomed."

"Doomed! Captain, we're practically kingpins already. Give me a break!"

"This happens to heroes. Illusions. There's all kinds of trials and a million temptations to sin."

"Sin. You call that a sin? You were just waving your pecker around like any other normal male. Jeeze, what do you think it's for?"

"The devil tries to make sin look like fun. In the Orange Home they warned us about the devil. His power is terrible to behold."

"Are we still talking about Mechelle's boyfriend?"

"A demon. He gave me such a clout on the head I nearly bit my tongue in half. Then he jumped on me, and pounded the bruises I got at Rock Springs. If he wasn't a demon, he was an alien."

"Well, at least you got to play knocky-knocky kneecaps with the massage girl. What do I, who tried to rescue you, get for my trouble? Nada but crap. That's how it goes for faithful companions – we get the shitty end of the stick. Hey – a drug store!"

Wonder Woman slammed the Coyote Mobile's brakes and ran into the drug store with the prescriptions. She returned in a few minutes with a tube of ointment and two bottles of pills. One was antibiotics, the other Demerol. She also carried a two-litre bottle of Pepsi to mix the drugs in, shaking the concoction as she ran back to Coyote Mobile. She jumped in and took a big swig.

"Hey, that's my medicine," Coyote protested.

"Quit bitching. You think you're the only one hurting?"

"You don't hurt like I do!"

"It's all relative, pal. I took a few hits too. And did you see me sinning?" She guzzled a few swallows and passed the bottle to Coyote. "No!"

The mixture tasted vile, but it immediately relieved Coyote's pain-wracked body and swollen tongue. Within five minutes, he was rambling again about Maritornes and massages and hermits and aliens, while Wonder Woman tried to find the Camelot Motel in the harsh light of late afternoon. Her driving was even worse than usual, veering through pedestrian crossings, over road medians, across sidewalks. She was trying to find the Cosmotower, but had forgotten whether it stood on the left or right.

"Hey Coyote. Why don't we go and stay in the Cosmotower? We can get a better security deal than we did with what's-his-face. Hey, even better, why don't we get a room at the MGM Grand, and take in the Sinatra shindig?"

"All our stuff is at the Camelot."

"Okay, then you find the way back. Dumb son of a bitch."

By squinting at the Cosmotower and lining its shadow up on the motel map of Las Vegas, Captain Coyote worked out the right direction. They wandered down to room 198, planning to sleep for the rest of the day, but the key card refused to open the door. They were locked out.

In a fury, Wonder Woman ran to Palomeque's office and demanded to know what was going on. He explained that he had checked with American Express, who informed him that Coyote's credit card had been cancelled at the account address. And as far as he was concerned, their security contract never existed, and until they paid for their room, he would hold onto their bags of stuff he'd locked up in his office.

"First we gotta talk benefits," Wonder Woman insisted. "Then there's the question of severance pay. And Coyote's injuries, which were suffered while engaged in his duties on security patrol. He will need compensation for all medical expenses."

"That reminds me," said Palomeque. "When you registered for the room, you signed a waiver of claim for my insurance company. We're not responsible for disputes you had with another guest."

"Dispute!" Wonder Woman snapped. "He tried to kill my partner, who was defending your business. We had an agreement, Palomeque!"

"What agreement?"

"Free accommodation plus meals and expenses, in exchange for security. That includes medical coverage and drugs. We kept all the receipts. I got them here."

"Ridiculous. You didn't provide any security."

"Palomeque, we negotiated a contract in good faith. If you're not happy with our service, file an official complaint. Business procedures have to be followed. You can't just grab our room! We had a deal. A contract! You gotta admit the Camelot Motel is secure since we took up our duties."

"If you don't pay the bill right now, I'm calling the police."

Wonder Woman blew her stack. "Come on, Dog Face. We're bailing out of this flophouse!" She grabbed Coyote's shirt and hauled him out the front gate of the palace. She loaded him into the Coyote Mobile and drove off in a spray of flying gravel.

"Well, got any more bright ideas?" she snapped. "It's already supper time, and we still haven't eaten."

"You think he'll call the police?"

"Not a chance. He owes us money, remember? Plus he knows we'll sue his ass off for your head gettin bashed in the massage parlour. He'd be delirious with joy if we just hit the road. So we're not. Mr. Palomeque hasn't heard the last from us."

"He has all our stuff. Our food. Our new sleeping bags."

"Here, have a swig of Pepsi Surprise."

"No thanks."

"Had enough, eh? Then you can be the designated driver."

"Oh, I don't think I can drive –"

"Then shut your mouth and quit bitching. Let's go and crash this Sinatra party. There'll be gallons of free booze. If we run into your friends the Reagans, maybe they'll wangle a room for us."

Fuelled by another hit of high-octane cola, Wonder Woman was transformed into a fearless road warrior behind the steering wheel, challenging every stop light along Lake Mead Boulevard. She swerved onto the I-15 by rocketing down the shoulder and cutting across three streams of traffic to the high-speed lane, holding it all the way to the Tropicana exit. Then she shut her eyes and powered the truck back across the veering traffic before roaring off the exit ramp. Hurtling out of the mass of cars like a pinball, the Coyote Mobile glided onto the southern end of The Strip, a vast shimmer of neon light and gigantic video screens.

All they could see in every direction was an extravaganza of flashing lights. Roller coasters leaped and whirled across the rooftops of buildings, looping through space before plunging back into the casinos, where vast fields of machines glittered and bonged, competing for attention. There was a new hotel or casino on every block, and an old one being torn down to make way for it. They passed The Oasis, built like a gigantic Egyptian pyramid. Facing it was a hotel in the shape of a jukebox thirty storeys high, and at the next corner was Indiana Jones's Temple of Doom. At the far north end of the Strip, the Cosmotower stood over the traffic flow like an obelisk. Pedestrians swarmed through the traffic, dodging street vendors and hustlers.

"Let's park this shitbox and walk," Wonder Woman said. "Get there a lot faster. Keep your eyes open for a parking spot. Bus stop, anything. They won't ticket cars on the night of Frank's Memorial."

Fat girls bursting from their costumes carried their slurpee cups in one hand, cigarettes in the other, parading down the noisy midway in a glazed stupor.

"I don't see any parking spots."

"Aaa, you can't see anyway. What's that?"

"It's a hotel driveway. Full of limos."

"Big deal – where they gonna go in this traffic? Take a chance, or we'll never get there."

Abandoning the Coyote Mobile in the driveway, they made their way on foot to the entrance of the MGM Grand, the world's biggest hotel. Barely two hundred yards from the entrance, they ran into a wall of frantic people, straining to reach the doors. Others were glued to the forty-foot video screen over the entrance.

"Fuck it," Wonder Woman said. "We'll never get through. Let's try the parkade."

There was a six-storey parkade two blocks behind the MGM, and a long line of cars waiting to enter. People were abandoning their vehicles and walking into the parkade, so the pair joined the flow heading to the Grand Garden Arena. Most of the people were impersonators and their wild costumes created a carnival atmosphere. Every fourth person looked like Frank Sinatra or Elvis Presley. The heroes also spied Liberace, Tina Turner, Sammy Davis Jr. and Dean Martin. There were a dozen Wayne Newtons.

In such a crowd, Captain Coyote and Wonder Woman did not attract too much attention. The guards at the door of the Garden Arena glanced at the tickets, waving people inside. For those who could not get in, TV monitors had been set up in all the bars and lounges around the complex. For those who did, a hologram image of the singer appeared on centre stage, a ten-foot image of Ol' Blue Eyes, singing all the songs he had ever filmed, looking more alive than he ever had in person.

Along the promenade to the Garden Arena, the heroes passed a door that said "Sinatra Memorial VIPs," where celebrities gathered before the show began. Coyote and Wonder Woman crowded to the door to see in.

And there, standing in front of one of the slot machines along the wall, was President Reagan. A couple of secret service agents hovered nearby watching for intruders, but Coyote barely noticed them. All he saw was the wizened face of the old Gipper, his greatest hero, grinning a grin handsomer than ever. The president was pulling the arm of a slot machine, nodding and smiling at everyone who approached.

Coyote rushed in and, drawing himself up to his full height, saluted the president on his best GI Joe style. Wonder Woman waited by the door to see the outcome of Coyote's bold initiative. She took the precaution of stashing the bottle of Pepsi Surprise beside the door. If Captain Coyote succeeded – they'd be in like Flynn.

The president grinned at him. "And who are you again?"

"Captain Coyote, sir! Volunteering for the secret service!"

"Excellent. Paiute, did you say?"

"No sir, Coyote. Or Coyotee, like they say down here."

"The writer Don Coyotee?"

"No sir, I'm not a writer. It's Coyote, like the wild dog. I'm a super-hero. From Canada. My partner and me have travelled to your country to offer our personal vows of allegiance. We are ready to serve the US of A."

"Coyotee. I can't stand coyotees – my insurance policy won't allow them on the property. Mangy pests. Worse than skunks. Worse than rats! Somebody deal with this son of a bitch."

Coyote was stunned into silence. He stared at the president's lopsided grin – a grin which took in not only Coyote, but the whole universe.

The president's agents pounced on Coyote and his accomplice, who was observed backing out of the room. They were hustled down the corridor and into a freight elevator so fast Coyote couldn't speak. Luckily, the agents decided that an investigation into their gross breach of security could only result in lame explanations in the full glare of television cameras. They deposited the two suspect heroes beside the bank of dumpsters at the rear service entrance, and told them to get lost. They did, galloping down the street in the wrong direction.

After two hours of wandering lost, they feel asleep on the lawn of the Liberace Museum. At dawn a security guard chased them off. At 9 a.m., when the tow-away compound opened, they were allowed to retrieve the Coyote Mobile. Their bruised carcasses throbbed in pain, for Wonder Woman had abandoned Coyote's medication. Now both their spirits plummeted into depression. Wonder Woman could no longer function, so Coyote got behind the wheel. He had never felt lower. The whole mission was a total disaster.

The insults from the biggest hero in American history – except for Superman – had felt like kicks to Coyote's stomach. He was so humiliated he could only repeat the president's hateful words in his mind endlessly. He tried to blame his hollowness on drug withdrawal, but his brain knew it was the President's cruel rejection. He felt stabbed through the heart.

"Where you goin now?" Wonder Woman moaned, gazing bleary-eyed at the passing maelstrom of blinking neon lights. "Back to the motel?"

"I hafta get outta here a while. Maybe we made a mistake comin to Las Vegas. I feel – like I swallowed some kind of poison."

"You wanna go back to the hospital and try for another prescription?"

"I'd like to get outside of town. Into the country. Maybe drive into the desert. I saw a place on the map, called Coyote Lake."

"Okay. Let's go."

They drove west of the city while the morning sun rose behind. Coyote felt some release from the tension of the traffic and lights, but waves of dizziness kept passing over him. Afraid he was going to faint, he pulled the truck over to the side of the road at the foot of the Spring Mountains.

"Lemme look at your tongue," Wonder Woman commanded, and Coyote opened his mouth wide. "Yuk," she said, prodding the tongue with one finger. Without warning Coyote vomited the bilious soup of his stomach into Wonder Woman's lap.

"Bloody hell!" she yelled. "The stuff stinks like dead skunk. Why'd you do that?"

"It's that medicine. I have to get some Firebrass, before I die."

"Now I'm covered in barf!" Wonder Woman tried to sponge the mess off with his cape, but the smell was so revolting she puked too, carpeting the seat, the floor, and part of the windshield. They stopped at Red Rock Canyon state park campground, and flushed the vehicle out with a hose.

"Now what?" Sandra said. "Head back?"

"I have to keep going."

"Where to?"

"I told you. It's in California – not far from Death Valley. I found it on the map."

"Coyote Lake?"

"I'm hopin there'll be some answers there."

"Answers to what?"

"About my past. Where my problems come from. Why nobody ever answers my prayers. You don't have to go. I just need to be alone for a while."

CHAPTER 21

A Burning Lake of Fire

The Coyote Mobile crossed the California state line at noon, descending the low mountain ridges into a landscape that looked even more desolate and sun-baked than the Nevada desert. Wonder Woman grew nervous about the way things were going. "Was that the road to Death Valley we just passed? Listen, I'm not crazy about travelling near that kind of place. It sounds dangerous as hell."

"Don't come. Maybe it's time we split up anyway."

"Well, who gets the truck then? And the hermit's bundle of dough?"

"I've been thinking. I could let you take the Coyote Mobile, but you better let me take care of the hermit's money. I'll arrange to get it back to him."

"You don't trust me? That's it! I'm quitting this stupid crusade! I'm outta here!"

"You'll go back to Moose Jaw?"

"As if! Hey, I'm practically an American citizen."

"So what will you do?"

"Go to Las Vegas and look for work, of course. Okay, it's not easy getting kicked, spit on, beat up, and discriminated against, but it's better than nothing. And without you charging like a bull in a china shop, I don't expect too many problems."

"Don't you miss your kids?"

"Naa – well, a little. I feel sorry for the poor little buggers – livin with Delvis!"

"I'd miss them if I had kids. You miss Delvis?"

"He'll have some other broad by now. If I went back home, I'd only have to kick her out, same as the others."

"I miss Doc, and Princess Di. A lot. So I want you to do me a big favour. If I let you have the Coyote Mobile, you have to take a message to P.D."

"To Moose Jaw? Ha. Be lucky to get as far as Vegas in this shitbox."

"The Coyote Mobile got us this far and she can get you back to Canada. If you do, I'll let you carry the hermit's money."

"Well, that's a fair deal. I could do that. What about the stuff in the van? You wanta divide that up?"

"All I need is some food. And I'll keep The Flash's helmet."

"It's all yours. By the way, who's buyin the gas for this trek to Moose Jaw? Me or the mission?"

"You can borrow what you need for expenses – as long as you stop in Utah and leave the rest for Carnahan. We have to give it back. It's like a curse. Taking the hermit's money was our first big mistake."

"Yeah, and the second one was letting you in on it. Where you wanta be dropped off?"

At Yerma, Coyote studied the map and turned down a back road that led to Fort Irwin Army Base. The road weaved across the sandy hills until it reached a turnoff where a crudely lettered sign said, "Coyote Lake, 12 miles, No Road."

"What're you going to find out there?"

"I just want to be alone and let my tongue heal up. I have to do some heavy-duty thinking. Maybe I'll find some sign of my ancestors. Coyote Lake might be some kind of home for me."

"Well, good luck. Don't worry, I'll be sure and thank the hermit, if I see him. You gotta quit punishing yourself just because you flattened that fruitcake."

"Thinking about him makes me feel horrible."

"Can we get back to our priorities here? Show me how I get back to Moose Jaw. I don't even remember where Utah is."

"Stay on the interstate as far as Beaver, Utah, then turn up into the mountains and follow the road till you see the pile of rocks below his camp."

"Got it. You really gonna walk to this lake?"

"If Carnahan could ride his bike from Salt Lake City, I can walk that far. Heroes go on quests like this all the time."

"Really? Name one!"

"The Lone Ranger."

"Okay – name another."

"How about Hercules? After he destroyed Thebes by mistake, he gave up his power and went on a quest to the Atlas Mountains."

"Big deal. Hercules was a loser from the word go."

"Jesus, then. He was another hero. They wrote the Bible about him. After he met John the Baptist, he took a big hike in the wilderness. 'And the spirit drove him into the wilderness,' the Bible says. 'He was in the wilderness forty days, tempted by Satan, and lived among wild beasts, while angels ministered unto him.'"

"Yeah, yeah, but they all had good reasons for buggering off to the boonies. All you did is beat up on a lunatic and lose your cherry in a Vegas massage parlour. That's no reason to disappear from society."

"I have to be alone and figure out what I need to do, where my instincts tell me to go. I'm hoping P.D. will come and help me sort it out."

"Oh, I see! This is all about Princess Di! If you're still mooning over her, you're crazier than the fuckin hermit!"

"Well, maybe I am crazy. And if Princess Di thinks I'm crazy, maybe she'll take pity and come and see me."

"And what if she doesn't give a damn?"

"Then I'll stay at Coyote Lake, living with the coyotes, where I belong."

"Here – take some food. Anything else you need?"

"Just the helmet. It's gonna be hot."

"For the last time, it's not a goddam helmet – it's an old wash basin! Jeeze, you're gonna drive me nuts! You got so much hero crap on your brain, you make up bullshit over every stupid piece of junk. Even the fucking convicts wouldn't take it! Here!"

"Take it easy, Wonder Woman. You don't know everything. You think being a hero and fighting injustice is bullshit – but you don't know anything, because you never read the stories! You don't believe there's alien beings from other planets, or angels, or worlds that human beings don't know a thing about. But how else do you explain UFOs, or the pyramids?"

"A wash basin is a wash basin is a wash basin."

"To you, it's a basin. To an alien, it could be something else, like a – a tuba. Angels and demons can make us think The Flash's helmet is an African drum, or an old basin, or anything they want."

"Sorry, I can't follow that."

"If it is The Flash's helmet, it's worth money, right? Crooks would steal it, if they knew about it. Maybe that's why some angel disguised it as a Depression basin. Maybe that's why the old man left it behind. If he knew what it was worth, he wouldn't have abandoned it so easy. The disguise was protecting it."

"Okay, I give up. Keep the fucking helmet. As long as I get the bag of money."

"Go ahead. Just make sure you keep an account of what you borrow."

"What're you doing now?"

"Taking my clothes off. Like Hercules did. You can have them too."

Wonder Woman was too stunned to speak. She'd never change Coyote's mind about his crazy quest, so she could hardly complain if his lunacy worked to her advantage. "You're going to walk out there all alone – naked?"

"Carnahan knew something. Living in the natural wilderness. I could live with the coyotes and other wild animals, and cactuses and wild flowers, and even rocks. Till Princess Di comes."

"How will she find you?"

"You have to tell her. I marked the lake on this map."

"You are a true nut case, know that?" She handed him snacks out of the food box: a couple of juice packs, a box of Chitos, a fistful of pepperoni sticks.

"You should observe me for a while, so you can describe my condition."

"I seen enough to give her a pretty good idea of your problem."

"Which problem?"

"Let's just say we don't need more evidence to put you in the funny farm. I'll tell Princess Di about all your stupid stunts on this goofy crusade. If she is interested, which I somehow doubt, I'll be happy to drive her back to Coyote Lake."

"Maybe I better send a note to explain."

"Couldn't you just phone her, save me a trip?"

"She still needs a way to get down here. And anyway, it's not the same. Phoning's not part of the tradition. Hercules never had a phone."

"Okay, okay! Write it out. Plus a note that says the money is in my care. In case I get stopped by the cops."

Coyote sat down on the truck bumper with a page torn out of Carnahan's tattered notebook. It took an hour of careful concentration, printing the letters carefully so P.D. could read them. Wonder Woman was impatient to get on the road, thinking about the bag of money and how she could stop in Las Vegas and trade the Coyote Mobile in on a decent car.

"Okay," Coyote finally said. "How does this read?

Wonder Woman ripped the note out of his hand and read it aloud. "My butifull Princess. Rite now Im am on the road to COYOTE LAKE thinking of you. All I think of is mameries of you. I hop you are okay and Doc too, but Im am not feeling so grate. Pleaze kud you come and visit. Wonder Woman will sho you the way. Im am not depressed, but this is seryus. Being away from you is offal. I kant handel it. I no you are busy writing your feeces but pleaz come. I will exept your advis, no matter what. If you kant come, my dead korps understands. Your faithful student, Captain Coyote."

Wonder Woman stared at him in amazement, her eyes wet and her nose running. "Jeeze, that's beautiful, Donny! It's better than the soaps! It might even persuade her! I had no idea you could write shit like that!"

Coyote raised his hand modestly. "Heroes have to be handy with words."

"Yeah. Now, the money agreement."

"How's this? 'To Hoom It May Cunsern. Be it none that Wonder Woman, AKA Sandra Dollar has purmishen to carry the bag of money to Utah.'"

"Okay, write the date and sign it! I'll fire up the van and be on my way. Sure you got enough food?"

"This will last a few days. I think these cactus plants are edible. That's how the Lone Ranger survived."

"Here. Take another handful of pizza pops. I'm gettin sick of them anyways."

"I'll be okay. On a vision quest, you're supposed to get hungry."

"What if I do persuade her to come? How will she find you?"

"Just take this trail to Coyote Lake. That's where I'll be."

They hugged each other awkwardly, then Wonder Woman clambered into the driver's seat and slammed the door. After a couple of dry wheezes, the Coyote Mobile started up and lurched through a turn on the highway before clattering off toward Las Vegas. She turned to give Coyote a final wave, and was astonished to see that he had removed every last stitch of clothing, even his winged running shoes and grey gym socks. He was leaping about in the desert like a jackrabbit, turning cartwheels and jumping in the air, as though he'd been attacked by a rogue swarm of bees. But his jumps looked suspiciously like leaps of joy. She rolled down the window, thinking she heard laughter. Maybe Coyote had gone over the rainbow! The sound of his maniacal laugh rattled in her head all the way back to Vegas.

Coyote's jubilation was brief, lasting only until the Coyote Mobile had disappeared down the road, and he was alone again. He still had to solve the main problem, to find his path for the future, whatever he was meant to do. He had to examine his past actions alone in nature, and wrestle the torment out of his mind. Coyote was nervous about mental activity, such as figuring out who 'Coyote' was, or what was the meaning of life, or why he felt so awful when his dreams turned to disasters.

It was a long hike to Coyote Lake, but he thought he could get there before nightfall. He plodded along the sandy track, trying to splice together the broken strands of questions racing through his head. The flakes of shale on the stony trail scraped his feet, turning them raw and bloody, but he hardly noticed. He had to connect all the questions and try to explain his own strange behaviour. Why was he always dreaming about naked women, including Princess Di? The answer had to be somewhere inside his head, like a memory.

Princess Di's face kept appearing in the sky before him. It was like a face carved from raw cedar, all beautiful angles and framed by clouds of red hair. He stopped his memory from looking at her naked body, which he had never seen, but which his imagination would not leave alone. Maybe this was grown-up love he felt – X-rated love – and not the deep warm affection he had always felt before.

If it was adult love, that would change everything. He would have to marry Princess Di, and dress like her boyfriends, and get a fancy car like a Corvette. There would be complications learning the customs of romance, such as picking the right deodorant and buying condoms. He shook his head to erase the image of Princess Di, and plodded on, his thoughts pounding like fury.

Who was he? Loser or hero? Donny Coyote or Captain Coyote? Or was he inhuman? A coyote condemned to live in a human body, but without a real brain to figure out what was going on. He had never doubted himself before, but the meeting with President Reagan popped his dream like a soap bubble. Maybe his soul had been swapped at birth with some alien's, and he only *thought* he was Captain Coyote, born to fight evil and correct injustice, but really just a pitiful human like everybody else.

There was no doubt he had failed his friends, people like Princess

Di and Doc, who cared about him. He had left Doc alone, fighting with his bottle in Moose Jaw. And how about beating up on the hermit? Then taking his money on top of it!

Why had Malachi Carnahan gone into the wilderness? Wasn't that also a failure of love? It was betrayal which had driven him like John the Baptist, the hermit who baptized Jesus. After forty days in the wilderness, refusing the temptations of Satan, Jesus had returned with his mission to drive the money-lenders out of the temple. Like the Lone Ranger, Jesus, and Hercules, Coyote limped across the wasteland, trying to answer these tormenting questions.

At sundown, he reached a ridge of sandstone that rose like a jagged red barrier across the desert. A crumbling spire of rock rose out of the centre of the ridge. He climbed to the top, the shale scraping his knees to the bone, until he stood at the peak. Far to the east, Coyote could see a smear of light across the horizon. It had to be the lake.

Coyote decided to spend the night up on the lookout as the sun slipped like a red hot biscuit below the horizon. Finishing his last pizza pop, he felt around till he found a chunk of old mesquite root. It was soft and weathered, a pillow for his aching head. Curling up in a depression in the rock, he tried to find a comfortable position, though his belly grumbled like crazy, and his tongue ached. His head pounded with fatigue, and he could not fall asleep, no matter how hard he tried. The faces of Doc and President Reagan and Princess Di and the hermit kept flashing through his head. Their questions jabbed at his soul as the stars turned slowly before his eyes.

When dawn crept across the cold grey desert, he still had not slept. He needed rest if he wanted to keep walking, but the rising sun made sleep impossible. Even through his closed eyelids, Coyote was blinded by the sun's white glare, which ricocheted off the sand, its heat magnified by his glasses. Maybe Fort Irwin was a nuclear test site for the US military, and he had been blinded by a hydrogen bomb explosion. He began moving toward the lake, a shimmering reflection across the horizon.

There were no coyotes, nor any other wildlife, except the occasional bird circling in the sun-bleached sky. The hunger pains in his gut started roaring aloud, and he stopped to forage in a clump of creosote bush and cactus. He scratched at the roots, looking for green fibers to chew on. He found and ate a few beetles. They got his saliva flowing, and he dug up more roots. They didn't taste too bad. Water could be a problem though.

He had figured there would be gallons of water in the lake, but the farther he walked toward it, the farther it receded. He was shuffling across the white dust of a dried-out slough that lay cracked and crumbling in a bed of alkali clay. The map had showed Coyote Lake to be about five miles wide. It must've been an old map, because Coyote Lake was a cruel mirage, another trick in the bag of tricks reality had foisted on him. Even cactus and beetles could not live in such an oasis. He looked back toward the tower of rock, but it too had vanished into the white glare. Then again, maybe it was just a long beach, and soon he'd be in the water, where there would be plants and other life. He shuffled onward.

By noon, the sun was unbearable. After a while, Coyote came across another set of footprints wandering through the chalky dust, and realized they were his own. He was going in circles. He slumped to the dust, the hot white light burning his eyes, making him dizzy and confused. He tried to hunch his sun-burned shoulders under the shade of The Flash's helmet. He decided to wait for sunset before walking any farther. At dusk, he might be able to see where he was going. He had to be near the trail when Princess Di came.

If Princess Di had arrived at Coyote Lake at that moment, she would not have recognized the figure squatting in the sand as Donny Coyote, his bare flesh scraped and barbecued. He started to think he might not get out of this fix.

Then he heard someone murmuring. "Coyote..." It wasn't a voice. It was like the whirring of air, or the drone of bees. "Donny... Coyote..." it came again.

"What is it?" Coyote stared out from under the helmet, but could not see beyond the searing fury of light. Was it the voice of God? Or was it Satan, with one of his weird impersonations? A shadow formed in the centre of the glare.

"Coyote..." The shape was not a person. It swayed and flowed in the heat waves like a wisp of smoke.

"Is that you, God?"

"Coyotl..." the voice sighed.

"You're not the devil?"

"I am Coyotl, Donald. I share the spirit of your ancestors."

"Really? I'm having a vision?"

"You are. We are joined together in the body of Coyotl."

"What happens next? Do I turn into a coyote?"

"That may come. First you must learn to stop abusing your human body, Coyote."

"I'll try. My head causes the problem. Thinking mixes me up."

"It is a superpower that can be learned. It will come. You must try harder."

"Should I go home and try? Or stay here at the lake?"

"There is no choice. The life of coyotes has ended here. They had to find refuge elsewhere, and abandoned this ruined paradise. To survive, they all learned to live like humans, scavenging and taking what they can. Your cousins have migrated to every corner of America, from the Arctic to the Gulf of Mexico. You can learn to co-exist with humans, grow tolerant of their faults and blindness. You are a test. You must go back."

"Princess Di is coming to meet me!"

"She is not coming. You will have to go to her."

"Jeeze. That could be hard. It's too far to walk."

"There is no end to the journey for reconciliation. You must control your physical desires. The love you desire is a deeper love than carnal, stripped of animal lust. It is the love of one spirit for another. Now go."

He tried to rise, but his legs failed. "Which way?"

"I will send three spirits to guide you. Follow their direction."

"Wait! Wait – Coyotl. Will they be angels?"

But the voice had fallen silent, and the shadow disappeared into the silver flame of Coyote Lake. Darkness fell.

CHAPTER 22

Doc Rides to the Rescue

That same morning, a gleaming Buick rolled out of the Avis rental lot at McCarran International Airport and sped along the Interstate toward North Las Vegas. It turned into the parking lot at the Camelot Motel and braked to a sharp stop in front of a wrecked camper with colourful licence plates that said: "Saskatchewan, Land of Living Skies." Doc Pearce stepped out into the afternoon heat and cautiously approached the broken hulk of the Coyote Mobile. It looked mortally wounded, its tires flattened and one wheel slumped to the ground. He had never seen the vehicle himself, but Princess Di had obtained a description from neighbours who had watched Coyote and Sandra pull up at his house weeks before.

The parking lot was nearly full at 6 p.m., except around the abandoned Coyote Mobile, where drivers had left extra wide space. The hood yawned open, exposing the engine's greasy parts. Plastic wrappers and bags littered the asphalt in all directions. Vandals had spray-painted graffiti in various colours across the back and sides. The doors were locked, but taped inside the windshield was a crudely lettered sign: CAMELOT UNFARE TO SECURITY WORKERS!! A skull and crossbones was drawn across it in black felt pen.

"Sandra Dollar's work," Doc said to the woman waiting in the

256

Buick. She was Dottie McKechnie, head of Special Needs Clients for Saskatchewan's Department of Social Services, a short woman with mouse-coloured hair and a beak of a nose that gave her a look of permanent indignation. She had been the supervisor of Coyote's social worker, the saintly Margaret St. Denis. She was also his legal guardian, and determined to have him returned to her jurisdiction.

"Sandra who?" she said.

"Donny's travelling companion. A woman named Sandra Dollar. She's the one I hold responsible for the whole catastrophe. She might be Métis. You know her?"

Dottie McKechnie's pale face turned paler upon hearing Sandra's name. The large round lenses of her glasses made her eyes look perpetually amazed. She was on permanent high alert, a committed public servant with a Master's in Deviate Psychology.

"I've had a few run-ins with her," she sniffed. "At first, I was sympathetic, but I soon discovered the woman can't utter two words in succession without lying. She's certainly not Métis, whatever else she is. I had her birth records checked. It's all make-believe. I investigated her claims, and none of them add up. You could say she has a pathological victim complex, but it's really just her way of getting attention. Or taking advantage. If she has influence over Donald, it's not good news."

"Well, there's no sign of them here. Let's check at the front desk."

An inquiry at the Camelot's registration desk brought the speedy appearance of the manager, Ernesto Palomeque. Once Doc identified himself, Palomeque provided a few details of the heroes' calamitous stay in the trucker's wing. Doc confirmed that the billings had appeared on Coyote's American Express account, which he had been monitoring for several days. Palomeque printed out a summary of the various charges and damages the two heroes had run up before they were evicted. Doc passed the invoices on to Dottie for payment. Palomeque demanded to know what Doc and the legal guardian planned to do about Wonder Woman's extortion campaign. She had shown up the day before to begin a protest demonstration in the parking lot beside the castle drawbridge. The news media had completely fallen for it, particularly the rabble-rousers at KIK-TV, who were taken in by her outrageous lies and obscenity-laden speeches. When she wasn't harassing customers in the parking lot, she was staging bizarre stunts in her costume to bring out more TV cameras. Through public legal aid, she had obtained a court order to prevent the motel from towing the vehicle away. He had finally obtained a counter-document the night before to have her removed from motel property.

"Where is she now?" Doc said.

"She's not at the truck? Try The Last Chance, the cheap casino next door."

"I'm really more interested in finding Mr. Coyote," Doc said.

"That maniac! We haven't seen him since his shenanigans in the fitness Center. He's lucky we didn't go to the police. Our masseuse is considering an assault charge."

Dottie McKechnie was writing furiously in her spiral notebook. "Was it sexual? Violent? Did he seem depressed? Show any signs of agitation?"

"He was in pretty bad shape the last I saw him. Nearly bit his tongue off. They skipped without paying the room charges, but I was happy enough to swallow the cost just to get rid of them. Then she turned up with this extortion racket. I won't pay her. She can rot out there in the parking lot!"

Ms. McKechnie explained that she would pay for all expenses incurred by Donald Coyote, but they did not cover Sandra's debts. She was concerned about his safety, and wanted to locate him as soon as possible. When Palomeque agreed to help, they booked in to the motel.

While Dottie settled in her room with her suitcases and files of papers, Doc went looking for Sandra at The Last Chance. He found her with surprising ease, the only gambler in the front section of the casino. She was working two entire rows of machines, staggering from one line back to the other with a pail of coins. As she reached a slot machine near Doc, he stepped in front of her.

"Evening, Sandra," he said.

Her jaw fell open as she gaped at him. "Dr. Pearce? What are you doing here?"

"What do you think?"

"Looking for Coyote?" She glanced behind the slot machines, as though the hero might be hiding. "I don't know where he is right now. His location might be confidential."

"Confidential?"

"Yeah – he's gone off on a personal 'vision quest.' Said he hadda sort himself out in the desert. Like this hermit he met in Utah. The only person who's supposed to know he's there is Princess Di."

"Sandra, I've come to find Donny. If you don't co-operate, I'm going to the police. I believe he's the registered owner of the truck you left parked across the street."

"Yeah, but that's cool. I have his written permission to drive it so I can take a message to Princess Di. I only stopped in Vegas to settle up our security contract at the Camelot, but the axle busted on the van. As soon as Palomeque pays up, I'm outta here. Hey, maybe you could take the message to her! Save me a trip."

"Sandra – where is Donny now?"

"Well, he's at a place called Coyote Lake. I dropped him off out in the Mojave, halfway to LA."

"You abandoned him in the desert?"

"Hey, I didn't dump him, if that's what you're saying. It was his idea! Don't blame me for his goofball tactics. Things were going great till he flipped out in the massage parlour. Well, I could see that coming. He was goin weird, eh? Then he decided to take a run around the desert to work out his problems. Like Hercules and Jesus. He gave me the Coyote Mobile in lieu of back pay."

"He's paying you a salary?"

"Not really a salary. Certain considerations."

"We can talk about that later. Right now I have to find him. Let's go before I lose my temper."

"Where we going?"

"Coyote Lake."

"How?"

"We can go in my rental car."

"I'll walk back to the motel with you. So how did you track us down?"

"Oh, Social Services got in touch with me. Margaret discovered he'd quit his job at Cansave Recycling, and got alarmed. The supervisor in Regina contacted Diana, and together they tracked me down."

"Tracked you down?"

"In Indian Head."

"What, Pine Lodge?"

"How'd you know that?"

"Been there, done that. The old detox centre, eh?"

"I promised the supervisor I'd find him and help bring him home."

"So – Social Services is paying the expenses for your trip."

"I'm covering my own expenses. They're paying Donny's though."

"They have to. He's a ward of Social Services."

"I called AmEx to get a computer printout of Coyote's charges along the way. This invoice was faxed two days ago from the Camelot Motel."

"Lemme just stop at the Coyote Mobile, and make sure my stuff is okay."

Wonder Woman unlocked the back door and unhooked the booby trap she had rigged up. "Nobody messes with this camper. Notice everybody gives me lots of space?"

"What message did Donny send to P.D.?" Doc asked.

"I got it here somewhere. He wrote it on a scrap of paper. I was going to get it typed, but didn't get around to it. Lot happenin in Vegas."

"I'm sure."

"It's here somewhere. I know he gave it to me! It was in the glove compartment. I musta put it in my pocket. Could be the other one. Anyway, there was two notes. One says I'm in charge of the money."

"Money?"

"Just a second, okay? One thing at a time! I had the freakin note right here."

But Wonder Woman could not find the paper in the Coyote Mobile, in any of the places she remembered it being, like the Lands End gym bag. Nor was it in her bra, or her shoes, or her underwear. She looked in every spare garbage bag, every pocket, before deciding the dumb bugger had forgotten to hand her the note before she left.

"He never gave it to me at all!" she declared. "The noodlebrain! And I need that note to get across the border!"

"What did it say?"

"Hang on. It's coming!" Sandra twisted her face, trying to force the words to pop up in her brain. "Son of a bitch!" she declared after a minute's futile effort.

"What?"

"Well, I forget the first words, but it went something, something, beautiful Princess, and then a bit about P.D. visiting him out in the desert, and ending, 'If you can't come, my dead corpse will understand.'"

"That doesn't sound good." Doc checked his watch. "Maybe we leave right now."

"No point even tryin. You'll never find him in the dark. It's black as Lucifer's ass out there. He'll be okay till the morning. He's used to campin out."

"It could be life and death."

"Well I can't stop ya goin. But you'll be better off after a night's rest and a fresh start in the morning."

Doc offered to pay for Sandra's accommodation in the motel, to keep her on task in the morning, but she flatly refused. "If I take a room from that Palomeque son of a bitch, it would wreck my whole plan. I'm not settling for a night's lousy accommodation. I'm in for bigger bucks! This is outright racism. I'll stay in the Coyote Mobile."

"Can I buy you breakfast?"

"Well, yeah, that's okay. The Camelot has a free all-you-can-eat continental breakfast, and if you take me in as your guest, we can both load up. And there's not a damn thing Palomeque can do about it! By the way, if you got money to invest, I'm running hot on the slots, and could get it back to you double in the morning."

"Here's twenty bucks. Just make sure you're ready to go first thing in the a.m."

While Wonder Woman dashed back to The Last Chance, Doc hurried back to the motel to report on her information. Dottie McKechnie was catching up on the accounting and record keeping. She had a notarized copy of the Canadian court order claiming Coyote's legal custody, and the group's entry visas from the US consulate in Calgary. The Social Services comptroller had issued her a credit card to cover expenses. Doc asked if that covered Sandra's expenses too. They were conferring over late night coffee in the Gwenivere Lounge, off the Camelot's Entrance Hall.

"For Sandra Dollar? Certainly not!" Dottie snapped.

"Won't she be going back with us?"

Dottie shook her head. "I can't responsible for her too. Let's focus on Donald."

"But we need her to find him. She's going with us to Coyote Lake at dawn."

"I predict she'll be more hindrance than help. Remember, he'll need gentle persuasion. We aren't allowed to use physical restraints. Will he be amenable?"

Doc told Dottie about Coyote's strange message to Princess Di.

"Hmm," Dottie said. "Intense post-adolescent sexual fantasy. Possibly confused with the masseuse. Could he be fixated on your daughter as an object of sexual desire?"

"It's possible," Doc said. "I've seen some indications. You don't think he could be – trouble that way, do you?"

"Hard to say. He seems to be control of the fantasies, for the most part. All our files indicate he's a well-socialized individual. It's important that he understand they are fantasies, and there is nothing wrong with that *per se*. I'd like to consult with Dr. Schwantzhacker in Regina when we go back. An excellent psychotherapist. My mentor. He practically wrote the book on post-modern adolescent fixations."

"Let's interview the masseuse. I got her card from the desk. We should hear what she's accusing him of."

"Good idea. Find out whether he exhibited any indicators of violence. Who initiated the encounter, etcetera."

Doc nodded with furrowed brow.

"Doc, would it be possible to bring Diana here – to persuade him to go back?"

"I can't ask that. She's right in the middle of defending her thesis."

"Is there anyone else he's fond of? Some 'damsel in distress'?"

"I can't think of anybody. Sandra, I suppose."

"It's just an idea. Donald finds it hard to resist the lure of a helpless female. His file shows a history of susceptibility. The right woman might persuade him to return to Canada voluntarily. And there's a nice Freudian logic about solving his problem with a fixation that caused it in the first place. We can channel his obsessions onto a path which allows him to objectify. Once he's home, we can place him in therapy and get the delusions under control. Dr. Schwantzhacker has resolved much more difficult cases."

Doc raised his eyebrows. "We could try Countess Dorothea of Micomicon."

"Countess who?"

"You don't remember her? She was in all the tabloids a couple of years ago, after the Princess of Wales burned up the front pages. A real soap opera. Donny was hooked on her tragic story – more sorrows than Princess Diana and Celine Dion put together. He was all set to fly to the Mediterranean and join her struggle."

"Well, I don't suppose she's available."

"No, but we could find a facsimile – say a theatre student – who could play the role of Countess Dorothea."

"That'll take too long. It's not a bad idea – but we have to act now."

"How about you, Dottie?"

"Me?" Her pale blue eyes dilated in panic.

"Sure – put on a bit of makeup, change your glasses. Discreet padding here and there. Voila – Countess Dorothea!"

"Oh, I don't think I could – deceive –"

"It's a long shot. But we have to take a chance. You'd make a great countess. There has to be a beauty salon in Camelot. They could fix your hair up in glamorous style, give it a few highlights. Are those your only glasses?"

"Well, I did bring a set of contacts, to wear on social occasions. And I packed an evening dress, in case there was some formal event where a pantsuit wasn't appropriate. But he'd recognize me! I interviewed him, when he left the Orange Home."

"With his eyes, I wouldn't worry about that. But you might try to alter your voice a bit. That's how he identifies people. We could test you on Sandra."

"Dr. Pearce, I hope this is not illegal."

"Well, I'm no lawyer or jurisdictional expert, but we're already on a different rule book here, so let's just do what has to be done. One step at a time. The first thing is to find Donny and make sure he's okay. Then we can bring him back to reality."

CHAPTER 23

The Micomicon Mission

The Lady of Shallott Beauty Salon was open 24/7, serving all-nighters from the blackjack tables who drifted in to restore their makeup. Then came the staff needing makeup for the morning shift at 6. When Doc arrived with Dottie McKechnie, the Maidens of Shallott declared their confidence in transforming her into a blonde cheesecake. "She's a perfect candidate for the make-over," the chief aesthetician gushed. "We'll enhance the hair, enlarge the flesh tones, and finish with some creative contouring of the eyes. Are these the clothes?"

"What do you think?" Dottie said.

"Give me your credit card number, and I'll order from Caesar's Salon."

"Go ahead," Doc said. He had time for a few hours' rest himself before rousing Sandra for breakfast.

Breakfast was served in The Dungeon, a grotto-like cell already jammed at 6:15 a.m. with motel guests groping for morning carbohydrates. Late arrivals were startled by the sight of Wonder Woman in the line in front of the coffee dispenser, cramming handfuls of donuts and pastries into her gym bag. Doc left her munching at the counter and went to retrieve Dottie, who was waiting in the beauty parlour. Her slight figure was now sheathed in a gown of silver lamé with a plunging neckline, and she wore chromium nail polish on her fingers and toes. Her bust had been enlarged dramatically. The Maidens of Shallott had also streaked her limp tresses, and pasted them into a structure resembling a stack of freshly blown straw. Her gleaming toenails peeked from the tips of a pair of high-heeled boa sandals. A pair of silver sunglasses reflected the stares of breakfasting tourists.

"Who the hell is she?" Sandra groaned. "Some movie star?"

"Close. She's actually the Countess of Micomicon, travelling incognito from Europe. I only met her last night. I think she can help us."

"Help? I don't think so."

"Well, you know how Donny can be influenced by some woman's sad tale."

"Tell me about it!"

"I'll introduce you. Countess!" Doc called. "This is a friend of Mr. Coyote, Sandra Dollar. Sandra, may I present Her Excellency, the Countess of Micomicon. She's come to North America to get help from Donny – that is, Captain Coyote."

"Right – and I'm the king of Turd Island. What help's Coyote to you, toots?"

"Delighted to meet you. Our problems in Micomicon are rather complex and difficult. I would prefer to explain them to Mr. Coyote."

"Just one question. Is this hero's work we're talkin about?"

"Yes. Yes, it is."

"Him and me are partners. You can ask me anything about security arrangements, money transport, detective work. We operate a rated service."

"Really? You have references?"

"Buckets of them. How's this? Ronald Reagan! Or the singing sensation Katie Kool?"

"I'd prefer to speak to Captain Coyote personally."

"He's out on a long hike right now, but I could take you to find him. She's not going out in the desert wearing that outfit, is she?"

"She can wait in the car. She'll be all right," Doc said, gesturing toward the motel driveway. His rented Buick was waiting at the entrance.

"I'm not leaving before I settle with Palomeque."

"We'll take care of it. Don't worry."

Doc led Sandra and the countess into the hot Nevada sun, which struck them like a blow from a fist. The countess eased herself carefully into the front seat, trying to keep her hair in place and her gown from wrinkling. Sandra crawled into the back, clutching the black gym bag.

The countess peered over her sunglasses at Wonder Woman's scruffy costume. "What's in the bag?" she asked. Doc was weaving through traffic, following signs to the interstate.

"Just food and stuff for the Captain. Personal stuff. Couple cans of beer."

"I hope there won't be any drinking on this trip."

"Hey, do I know you from somewhere? You look kinda familiar."

"Probably on television," Doc said. "The countess's story was in the news for years. She's a second cousin of the princess of Monaco, on her father's side."

"Yeah, I remember. You're the one who was boinking the chauffeur, right?"

"A fiction of the gutter press," the countess sniffed. "Ferdinand is a loyal employee, and already married."

"So how come you wear the mirror shades?"

"You can't imagine the hell my life has been, since the disasters in my country. Hordes of paparazzi chase me all over Europe."

"You better switch clothes. Nobody'd notice you then."

The countess looked pointedly at Wonder Woman's XXL T-shirt, which proclaimed BULLSHIT RULES!

"How far till we turn off?" Doc said. The Buick was already approaching the California border.

Wonder Woman leaned forward from the depths of the back seat. "Keep going till you pass Baker, and turn at the sign that says Fort Irwin."

"Tell me about this incident in the massage parlour. Palomeque said Donny was seriously injured."

"I was gonna tell you about that, but I was kinda worried you'd blame me."

"Well, what happened?"

"Had nothing to do with me. I took him to his room after he fell asleep in the massage parlour, and I guess he walked back in his sleep. Listen, if Coyote gets back safe to Moose Jaw, is there a reward for finding him?"

"There's no reward, but I'll compensate you for any help you can give us to get Donny home."

"See, the thing is I probably won't be going back to the Jaw. I'm planning to stay in Vegas and take up a career in crime prevention."

"Career changes are wonderful opportunities," Dottie observed.

"The massage parlour," Doc said.

"Yeah, so Coyote got attacked by a boyfriend of one of the massage girls."

"Whose idea was the massage?"

"He went on his own! Him and Mechelle's boyfriend had issues, and the guy practically chopped his tongue off! Ugly scene. Coyote thought Trevor was an alien acting for the hermit."

"Hermit?"

"The Hermit with the Hairy Ass. Now that guy was a total nutbar, Doc. Went off to live in the mountains like the Unibomber – excaping human society. He was in politics too, until Nixon got the can. That's what drove him over the edge. Coyote tried to help the poor bastard get a life, maybe recruit him for our mission. I told him the guy was a complete loser, but of course 'Captain Coyote' doesn't listen to a lowly female employee.

"Anyway, the hermit threw a hissy fit there in his camp, and we had to take him down or get the crap beat out of us. All we were doing was holding him, really – but he took a leap off the cliff. That kinda knocked Donny for a loop."

To explain how they'd met the hermit, she had to tell Doc about

Butch Cassidy, and about their incredible escape from the gang of convicts, and Coyote's defence of the wilderness in Yellowstone Park. By the time she got as far back in the story as the Yankee vigilantes and the battle of bikers at Wood Mountain, Doc lost patience with the absurd tale. Countess Dorothea of Micomicon took notes for a while, but worn out by her all-night session in the beauty salon, she soon fell asleep.

It was noon when they reached the road sign pointing to the Coyote Lake trail. Sandra found a few shreds of pepperoni wrapper abandoned nearby, then the bits of clothing Donny had thrown off: his shoes and Coyote jersey. There was no sign of his jockey shorts, so she figured he must have put them back on before starting his quest. It was a typical Coyote move, trying to protect his modesty. Doc picked up the clothes and put them in the car to take along. If Donny had nothing to cover himself against the brutal desert sun, he'd be fried to a crisp.

They set out across the sand flats, though the horizon kept disappearing into the shimmering haze of heat. The trail also petered out, but Doc kept pushing the Buick across the rocky sands. "We'll drive as far as the car will go," he said. "I've got a cell phone if we run into trouble." His map indicated that Coyote Lake was about ten miles off the road, but the car had plenty of gas, and the air conditioner kept the inside cool. Doc had packed a thermos jug of water and a bag of sandwiches.

At length they reached the great ridge of red sandstone that Coyote had crossed. It was a rocky barrier which had formed the shoreline of Coyote Lake in ages past, and was impossible to drive around. The three of them got out and climbed to the top of the ridge to look for the lake, though the countess was seriously hampered by her fancy costume.

They could see no water, just a vast crater of dusty clay, devoid of vegetation. Once an oasis of wildlife, Coyote Lake had become a waste of white alkali. Its last pools of water had evaporated decades ago, around the time the coyotes disappeared. Little dust devils of wind swirled fitfully across its dried-out gullies and arroyos, scorched of all but the most tenacious forms of life. From the height, Doc could make out a set of footprints emerging from the haze of salt and dust. The tracks wandered the grey surface, weaving this way and that, apparently heading for the stone tower in the centre of the ridge.

"That must be his tracks. They're heading for that pile of stone."

They scrambled toward the peak of the ridge, but found no sign of him. When they descended on the north side of the tower, they found Coyote slumped in a thin patch of shadow against the rock face. He looked as though he'd been skinned and flayed, his back and shoulders blistered by the cruel sun. He was curled beneath the scant shade of The Flash's helmet.

Doc reached him first. "Donny! Are you okay? Donny!"

"Jeeze, he even looks like that crazy hermit! How is he?"

"Alive – barely conscious. Here, Don, here's some water." Doc pulled the water bottle out of his shoulder bag and tilted it over his friend's cracked lips.

Captain Coyote's eyes slowly opened, squinting at the moving shadows in front of him. They had to be the angels Coyotl had promised. One wore a white shirt and canvas Tilley hat like Doc's. Another was wearing a clown outfit, and the third angel was a famous movie star he had seen somewhere. She was carrying a shopping bag with his clothes in it.

"How are you, Don?" Doc said, lifting The Flash's helmet. The angel gently pulled the Phoenix Coyote shirt over his neck and drew his arms into the sleeves. Doc covered Coyote's head with his own hat, the Tilley.

"Doc...!"

"Yeah, it's me."

"Did Princess Di come?"

"She couldn't make this trip, Don. She sends her regards."

"I'll wait for her here."

"She's very concerned about you, Don. We all are. Come on, let's move out of the sun."

"Hey, Captain. How's it hangin?"

"Wonder Woman?"

"Yours truly. Doc and me came to see how you're makin out."

"Did you deliver the message to P.D.?"

They all looked at Wonder Woman, who looked blank. Doc said, "P.D. wants you to come to Moose Jaw with this friend of hers. She needs help."

"P.D. needs help?"

"Her friend does. This lady here. She came from Micomicon to ask for your personal assistance. Countess Dorothea."

Coyote's broiled face turned to the third angel standing before him like a mirage – a beautiful countess in a silver dress that dazzled in the powerful Mojave sunlight. Was she the messenger sent to answer his prayers? As the angel tottered in her high sandals, he turned onto his knees and tried to bow before her.

"Countess Dorothea of Micomicon? You came to see me?"

Dorothea gestured for him to stand, but he couldn't, so she bent down and took his ravaged face in her cool fingers. "You poor man. Come to the car. We have to get you back to Las Vegas."

"You came from Micomicon?"

"Captain Coyote is a legend in my country. Along the entire Riviera."

"What do people there say about Captain Coyote?"

"They say you are a defender of the weak, a patron saint of abused children, a staunch protector of Mother Environment and all her creatures. The Royal House of Micomicon has delegated me to request your help. We are trying to preserve our culture and estate against a multinational corporation, a cartel controlled by my father's old enemy. When I tried to defend our property, they attacked me in the press."

"Can you speak up, countess? I can't hear so good."

"Come and join our cause! The oppressed people of Micomicon are crying for help in their struggle for justice, and they won't accept no for an answer."

"I'll go – but first I have to see Princess Di."

"That's a good idea. Of course, she approved this mission."

"What do you say, Doc?"

"The countess is right. First we have to get out of the sun. Then drive you to a clinic and get a medical check-up. You'll need time to recover."

"I could do that in Moose Jaw."

"We'll leave as soon as you can travel. Come on – there's more water and sandwiches in the car. You must be starving. We'll head back to the Camelot Motel."

"The Camelot!" Coyote groaned. "I can't go there!"

"We have to go there!" Sandra insisted. "I'm not leaving till I collect from that bastard Palomeque. He owes us big-time!"

"That's not relevant now," Doc said. "We've already booked the rooms. The government is taking care of it, so we might as well. It's comfortable, and less expensive than downtown."

Carrying the sun-baked hero between them, Doc and Wonder Woman struggled down the rocky outcropping to the waiting Buick. By the time they reached the car, Coyote was fading from heat stroke, his eyeballs turned up in his head. He sank with a groan into the back seat. The countess climbed in to comfort and revive the stricken hero. Doc turned the car around and aimed it back toward Las Vegas.

Along the way, Wonder Woman began thinking about the proposed trip to Micomicon, which could include staying in a ritzy hotel on the Riviera. She turned to the countess. "This Momicon gig will be all expenses paid, right?"

"We can discuss all that later," the countess said, glancing nervously at Doc.

"And what's the drill at Momicon customs? Do the border cops hassle people over their juvenile record and such?"

"What sort of juvenile record?"

"Aaa – minor stuff. A few B and Es. Impaired driving. Assault. Petty stuff."

"Well, that could be a problem – you'd have to apply for a visa."

"Let's get to Moose Jaw first," Coyote said. "Are we going in this car?"

"I think we'll be flying," Doc said. "I have to book your airline tickets."

"Couldn't we fix up the Coyote Mobile? There's room for all of us."

"I don't know. That Coyote Mobile's in pretty rough shape." Doc remembered the heap of wreckage on the Camelot parking lot. "It's headed for the junk yard, I'm afraid. It would take a week to repair – if we even found a shop that would tow it in."

"We have to fix her!" Coyote cried. "That vehicle is part of me! I've got to take her home to Moose Jaw!"

"Well, we could go to a garage for an estimate, I guess."

"The problem," Countess Dorothea pointed out, "is that we have to get to Moose Jaw right away. There's no time for sentimental attachments. We have to be practical."

"Well, hang on," Doc said. "If it was running and we took turns driving, we could be there almost as fast as by plane. I'll get it checked out. First, we need to make a medical appointment for Donny. He is seriously dehydrated."

Arriving back at the Camelot Motel, they took Coyote to Doc's room until the doctor could be summoned. Doc got the name of a doctor from the manager, and reserved two additional rooms in the main tower. Doctor Aziz Haq showed up and gave the hero a complete physical. Except for an anti-inflammatory prescription for his swollen tongue, sunburn cream, and a steady diet of fluids, Coyote was pronounced in better shape than he looked. He could travel in three days. Dr. Haq said the group might as well explore the delights of Las Vegas in the meantime.

"By the way," Doc said to the others. "The management has agreed to give Sandra a room on one condition. She has to drop her protest."

The countess looked sour, but Sandra said, "Fine by me. Let bygones be bygones."

"Don, by way of apology for all the aggravation, the Camelot is going to provide you a luxury room – actually a pair of rooms – called the Lancelot Suite. Normally reserved for VIP guests. Complete entertainment console. It'll be a good place to get some well-deserved rest. Okay, Don?"

"Cool. Tonight we could hear the countess's story."

Doc glanced at the countess, who shook her head. "Tomorrow," Doc said. "I'll organize everything tomorrow. First thing in the morning, I'll see about the repairs, and cancel the airline tickets. The rest of you can relax by the swimming pool. Let's do our planning tomorrow."

CHAPTER 24

The Countess Drops A Veil

The next morning, the Canadian expatriates relaxed in the sun by the Pool of Excalibur, located on the roof of the Camelot Lounge. The concrete tank had been decorated to look like a lakeside glen in Sherwood Forest, with a stand of artificial oak trees, and stone edges around its rim. Coyote and the countess sat at an umbrella-shaded table while Sandra stretched out on the Astroturf by the pool, sucking on her first beer of the day. Doctor Haq was due at 2 p.m. for another examination of Coyote's tongue.

Doc had left early to cancel the airline tickets. He promised to be back at eleven, so they all watched the hours pass on the antique clock mounted on the castle tower. Every fifteen minutes, a quartet of medieval figures popped out of door on the clock and paraded onto the seventh floor platform. They turned in a circle, and every quarter hour one of them would strike a bell on the clock face: the knight in armour, the lady, the king, or the clown. When Doc got back at noon, the clown gonged the bell twelve times.

"Exquisite," the countess sighed.

"Awesome," Sandra belched, pulling a fresh can of beer from a waiter's hand. She took a long guzzle, enjoying her status as a paying guest.

The green Astroturf around the pool was dressed here and there with beds of plastic flowers and fibreglass shrubs. Medieval waiters in leather jerkins and shorts dashed among the bushes, bearing trays of drinks and sandwiches to Camelot's guests. A woman's plastic arm rose from the depths of the pool every ten minutes, dripping seaweed and wielding a gigantic sword. The arm belonged to the Lady of the Lake, and fountains of water spouted around it while the theme from Camelot played on the loudspeakers.

"Could we hear about the Micomicon mission now?" Coyote asked.

Countess Dorothea settled her sunglasses and began. "My father, the Count of Micomicon, is remembered in our tiny state for his generosity and wisdom, though the French newspapers reviled him as a royalist charlatan. He was gifted with prophetic ability, and predicted natural disasters. He became famous for forecasting election results, and the future winners of the Micomicon Grand Prix."

"Cool!" Wonder Woman said. "Can we meet him when we go?"

"Unfortunately, His Excellency my father passed away some time ago. His gift of prophecy brought him no fortune or pleasure. In fact, it was a curse. Six months before I was born, he had a premonition that my mother the Countess Sybille would die in childbirth. Like his other prophecies, this too came to pass. I was her only child, the child who killed her. My father never remarried."

Tears of pity welled in Coyote's eyes, and even Doc seemed moved by the tale.

"I had a fortunate childhood – no luxury was too great for him – but I watched his soul wither away. He became obsessed with death, my mother's death, his own death, and worried that I would be left a helpless orphan. He devoted his life to building my inheritance."

"How much would that be?" Sandra asked.

"Quite a lot. He became terribly anti-social. By the time I was an adolescent, he had withdrawn to a tiny office in the attic, refusing to see anyone but his accountant and myself. One day, alarming news arrived from his lawyers in Paris – news he had not prophesied. A

Belgian corporation was claiming the entire estate of Micomicon, through a disputed bank mortgage taken out by my cousin Julian in the 1970s. Julian was on the board of a multinational conglomerate called Panda Filando, based in Brussels. This company plotted to seize my family's estate, to build a cement factory over the limestone catacombs where our ancestors have been buried for over four centuries."

"Bastards!" Coyote muttered, his fingers groping for the heft of a good cudgel.

"The legal battle against Panda Filando consumed all our assets. They were financed by the Bank of Europe, whose reserves went even deeper than Julian's greed. At one point, they offered Father a lifetime management position, if he agreed to surrender the property. He threw the offer back in their teeth. They proposed to establish an international chair at Sorbonne in his name, but he refused all such bribes, and maintained his struggle to the death against the Panda Filando."

"Good for him," Coyote declared.

"Unfortunately, Father's nerves were affected by the relentless struggle, and he died tragically last year of a self-inflicted gunshot wound, as you may have read in the press. He left me the deed to the estate, a deed signed by the King of France in 1562, with instructions to seek help in North America. He said to look for a hero to take up the Micomicon cause – one Donald Coyote."

"Coyote!" Sandra exclaimed. "It's him!"

"Undoubtedly. I found Mr. Coyote's résumé on the internet, on a Local Heroes page of a website set up by the city of Moose Jaw. So I contacted Princess Diana and Doc, who agreed to bring me along."

"Princess Di recommended me?"

"She did. So did the mayor, and the chamber of commerce. They would all be delighted if you returned home, even for a few days, before going to Micomicon."

"Let's take it one step at a time," Doc cautioned.

"Only such a hero could restore the Micomicon estates."

"And how much do we get paid?" Wonder Woman asked. "I usually negotiate our contracts."

"Well – if the captain were successful, there would be a substantial reward – and perhaps my hand in marriage."

"Yeah? That's not too shabby, either, Coyote. Better get that written down. Draw up a real marriage contract."

"I don't think I could agree," Coyote said. "I'm already committed to someone else."

Wonder Woman stared at him in shock. Coyote had refused the hand of this bubble-brain and given up his best chance of becoming a millionaire! Would he turn the countess down and abandon Wonder Woman to a life of poverty in the streets of North Las Vegas? She swelled to her full dwarfish height.

"It's a deal!" she declared, smacking Coyote across the head. "Snap out of it, Coyote! Let's go kick the shit out of this Panda outfit, run them out of business, and save the countess's estate. This is the best deal we been offered so far, a high-class appointment. Play your cards right, and you could be the next King of Micomicon!"

"I don't mind the work," Coyote said. "But I'm not available to get married."

Sandra shoved him aside and rasped to the countess, "Don't worry, I'll talk sense into him. He just needs to see the good points. Give us a minute.

"Are you nuts?" she hissed, pulling Coyote to the side of the lake. "You'd kick a billion dollars out of bed? You will never get a deal like this again! What are you thinking about? This one's better-looking than Princess Di!"

"Hey!"

"Okay, she's not great, but she's dying to get stuffed. Sign the contract, and we'll go kick some Mocomian butt. If they make you King, the bank vaults will be yours. We'll be rich as movie stars! When it comes to money, P.D.'s not in the same league."

"Will you shut up about Princess Di?" Coyote was so annoyed he almost pushed Wonder Woman into the waterfall. "If I help the countess, it's only because she's P.D.'s friend!"

"Okay, okay. It's your decision. Don't shoot the messenger. I'm just saying a princess in the hand is worth a dozen in the bushes. You can keep Princess Di in reserve, like Charles did. But now you gotta be a man and take the countess riding on your baloney pony. She's practically begging you! This is a gift from heaven!"

"Wonder Woman, did you take my message to Princess Di or not?"

"Well, not directly, no."

"But you said she sent a message!"

"Kind of. Doc brung it. I just exaggerated, is all. Jeeze I hate it when you accuse me of lyin!"

"You never even spoke to her? "

"Well, I lost the letter before I hit Vegas. Then one thing happened after another.... Let's just go schmooze the countess, okay? I don't mind suckin up, if it gets you a job. This could be worth mucho buckos, Donny Boy."

They went back to the patio table, where Doc and the countess were going over the travel plans. Sandra opened another can of beer and plunked herself on the chair beside the countess. "Okay, I think we're close to a deal. One more question. Before we agree to go to Momicon, we'd need some kind of retainer, paid in advance."

The countess looked up. "I wasn't really planning to take you along, Sandra."

"Hey, Captain Coyote and me are a team."

"I just don't think that would be possible."

"Why not? I can bash heads as good as he can. Or is it because I'm a woman?"

"No, no – it's just that – you find it hard to take direction."

"Hey, countess! I know which side of my bread's buttered! You're the boss!" To demonstrate her subservience, Sandra knelt before the countess's deck chair. She reached to kiss her hand from a kneeling position, but her feet slipped on the artificial turf, and she shot over the edge into the Pool of Excalibur. She bobbed up for air, coughing and spewing water, still clutching her Budweiser.

"Then it's settled?" she sputtered. "We go as a team?"

"You're not going. That's all there is to it. I can only take Donald."

Outraged by the countess's rude rejection, Wonder Woman stormed back to her room, dripping wet. The countess escorted Coyote back to his room for the doctor's appointment, while Doc drove out to the garage where he had towed the Coyote Mobile. They reported that even with a new engine, its future was doubtful. The transmission was leaking oil, the ball joints were shot, and the three remaining tires were road hazards. Four thousand dollars would be needed for bodywork, not counting the paint job. They said Doc could buy a good used RV for less cost than repairing the Coyote Mobile.

That evening, Doc shared his disappointing news with the countess in her room. He sighed. "So, we may have to fly back after all."

Dottie had an idea, though. "Let me call Regina, and see if there's another alternative. Maybe we could lease a Coyote Mobile."

"That's not bad. If we found something so cool he couldn't turn it down, he might give up his attachment. Could be good for his self-esteem."

"That's true. It might be better than a trip to Europe. I'm ready to abandon the whole Micomicon business. It's getting out of hand. Taking Sandra along?"

"Don't worry, you can slip back to your old identity as soon as we're back on Canadian soil. You're doing a wonderful job."

"It's strange. I'm starting to feel good in this outfit."

"You do look sexy."

"You find this – attractive?"

"Coyote is certainly charmed."

"He's so gullible. People must take advantage of the poor guy all the time."

"Donny Coyote can be streetwise when he has to be. Not a lot of BS gets past his instincts. But certain stories – beautiful damsels in distress for example – do turn him into a veritable fool."

"He is a character," she agreed. "You couldn't invent a Donny Coyote."

"It's the old cliché – truth is stranger than fiction."

"Doc, are you concerned about Donald's infatuation with your daughter?"

"It's not bad now. P.D. used to tease him something terrible when she was young. I worried about his interest then, that he might end up doing something – unfortunate. Perhaps it was a factor in his breakdown. Somehow Diana got mixed up in the masseuse incident."

"He clearly suffers from erotomania. He seems normal otherwise."

"Did you see the newspaper article about him this spring?"

"Yes. He sounded like he knew exactly what he was saying. Very articulate, even eloquent."

They agreed that Dottie would continue in the role of Countess Dorothea, until they got on the road. Her makeup was high maintenance, but an effective disguise. It would be at least three days before they could leave, so they decided to relax and take in some Las Vegas shows. They could explore the wonders of the Cosmotower, or go to the *Elvis Live!* hologram performance. Dottie thought she'd enjoy a good show.

Meanwhile, enraged at being kicked out of the Micomicon mission, Sandra spent the evening in the Last Chance Casino, brooding over her injustice. She had money in the gym bag, but there would have been more if Doc hadn't wrecked her plan for revenge on Palomeque. The motel had been on the edge of a cash settlement in five digits, before Coyote's protectors arrived and interfered.

When the bartender at the Last Chance cut Wonder Woman off, she returned to the Camelot Motel in an even fouler mood than she'd left. She had spent more of the hermit's money, and wandered drunkenly down the corridors, looking for the countess's room, banging on doors and rousing other guests. At Room 602, her strategy paid off.

Countess Dorothea answered, straightening her wig and pulling up her dress. Wonder Woman was stunned. It was old Dottie McKechnie, her enemy from Social Services!

"Yes?" she said, her smeared lipstick spreading in a smile.

Wonder Woman caught a glimpse of Doc in the room behind her, doing up his tie and jacket as he disappeared into the bathroom. Even blind drunk, she recognized a game of patty cake going on when she saw one.

"Hey! Whass happenin here? You guys havin a party?"

"We were discussing the travel plans back to Canada. What is it?"

"Ran outta money. Time to pay up!"

The gist of her drunken rant was that she wanted compensation from Doc for the money Palomeque owed on the security contract, because Doc had scuppered her negotiations. "I hafta get paid. That shoulda bin part of the deal!"

"We agreed to pay Donald's room expenses only. You weren't even registered!"

"No, but it was me who got the deal on the room with Palomeque! Not Coyote. If I don't get paid, I'm not leaving Las Vegas."

"That's fine with me!" the countess snapped. "I'm not giving you one more cent." She pushed Wonder Woman out the door. "Good night!"

Sandra staggered down the hall to Coyote's room and banged her fist on his door until it opened. Coyote stood blinking in the light.

"Sorry a bother you, Captain old buddy, but – I gossum heavy news."

"Let's talk tomorrow. You're awful drunk."

"Don't gimme that moral superior bullshit! Get this – there's no Riviera!"

"What?"

"'S a trick. The countess – the whole country of Micromiton's a crock of shit!"

"Don't talk crazy."

"I can prove it. It's a lousy con game to ship you back to Moose Jaw and have you committed to the loony bin. You know who the Countess is? A shrink!"

"A psychologist?"

"Worse! One of the bosses, a supervisor. A welfare cop. I ran into her years ago! Ditsy McKechnie."

"Jeeze, I knew she sounded familiar! That's her! But what's Doc doing with –?"

"Good question. I dunno why he's here, unless it's keepin you away from his daughter, ever since you got your shorts in a twist. After you lost it in the massage parlour, Palomeque obviously called them to hook you back to Moose Jaw. The whole Momicant scheme was a hoax – and you fell for it like a ton of bricks! What a dodo! You're such a sucker for women, that McKechnie put on a dolly costume and – bingo."

"How do you know this?"

"Aaa, I smelled a rat all along. Reckanized her right off the bat, just went along with the gag to see what they were up to. I was worried, okay? I thought you were gonna barbycue yourself out at Coyote Lake!"

"Doc wouldn't go along with this."

"They both made it up! Her and Doc. She's the one pulling the strings, though. So I been gathering evidence as soon as I saw they had you completely foxed! The bastards can't cut me out of the action! I got rights too!"

"Don't start badmouthing Doc, okay? It was me who decided to end my vision quest, not Doc. Now if you don't mind – I need to rest."

"I'm giving you the straight goods. They're not draggin me back to Canada."

"You don't have to go. But I want to. And Doc's fixing the Coyote Mobile."

"Okay, they got you snookered. But it took me thirty fuckin years to make it across that border, and now that I'm finally in the land of the free, I'm not going back without a fight! Maybe the streets aren't paved with gold, but at least they're paved!"

"But how will you live?

"Don't worry, I'll collect from Palomeque."

"Is the hermit's money gone?"

Wonder Woman waved vaguely toward her room. "I got it put away."

"I can't leave you here with all that money. You'd self-destruct in no time. You have to think about your long-term future."

"What bullshit! It's you that's in denial, Coyote! They confiscate our wheels, deny our rightful demands to full employment, practically imprison us, because some shrink wants you to get psychiatric treatment in Saskatchewan."

Coyote sighed. "Also I want to see Princess Di."

"You are a certifiable loony-tunes! I work like a maniac to expose their rotten scheme, and you still believe them!"

"Well – lots of things people say aren't true, and I still believe in them. Like Santa Claus. Doc has lots of weird theories I don't believe in, but I still like to hear him talk about them. He can keep all kinds of different worlds in his head. He can tell you stuff about ancient Greece and Mongolia, or how music works or why people worship numbers. I get pictures of them in my head – then I'm in Doc's world too.

"That was why I had to go to Coyote Lake. To find my own world. We live in other people's worlds too much. I'm trying to find mine."

"I'm not interested in your crackpot theories about other worlds. All that illusion and reality crapola. My philosophy is, take what you see here and now. Grab the bottle and suck it dry. Survival of the fastest. You think too much, y'know? Lookit all the trouble we got into because you started thinking about stuff. Remember the Russian Drones? And you thought this motel was a governor's mansion!"

"You said the Camelot wasn't a castle."

"It's not a castle, it's a fucking motel!"

"But it's both at the same time! I mean, it's a fake castle but it's as real as an old one in England. And if finding a castle in Vegas isn't a miracle, what is? It's just another world. Everything that happens has its own rules, which only seem weird to us because we're not totally in that world yet. That's how I see it."

"Some shithouse philosopher you are! You never used to spout this kinda crap in Moose Jaw. The bullshit here is so thick it's plugged up your brain. Maybe if you hung out in the 'other world' long enough, you'd be Albert Einstein!"

"I guess I might. Anyway, everybody's got their own private little world. Some are happier than others, that's all."

"So are you gonna stay in Las Vegas, or go back with those turkeys?"

"I agreed to meet the countess for breakfast. I'll ask her what's going on."

"To hell with you, then. I give up. You're on your own!"

CHAPTER 25

An Adventure in Camelot

Countess Dorothea appeared at the Nights of the Round Table Café for breakfast in a new travelling suit, a trim combination of teal blue. She was startled to see Coyote standing at attention by one of the stone pillars at the entrance. The Flash's helmet was perched on his head, and he proudly wielded a mop handle for a cudgel. He was decked out in as much Captain Coyote regalia as he could cobble together that morning. Around his shoulders flowed a white cape of motel towel, and over his jeans he wore a pair of white jockey underwear Doc had bought at the shopping mall. The serving wenches of the café looked a little shocked by Captain Coyote's appearance, and scurried about with many sidelong glances, but he was a hit with the morning breakfast crowd. A pair of Japanese tourists took him for a castle guard, and asked him to pose beside them for photographs.

He saluted grandly as the countess arrived. "Good morning, Countess. Captain Coyote at your service!"

After Sandra's drunken intrusion during the night, Dorothea was prepared for trouble, but not this. She observed Captain Coyote's costume from head to foot, and shook her head dubiously. "What's going on, Donald? Why are you wearing that getup?"

"This is my uniform for the Micomicon mission."

"Well, you can't go dressed like that!"

"No? Then I guess the deal is off – Countess Dottie!"

"Pardon me?"

"Wonder Woman told me who you are. That Micomicon story was just a trick to send me back to Moose Jaw. You're a government shrink."

"Donald! You mustn't believe what that woman says!"

"I remember your voice! You phoned me when I was at the Hustons."

"Well, you've got a remarkable memory, Donald. All right – I'm Dottie McKechnie."

A crowd of Asian tourists had gathered at the café entrance, drawn by the noisy argument, perhaps hoping to see a fight. They began digging cameras and autograph books from their backpacks, and a line formed to take the mascot's picture.

Dottie tried to collect her wits. "Let's go and sit down for a coffee," she said. "Is Sandra coming down for breakfast?"

Coyote shrugged. "She was drunk as a skunk last night. Hard to tell where she ended up."

As the serving wench brought their coffee, Dottie asked Coyote to remove his helmet, but he sullenly refused.

"I'm sorry about the deception, Donald," she began hesitantly. "But we – Doc and I – thought your fantasies were the best way to get you home and into a treatment program. We could have just grabbed you with a custodial order and dragged you home. But we thought a heroic mission might be the best way to get you back."

"What sort of treatment program?"

"Well – I've made an appointment for you with Dr. Erhardt Schwantzhacker. For reality therapy. To resolve your – imaginary adventures."

"You think my adventures were imaginary?"

"Well – partly, perhaps. They are an exaggerated form of reality. You are also manifesting a tendency to erotomania. You don't know what that means of course, but – love, well, takes many forms –"

"I don't want to know what it means. I don't believe you."

"I am truly sorry, Donald."

"I fell for your lies. But not any more. I'm not going to Micomicon – or Moose Jaw either."

"Let's not be hasty, Donald. Doc is fixing up a new Coyote Mobile so we can travel back together."

"New –?"

Dottie regarded him steadily. "State of the art emergency vehicle." She let that sink in for a few seconds and continued, "No more pretending, I promise. But you yourself prefer fantasies over reality – and we thought it was a way of talking your language. Anyway, we'll end the charade – if you're ready to live in the real world, and not the world of comic books. Believe me, Donald, we did this for your sake."

"Did Princess Di agree to this?"

"I don't see what difference that makes. I played the role of the Countess to get access to your traumatized psyche. You could have died out there in the desert, Donald! If my role-playing helped get you back together with Doc, surely it was worth it." She reached out a soothing hand and touched his arm. "I learned a lot, too."

"You learned I'd believe *anything*, is that it?"

"No. I learned about you. As the countess, I could get close to you and see you for the first time. As Dottie McKechnie, I now understand why Doc wants you to live a life of independence. That you can be trusted to make your own decisions. As a civil servant, I am your official guardian, and now I can be a much better advocate for you. That's my responsibility. Doc and I will help you together. Coming to Las Vegas has opened my eyes. A more compassionate Dottie McKechnie has emerged from her cocoon. Thanks to you and Doctor Pearce I've become a better person."

"Yeah?"

"I don't even want to go back to wearing my old outfit. So you see, you've helped me too. I'll be taking a whole new personality back to Saskatchewan."

"So you might join our campaign for human justice?"

"One thing at a time. For now, I want to enjoy just *being*."

"In Las Vegas?"

"Anywhere. It's like entering a new dimension, where doing the right thing counts. I look forward to going back to Moose Jaw, and working with you to help other special needs adults in the community."

"Then don't go wrecking my identity! I want to be Captain Coyote."

"What do you mean?"

"Well – after all these disasters, I finally realized I can't change everything in the world. In the States, there's literally millions of victims and criminals and environmental catastrophes, and I don't have time to fix them all. So instead of trying to do what I can't, I'll just try to set an example. One thing I thought of is to go around giving medals to people who act heroically and unselfishly. I'm going to design a brand new medal. The Coyote Medal of Courage."

"That's a good idea, Donald! A living role model."

"If you committed to our mission, you could get one."

"I will commit, speaking for our department. This would be an excellent application of our self-help program, which prepares adults with special needs to become good citizens. I could probably get you an office...."

"Jeeze, that'd be neat! Okay, let me think about it. I'll discuss it with Sandra."

Doc rushed into the café at that moment, back from the garage on Red Canyon Road. It would be two days before the new Coyote Mobile was roadworthy. However, Dottie had to inform him that Sandra had exposed their ruse.

"Oh. Well, I'm sorry, Don, but –"

"It's okay. She explained. I'm still going home."

"Ah, good. It'll take you a while to bounce back. And of course, we can rest up here for a couple days. What about Sandra?"

"We have to get her out of here for her own good," Coyote said. "Her habits are completely falling apart."

"The real problem will be to find her. She could be in any of a thousand bars."

"Oh, she'll be in the neighbourhood," Doc said. "I could track her down and try to talk some sense into her."

Ten minutes after Doc went looking for Sandra, a commotion broke out in the lobby outside the entrance to the Nights of the Round Table. A Chinese man came dashing frantically across the drawbridge, shoulder bags and cameras flapping around his neck. He was being chased, perhaps attacked, by a tiny woman in a bright yellow ski jacket. She shrieked at him in Chinese as she yanked on his bags and the hem of his jacket. When she finally stopped him, she proceeded to slap and kick him until he ran into the Camelot mall, dashing from one shop door to another, seeking protection.

Instinctively, Captain Coyote rose to intervene. Trapped between the Nights Of The Round Table Café and Sir Galahad's Souvenir Shoppe, the man looked frantic and confused. He was about fifty, and the woman looked younger but could have been any age – his daughter or his wife, perhaps a girlfriend. Her fury indicated some kind of domestic relationship. After several minutes of verbal abuse, the man broke free and ran toward Coyote.

"You have room?" he demanded.

"You mean a hotel room?"

The Chinese man nodded. "We need big room. You got big room?"

"The registration desk is down that way," Dottie pointed out. "They can help you."

"No speak English! You got room?"

"*Front desk!*" Dottie repeated. "That way! Donald, could you show these people to the front desk?"

Coyote was glad to help, for they were obviously visitors from a foreign country – probably refugees from Communist oppression seeking freedom in the USA. The desk clerk determined that they were from Hong Kong, though the wife had a passport from mainland China. They were on their honeymoon. The man was barely understandable, and she did not speak a word of English.

Coyote helped him explain his story to the desk clerk. It seemed that their travel agent in Hong Kong had booked them into a North Las Vegas hotel that turned out to be a drug-dealers' front. They had been deposited there by taxi from the airport, and barely escaped with their lives. Despite their jet lag and exhaustion, they had leaped onto a shuttle bus with their suitcases and ridden till it stopped in front of the Camelot Motel. Coyote remembered what it was like pinballing through the city's frantic streets the night of the Sinatra Memorial, and felt sorry for them. The little Chinese bride's frantic hysteria was subsiding. She sat down on the floor and fell asleep, bundled in a yellow ski jacket despite the oppressive heat.

Mr. Palomeque arrived at the desk and informed them the Camelot Motel was fully booked. Not a room was to be found.

"Even in the trucker's wing?" Coyote asked with a raised eyebrow.

"That's right. Even in the trucker's wing."

Coyote thought for a moment. He formed a plan to save the Chinese honeymoon.

"Look," he said to Palomeque. "I'm staying in the Lancelot Suite, two monster rooms on the sixth floor. These people can bunk in with me, okay? They can have the king-size bed, and I'll sleep on the pull-out sofa in the living room."

The manager raised his own eyebrow. Such an arrangement was unusual, but possible. The Hong Kong tourist was overwhelmed by Coyote's generous offer to give up his own privacy.

"It's no big deal," Coyote insisted. "The room is bigger than I need. It's paid for. But only for two more nights. You'll have to find another place after that."

The man and his bride knelt on the floor, hugging Coyote's knees and weeping.

"You get reward for this," the man said. "My father rich Hong Kong guy. Lee Family. My father own Peninsula Hotel. Lee family hotel. My name Lee Jun. This my wife Bing Bing."

"Hello, Bing Bing. Pleased to meet you."

She erupted in a fury. "No Bing Bing!" She scowled at the hero. "I
Rosalind!"

"Sorry," Coyote said. He went with Lee Jun to help move their bags
from the sidewalk up to the sixth floor.

Lee Jun was so grateful for Coyote's generosity that he insisted on
treating him and his friends to a medieval banquet that evening in the
Jousting Hall. The group agreed to meet at six o'clock by its stone-pil-
lared entrance. Doc had located Wonder Woman sleeping in one of the
women's toilets at the Last Chance, and persuaded her to join the
group for dinner.

They were all ushered to the VIP ringside table Lee Jun had
reserved. The table overlooked a jousting arena the size of a football
field, filled with two feet of sand. The Master of the Tournament came
out wearing a felt hat and a pair of bloomers and said they were about
to witness the spectacular Tournament of Kings. The Kings of France,
England, Spain, and Italy were at that moment preparing to do battle
for the Holy Grail, a monstrous platinum mug being lowered on gold
chains from the ceiling. As the guests sat, a throng of serving wenches
brought them bowls of barley soup and mugs of Nut Brown Ale, plus a
roasted Cornish game hen each.

Hundreds of spectators chewed on the tiny drumsticks as the
crowned heads of Europe, dressed in their national colours, came
charging out on horses from the four corners of the arena. The audi-
torium was divided into colour-coded cheering sections. They urged
their monarchs on by screaming and waving their drumsticks in the
air while the kings clobbered each other off their horses with long
poles. It was better than the Super Bowl. On foot, the kings pounded
each other with maces and cudgels and broadswords, while the spectators cheered and licked crumbs off their fingers. There were special
effects like fireworks and rock music, even a big dragon at the end
that charged into the arena and breathed fire at the audience. When
the smoke had rolled away and the dust settled, the King of Spain
went to the centre of the ring and kissed the holy grail. His wounded
enemies were carried off to die in a chamber in the castle. The spot-

light came back on the Master of the Tournament with his cordless microphone.

"Ladies and gentlemen, we know you enjoyed tonight's spectacle of entertainment. Now sit back and relax with drinks and desserts, which the serving wenches are bringing out. I would like to take this moment to introduce a Good Samaritan who appeared in the hotel today. Mr. Lee Jun and his wife Rosalind arrived on their honeymoon from Hong Kong, and in an emergency situation, ended up at the Camelot Motel. Alas, there was no vacancy, but a guest staying in our luxurious Lancelot Suite immediately offered to share his room with them! Isn't that wonderful? Please put your hands together to honour our generous benefactor – Captain Donald Coyote."

The spotlight suddenly swooped at Coyote, who was stunned by the unexpected introduction. The crowd applauded wildly as he stood up.

"You big hero," Lee Jun burbled at him. "You talk." He took the microphone from the tournament MC and handed it to the bashful Captain Coyote.

"What should I say?"

"Tell them – who you are. Why you great hero."

"Go ahead, Donny – now's your chance."

"Well, I guess this is really a kinda farewell speech to the USA. I came down here to be a superhero, but it turned out to be a tough assignment. Anyway, I'm going back to be a community hero, an ordinary hero. It's weird being a hero. It's kinda dangerous, and full of all kinds of PR challenges. Most people have no idea how hard a hero has to work. But since I came to Las Vegas, I'm starting to see how the world goes, and maybe why the public has lost faith in its heroes."

Coyote felt a little shy speaking his thoughts in public, but he gradually warmed to the audience. The hall was paying attention, even the King of Spain's rowdy cheering section on the far side. There were more people than at Coyote's initiation in the Billard Hotel, which seemed a hundred years ago. He decided to get a few things off his chest.

"You probly don't know this," he went on, "but I'm a famous crime fighter up in Canada. Of course just one of many, but I know most heroes never get recognition, yet they keep plugging away. Any of you or your neighbours could be a hero, or a friend at work, someone you think you know but really don't. So get to know them. The more people recognize heroes, the sooner we can halt violence and all the sickness in modern society. Drugs and crime and abusing little children. If that is the way modern society is going, I say to heck with modern society!"

Some in the audience emitted a half-hearted cheer, but most began standing up and asking for their bills. Doc shifted nervously in his seat. Dottie put a hand over her face. Only Sandra and Lee Jun clapped with any enthusiasm.

"I got nothing against theories and ideas, but they're not the same as taking action, like an action hero has to do. Action is more than just beating up on gangs of crooks, too, or crawling inside a burning house. It takes guts and brains. Only a solid brain can out-think criminals and low-lifes who hang out in the gutters. I'm lucky to have a good working brain. Ask my friend Wonder Woman. Being a hero takes smarts. Maybe more smarts than your average professor or lawyer. Who has to think the most, eh? The guy who reads books, or the hero who faces a thousand dangerous decisions every day? The action hero! A hero like Superman or Goldhawk!"

Another smattering of applause went round the arena, but more diners headed for the exits. The serving wenches had cleared the tables and were hovering for their tips. Doc edged toward Coyote, as though he might have to shut him down.

"Of course, you have to use your brain to be a hero. Thinking how to take care of the weak and the downtrodden, the environment and helpless animals, let alone pay equity and handicapped rights and everything else. Politicians and teachers have been trying to change things for thousands of years, but how far did they get? Nowhere. Out there in the streets of Las Vegas, there's a war going on. And if people want peace and justice, they're going to have to kick butt!"

Lee Jun leaped to his feet clapping, but most of the crowd had left for the casino.

"Everybody has to become heroes. But why don't they? Because kids don't read comic books any more! It's not easy, either. I grew up sharing a comic book with ten other kids! I never had the chance to go to high school. Heroes have to get along on nothing. The pay is ridiculous."

"Right on, brother!" Wonder Woman chimed in. She had downed at least three jugs of Nut Brown Ale.

"We work for peanuts, and wear cast-off uniforms. We scrounge for stuff to recycle, and half the time it already belongs to somebody, and we have to give it back or get arrested for stealing! But say I get lucky after a few years and end up on TV with Superman and the other superheroes in a showdown with evil. Every hero has to mentally prepare for this battle, hoping he doesn't get his head bashed in first, or his leg chopped off, or poisoned in toxic waste.

"People sometimes say to me, 'Heroes must be rich, with all the money from comics and television shows.' Well, the heroes don't get it. It goes to publishers and T-shirt factories and toy makers! Millions of dollars, if you take Superman for example! But does he get paid? Not a dime. Heroes have to struggle just for enough to eat."

"Look, you did okay," the MC observed snarkily, reaching for the microphone.

Coyote cranked up the volume a notch. "It's different than it used to be! In the olden days, when knights fought on horses and ships, with catapults and slings and bows and arrows, fighting was easier. Heroes were all comrades. When they fought in the line of battle, their brothers would defend them from the enemy swords. When one fell in combat, another rose to take his place!"

"Thank you, Mr. Coyote," the announcer said, trying to wrestle the microphone from Coyote's grip. Doc stood on the other side, his hand on Coyote's elbow.

"That's all gone!" Coyote shouted. "Now it's guided missiles and laser beams and smart bombs and weapons of mass destruction. Is that Progress?"

Coyote was hitting his stride, though the audience had shrunk to a few people tilted over their drinks. He had forgotten about his meal. Wonder Woman had long since grabbed the game hen from his platter, along with his cob of corn, even the handful of french-fried turnips. She had downed his tankard of ale. Now she reached for his dessert, bread pudding with real custard. He reacted by slapping her fingers, and the MC jerked the microphone out of his hand.

"Thank you, Mr. Coyote," the MC said, as Doc and Dottie guided the hero toward the exit. "Thanks for your generosity. Remember folks, the next banquet sitting arrives in five minutes, so – another round of applause for the hero, Donald Coyote!"

In the foyer, Doc suggested that they go back to the motel. He was worried about Coyote exhausting himself, and thanked the Lees for the night out. Mr. Lee, who was a little drunk, insisted that it was his duty, as the son of a rich Hong Kong businessman, to repay Coyote for his kindness. Tomorrow, Lee Jun insisted, he would take them all to a matinee of *Elvis Live!* at the Rio Nevada Lounge.

For later that evening he had booked tickets for another hot show called *Viva Las Vegas* at the Late-Nite Revue Bar, next to the Golden Nugget. He showed them a brochure, a full-colour foldout from his tour package. The headliner was an exotic dancer named Gweneth Deevine, a star 'in the tradition of Liberace and Elvis,' who was already a Las Vegas legend. It cost $400 a ticket, but Lee Jun's credit card had such deep reserves that even Wonder Woman was invited along.

They all agreed to this plan and wandered off to their rooms. The Lees were so happy for their honeymoon haven in the Lancelot Suite they kept thanking Coyote again and again. He finally had to close the door to the front room so he could go to bed and sleep. At least he had made the Chinese couple happy. Maybe he was on the right track at last.

CHAPTER 26

Naughty Night in Camelot

The next afternoon, Gweneth Deevine was taking deep massage in her private dressing room, upstairs in the Revue Bar. She had thrown her back out at the Sinatra Memorial, performing her erotic art for the first time at the MGM Grand. The pain in her sacroiliac had required the talented fingers of the Camelot Motel's ace masseuse, Mechelle Baxter, the same Mechelle who had confused Coyote for her boyfriend Trevor and set off the ugly chain of incidents which had nearly silenced him forever.

Before a sex change operation in 1996, Gweneth had played two seasons for the Toronto Raptors as a shooting guard named Mike Harass. After a team hypnotherapist helped her discover her true transgendered nature, she staged a sensational public coming out during the halftime show at the Air Canada Centre. Following a program of transplants and hormone treatments, Gweneth began a second career as an exotic dancer. Her towering stature and astonishing cleavage quickly made her a top draw of Las Vegas entertainment.

In the course of her remedial massage, the subject of male organs arose, causing Mechelle to wax enthusiastically about Coyote's sexual equipment. "I've seen well-hung?" she confided to her client. "But this guy was incredible! Like a Genoa salami?"

"The question is – does he know what to do with it?"

"The answer is, does it know what to do with him? He was kinda slow getting there – the poor guy seemed to be in a coma at first? – but he came to life like a booster rocket. That's when Trevor busted in and all hell broke loose?"

"Oh, you poor thing. What happened to Captain Coyote?"

"Well, it wasn't good. He practically bit his tongue off."

"Oooo."

"Mr. Palomeque kicked him and his weird partner out, and the last I saw, they were driving to the hospital to get his tongue stitched. He was swallowing blood and everything?"

To satisfy Gweneth's curiousity, Mechelle described Coyote's dog-like face, his magnifying lens eyes, his muscular physique, even the little coyote-shaped tattoo on his butt. For the rest of the day, Gweneth fantasized about the well-endowed Canuck, and imagined herself fondling various parts of his body. The guy sounded like a noble stud, which Gweneth's imagination began to embellish with images of bondage, flagellation, and torture. Limping toward the stage at the Late-Nite Revue that night to begin her performance, she could hear the audience already chanting. Clouds of cigarette smoke drifted across the lounge. The fans were roused by the pulsating music, yelling and pounding on their tables as the speakers blared, "And now – the Amazon queen you've been waiting for – the heavenly – Gweneth Deevine!"

On the cue, Gweneth gritted her teeth and strutted onstage, bathed in the crowd's euphoric uproar. She threw them a look of extreme contempt and saw, only twenty feet from the edge of the stage, the noble stud himself, Captain Coyote. She recognized him right away: his hard-muscled body and long nose, framed by the pair of thick glasses. He was seated with a group of tourists in the front row, staring at the nylon string that more or less covered her jewel box.

Gwen halted in mid-grind, the pain of her back evaporating in a euphoric flare of lust. The Revue audience cheered and whistled, fanning the flames of her desire. She turned her complete attention on

Coyote with a full-frontal appeal, shimmying toward him and cooing with her lips, ignoring the crowd. She had all the moves needed to blow his pants off, and make him come crawling on stage begging for her gorgeous body.

Gweneth Deevine was soon splayed out on the stage at eye level, hips pumping and gyrating in orgiastic contractions. She craned her neck to watch Coyote, hoping to see him bug-eyed and hyperventilating like the others.

What she saw was a toad-like creature in a garish T-shirt, standing at the front of the stage. "Degrading to women!" she yelled. "No strippers! No strippers!" She urged the crowd to join her chant, but they quickly fell silent. The music stopped. Gweneth stood up, her back pain jabbing viciously, looking for the security officer.

The woman kept shouting incoherently, "Degrading to women. You people should be ashamed. Go home. Get outta here."

Uniformed guards were running down the aisles to centre stage as Captain Coyote grabbed the woman by the hand and pulled her out the front exit. Others at their table followed in the confusion, with a Chinese man throwing money on the table. Gweneth staggered off stage, humiliated and confused. Captain Coyote had taken a powder. Just spurned her and walked out!

The audience was aroused to a bestial frenzy. They howled at her across the footlights as she slumped toward her dressing room. It was worse than the time the Raptors had walked off the basketball court to protest her new identity. Her humiliation slowly boiled into a cold fury.

So Coyote thought he was an extreme stud, did he? Well, she would give him a lesson in rejection! She phoned Mechelle at the Camelot Massage Center, where the masseuse was expecting late-night arrivals from El Paso.

"Mechelle? I need info on your boyfriend Coyote. Do you know what room he's staying in?"

"I think in the Lancelot Suite! Palomeque had to give it to him in compensation."

"I've got a fantastic idea. You and me and him – one big orgy. Cancel your appointments for tonight. Get ready for a party."

"What shall I wear?"

"A gown, a frock – something feminine and ye oldie. Frilly underwear."

"Sounds good. Shall we take him to the clock tower?"

"Good idea. Get the entry key for King Arthur's."

King Arthur's Throne Room was on the seventh floor of the clock tower, a penthouse turret diagonally above the Lancelot suite. Arthur's Throne Room was reserved for special guests such as foreign royalty and executors of the estate of Howard Hughes. The two had partied there with many clients and they agreed it would be the perfect venue for Gweneth's revenge. The balustraded platform in front of the clock – where the medieval manikins marched – looked out over the glittering streets of Las Vegas.

Confirming from the front desk that Coyote had returned for the evening, Mechelle used her security key to take the elevator directly to the seventh floor. King Arthur's Throne Room was vacant for the night. The party room contained a large selection of chains, ropes, whips, and other devices which would keep them amused for hours.

In the meanwhile, Doc and Dottie and the Lees were on their way to the late performance of Cirque Du Soleil at Treasure Island. Dottie was concerned about Coyote's abrupt departure from the Late-Nite Revue Bar, but the others accepted his explanation about getting Wonder Woman out, and going back to his room for some rest. They couldn't turn down a chance to see the famous acrobatic troupe from Québec.

Gweneth and Mechelle stepped onto the parapet. Mechelle placed a finger to her lips and pointed down to the Lancelot suite. There was the scoundrel on his outdoor balcony, pacing among the plastic lawn chairs. Despite the noise of traffic seven floors below, they could hear him muttering, and edged close to the railing to listen.

"Oh Princess," he moaned. "I miss you too much...."

They giggled, and Gweneth called out, "Captain...Coyoteeee..."

"Who's that?" He looked around for the mysterious voice.

"This is your princess speaking, Coyote."

"Princess Di?" he gasped.

"Can you hear me, Coyote?" The two pranksters giggled and snorted, almost wrecking their scheme.

"P.D. Is that you laughing? You sound so close."

"I am, I am! I'm very close. And I want to get – closer to you."

Gwen dropped a pink ribbon of her silk gown over the edge to float over Coyote's balcony, high above the flash of the Las Vegas lights.

Though Coyote saw it, he was still looking for the voice. "You don't sound like P.D.," he said.

"I'm the spirit of Princess Di. I need your help."

"How can I help?"

"You have to help me escape from the tower."

"What tower?"

"The clock tower! Above you, to the right. Look up toward the clock, and you can see the door to my room."

Coyote leaned over the railing, far above the frenzied stream of traffic. "Jeeze – it's kind of high."

"That shouldn't be a problem for a hero. Climb onto the ledge."

Heights sometimes made Coyote dizzy, but he stood on one of the chairs and stepped onto the balcony railing. He avoided looking down at the turmoil of taxis and tour buses, and raised his eyes slowly to the platform above. "I still can't see you."

"Of course not. I'm a prisoner in the tower, locked in by the manager!"

"That creep, Palomeque?"

"Yes. He's holding me hostage and forcing me to service his customers in all kinds of perverse ways. Please – rescue me!"

"Okay."

Coyote edged along the railing, reaching overhead to steady himself on the ceiling of his balcony. Then he stretched precariously toward the bottom of the seventh storey platform and grabbed it with his fingertips. He was stretched out between the two balustrades on a 45-degree angle, but unable to go up or down, forward or back.

"Can you give me a hand?" he gasped.

"Of course I can," Gweneth cooed, pushing her arms through the railing. Before he could react, she had snapped a pair of handcuffs onto Coyote's wrists, locking him to the upper floor.

"Hey, that hurts!"

"It does? Could I please hear a shriek of pain!"

"Huh? Who are you?"

"You don't recognize me? Or my friend Mechelle? Come on, Coyote – one little yelp of pain. What's the matter? Doesn't a hero feel pain?"

"Hey! Is this some kind of trick?"

"You tricked yourself, you silly coyote."

"It's not fair! Unlock me! Help!"

The two playgirls not only ignored his yells, they ran giggling to the elevator and descended to the sixth floor. Using Mechelle's master key, they scurried onto Coyote's balcony. Reaching out with her long arms, Gwen grabbed the belt loops on Coyote's jeans and pulled them down to his ankles. She did the same with his shorts, ignoring his yells and pleas. They laughed as Mr. Private fell and dangled into space, growing stiff in the cool evening breeze.

Coyote was stretched between the two balconies as though he was on a *strappado*, a medieval torture rack he had first seen in the comic of *The Count of Monte Cristo*. It was a device that lifted the victim's body from the ground until his toes barely touched the surface, and caused terrible pain as the victim twisted to relieve the agony in his arms. Coyote was stretched to the limit, manacled to the platform of a clock tower seven storeys above the courtyard. But the pain of his *strappado* was not the worst part. The worst part would be the humiliation of being discovered. In another minute, the floodlights on the clock tower would switch on for the striking of midnight.

No one answered his yells for help. He had to think of a solution and, above all, stay calm. The Lees would soon return to the suite, and they could call Doc to rescue him.

The minute hand touched XII, as the armoured knight emerged from the portal. He struck the bell with his mace, producing a deep resonant gong, and thousands of eyes turned up toward the tower. There was Coyote, his manhood revealed in sad display as he stretched naked between the balconies. A moan rose from the throats of the watchers, and a small around of applause for the daredevil act Coyote was attempting.

Fortunately for Coyote, his predicament was also observed by a paparazzi cameraman at the Bed Rock Inn, a Flintstones theme hotel two blocks away from the Camelot. He was a sex tourist from Stuttgart, Germany, who specialized in pictures of indecent acts performed by the residents within the city's hotels. His digital camera had a high-power telephoto lens, and he had spent the evening taking snapshots from the Barney Rubble Penthouse for his voyeurs' website in Germany. He snapped a roll of film of the half-naked Coyote before dialling Emergency 911 to report a fetish suicide jumper, and followed it up with a call to KIK-TV, a local station which paid for hot news tips and photos.

As the shriek of fire sirens rose in the distance, people gathered in the streets below. Coyote felt a twinge of horror as he realized the fire trucks were heading for the Camelot Motel. The ladder truck screeched to a stop far, far below Coyote's draughty perch, and several firemen in yellow helmets jumped off, staring upward.

"It's okay!" Coyote yelled. "Never mind me. My friends are coming to get me!"

A fireman aimed his bullhorn at the clock tower. "Okay, buddy," his voice boomed. "Just stay calm and ease yourself back onto the balcony!"

"This isn't what you think!" Coyote called. "Doc will be here any second!"

"Stay calm and – don't – panic. We're sending up a ladder!"

As he spoke, the truck's extension ladder pivoted around and began elevating skyward, section by section, toward the seventh floor. Other firemen spread a safety net across the courtyard below, to catch him if he jumped. A huge crowd of people had streamed into the courtyard of the motel, pointing up. Cars pulled out of traffic into the park-

ing lot across the street, and Coyote could hear the clatter of a helicopter beating closer through the night sky.

"I'm okay!" Coyote yelled. "Go back to the fire station. It's not a real
emergency!" He felt terrible that the fire department was sending valuable manpower to a ridiculous prank done by somebody he barely knew.

"Don't – move – sir!"

"Doc is coming. He can explain everything."

"Is anybody up there with you?"

"I'm a hotel guest. Ask Mr. Palomeque!"

"Just – stay – calm, mister. The crew's nearly there."

Just then he heard a knock on the door of his room behind him.

"Come in!" he shouted. He tried to jump back to answer the door,
but the handcuffs jerked on his arms, leaving him swinging from the
clock tower. He dangled on the handcuffs like a plucked turkey, his face
flushing red in the hot glare of the spotlights. The biggest crowd he had
ever seen filled the courtyard, and packed the streets for two blocks in
each direction. Traffic had ground to a halt as people abandoned their
vehicles in the street to stare at the naked figure dangling from the
Camelot tower.

"Don't struggle, sir! The team's right there! Hang on. Don't let go!"

"I can't let go! The handcuffs –!"

Three firemen were standing on top of the extension ladder, barely
inches away. The nearest fireman lifted a plexiglass face mask. "Are
those handcuffs, buddy?"

"Somebody handcuffed me to the clock railing. It was a joke."

The fireman's helmet said his name was Brent. "Hang on, we'll cut
you loose."

"You've got bolt-cutters?"

"Better – a propane torch," Brent said. "Don't worry, I'll be careful.
Okay, try and step onto the ladder, bud."

Despite the pain of his arms, Coyote swung out and stretched his
foot as far as he could. He still couldn't reach the ladder. The men with
the net skittered around below, anticipating the arc of his fall. The net
looked about four inches wide.

"You guys are fantastic, but really – I can get down by myself."

"Just doing our job, buddy. No big deal."

"I'll make sure you get an award from the President for this."

The two female pranksters had been watching from their portal, but stopped giggling when they suddenly realized what they could be found responsible for. Crouching beyond the beams of light, Gweneth reached through the railings and unlocked the handcuffs. The cuffs separated, and Coyote plummeted toward the cobblestones seven storeys below, his pants streaming behind like Superman's cape.

The firemen on the ground dropped their safety net and ran for their lives, afraid he would score a direct hit. However, at the instant the cuffs parted, Brent had snapped a heavy-duty nylon cord onto Coyote's belt around his ankles, a timely act that saved his life. The other end was fastened to the top of the ladder. The nylon stretched like a bungee cord when Coyote hit the bottom, but his belt loop held. He soared back into the atmosphere like a rubber ball, smacking his head on a lower rung of the ladder and splitting his scalp.

As he bobbed at the bottom of the rope, Coyote felt grateful to his rescuers, despite his pain and embarrassment. He still couldn't figure out what had happened.

The extension ladder slowly lowered him face first toward the courtyard, to a hearty round of applause from the crowd. The KIK-TV news helicopter hovered overhead, recording the scene of Las Vegas's latest news sensation. Tomorrow, the footage would run incessantly on the video waves of America, as Coyote's adventures finally found an audience.

CHAPTER 27

Wonder Woman's Bombshell

Dottie McKechnie was in shock. She had witnessed Coyote's terrifying plunge from a block away, his falling body caught in the lights of the helicopter and rescue crews as it swanned toward the pavement. Dottie ran with Lee Jun and his bride across the drawbridge to the fire truck and was relieved to find him alive, though dazed. His glasses had disappeared. She would have to protect him from the news media now racing toward the Camelot from every outlet in Las Vegas. Dr. Pearce was still at the Cirque du Soleil entertainment.

As Coyote was laid out on the cobblestones, Dottie arrived and pulled his jeans back up. "Thanks," he whispered. She and Lee Jun lifted the hero by the arms to help him back to his room.

A policeman stepped out of the crowd and stopped them. "Hang on a minute," he said, turning a powerful flashlight onto Coyote's face. "I have to ask this guy some questions."

A few people in the crowd booed, and a second policeman appeared, pulling a gun from his holster and pointing it at the dazed hero. "What's your name, fella?"

Without his glasses, Coyote had no idea who he was facing. He was struck dumb, blinking in the harsh glare of the flashlight.

"His name is Donald Coyote," Dottie said, stepping protectively in front of him.

"And who are you, lady?"

Dottie handed the policeman her business card. "Dr. Dorothy McKechnie. I represent the Province of Saskatchewan, Mr. Coyote's legal guardian."

"That up in Canada somewheres?"

"Officer, couldn't you interview him inside? He's in shock, and that cut on his head needs medical attention. We're all registered guests at the Camelot Motel. Mr. Palomeque will vouch for us." Half a dozen policemen with batons were now pushing the hordes of onlookers back from the drawbridge.

"All right – bring him over to the police car." The policemen shoved some defiant street people to one side so Dottie could escort Coyote through the crowd. Palomeque arrived in an anxious state, glancing nervously back at the castle portcullis. He was worried the mob would flip out of control, attack the police car, then ransack his motel. It was practically a Las Vegas ritual.

As the hero was being rushed across the courtyard, two veteran players in Coyote's adventures suddenly reappeared. Mr. and Mrs. Vance Bullinicks had taken a scenic detour off the I-15 to drive along the Las Vegas Strip, only to run smack into a snarl of police barriers, fire trucks, emergency medical teams, and hordes of rubberneckers surrounding the Camelot Motel. Traffic was completely stopped. Shunted into the parking lot, the Bullinicks got out of the old Chevy to watch the action.

Vance suddenly spotted Coyote stumbling toward the police car with a crowd yelling behind him. The Bullinicks went berserk. They had reached Nevada that morning after two weeks' delay in Jackson Hole, completing police reports and insurance claims over their stolen basin. And here, at the centre of a mob scene on Western Avenue was the maniac who had stolen their antique – in the hands of the police!

They pushed through the throng to the squad car, with Vance yelling, "Grab that man! We're charging him with robbery and assault! That's the son of a bitch who stole our depression basin!"

The policemen turned to Coyote, who seemed stunned by the accusation. What could he say? Dottie threw her hands up in despair, ready to flee the scene. Mrs. Bullinicks was shrieking hysterically at the police. Coyote's arrest seemed certain.

Wonder Woman suddenly appeared like an American cavalry charge, her voice bugling across the courtyard as she charged, waving a six-pack of beer. Mrs. Bullinicks was still screeching accusations when Wonder Woman slammed her over the head with the beer, silencing the old lady. She turned her fury on the cop holding Coyote.

"Let him go!" she yelled. "You got the wrong person! He rescued a famous relic from these old turkeys! They're the criminals! We took it from them in a fair fight!"

"Thieves!" the old man hissed.

"Racists!" Wonder Woman shot back. "Perverts!" It was like throwing a match into a can of gas, the catalyst the mob had been waiting for. They had been clamouring for the police to free the nude bungee diver, and now they joined his cause, whatever it was. The seething mob of street vagrants – hustlers, hookers, bikers, shills, pimps, and assorted tourists – exploded into a full riot. They pulled Coyote out of the hands of the police and, roused to mania by Wonder Woman's taunts, prepared to rip the pensioners limb from limb. Bottles, cans and rocks began whistling through the air. The Camelot courtyard looked like a WWF wrestling arena – rampant confusion with no clear lines of action – when Doc arrived on the scene. Punks and police were kicking and punching each other, hookers and tourists alike drawn into the fray.

As the police tried to drag Wonder Woman and Coyote to the squad car, Doc fought his way to the centre of the storm. He told the police it would be faster and safer to go into the motel, where they could investigate the accusations in a rational way. First they had to pry Mrs. Bullinicks out of the tattooed hands of a squeegee kid. Doc led them to Palomeque's office, where the two seniors were asked to state their complaints. By then the old man was unhinged, confused about what city he was in. Mrs. Bullinicks had a clearer line on things, having nursed revenge several hundred miles, and was determined to have the basin for the San Diego Antique Roadshow. She grabbed Doc by his shirt collar, yammering in his face, and ending her tirade with, "And he says it's not a basin at all, but some idiotic helmet!"

"It is The Flash's helmet!" Coyote insisted. "I have to return it to its rightful owner."

The policeman turned to Doc. "Have you seen this thing? Is it a helmet or a basin? You're a professor, right?"

"I am not an expert on basins," Doc said. "But if Donny says it is The Flash's helmet, I accept the statement at face value. I haven't examined the object."

"If it's a helmet, where's the chin strap?" the old woman demanded. "You ever seen a helmet that had no chin strap?"

"The Flash never used a strap," Coyote retorted. "That's how I know it's genuine. If it had a strap, it would be a fake!"

"I'll tell you what, mister," Doc said to Vance, whose eyes had crossed in confusion. "I'll give you forty dollars for the basin and we'll call it square."

Mrs. Bullinicks was outraged. "If it belonged to The Flash, it's gotta be worth more than forty lousy bucks!"

"Well, you can't have it both ways. That's my offer. Take it or leave it."

Doc finally calmed the Bullinicks family by compensating them for the time wasted with police and insurance claims, and obtained a written bill of sale waiving all claim to The Flash's helmet. The police accepted Dottie's authoritative account of Coyote's history, but insisted on taking Wonder Woman to Clark County Women's Jail, on a charge of inciting a riot. They said she could be freed on bail when she sobered up in the morning, if she could make bond.

Even Doc was beginning to doubt the merits of his rescue mission. Would they ever escape from this place? What else could go wrong? Dottie got Coyote's Social Services file from her briefcase, and this satisfied the police need for official identification. Doc provided the LVPD with a guarantee of Coyote's good behaviour until he left the city, and they agreed to overlook his illegal entry into the USA as long as he left the county within 48 hours. With the signed waiver from Mrs. Bullinicks, the police released Coyote into the custody of the Government of Saskatchewan representative, Dottie McKechnie. They handed him his glasses, scratched and twisted but still intact. Someone had found them lying beside the moat.

Doc walked Coyote up to the Lancelot Suite, where Lee Jun and Rosalind waited anxiously for their host.

At the door, Doc said, "The new Coyote Mobile will be ready to roll in the morning. You're set to go, Don?"

"I have to get out of here," Coyote replied. "I'm so mixed up I hardly know who is who any more, or who they aren't, or even what's real. I think this castle is haunted."

"I wouldn't be surprised. It sure hasn't been very good to you."

"Both times I stayed here, weird stuff happened. It's like the place is jinxed, or possessed by an alien power. Sometimes I feel like it's – taking over. Maybe Camelot really is enchanted, like the song says."

"What do you mean?"

"I don't know. I'm not even sure what I'm saying is what I want to say, know what I mean? I had weird dreams last night."

"Donny – what happened tonight? How did you get up on that ladder?"

"I was out on my balcony, waiting for the Lees to come home. I was thinking about Princess Di, and her voice just came out of nowhere. At least I thought it was her voice, but it turned out to be a friend of Mechelle's."

"Mechelle of the infamous massage centre?"

"Yeah, she was getting crazy about me, just like that dancer in the Revue Bar. I had to get out of there. It was like a bad dream. They were up on the clock and tricked me into climbing the tower, and then they locked me on the railing with handcuffs."

"Hmm. Well, you'll be safe in here now. The Lees can help you if anything goes wrong. I'll make sure the windows are locked and the security system is set on the door. We'll be free of this place tomorrow. Meantime, get a good rest."

In the morning, Doc had to settle the motel account with his gold card. Having noticed Doc's generosity to the Bullinickses, Palomeque had added on the damage to the courtyard during the previous night's incident, outstanding invoices and damage claims from Coyote's previous stay, as well as all the surcharges he had to pay on his insurance.

Doc had risen even earlier to spring Wonder Woman from the police station, a mere formality once she had sobered up. They had breakfast together with the Lees, who reported that their friend Captain Coyote had spent a quiet and restful night. Dottie was more cheerful in the light of a new day, wearing a summery outfit she had discovered at the Bellagio Esplanade. She sat at the far end of the table from the grouchy Wonder Woman. After breakfast, they said goodbye to the Chinese honeymooners. Doc brought the rental car to the door and drove them to the car dealership on Red Canyon Road.

"How do you feel about heading back home, Donald?" Dottie asked.

Wonder Woman sat beside him in the back seat, clutching her gym bag. "Ha!" she said. "Under duress."

"Kinda mixed feelings, I guess," Donny said.

"How's that?"

"I hoped to get a lot more accomplished in the States. We just got started, and we're already leaving. And I'm thinking maybe it's a mistake to go now, with all the publicity on TV last night. It could've been a boost to our PR."

"Hey! Now yer talking, buddy," Wonder Woman chortled, clapping an arm around him. "Strike while the iron's hot! They were showing your hound-dog mug on all the news channels this morning! Never mind if you looked like an idiot on that bungee cord. You were on the front page of the morning paper! Now's the time to grab the brass ring!"

"You think so?"

"It's not an option, Donny," Doc frowned. "We're going to pick up the Coyote Mobile at the garage."

"The transportation is costing a fortune," Dottie frowned.

"Donny – don't get sucked in by this fancy vehicle offer. Think for yourself!"

"Sandra, we can't change travel plans now," Doc said. He eased the car into the heavy traffic, heading for the west side of the city.

"Well, then, I better shut my mouth, or I might get tossed out of the ark."

"That's right, lady," Dottie murmured. "Don't push your luck."

"This social worker waltzes in here and pulls the wool over your eyes so bad your head shrank – and now she's going to run your life!"

"She's just doing her job," Coyote pointed out.

"Her job!" Wonder Woman howled. "You call shacking up with Doc a job?"

Wonder Woman hurled her accusation at the conversation like a live grenade, and sat back in her seat to watch it explode. She had been waiting two days for the moment of attack, knowing Coyote would never suspect his mentors of carrying on behind his back. And if they'd been boinking all along, they were capable of any dirty trick.

Coyote turned in shock to Dottie, blushing pink with embarrassment and horror. Doc slammed his foot on the brake, squealing the car to the side of the road.

"How can you say such a thing?" Dottie huffed. But Coyote could tell from her red face that Wonder Woman's shot had hit the mark. *Something* was going on.

"I'll tell you how I can say it! I saw Doc tippy-toeing out of your room at one o'clock – trying to pull his pants back on!"

"That's ridiculous!" Doc snapped.

"She's a liar," Coyote said without conviction. "There was a reason, right Doc?"

Doc glared at Wonder Woman in the rear-view mirror, while Dottie began to cry, pulling tissues out of her handbag.

"That's the kind of treatment they give you!" Wonder Woman said. "Lies and sneakiness. All you were trying to do was earn a few honest bucks, fighting crime and pollution, and that's the respect you get. You wanted to go to Vegas. I got you here. But you've been tricked into leaving by these two con artists!"

"Be quiet, Sandra!" Donny said. "You sound like a pot calling the kettle black."

"Get serious!"

"I am serious. Shut your mouth, or I'll kick you off the action team. You're always causing trouble – making up lies and stories about Doc. You're a shit-disturber and a rabble-rousing good for nothing! You belch and fart and swear in public, and never brush your teeth. I'm getting sick of the sight of you."

Everyone was shocked by Coyote's outburst. No one had ever heard him speak with such vitriol. Looking stern, Dottie held up her hand to still the turmoil and said, "We won't get anywhere with name-calling and aggression, Donald. I can't comment on my relationship with Dr. Pearce, but whatever happened in the privacy of my room has nothing to do with our plan to drive back to Moose Jaw. Now apologize to Sandra, and maybe Sandra will apologize to Doc, and we can continue on our way."

After a round of sullen apologies, and no clear agreement except that the Camelot Motel was jinxed, a place where bizarre and dangerous things happened, they set out once more for the car dealership. There Doc revealed the surprise he had been preparing for three days – a new Coyote Mobile. This had not been easy. Dottie had arranged for the leasing of an ambulance for the Regina Health Region, and ordered an EMS vehicle straight from the factory in Anaheim. It had been customized with racing stripes around the medical insignia. A panel on each side declared in big bold letters, "Coyote Mobile II!"

"It's a trick!" Sandra huffed. "They're trying to buy you off with this expensive toy!" But she could tell from Coyote's face that he had fallen for the bait. He could already see himself driving along the interstates, lights flashing and sirens blaring, looking for victims to save.

"Neat-o!" Coyote said, running his hands over the windshield visors and gleaming panels. He ran to the driver's door and threw it open. The dashboard was bigger than the Batmobile's, with dials, lights, and switches on three separate decks, and a console with rows of functions. The seat had four separate levers for driving comfort.

"Can I drive?" he asked.

"I'm afraid Doc is the only one properly licenced," Dottie pointed out.

"Darn!"

"You and Sandra will be comfortable riding in the back. It's completely customized. There's a built-in video panel and a refrigerator full of snacks and drinks."

"This is better than a Southwind!"

"What's this?" Wonder Woman said. "The back door is locked!"

"It's just a safety feature. All EMS vehicles have locks on the doors."

"So we're prisoners being hauled back to Canada!"

"Nonsense," Doc said. "We're just making sure Donny is comfortable going back. There's no restraint of any kind."

"Not yet maybe!"

"We'll be driving straight through to the border, so relax and get comfortable," Dottie said tightly. "There's fruit juice and pop in the fridge."

"No beer?"

"That's right, Sandra. No beer. We're going sober all the way."

"This is against our human rights!"

Dottie ignored her. "Donald, I know you won't be difficult. We only intervened so you could function again, and enjoy normal relationships with people. I believe you want to see Princess Di and enter rehabilitation."

"Yeah, I guess so."

"Once you're back on an emotional even keel, you can take up a hero's career again in Moose Jaw, and do all kinds of wonderful things for people less fortunate. But it might mean putting your Captain Coyote outfit in storage for a while."

"I don't get it. I like being Captain Coyote."

"Dottie has a point," Doc said. "Maybe it's time to go back to plain old Donny Coyote."

"What do you say, Sandra?"

"Hell, no. I won't go! Never!"

"If that's your final word," Dottie said, "can we drop you off at the motel?"

"Fuckin aye! I know my rights!"

After returning the rental car to the airport, they drove the Coyote Mobile II to the gate of the Camelot. Coyote and Doc loaded the bags, while Wonder Woman stomped off toward the Last Chance Casino. She was nearly broke, but planned to make enough on the slots to buy the beer she'd need to go looking for work.

Coyote, in the meanwhile, got comfortable in the back of the Coyote Mobile II. Doc had picked out some movie videos, and packed the refrigerator with snacks like pears and cashew nuts. Two comfortable bunk beds were set up in the back, and a small bathroom. They were all set for the thousand mile, non-stop drive to the border. Unless something else happened.

CHAPTER 28

Kidnapped

Four hours after the new Coyote Mobile departed for points north, Wonder Woman's outrage boiled over. She'd drunk several rye whiskeys while stewing over the injustice of Coyote's kidnapping, and could now detect Palomeque's double-dealing treachery behind the whole screw-up. She called KIK-TV, the 24-hour news channel that offered cash rewards for breaking news tips. So Coyote wanted to make his story public, did he? Well, she could give it profile!

"KIK Tee-Veee!" the receptionist's voice perked at the other end of the line. "Only news, but all the news!"

Wonder Woman was standing at a pay phone in front of the Last Chance. "Zat right you pay five hundred bucks for hot news tips?"

"Well – up to five hundred. Is this a fire or an accident?"

"That's just kid stuff. I'm reporting a hostage taking."

"One minute, please."

Wonder Woman saw Palomeque as the mastermind behind the Mafia plot to ship Coyote back to Canada like a lamb to slaughter. She saw it with a clarity which had been denied her in her drug-addled state the week before. Palomeque had summoned Doc and the pesky social worker to Las Vegas, as part of a back-stabbing move to tear up the security contract and force Wonder Woman out of the parking lot.

Palomeque and his Mafia pals had probably supplied the glorified paddy wagon hauling him back to the border.

"Hi, Kevin Breezely on the news desk. You're reporting a hostage taking?"

"That's right. This morning. From the Camelot Motel."

"Who is the hostage?"

"Captain Coyote."

"Coyote. The guy who jumped naked off the clock tower? Is this some kind of publicity stunt?"

"No, no – it's true. He's a hero from Moose Jaw. They grabbed him and they're deporting him back to Canada. You've got to stop them!"

"Who are we stopping?"

"His so-called guardians. One of them's an old drunk, Doc Pearce, and the other's a shrink from Social Services, Dottie McKechnie. But they're just stooges for Palomeque and the Mafia!"

"Just a minute. Who are you?"

"Well, my professional name is Wonder Woman, AKA Sandra Dollar. That's D.O.L.E.U.R. I'm Coyote's business associate. We were security at the Camelot until this gang showed up from Canada."

"Okay, we'll come and check it out. Are you calling from the Camelot?"

"Just down the street. A payphone in front of the Last Chance."

"Hang on. We'll be right there."

Kevin Breezely was the deputy news producer for KIK-TV. He was only an hour from the Evening Report, and had nothing in the can but a freeway pileup at the Tropicana exit, and the forty-third consecutive day of the city's heat wave. Another record.

The informant sounded like a complete nut case, but that didn't mean there wasn't a hostage taking. It was suspicious that it was the same guy whose cock they'd been exposing every half-hour since the photos arrived. But even if it was another publicity stunt, it could be hot news. CNN news. He called his ace shooter and sound-man, Nicky Tinos, and in seconds, the KIK-TV mobile unit was waiting loaded at the front door. Grabbing his KIK-TV camouflage jacket off the rack, Breezely flung himself into the van.

They pulled up in front of the casino five minutes later. Beside the pay phone was a troll-like woman wearing fishnet stockings, silver cowboy boots, with a T-shirt that read LIFE SUCKS!

"You're Wonder Woman?"

"Yeah. Got the five hundred bucks?"

"First let's see the hostage. Have you called the cops?"

"That's not my job. I just blow the whistle. They've already skipped town. They're taking the I-15 to Canada, through Utah. Driving a customized ambulance. How about four hundred for the tip?"

"If I see a hostage, I'll make it a thousand."

"We can track them down, easy. Where's your chopper?"

Breezely called the station on his cell phone to summon the KIK-TV helicopter, which was aloft on traffic duty. Within minutes it picked them up at Number 3 landing pad along the Strip, and they were clattering through the afternoon heat haze over Lake Mead. Following the I-15 past the Valley of Fire to Mesquite and across the northern tip of Arizona, they pursued the disguised ambulance. And as they climbed the twisting canyons of the Virgin River into Utah, Breezely interviewed his informant.

To explain how Coyote had been kidnapped, she had to tell him about the mission from Moose Jaw, and her brilliant plan to get them across the border into Montana, and how they had smashed the Yankee Freemen and liberated the chain gang, and various battles they had won, or nearly won. She wove such a fascinating tale that Breezely – who had covered many incredible events in his short career – knew he either had a bag of wind, or something sensational. He ordered Nicky Tinos to tape footage of their flight into the great Utah basin.

They caught up to the Coyote Mobile II speeding along the freeway just outside Provo, Utah. "That's it!" Wonder Woman cried. "There's Coyote!"

The ambulance looked like O.J.'s white Bronco driving along the highway, its fresh colours glistening in the sun, unaware it was being followed. In seconds, Nicky had the vehicle in his viewfinder, and Kevin was preparing for a live feed to the KIK-TV audience, 19% of viewers in Las Vegas and Clark County. He told the station manager to alert CNN.

"You gotta stop them!" Wonder Woman yelled.

The helicopter pilot called, "They've seen us! They're turning off at that rest area."

"Is there room to set down?" Breezely asked.

"No problem."

"Okay, let's go see who's inside that ambulance."

The pilot set the helicopter down in front of the stopped ambulance. Its rotors were still turning as Breezely jumped out, with Nicky following in his wake. He ran to the emergency vehicle and rapped on the tinted passenger's window, which lowered to reveal Dottie McKechnie's pale face.

"Yes?"

"KIK-TV News," Breezely declared crisply. "Mind answering a few questions?"

"What about?"

"About a hostage you are alleged to be transporting in the back of the ambulance."

"A hostage? Absolutely not. Are you the police?"

"No ma'am. Kevin Breezely. Associate producer of KIK-TV news. We have been reliably informed that you are transporting a hostage named Captain Coyote against his will. Do you deny the allegation?"

Doc leaned over from the driver's seat. "Who told you that?"

"His, uh, partner, uh, Miss Douleur."

"I thought as much." Doc stepped out to face the KIK-TV news team. "That's ridiculous. We're not committing any crime. And this is an invasion of Mr. Coyote's privacy. Now if you don't mind – !"

"You admit Captain Coyote is inside that vehicle?"

Dottie spoke up. "We have the legal authority to transport a ward of the province in need of medical treatment. Here is my card."

"Thanks. But is Captain Coyote...?"

Doc took Breezely to one side, away from the video camera. "Turn off your camera, and you can meet Donny Coyote. He's perfectly capable of speaking for himself. However, he's recovering from a serious accident – and we don't want to add stress by putting him on television news. The fact is, you've been conned by a blatant sociopath."

"Hey – her story checks out! And your man's big news since his highjinks on the clock tower last night. This is the same guy who sprang Gino Pasamonte out of prison, right? If he confirms –"

"You can ask him anything you want – without the camera."

"Do you think that's wise?" Dottie said.

"He has to learn to handle these situations. That is, situations of his own creation. I'll step in if it gets out of hand."

Once the equipment was turned off, Doc opened the rear door and leaned inside. Coyote was watching the new *Spiderman* video. "Donny? There's a television reporter who'd like to talk to you."

Coyote's spectacled face emerged in the late afternoon sunshine. "Did I hear a helicopter?" he said. "This probably has something to do with Wonder Woman."

"Ta-*daaa!*" Sandra's voice sang out. She came running across the asphalt from the helicopter, her bloodshot eyes ablaze with victory. "Wonder Woman to the rescue!"

Nicky switched his camera on again to catch the action.

"It's me, hound-face! I called the TV guys to snatch you to freedom, buddy. Try and look a little grateful!"

"But I told you, I *want* to go home now! You gotta cut out this crap, Sandra."

"It's not true you're being taken to Canada against your wishes?" Breezely asked.

"No, it's not. She's a big fat liar."

"Do you know these people?"

"This is my friend, Doc, who gives me advice. That lady's from Social Services."

Shocked by Coyote's denials, Sandra swelled up defiantly. "He doesn't know what he's sayin! How come they're haulin him in a locked ambulance? How much more proof do you need?"

"We have full documentation," Dottie said, reaching into the ambulance for the file folder. "We can account for the purpose of our travel in the US, if the police or some authority is concerned. I have a court order defining our custody rights, plus we all have identification – which is more than she has."

Breezely turned back to Wonder Woman.

"Well," she sighed, "I don't have my ID on me. We lost it in Wyoming. Coyote's the official spokesman. Say something, shit-head."

"About what?"

"Tell them who you are, and our work smashing gangs and saving the environment, eksetera."

"To tell you the truth, I'm not sure *who* I am these days," Coyote said.

"But you use the name Captain Coyote?"

Coyote glanced at Doc. "Yeah, sometimes."

"I told you! That's him. And I'm his partner, Wonder Woman."

"Let me get this straight," Breezely said, elbowing her off camera. "You're a Canadian hero who specializes in saving people and busting crime, right?"

"Well, I try," Coyote admitted.

"And you're the guy who took the bungee leap off the Camelot Motel, and freed the illegal aliens up in Wyoming?"

"Well, there was more to it than that."

"Never mind, that's enough. Did you know Gino Pasamonte has been robbing banks and breaking convicts out of jail in two states?"

"Oh, no."

"He calls himself the new Butch Cassidy! He's been getting more press than Saddam Hussein. He pops up somewhere every day to give media interviews. Last week it was Elko, yesterday Cheyenne! He claims you are his inspiration after you gave him his freedom. You – Captain Coyote. That must make you pretty proud, huh?"

"Well, that wasn't really my idea –"

"What if KIK-TV could set up a combined interview with you and him? Back in our Las Vegas studio. A kind of celebrity matchup."

"Wait a minute," Doc said.

"Forget Pasamonte," Wonder Woman snapped. "One thing at a time. First we liberate the hostage! We can organize the reunions later."

Nicky brought the camera in close on Wonder Woman's battered face as she grabbed the microphone and turned on Breezley. "You saw for yourself – that door was locked! They're taking him back in a padded cell! And all he wanted was to be an all-American hero, to live in the land of the free and the home of the brave. He has more right than those assholes in Wyoming."

"So will the two of you be making a formal claim for refugee status?"

"Hey – that's an idea! Good thinking, Breezely! How does it work?"

"Well, if you have been threatened with murder, torture, or genital mutilation in Canada – and the INS believes you – they'll issue you a resident's permit in six months."

"Hallelujah! There's the solution, folks! What do you say, Donny? We'll stay?"

"Donald will not be claiming refugee status, Sandra. You could jeopardize his getting home at all!"

"That's too bad. You should've listened to me this morning."

Doc placed his hand over the lens of the KIK-TV camera. "Breezely, this has gone far enough. Ms. McKechnie and I here are on an international errand of compassion – taking Donald Coyote home for medical treatment. We're not responsible for Sandra Dollar or Douleur, or whatever she calls herself. She can stay in the States if she wants. She'll be happy to tell you her life story. Take her, and good riddance. But she can't have Donny Coyote."

"You're so good at speeches!" Wonder Woman sneered at Doc. "While you're at it, why don't you tell these guys how you stole Coyote's comic books?"

"Comic books?" Breezely's voice rose an octave.

"Donny's comic book collection. Worth a fortune. He had a copy of *Action Comics Number 1,* valued at fifty thousand dollars! Not even insured. And this so-called 'friend' of his went and stole it!"

"Sandra, you don't know what you're talking about."

She pushed her chest out defiantly. "Well, I'm not gonna bite the shit end of this stick, Doc. Donny never would of run away on this adventure if somebody hadn't ripped off his comic books, and you know it. That's why he took off. Had nuthin to do with me."

"The comics were not stolen," Doc insisted as Breezely swung the microphone toward him. "They're in a safe place for protection. They represent all his life savings."

"They weren't stolen?" Coyote said.

"I placed them in a safety deposit box – so you wouldn't be tempted to sell them."

"But why didn't you tell me, Doc?"

"I couldn't. I felt terrible about it. Then I fell off the wagon and went crazy for a while. It was rough."

"But we agreed I could look after my own stuff! P.D. said I could."

"If you'd pawned it that day, it would be gone, and you'd have nothing."

Breezely turned the microphone to Coyote. "Excuse me, Captain, but are you accusing Doctor Pearce of – theft?"

Doc flushed angrily. "There was no theft, there is no hostage, and the interview is over, sonny. We've driven a long way today, and we expect to be driving all night, so we have to go. Interview Sandra if you want a colourful story."

"Ha! You're not getting rid of me that easy, Doc! If Coyote goes back in chains, I'll have to join him to give him support and courage. Keep the camera running, Hotrocks! I wanta make another statement."

"About what?"

"How the hell do I know? You're the one asking the questions. Fire away."

"Well, could you verify the rest of your story? Like stopping the attack on Katie Kool – or the connection with President Reagan, or the captain's affair with Princess Diana. To be honest – it sounds a bit off the wall. Are you sure he's sane?"

"Coyote? He's saner than I am! Just not as smart."

"Hey!"

"Anyway, he's obviously not a hostage, so we won't be paying for the news tip –"

"What? After all that tape you shot? And the helicopter expense?"

"However, I have another idea, if you could give me a few more seconds of your time, Dr. Pearce. It occurs to me we *could* make an interesting documentary about Captain Coyote, so as not to waste the footage we've already shot. Dr. Pearce – if we dropped the hostage angle, and any reference to the missing comic books, how about an interview with Mr. Coyote? KIK-TV could profile this unique Canadian hero and his activities. It could make an awesome little *Sixty Minutes* type human-interest feature. Maybe get it onto Fox or CNN."

"No, I don't think so –"

Coyote spoke up. "It's not a bad idea, Doc. What have we got to lose?"

"Well, a few hours travelling time, for one thing. We have a deadline."

"It's a way of promoting direct action. P.D. would approve it."

"I don't believe this is in Donald's interest," Dottie objected.

"It wouldn't go to air until long after you're back in Canada, Dr. Pearce. Could we stop somewhere for a drink and discuss it? My treat. I just have to call the station manager to okay it. I'm sure KIK-TV would make it worth your while."

Everyone agreed that a supper break was overdue, so Doc drove them in the Coyote Mobile to the next highway interchange, where there was a Chucky Cheez restaurant and bar. The pilot had to stay with the helicopter for security, and although Coyote volunteered to take his place, they insisted he be part of the discussion.

Over burgers and fries, Breezely outlined his exciting new plan, which had been conditionally approved by his manager. "It hit me like a truck when Captain Coyote mentioned comic books! I thought, *Wait a minute!* I used to be a comic book collector. I know how this guy thinks. I have this vision of Captain Coyote as a comic book hero. If I can interview him about his adventures, and intercut it with our helicopter shots of the Coyote Mobile zooming along the highway – it would be a breeze to slap together. It's perfect Reality TV. And if we could tag along with you as far as the border, something dramatic will no doubt happen along the way! You seem to have a knack for trouble –"

"That's it – just like The Flash."

"Never a dull minute," Wonder Woman observed.

"This could make a bitchin documentary! I'll send the helicopter back and we'll rent a van in Salt Lake City. Nicky can get a few tracking shots to go with the aerials. And I'll interview you inside the Coyote Mobile as you travel."

"You really think your television station will show this?" Doc said.

"Hey, if they don't, we'll sell it somewhere else! I have my own production company too, dig? If KIK-TV doesn't jump on this like a trampoline, I'll take it to a specialty producer I know in LA. With all the Reality TV, this show is a natural. The last one I did for him was a feature called *Bumfight*. Two homeless winos on the street in North Vegas decided to beat the shit out of each other. Now I'm ready for bigger things. 'The Last Action Hero of America,' featuring the legendary Captain Coyote –"

"And his partner, Wonder Woman!"

"Of course – we need a loyal companion. I mean, the potential is *incredible*. We'll locate Pasamonte, maybe the hermit if he's still alive, and get them into it too. The portrait of a people's hero. All *cinema verité* – just like *Survivor*. We'll tape you as you race for the border, recording your victories over evil and disaster."

"Complete and utter nonsense," Dottie sniffed.

"It's not a bad idea," Coyote repeated.

"We might agree to an interview," Doc said. "But no fake dramas."

"Did you say you were a comic book collector?" Coyote asked.

"Yeah, I grew up on them! I don't have any *Action Comics,* but I do own an early *Spiderman*. A lot of the newer stuff – *X-Men, The Incredible Hulk, The Terminator*. See, I majored in movie action heroes at UCLA! Wrote an honours paper on the influence of comics on the American hero as a political propaganda figure. I called it 'SuperSam: Literature of the New World Order.' Solidarity, Hungarian Freedom Fighters, the *mujahadeen* in Afghanistan, and so on. Canadian heroes probably follow the same pattern – if they're not anti-American. Hell, this'll make you a Hollywood icon, Captain!"

"All right, let's cut to the bottom line," Wonder Woman said. "How much?"

"Well, I could offer you interview fees. My production company is a fully accredited member of the Las Vegas Cineaste Co-operative. Standard independent production agreement. I could also guarantee you, let's say, ten percent of net profit."

"Forget it! Twenty-five or we take a hike."

"Okay, twenty-five percent of net profit."

"How much cash out front?"

"Jeeze, what do you want?"

"I want to get rich, Breezely!" Wonder Woman said. "The same as any other refugee. Isn't that the point of democracy? Welfare cases in the States get more than doctors in most countries of the world. Where else can you get hit by a truck and sue somebody's ass off? Can't do that in Russia, Kevin."

"How about it, Doc?" Coyote said. "If we got to tell our story, then our mission wouldn't be a failure. It could make P.D. proud!"

"I'm afraid we don't have room for all their equipment."

"Oh, I won't take up much space. Honest. Plus I can subsidize your travel expenses. You'd like to stop for a night's rest, right? I'll pay for your motel! And if this documentary makes it to air," Breezely enthused, "we won't stop there! I have credits as an indie producer. I know we could do this as a reality series – Captain Coyote travels across America, doing heroic deeds. A true road serial!"

"This is getting totally out of hand," Dottie said. "It started out as an interview. Now there's a whole production...."

"One question," Doc said. "Is there any redeeming social purpose to this film?"

"Absolutely! To demonstrate the benefits of comic book literacy! It was Captain Coyote's love for comic books that led to his dream of being a superhero. Okay, he's a little strange, and he makes a few mistakes along the way – but who doesn't? That's normal. The point is, he comes to the aid of people in despair, people who've lost hope. We'll just find one or two and show him doing his thing! A genuine professional hero!"

"Sounds good!" Coyote nodded. "How about it, Doc?"

Doc glanced uneasily at Dottie, who was pacing in agitation, anxious to get back on the road. "It's just another outrageous fantasy," she muttered.

"Of course it is!" Breezely said. "But I can make it real! The fantasy of an amazing street hero. That's why it's such a great idea – a regular guy becomes a Hollywood superhero!"

"Donny's not so easy to pigeonhole. He's old-fashioned. If you just showed that."

"So that's a yes?"

"You can tag along," Doc said. "On condition that Dottie or I approve the final cut."

"You got it, Doctor. The final cut. You won't regret this."

CHAPTER 29

Breezely's Big Shoot

Rue to his word, Breezely arranged their night's accommodations in the Salt Lake Travelodge, on a budget approved by the KIK-TV manager. While the helicopter returned to Las Vegas the next morning for more mundane duties, Nicky rented a van to carry the KIK-TV equipment. He proceeded to set up his camera and sound recorder in the Coyote Mobile for Coyote's interview, while Breezley and Wonder Woman negotiated a contract for her to drive the film-makers' rental van. They set out for the Canadian border after breakfast, driving over the Malad Summit into Idaho.

Nicky had a case of blank videotapes, and kept the Betacam rolling as they passed through Pocatello and Idaho Falls. They tacked across the Continental Divide to Montana, through Butte and Helena, as Coyote described his battle with the Yankee Freemen. He told of the bizarre sojourn with the Mormon hermit, and relived his horrific discovery of the parking lot in Yellowstone Park. The caravan stopped for a supper break at Great Falls, at an A&W looking out across the Montana plains. The two heroes had crossed the state only weeks before, but it already seemed like years.

Breezely was so excited by Coyote's tales of adventure, he could hardly eat his Grandpaburger. He had struck video gold – the fable of the century. If it panned out, Breezely would produce not just an award-winning documentary, but a Hollywood feature blockbuster. "This could be bigger than *Titanic!* More powerful than *The Magnificent Seven!* Coyote, we're going to make you famous!"

"I already am famous," Coyote said.

"Maybe in Canada. So what? Except for Las Vegas, Americans have never seen you. I'm going to blaze your name across the cultural land-scape of the USA. And that's just a start. Once Hollywood gets on board, we'll unleash you on the entire world!"

"Let's see how the documentary turns out first," Doc cautioned.

"Hey, it's already fantastic! As soon as I edit the interviews, I'll go and track down the various characters Captain Coyote met. Pasamonte, the people in Vegas. Maybe we can find the hermit. We'll get all their stories! Hey, I'll cut a deal with Katie Kool to compose the score! The only problem is, I need more action footage. Helicopter shots and talking heads aren't enough. We need live action."

"Like what?"

"Oh, a rescue of some kind. Where could we find people in trouble at this time of day?"

"Forget it," Doc said.

"Listen, as soon as I cut the documentary, I'll start writing the fea-ture through an agent I know. He's got connections at Sundance. When we score some development money, I'll bring these guys down to Vegas to work on the script. We'll put Captain Coyote up on the *big* screen. Get these guys regular work permits. We'll shoot *the real thing.*"

Doc looked sceptical. "Don't you think the story's – far-fetched?"

"Far-fetched! Have you seen the shit they put on screen these days?"

"It just doesn't seem very realistic."

"This is great realism, if you compare it to the crap they call real-ity – survivor contests, the Springer shows, losers sitting in prisons. I ask you! At least our bum fight had real blood. These things are so phoney, realism has been completely reversed. *Survivor* is so fake it makes *Lord of the Rings* look like kitchen-sink drama. Don't worry, when Vegas meets Captain Coyote in all his glory –"

"With his partner, Wonder Woman –"

"Hey – no sweat. I can make it happen! But I need some action before we hit the border. All I have now is the captain stepping out of the Coyote Mobile. We need to find a chain gang or something – somebody in desperate need of help."

"Don't even think about it," Doc said.

But Doc thought about it, driving across the plains ahead of the setting sun, as Dottie napped in the passenger seat, her head bumping gently on his shoulder. He could not allow the smooth-talking film-maker to exploit his friend Donny. He decided the best defence was to head straight north to the nearest border crossing. Breezley's van and equipment would not be permitted to cross the border without a pro-duction permit, and they would be rid of them.

But it was 9 p.m. before their caravan reached the customs post at Coutts, Alberta, and the border crossing had already closed for the night. It would not open until 8 a.m. the next day. They had to drive back into Montana to the nearest campground. Sweetgrass Hills State Park was as far off the beaten path as Doc could get, as he planned to spend their last night in the US as quietly and undramatically as possi-ble. Crossing the border with Wonder Woman in the morning would provide enough action for videotaping.

The campground was located in a remote corner of the park, and a scarcity of campers improved Doc's spirit. It was only a $1 admis-sion, but the facilities did not include a gate, or toilets, or showers. Each site consisted of a rough plank table set in a thicket of poplar trees. Fortunately, the Coyote Mobile II was designed to camp anywhere, with its diesel generator, extra propane canisters, and an ecologically correct self-composting waste system.

In the semi-darkness, Doc hung some halogen lights to illuminate the campsite. Dottie volunteered to cook a big pot of chili on the propane stove Coyote set up on the table. Breezely huddled with his cell phone in the van, muttering to his manager. "I tell you we got a world-class documentary – it'll get nominated for Emmy awards.... No, wait a minute, Mike, I arranged for Corbin to do the traffic reports. Anyway, don't worry about that now. No, I still don't have the action shots. We're hoping some local wildlife might show up. We'll be back tomorrow night, okay, Mike?"

A honking sound suddenly burst out of the chokecherry bushes behind their camp. It sounded like an animal in distress.

"Hang on, I'll call back," Breezely said crisply. "I think we got action."

Captain Coyote edged toward the noise in the bushes, using Doc's powerful flashlight to light the forest of scrub. He could see nothing but gloomy shadows, and hear only the sound of a creek running beyond them. Suddenly a donkey lunged out of the vegetation, braying frantically. It was coated with mud and dragged a length of rope from its neck halter. For a moment the donkey stood bawling lustily, but when Coyote approached with his hand extended, it turned and fled into the trees.

"Follow the mule!" Coyote shouted. "I think somebody's in trouble!" With the camera crew and Wonder Woman in hot pursuit, he chased the sound of the animal plunging through the tangle of fallen spruce trees. As they came to a bend along the creek, the donkey disappeared and they lost the trail. Coyote stopped, holding his hand up for silence. He thought he heard a faint cry for help. A human cry. The others paused, panting for breath. The moan came again, drifting like a sigh through the tangled bush. *"Helllp..."*

Wonder Woman backed up toward the camp. "It could be a trap. Let's get Doc."

"Hellooo!" Coyote called.

Breaking out of the brush to the creek bank, he heard the mule braying again, and a voice saying, "Good girl! Don't panic, sweetheart. We'll get out of here yet!"

Coyote shone the flashlight around the misty darkness till he spotted the mule standing near a deadfallen tree in the water. He slid down the bank into the murky swamp that had filled in behind a beaver dam. Holding the light overhead and wading toward the donkey, he found a cowboy pinned under the tree, mired in the thick silt of the creek bottom.

"You okay, mister?" Coyote called.

"Thank God you came! I was gonna drown for sure. Bernadette was trying to pull me out!"

He was a big man, but near the end of his strength, struggling to keep his head out of the muck. He must have fallen off the mule while crossing the beaver dam.

"Wonder Woman, come hold the mule while I try and get a rope around this guy."

"Hey – you guys sound Canadian," the cowboy said.

"That's right – Canadians," Wonder Woman said. "There a problem with that?"

"Relax for a minute, mister. We'll get you out."

Breezely and Nicky started setting up their lights and camera to record the dramatic rescue. As Coyote slogged through the mud to the struggling cowboy with the halter shank, Breezely shouted from the edge of the swamp, "Hang on a minute, Captain! We want to get this on tape! Okay. We're recording and – Action!"

Coyote knotted the rope under the cowboy's shoulders and secured the line to the mule's halter. They all heaved at once: Wonder Woman, Bernadette, and Captain Coyote, who was kneeling in sludge up to his chin. With a long sucking noise, the cowboy popped out of the muck and was dragged up onto the creek bank. He laid there in a sodden heap, gasping for breath.

Coyote staggered onto the ground beside him. "You okay?"

"Yeah, thanks."

Wonder Woman pulled the donkey into camera range. "That is a great mule!"

Oddly, the cowboy took offence. "Bernadette ain't a mule, she's an ass."

"A jackass?"

"No, a jenny – a female ass. And the bitch is in trouble now!" He seized a tree branch off the ground and to Coyote's horror, began clubbing his faithful mount over the back. "Take that, you filthy slut! There! You pig-headed old jezebel!"

With a fury surprising in a man only a few seconds away from death, he slammed the club on her head. Bernadette reared on the halter, nearly pulling Wonder Woman's arms out of their sockets.

"Hey, take it easy!" Coyote said.

Grabbing the rope from Wonder Woman, the cowboy punched the animal in the face with his huge fist. "Leave me to die, would you, bitch? Stand still, or I'll smack your brains out!"

"Stop!" Coyote cried. "It wasn't her fault."

"To hell! The sleazy whore almost killed me!"

"She came and alerted us, and saved your life!" Coyote protested. "I think you're in shock. Better sit down and rest."

"Who the hell are you? And what are they doing?" He pointed to the television crew on the creek bank, recording the scene.

"I'm Captain Coyote, and that's a TV show about the rescue. We're camped in the park, waiting for the border to open. You're lucky we found you. How did you get into this jam?"

"Me and Bernadette live a couple miles up the coulee with a herd of beef. We were chasing a calf across the beaver dam when this jade threw me off under that tree." He extended a paw to Coyote. "My name's Eugene Klatt. Giss I owe you some thanks."

"Maybe you should thank your ass. She's the real hero. We do this professionally, eh? Me and Wonder Woman. That's why they're making the movie."

"Well, I appreciate it. You travelling by yourselves?"

"My friend Doc's up at the camp and my supervisor's making chili. You should come up and get something to eat. We don't mind sharing. You can bring Bernadette along."

"Well, I wouldn't turn down a bite of supper. Not if somebody else's cookin'."

Nicky walked backward ahead of them, for a long tracking shot as they crashed through the bushes. He filmed Coyote ladling out bowls of chili to the famished cowboy and the rescue team. Breezely was pleased with the action sequence, and decided to keep the tapes running. In the morning, they'd take it all back to Las Vegas.

"Listen guys, I think we got something special here. Mike will love this stuff. And when we cut the documentary, we'll fly you down to Vegas to have a look. Maybe do some more shooting."

"Whatever happens, happens," Coyote said. He wouldn't get his hopes up till he saw the result. President Reagan had struggled in the film business for years before he finally got a decent part in politics.

Eugene was enjoying the chili and corn bread, sharing it with Bernadette, who was curled up beside him like a faithful dog. "Is that coffee I smell?"

"Yeah," Doc said. "Dark roast." Dottie poured the cowboy a mugful.

"Get a sniff of that, Bernadette – real coffee! After a winter of that powdered shit."

"She drinks coffee, too?"

"Oh, we share everything, Bernadette and me. She's a wonderful companion. Sweeter than a woman."

Wonder Woman bristled. "What the hell's that supposed to mean?"

"He just means she's good company," Coyote said.

"Oh, she keeps me warm on long winter nights." He stroked Bernadette's nose and she breathed a sigh of contentment. "We cuddle up like a pair of newlyweds."

"Sounds sick to me," Wonder Woman said.

"You guys probably think I'm a pervert, talking like this about Bernadette. But before we met, I was a psychological wreck. She understands human weakness, especially in men. Okay, I smack her over the head once in a while to get her attention, but those are just love taps. A kind of bonding. This gal gives me all the affection I need."

Doc glanced at him curiously. "You and your ass – sleep together?"

"You've heard about horse-whispering?" Eugene said smugly.

"Yeah," Wonder Woman said. "I seen that movie."

The cowboy nodded. "Robert Redford stole it from my life story. Except I'm an ass-whisperer. You probably didn't know that ass-whispering came first, long before they tried it on horses. My lawyer in

Shelby is suing Redford unless he apologizes like a man."

"And if he doesn't?"

"We hit him for two million bucks in damages. You seen the movie. He didn't look like me at all!"

"He was way older," Wonder Woman said.

"Anyway, it's not what you whisper to them, it's what they whisper. You can get a lot of philosophy from an ass."

"You don't say?"

"Understand your ass and you'll know everything. You'll be a success!"

Doc smiled. "And what would you call a success, Mr. Klatt?"

"Oh, just being alive one more day in the Sweetgrass country, watching the sun go down at night, tending cattle and my sweet Bernadette." He gazed into her dark heavy-lidded eyes. "I have found the purpose in being."

"You're a real cowboy?"

"You bet. Me and Bernadette herd about twenty beeves, fixing fences, putting up hay. But we work to the ticking of an Almighty clock. And my purpose is to enjoy each day to the fullest. This coulee is as close to paradise as I'll find on earth, so me and Bernadette are planning to stay as long as we can."

"How long so far?" Doc asked.

"Bout four years. Came out here to escape the female species."

At this point Dottie said the mosquitoes were getting intolerable, so she went and sat in the back of the Coyote Mobile.

"What was that about women?" Breezely prompted.

"You gonna put this in yer movie?"

Breezely turned to Nicky who shrugged and said, "We're nearly ready to wrap."

"What's the angle?" he asked Eugene.

"It's a long story."

"Before you start," Sandra said, "I'm dying for a beer. Anybody interested in going to the next town to hunt down cold beer? We might find Bushwakker this close to the border."

But Eugene was not interested in beer. Neither was Doc or Breezely. Nicky said he could take it or leave it. They all wanted to hear Eugene Klatt's story of bestial romance.

With Bernadette's huge head snuggled in his lap, Eugene began his fateful tale.

"I grew up east of here a few miles, in the heart of ranching country. My folks had a place in the badlands, on Jumping Deer Creek. Our coulee was mostly federal reserve land that Old Bill Henderson leased for horses. Him and his son Clayton bred the most beautiful Appaloosas in the state, and made a fortune on the rodeos. They cornered the market for bucking stock. Clayton eventually got hitched to the daughter of the hotel owner, and they had a girl as beautiful as a morning sunrise."

"Wait a minute," Coyote interrupted. "Was this somewhere near Opheim?"

"Yup."

"Was the girl's name Marcella Henderson?"

"You know her?"

"I met her there. At a funeral."

"Ain't she something? Pride of Montana. She could ride anything with four legs, and swing her lariat like a man. First woman to ride a bull in the Miles City Stampede. I fell in love with her when we was in school. Course, I was kinda shy with the ladies and never worked up the nerve to ask her out, but she knew my feelings and tole me to be patient while she went off to the university in Colorado."

Coyote nodded. "We met at the Opheim rodeo grounds."

"Three times Queen of the Opheim Rodeo! She's a stunner."

"Course, she might not remember me," Coyote said. "She didn't seem to care much for men."

"She used to before she met Rocco."

"Who?"

"Vince Rocco was the son of the shoemaker in Malta. Italian family. He'd joined the army and went on the mission to Somalia, then the Gulf, and God knows where else. Demolition expert, blowing up mines and shit. Dirty work, but somebody had to do it, right? He'd lost two fingers on his left hand, and the use of an eye, I forget which one. Anyway, he showed up in Opheim, messed up as a runty hog, probably post-traumatic stress or uranium poisoning. Couldn't quit talking about it. Oh, he had all kinds of medals and special badges, rows of them – one for every explosion."

"A war hero?"

"They wrote him up in the Malta *Gazette*. That's all he talked about, day in and day out. Mines exploding. Bombs exploding. Shells exploding."

"That could get monotonous, okay."

"He'd sit in the Opheim Bar every night, describing each one in detail. All the blood and gore he'd seen. Kids blown apart. Soldiers gutted by mortar shrapnel."

"Jeeze," Coyote said.

"He loved playing the hero. But he was a bullshitter, showing off in the bar. Then Marcella came home from university one weekend."

"I knew *she'd* be part of this," Wonder Woman muttered to no one in particular.

"I remember it like yesterday. Day of the fall turkey shoot. She walked into the Opheim bar – and there was Vince Rocco, his sleeves rolled up to show off his tattoos."

"She fell for him?"

"Like a straw shithouse. Her old man never got the chance to intervene. She walked out of the bar with Rocco that afternoon, climbed onto the back of his motorcycle, and they headed for Reno to get married. They got as far as Great Falls, and shacked up in some fleabag motel until her credit cards were rung up to the limit. After she hocked her watch and everything, he kicked her out and took off for the west coast."

"Just like a man," Wonder Woman sniffed. "What did Henderson do?"

"Well, Marcella claimed Vince never laid a land on her in Great Falls – that all he took was her money, but Clayton wouldn't believe her."

"Didn't you believe her?"

"Vincent Rocco wasn't the type to sit in a motel five days playing cribbage. Clayton, he lit up like a Chinese cracker. He tried to hire me and Jimmy Wessel to track Vince down in California and deep-six him. Gave me his old 45, but I never had the guts to actually do it."

"Poor Marcella," Coyote said. "She had no one in her hour of need."

"She made a mistake running off with Vince Rocco, that's all. Things might have been different if I had declared my love when I had the chance. Cast away my only pearl. Same old story – men and woman and the folly of love. Oh, it can ruin your life. I was strung out on booze for a long time, rammin around all the bars in Idyho. I did some wrangling up in the mountains – then I met Bernadette. She's the light of my life. Show them your ring, honey."

"You married your ass?" Doc gasped.

"Well – we never formalised it. Couldn't find a church that would bless us. Course I appealed to the human rights tribunal, but that takes a fearsome long time."

"You live as – man and wife?"

"Compared to most wimmen, Bernadette's a devoted companion."

"That is a sad story, Eugene," Coyote said. "But surely – it's not too late."

"What's not too late?"

"To find the woman of your dreams. Marcella Henderson. I know she still needs a man – a true cowboy. If you declared your love, she might restore your faith in women."

In his imagination, Coyote was riding across the prairie on horseback, picking up Marcella's trail in Lewiston and following it wherever she rode. He could prove to her there was one man in the world she might trust. "Besides," he said to Eugene, "you can't sleep with an animal. It's too – disgusting!"

Eugene looked sharply at Coyote. "Disgusting? Animals not good enough for you, that it?"

"I just don't like it when people mess around with animals. Taking advantage of poor dumb creatures that don't know any better –"

"You ass-ist son of a bitch!" Eugene spluttered, jumping to his feet. Without any warning, he clouted Coyote a ferocious blow with his fist.

Eugene's punch was no big deal to Coyote, who had taken more poundings in the last few weeks than he'd seen in his entire childhood. But to be attacked as anti-animal? That was the final straw. Coyote felt himself turning green with rage, like The Hulk. Doc could see danger and moved to restrain him before he snapped, but was too late. Coyote grabbed the coffee pot, the only weapon at hand, and hit Eugene in the face, jamming the spout up his left nostril and sending a blast of hot coffee through his sinuses. With a shriek of pain, the ass-whisperer seized Coyote by the throat and would have choked the life out of him if Wonder Woman had not leaped onto the cowboy's back. She sank her few remaining teeth into his neck, clamping down on it like a wolf trap.

Breezely and Nicky kept the camera going as the brawl spun out of control around the picnic table. The scene was better than Breezely had hoped, and he urged Nicky into the heat of the fray, demanding tight close-ups of blood and gore. Terrified for her life, Dottie McKechnie locked the inside doors of the Coyote Mobile II.

Eugene tried to claw Wonder Woman off his neck, and executed a wild back flip which sent all three combatants crashing onto the camp table stacked with the supper dishes. The table snapped in half as dishes, brawlers, and propane stove crashed to the ground. Wonder Woman was hurled over the end of the table upside down, piling into Nicky and the KIK-TV camera.

Coyote landed somehow on top of the pile, trying to pry Eugene's fingers from his throat and taking several kicks in the face from Sandra's flailing cowboy boots. She was aiming her shots at Eugene's head, but he'd scrambled out of her range, trying to grab a kitchen knife lying in the dirt. Doc spotted the move and kicked the knife out of reach.

Coyote jumped on Eugene to deliver his *coup de grace*, a deadly *tae kwon do* chokehold to render him unconscious. He jammed his forearm under the cowboy's chin, eliciting a howl of pain.

Unhinged by the sound, Bernadette spun round and, planting

both front feet, hoisted her powerful hams into the air and drove her rear hooves straight at Coyote's head. There was a frightening *crack* and he fell with a crash to the ground, twitched once and lay there lifeless.

"*You jackass!*" Wonder Woman screeched. "*You killed Captain Coyote!*"

CHAPTER 30

An Ultimate Adventure

Everyone stopped moving, as if caught in a freeze frame. It was a tableau of death, focused on Coyote's body lying in the moonlight: Wonder Woman, Doc, Breezely, Eugene, and Bernadette. Nicky kept his camera framed on the prostrate figure on the grass.

Eugene was the first to break the tableau, leaping onto Bernadette's back and galloping into the bush the way they had come. The path to the creek was a ghostly shadow among the poplars. The two outlaws disappeared out of sight, as though into another dimension.

"Donny!" Wonder Woman cried, running to his tattered body. After all the battles they'd fought together, the trials they had endured side by side, she couldn't believe he was dead. She had never seen him defeated. She lifted the smashed glasses gently from his face. "Come on – you're okay, Donny!" she urged. "Open yer fuckin eyes."

Doc Pearce could still not move, stunned by the awful sight, and feeling a burst of panic because he didn't have a bottle on hand. He fought the anxiety down. Dottie emerged from the ambulance, terrified that she had failed her young charge.

Wonder Woman grabbed Coyote's shoulders and shook them till his head rolled. "Coyote, don't play around!" she wailed, wiping blood and chili sauce from his face. "You can't be dead! Come on, we're going to Moose Jaw!"

Coyote's eyes fluttered and squinted open. "It's my fault," he muttered. "I never should have left."

"Coyote! You're alive!"

"Jeeze – I am! Where are we?" He sat up groggily. "Where's P.D.?"

"She's waiting in Moose Jaw, Donny!" Doc said, tears of relief starting in his eyes. "We're going home. Tonight. Will you be okay?"

"My head feels like a bomb went off inside it. And I think my shoulder's busted."

"Lift gently, Doc," Dottie said. "Get him to the vehicle."

"Hang on," Coyote moaned. "Let's wait for this wave of bad luck to pass."

"We got it all!" Breezely called. "Keep going. Nicky's just changing a tape."

"Okay, no more screwing around!" Sandra announced. "We're taking him back to Saskatchewan."

They helped the dazed hero to the Coyote Mobile and laid him on his bunk. Breezely hollered, "Cut!"

Nicky called out, "Can we help?"

"Yes, you can," Doc said. "Take your goddam camera and get out of my sight! We've had enough." Wonder Woman and Doc piled the camping gear in the Coyote Mobile, while Dottie took the driver's seat and looked at the map. The border at Coutts was closed, but in the morning they could cross the 49th parallel at Coronach. It was two hundred miles further east, and straight south of Moose Jaw. She and Doc could drive all night across the Montana badlands if they had to.

A fuzz of darkness spread out before them, the yardlights of farms and ranches winking in the distance like fireflies. The Northern Lights shimmered like a band of green fire along the curve of the dark horizon. In their flickering pale display, Coyote could see Princess Di's smile glowing in the sky, guiding him along the road.

They reached Coronach at dawn, and had to wait for the gate to open at 8 a.m. The crossing was simple. Coyote and Wonder Woman were asleep in the back, and the Canadian customs officer was only interested in the new ambulance, on which she had to collect customs and excise fees.

A few miles north of the border, they stopped for breakfast at a coffee shop in Willowbunch. Coyote's appetite had revived, and he was able to put away a full order of pancakes and sausages, covered with maple syrup and poutine.

He was surprised how perfect everything seemed – things he had forgotten about, like kilometres on the road signs, and grain elevators popping up across the horizon, the fields of green wheat ripening in the sunshine. Would Moose Jaw be the same, too? Or so full of changes he wouldn't recognize it? Would Princess Di greet him with a big hug on his return?

One of the first things he had to do was find a new place to live. He had given notice on his apartment above Kwikprint.

"Don, you're welcome to stay with us until you find a place," Doc said.

"Thanks Doc. How about you Sandra? Lookin forward to seein your kids?"

"I won't recognize the little buggers, they'll be grown so big. Be just my luck if Delvis is still there. You gonna go to Cansave and try to get your job back?"

"First he'll be taking a complete medical exam," Dottie said. "Then re-assessment, to determine the appropriate therapy."

By noon, they could see the tall buildings of Moose Jaw from the hills south of the city. They drove past the former air base and the old Moose Jaw Wild Animal Park. At the edge of Moose Jaw, along the highway, they could see a colourful display of banners and flags greeting them. The parks were full of people playing softball games and setting out their barbecue equipment.

"It must be Canada Day," Doc said. "I can't imagine what other celebration would be going on."

As they entered town, the streamers confirmed that it was indeed the First of July, Canada Day, but these banners were no mere display of patriotism. They had been erected by the Chamber of Commerce to promote Sidewalk Daze, an outdoor sale across the city.

It was especially lively on South Hill: Costa's Pizzeria, Karl's Konfectionery, Merle's Beauty Salon – all had outdoor stalls on the sidewalk to promote their products. At the Billard Hotel, Mr. Klovik had that morning unveiled his underground tunnel under the CPR tracks to the old Robin Hood Flour mill, and was charging ten bucks a head for public tours.

"Hey – an ambulance!" someone shouted.

As the Coyote Mobile II approached, crowds lined the sidewalk. Doc called Coyote to sit in the passenger's seat like a royal person. He couldn't see individuals too well without his glasses, but he could greet the cheering crowds with a friendly wave. The Coyote Mobile stopped at the red light in front of the Mohawk gas station.

"Who's that funny-looking dude?" a child asked.

"You don't reckanize him?" his father said. "That's Captain Coyote – the guy who saved the popcan kid! Hero of the week three times running."

"That's the guy who ran the Hells' Angels out of town," another citizen chimed in.

"Captain Coyote? Hey, were you there the night of his initiation at the Billard?"

Already festive because of the holiday, the atmosphere of Moose Jaw turned jubilant. Coyote's name buzzed through the crowd, up and down the sidewalks, spreading in a wave all the way to the grounds of Empire School, where it echoed among the children playing on the softball diamonds.

Sandra's partner Delvis was waiting at the door of their shack on Maple Street as the Coyote Mobile stopped out front. At least Coyote assumed he was Delvis, a rabbity little man who looked nothing like the monster Sandra had described in times past. He seemed to be a regular guy, with all the kids clustered behind him looking out. Doc gave a blast on the ambulance siren, which brought the Dollar children running into the front yard like chickens.

"Hi, guys!" Wonder Woman called.

Four-year-old Denby ran out dragging a one-eyed kitten, while Fonn, seven, lingered behind, sucking on a Freezee bar. Baby Brent crawled across the barren flowerbeds in a fresh pair of Pampers.

"Wait a minute, okay?" Wonder Woman said to Doc. "I'll just say hi, and catch a ride downtown with you. I need to pick up some beer to celebrate my homecoming."

"Mummy?" Denby asked.

"Where were you?" yelled Fonn.

"I was on the road with Coyote for awhile."

They all stared at the Coyote Mobile. "Did you bring any money?" Delvis asked.

"What kinda question is that? Asshole! That's the first thing you want to know? You don't care if I'm okay?"

"You said you were going to bring home a pile of money."

"Well, I made a few bucks but it's gone. So don't start looking for handouts. I'm working on a movie deal that could turn into a goldmine. We might have to go back to Vegas to finish it off."

"Movie?" said Delvis. "I thought you were doing security."

"Aaa – you don't know shit, Delvis. Yer lucky I'm even talking to you, so shut your trap. I wasn't runnin some lousy protection racket, I was being a hero, which is a hell of a lot harder than you think."

"Why? How much do heroes get paid?"

"Fuck all. But there's perks, like stayin in swank hotels, havin a few laughs. You need luck to hit the big leagues. Where Coyote and me are heading as soon as our movie comes out. That's the States, eh? One minute you're rich, the next you're flat broke. They offer a future for people with talent."

"I wanna go to the States," Fonn whined.

"Sandra, we'll leave you to get re-acquainted with your family," Dottie called.

Doc was revving the engine and shifting gears, wanting to get under way. The Coyote Mobile proceeded down the street in a blaze of flashing lights, crossing Thunderbird Viaduct and into the centre of Moose Jaw.

News of Coyote's return spread like a prairie fire, leaping across the web of CPR tracks and racing through the streets. The workers at Cansave Recycling Depot put down their brooms and plastic bags and ran to the sidewalks to cheer as the Coyote Mobile II drove past. They were all wearing heroes' costumes. Coyote was their greatest hero, ever since he quit and drove off in his own car. Now he'd returned – waving from the window of a brand new Coyote Mobile! Dwayne had applied to get his job back when he heard he could dress like The Punisher.

The Coyote Mobile rolled past the railway station, the new casino, and the old Moose Jaw Light and Power building. Hundreds of Moose Javians thronged the sidewalks to see Captain Coyote's triumphal procession up Main Street.

Coyote, however, was thinking only of the person he hoped would be waiting at the end of the journey. "You think P.D. will be at home, Doc?"

"I do. I phoned her yesterday from Great Falls. She was driving down from Saskatoon to put the house in order, and make sure the guest room is ready for you."

When the ambulance rolled to a stop in front of Doc's house on Redland Avenue, Coyote knew he was home. Doc's house was a rambling brick house of two and a half storeys, shaded by three big crabapple trees in the front yard. They were bursting with red and white flowers, whose petals dusted the lawn with a layer of pink. Coyote realized how comforting the place looked. And there was Princess Di – waiting on the porch swing as though he had never left! She ran down the walk to embrace him.

"Donny!" she cried. "Welcome home!"

"Jeeze – it's good to be back, P.D.," he said. Even without his glasses, he could see her beautiful smile and tumbling red hair.

"I'm sorry I couldn't go to Nevada," she said. "My thesis defence was scheduled for last Saturday."

"Now you're P.D., Ph.D.?"

"I'm just happy to see you, Donny! I want to hear about all your adventures."

"Well, some were good, some were a bit ugly. Are we still friends?"

"We'll always be friends, Donny. For the rest of our lives. That can't change."

Doc introduced his daughter to Dottie McKechnie, though something about the way he blushed and stammered made P.D. realize that Doc was beginning a new relationship. They carried Donny's bag into the house, and put him in the guest room on the second floor. His comic book collection was already there, stacked in boxes beside the dresser. The doctor came to give Coyote a complete physical, and declared that except for a mild concussion, he was as healthy as a horse. He could start back at Cansave in a few days.

"Actually, I don't plan on going back to Cansave," Coyote said.

"That's right," Dottie said. "He's going to be starting a new position. I'll have his new office ready in a couple of weeks."

"What office?" Princess Di asked.

"Donald is going to initiate a new community program, setting an example for challenged adults. He wants to find and celebrate heroes in the community. I thought he could start with a fitness class for teenagers."

"What a fantastic idea!" P.D. enthused. "I could help too."

"That's great!" Coyote said. "At least until I receive a higher call. When Kevin Breezely's TV show is finished, I could be getting a summons from the States. To be a superhero."

"TV show?"

"It was a nightmare," Doc said. "I'll tell you about it later. Donny, those clowns will never finish that documentary –"

"Ssshh!" P.D. warned. "Don't be negative. Whatever Donny wants to do, he should do."

"I could become a legend, Doc. Another Superman. I can't give up just because I lost the first round."

"Maybe we should encourage him," Dottie said. "Ultimately, he has to be his own person, making his own decisions."

"The world is hoping for somebody like me, Doc. I won't be able to turn it down if the call comes to take action. It's the way I am. I can't help it."

Doc smiled grimly.

"Besides," Donny went on, "you always said, 'Better to lose by a card too many, than by a card too few.'"

So Donny Coyote decided to remain for a while in the little city of Moose Jaw, a place of exile and a place of comfort, a place to gather his wits and resources, before once again making a stand against the world's injustice and cruelty.

Acknowledgement of assistance and support for this adventure goes to Rick Gaudio, Garry Sherbert, Britt Holmstrom, Nels Bird, Jerry Deshaye, Leslie Griffin, Jeff Pfeifer, Kevin Mitchell, Andrew Stubbs, June Fox, and the Vintage Book Club of Perth, Australia.